We Free the Stars

HAFSAH FAIZAL

FARRAR STRAUS GIROUX · NEW YORK

To Azraa—

Sometimes friend,

Sometimes foe,

Sometimes ferocious,

Forever my sister.

Farrar Straus Giroux Books for Young Readers
An imprint of Macmillan Children's Publishing Group, LLC
120 Broadway
New York, NY 10271

Text copyright © 2021 by Hafsah Faizal
Map credit © Virginia Allyn
All rights reserved
Printed in the United States of America
Designed by Elizabeth H. Clark
First edition, 2021

ISBN 978-0-374-31157-5

5 7 9 10 8 6 4

fiercereads.com

Library of Congress Cataloging-in-Publication Data is available.

Our books may be purchased in bulk for promotional, educational, or business use.
Please contact your local bookseller or the Macmillan Corporate and Premium Sales
Department at (800) 221-7945 ext. 5442 or by email at MacmillanSpecialMarkets@macmillan.com.

Honor before heart, said the girl.
Delicacy fosters death, said the lion.
Destruction follows darkness, said the boy.
Power begets pain, said the king.
And they were all horribly right.

Anadil

Abal

Alhena

The Wadi Sea

Alderamin

Umas

The Wastes

Hessa Isles

Sharr

The Baransea

Abia River

Pelusia

Guljul

Zaram

ACT I

DARK AS A HOLLOW GRAVE

CHAPTER 1

DARKNESS SURGED IN HIS VEINS. IT EXHALED WISPS from his fingers and feathered his every glance. And when he thought too hard too fast, it bled up his arms in streams of black.

Fear becomes you.

The high sun drew Nasir Ghameq's shadow across the planks of Jinan's ship as he slid, for what felt to be the thousandth time since they'd left Sharr, the crate's lid back in place. A steady pulse thrummed against his fingers, emanating from the four hearts resting inside. Hearts that once belonged to Arawiya's founding Sisters of Old, sourcing the kingdom's magic from the five caliphates' royal minarets, amplifiers that rationed morsels of magic to the masses. And until the organs were restored, magic was as good as gone—as it had been for the past ninety years.

Yet magic continued to exist in him, a fact he couldn't keep to himself because of the shadows ghosting his presence.

"The fifth heart isn't going to materialize the harder you look. Neither is he, for that matter," Kifah said, lithely climbing down the crow's nest. The cuff on her upper arm glinted, the engraved crossed spears a reminder of who she once was: one of the Nine Elite who guarded Pelusia's calipha. With a pang, Nasir realized he was waiting for a certain golden-haired general's response to her lightning-quick words. Something silly, or clever, followed by an endearing *One of Nine*.

The silence that echoed was as loud and unsettling as the Baransea's crashing waves.

Nasir made his way to Jinan. The gash across his leg, courtesy of an ifrit on the island of Sharr, forced him to limp about the ship.

"We've been at sea for two days. What's taking so long?"

The Zaramese girl squinted at him from the helm. Unruly dark curls slipped from the folds of her checkered turban, the cloth casting her brown eyes in a reddish glow. "*'Anqa* is the fastest ship there is, your highness."

"Not that there *are* any other ships, kid," Kifah pointed out.

Nasir tucked the crate with the hearts safely into a nook near her as Jinan frowned. "I'm not a kid. *'Anqa* means 'phoenix.' You know, like the immortal bird made of fire? Named after my favorite star. My father—"

"No one cares," Nasir said, gripping the rough wood as the ship rocked.

Jinan gave an exaggerated sigh.

"How much longer?"

"Five days," she pronounced, but her pride deflated at Nasir's withering stare. "What, his highness's ship took six days, at most? Forgive me for not having the sultan's might at my back."

"My ship," he said slowly, "took less than two days to reach Sharr, even with the dandan we defeated along the way."

Jinan whistled. "I'm going to need to take a look at those ship plans when we get to the fancy palace, then. What's the rush?"

Irritation flared beneath his skin, and a streak of black unfurled from his fingertips. Jinan stared. Kifah pretended not to notice, which only irritated him further.

"Did you go to school?"

Jinan's eyes narrowed. "What does that have to do with anything?"

"Then you would know how dire it is when I say the Lion of the Night is alive," said Nasir, and the assassin in him reveled in the fear widening her eyes. He didn't tell her of the heart the Lion had stolen. He didn't care about that, or even magic—not as much as he cared about Altair, but the girl wouldn't understand. Nasir himself didn't understand the strange compulsion in his blood, this concern for another human that he thought had faded with his mother's supposed death. "Did you think Benyamin tripped on a rock and died?"

Jinan turned away with another frown and Kifah leaned against the mast, crossing her arms as she studied him. "We'll get him back."

It wasn't Benyamin she spoke of.

"I wasn't worried." He didn't look at her.

"No, of course not," Kifah drawled. "I'm just reminding myself aloud that he's Altair and he can handle himself. He could talk so much the Lion would beg us to take him back. I wouldn't be surprised if he left the bumbling fool somewhere with a sign saying 'He's all yours.'"

It was a lie, and they both knew it. Uncertainty rang painfully clear in her normally grounding voice.

Nasir looked to the sea beyond, toward the island of Sharr. Part of him expected to see another ship in pursuit, dark and fearsome as the Lion himself. A fortnight ago, Nasir had been ready to kill Altair—he was ready to kill *anyone* in his path, but when he closed his eyes now, he saw the blinding beams of light extending from Altair's open palms. He saw the sharp facets of the Lion's black stave protruding from Benyamin's heart.

Sacrifice, Benyamin had murmured. Sacrifice was nothing but death in a romantic farce. Nasir knew—he'd been born for death and darkness, and it was hard to have a heart when one had stopped that of so many others. It was hard to do good when it would be shadowed forever by his wrongs.

Somewhere on Sharr his heart had found a beat, and he intended to keep it going. He intended to make himself worthy of it, even if it meant restoring the very magic that had destroyed his family.

And he would start by rescuing Altair and vanquishing the Lion.

He looked at Jinan. "Five days is too long. Make it three."

Jinan sputtered. "That's impos—"

He was already turning for the steps leading belowdecks. "Make it three and I'll double Benyamin's silver."

The young captain's shouts were instant. Chaos erupted as her ragtag crew leaped to attention, the rough inflection of Zaramese at home with the crashing sea. He didn't know what the girl would do with so much coin, but he didn't exactly care. The throne had enough to spare.

Nasir limped down the steps. Three days was still three days too long. Now that the Lion was no longer shackled to the island, he had no reason to remain there, particularly when the Jawarat—the key to what he wanted most—was getting farther and farther away from him. The zumra needed to reach shore before the Lion did, or their troubles would be infinitely worse, and if there was anyone who could quicken their journey, it was no mortal girl from Zaram.

The must of burning oil clung to the salty air within the ship. Lanterns flickered as Nasir made his way past cabins cramped one against the other like a mouthful of teeth, bolted beds and other sparse furnishings dark in the dim, reminiscent of the palace.

His exhale broke and suddenly he was standing in front of Ghameq, telling him of the mission. How he'd failed to kill the sultan's general. Failed to kill the Hunter. Failed to bring back the Jawarat.

Failed, failed, failed.

He shook his thoughts free. It was different now, he reminded himself. The leash between him and his father had gnarled, tangled in the lives of many more. Zafira, Altair, Kifah, his mother, and most important, the

Lion of the Night, who had sunk his claws into Ghameq, controlling his every move.

His gaze flicked to the farthest end, where Zafira's cabin stood like a ledge just out of reach.

During her rare emergences on deck, the Jawarat was always clasped to her chest, her gaze distant and detached. It worried him, seeing the ice in her eyes fading as something else took its place, but coward that he was, he couldn't approach her, and as the insanity of their final moments on Sharr continued to recede, Nasir didn't know how to halt the rapidly swelling distance between them.

He paused to rest his leg, leaning against a splintering beam. The Silver Witch—*his mother, rimaal*—had chosen a cabin just as far as Zafira's, and when he finally reached her door, a dark gleam on the floorboard made him pause.

Blood?

He tugged his glove free and touched two fingers to the splotch, bringing them to his nose. Sharp and metallic—most certainly blood. He wiped his fingers on his robes and lifted his gaze, following the haphazard trail.

To where it disappeared behind the door to the last cabin: Zafira's.

CHAPTER 2

Power bled from her bones. It leached from her soul, dregs draining into some unseen abyss. Emptying her. Zafira Iskandar had ventured into the cursed forest known as the Arz for as long as she could remember, magic gradually sinking beneath her skin, always there, within reach.

And now it was gone.

Stuffed into a crate, shoved beneath a rotting nook beside a too-sure Zaramese. The Jawarat echoed her angry thoughts.

"I planned to destroy that book after magic was retrieved." Anadil, the Silver Witch, Sultana of Arawiya, and Sister of Old pursed her lips at the green tome in Zafira's lap. The lantern cast the angles of her face in shadow, white hair shimmering gold. Zafira's cabin paled in her splendor.

She does not like us, the Jawarat reminded.

Zafira no longer flinched at its voice. It was nothing like that soothing whisper that once caressed her from the shadows near the Arz. The one she had thought belonged to a friend, before she learned it belonged to the Lion of the Night.

No, this voice was assertive and demanding, yet it was filling the void that magic had left behind, and she couldn't complain.

No, she does not.

Instead, she had begun speaking back to it.

After all the trouble Zafira had gone through to retrieve the forsaken thing, she wasn't going to let a scornful witch destroy it. Skies, was this why the woman had come to her cabin? "You're afraid of it."

"The Jawarat is my Sisters' memories incarnate," the Silver Witch said with a withering stare from the cot. Now that Zafira knew the woman was Nasir's mother, she could see the resemblance in that look. "What have I to fear?"

She does not know. She is oblivious to what we gleaned upon Sharr.

The reverberation in her lungs was an order of silence as much as a reminder: *Zafira* didn't even know the extent of what she had gleaned on Sharr, in accidentally slitting her palm and binding herself to this book. For the Jawarat was more than the Sisters' memories.

It had steeped on Sharr for ninety years with the Lion of the Night. It held some of his memories, too, and the Silver Witch hadn't the faintest clue. *No one* did.

Tell them. Her conscience was barely a whisper beneath the Jawarat's weighted presence, but that was not the reason why she didn't heed it. She simply *couldn't*. She could not tell them of the Jawarat any more than she could tell them of the darkness that once spoke to her. Fear mangled whatever words she summoned. She was afraid of them. Afraid of how the others would see her.

She had been judged long enough simply for being born a woman.

"But we need it," Zafira said at last, smoothing her features. The trunk beneath her had been bolted to the ship, but her stomach lurched with the waves. "To *restore* magic."

"I'm a Sister of Old, girl. I know how magic must be restored. It is the book I know little about, for it was created in their final moments, in their last attempt to triumph over the Lion."

And they had. They hadn't been strong enough to destroy him, but they had trapped him upon Sharr and created the Jawarat. The way Zafira saw it, the book had been created for a single reason: to house their memories so that one day their story would be known. To say why magic had been severed from Arawiya that fateful day, why they had died, and most important, where the hearts were located.

"The removal of the hearts from the minarets left Arawiya without magic, but the spell entrapping the Lion drew upon so much that it cursed the kingdom, leaching energy from every caliphate and causing havoc. Snow in Demenhur. Darkness in Sarasin. Sharr became frozen in time," the Silver Witch said, catching Zafira's surprise. "Indeed, life spans stretched beyond reason. Death became an impossible wish. By freeing the Jawarat and the hearts, you freed Arawiya, including those trapped upon the island. They were at last given the peace they sought."

"Then the kaftar . . ." Zafira trailed off, tugging at the fringe of the scarf around her neck. She hadn't been fond of the way the men who could shift into hyenas had leered at her, but they'd come to the zumra's aid. They had helped fight off the Lion's horde of ifrit.

"Dead."

Zafira released a breath. How long did one have to live before death became a wish?

Jinan's shouts echoed in the silence, the crashing waves muffling the rushing of feet on deck. Her contract with Benyamin would only take them to Sultan's Keep, but they were heading for the mainland, close enough to Demenhur to rile a restlessness in Zafira's blood.

"If you know how to restore magic, then you won't need me," she said. *Or the book.* "I can return home."

She had left everything she'd ever known for magic. Journeyed across the Baransea. Trekked through the villainous island of Sharr. But that was before time and distance had created an insatiable yearning that came laced with fear.

Because she would need to face Yasmine.

"To what?" the Silver Witch asked without a drop of sympathy. "The Arz is gone. Your people have no need for a hunter."

Her words were pragmatic, rational. *Cruel.* They stripped Zafira bare, reducing her to an insignificant grain in the vastness of the desert. Bereft, she reached for the ring at her chest—

And dropped her hand back to the Jawarat, running her fingers down the ridges of its spine. Almost instantly, she was filled with a sense of peace. Something that lulled the disquiet.

"When I bathe, will the pages melt?" Tendrils of sorrow lingered at the edges of her mind, too distant to grasp. She couldn't remember being sad now. Nor even the reason for it. The Jawarat purred.

The Silver Witch paused. "I sometimes forget you're only a child."

"The world thieves childhoods," Zafira said, thinking of Baba's bow in her still-soft hands. Of Lana, brushing a warm cloth across Umm's forehead. Of Deen, a ghost after his parents became bodies in a shroud.

"That it does. The Jawarat is a magical creation, immune to the elements, or it would have crumbled to dust within its first decade upon Sharr. Its life force, however, is now tied to yours because you so foolishly bound yourself to it. Tear out a few pages, and you may well lose a limb."

Zafira hadn't asked to be tied to the book. The Silver Witch was the one who had asked a *child* to go on this journey. It was her fault that Zafira was now bound to this ancient tome, and she hadn't even *needed* Zafira for this quest. Only someone strong enough to resist the Lion's hold. Unlike the Silver Witch herself, who had fallen deeper than any of them even realized.

Zafira had been certain Sharr had given them enough revelations to last a lifetime, but that was before Kifah's pointed question. Before they'd learned Altair was the Lion's son as much as he was the Silver Witch's. Strangely enough, learning his lineage had only made her *more* partial to the general.

She bit her tongue. "And there's no way to undo the bond?"

"Death," the Silver Witch said, as if Zafira should have known. "Drive a dagger through the tome's center, and you'll be free of it."

"How kind," Zafira ground out. "I'll be 'free' of everything else, too."

She brushed her fingers across the green leather, thumb dipping into the fiery mane of the lion embossed in its center. The Silver Witch only hummed, studying the girl who knew the Lion almost as well as she did.

She envies us.

Zafira began to agree, before she clenched her jaw against the Jawarat's whispers. They could be far-fetched, she realized. Why ever would a Sister of Old envy a mortal girl?

We will align with time.

Whatever that meant.

She jumped when the two lanterns struck with a sudden clang. Her quiver tipped, arrows spilling and dust swirling like the sands of Sharr. The Silver Witch didn't flinch, though Zafira noted the tight bind of her shoulders, so unlike the languid immortal, before the door swung open, revealing a silhouette in the passageway.

Zafira recognized the mussed hair, the absolute stillness she had only ever seen in deer before she loosed a fatal arrow.

A cloak of darkness followed Arawiya's crown prince inside. He was effortless, as always. Almost careless, if one wasn't paying close enough attention to his deliberate movements. His gray gaze swept the small space and she couldn't stop the flitter in her chest when it locked on hers.

And strayed to her mouth for the barest of moments.

"Are you hurt?" Nasir asked, in that voice that looped with the shadows, soft and demanding. But there was a strain to it, a discomfiture that made her all too aware of the Silver Witch watching every heartbeat of this exchange.

Zafira had known the context behind that question, once. When she was an asset that needed protecting. A compass guiding his destructive path. What was the reason for his concern now that they had retrieved what they once sought, rendering her purpose—on Sharr, in Demenhur, skies, in this *world*—obsolete?

Before she could find her voice, he was looking at the Silver Witch and gesturing to a dark trail on the floorboards that hadn't been there before. Red stained his fingers.

"So this is why the ship isn't going any faster."

Waves crashed in the silence.

"I can perform the mundane tasks any miragi can," his mother said finally, "but time is an illusion that requires concentration and strength, neither of which I currently have."

"And why is that?" His tone was impatient, his words terse.

The Silver Witch stood, and despite Nasir's height, everything shrank before her. She parted her cloak to reveal the crimson gown beneath, torn and stiff with blood.

Zafira shot to her feet. "The Lion's black dagger. Back on Sharr."

Beneath the witch's right shoulder gaped a wound, one she had endured to protect Nasir. It was a festering whorl of black, almost like a jagged hole.

"The very same," the Silver Witch said as another drop of blood welled from her drenched dress. "There is no known cure to a wound inflicted by cursed ore. The old healers lived secluded on the Hessa Isles, and if any of them still remain, my only hope is there."

"What of Bait ul-Ahlaam?" Nasir demanded.

Zafira translated the old Safaitic. *The House of Dreams.* She'd never heard of it before.

"You can easily cross the strait from Sultan's Keep and find what you need there."

"At what cost? I will not set foot within those walls," she replied, but Zafira heard the unspoken words: *Not again*. She had been there before, and it was clear the cost had little to do with dinars.

The Silver Witch was not easily fazed, so the flare of anger in her gaze and the frown tugging the corners of her mouth was strange. Notably so.

"Then you'll leave us," Nasir said, and Zafira flinched at his harsh indifference.

"I will be a walking vessel of magic. Of no use to you, but of every use to the Lion when he inevitably gets his hands on me," the Silver Witch replied. "With my blood and his knowledge of dum sihr, no place in Arawiya will be safe. There is only so much he can do with my half-si'lah sons."

Nasir looked down at his hands, where wisps of black swirled in and out of his skin. Almost as if they were breathing. His shadows hadn't retreated like Zafira's sense of direction had. He didn't need the magic of the hearts when he could supply his own. He didn't have to suffer the emptiness she did.

Something ugly reared in her, choking her lungs, and Zafira nearly dropped the Jawarat in her panic. Just as suddenly, the rage cleared and her heartbeat settled.

What— Her breath shook.

"This mess began because of you." Nasir's words were too cold, and she had to remind herself that he was speaking to his mother, not her. "We left Altair in the Lion's hands because of you."

The Silver Witch met his eyes. "There was a time when the steel of your gaze was directed elsewhere. When you looked to me with love, tenderness, and care."

Nasir gave no response, but if the tendrils of darkness that bled from his clenched fists were any indication, the words had found their mark. He loved her, Zafira knew; it was why his words manifested so hatefully.

"I've taught you all that you know," his mother said gently. "There is still time—I will teach you to control the dark. To bend the shadows to your will."

"Just as you taught him?"

The silence echoed like a roar. Nasir didn't wait to hear the rest. He turned and limped away, shadows trailing. Zafira made to follow, careful to keep her gaze from sweeping after him, for she was well aware that nothing passed the Silver Witch's scrutiny.

"Heed me, Huntress," the Silver Witch said. "Always carry a blade and a benignity. You may never know which you will need."

Zafira felt the stirrings of something at her tone.

"And you cannot return home."

Purpose. That was what she felt. Something dragging her from this sinking, burrowing sense of being nothing.

"If you do, your entire journey to Sharr—including your friend's death, Benyamin's slaughter, and Altair's capture—will have been in vain."

Perhaps the witch had always known someone with the rare affinity of finding whatever they set their heart to—a da'ira—wasn't needed for the job. Perhaps she saw in Zafira what Zafira could not see in her, but knew from the memories of the Jawarat to be true. Someone like herself, guided by a good heart and pure intentions, before she fell prey to a silver tongue.

"The hearts are dying. They are organs removed from their houses, deteriorating as we speak. Restore them to their minarets, or magic will be gone forever."

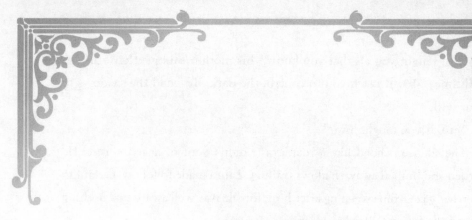

CHAPTER 3

U NDER HIS PHILOSOPHY, RETROSPECT WAS THE AN-
tecedent of wrinkles. Yet shackled and shoved into the dank
bowels of the ship, Altair al-Badawi could do nothing else.

He had spent most of his life vying for his mother's love, trying to
atone for the curl of her lips every time she turned his way. Though it
hadn't taken long to understand that she saw him as the culmination of
her failures, it wasn't until Sharr when he learned the extent of it: that she
was a Sister of Old and the reason magic was gone, that she had—

Altair halted the thought with a grimace.

It wasn't often one learned he was the Lion of the Night's son.

The sun crawled through the tiny excuse for a window, marking two
days since he'd labored with the ifrit on Sharr to salvage the ship they now
sailed in. And in the two days since, he'd been fed and given a chair to sit
upon. Not bad for a prisoner.

If he wasn't being milked like a prize goat.

Every so often, an ifrit would come to secure his chains to the wall, rendering him immobile before slitting his palm to fill a tankard for the Lion to get drunk on. He loathed being the fuel for his father's dum sihr, forbidden magic that allowed one to go beyond one's own affinity. But worse than the chains and the bloodletting, perhaps, were the shackles, spanning at least a quarter of the length of his forearms and suppressing his power. Heavy black ore wrought with words in the old tongue of Safaitic.

The odd push and pull in his veins was taking its toll. It slowed his mind, a thought more troubling than the loss of his physical strength— for it meant the Lion would always be one step ahead of him.

Laa. *Half* a step.

A latch lifted, and he flopped back in his dilapidated chair, propping his feet atop the worn table despite the rattle of his chains, and when the Lion of the Night stepped into the hold, the flare of his nostrils pleased Altair far too much.

"Your horde is slow," Altair announced as if he were speaking to his uniformed men. Simply because he was in chains didn't mean he had to sacrifice dignity. The rich flaunted chains all the time. "We're nowhere near shore, and with the Silver Witch on Nasir's side, spinning illusions as well as you do shadows, they're guaranteed to reach the mainland before you. Time is merely another mirage for her to bend. And when we dock wherever it is you plan on docking, my brother will be waiting."

This was where Altair's bluster faltered.

For his half brother was the same Prince of Death he had accompanied to Sharr, fully aware that his orders were to bury Altair upon that forsaken island. He had left him instead.

Nasir and the zumra, strangers who had become family, had turned and fled, abandoning him to their foe. Laa, he didn't truly know if his brother would be waiting.

But if there was one thing he did better than look impeccable, it was bluff.

"Your freedom, Lion, will be short-lived," Altair finished somewhat lamely. Akhh, valor was a fickle temptress as it was.

The Lion gave him the phantom of a simper that Altair himself had worn far too many times. *Like father, like son.* It was unnerving to think the man was his father when he looked barely a day older than him. Then again, Altair himself was ninety, the exact age of Arawiya without magic. More than four times Nasir's age, and if he was being humble, he'd say he looked a year younger than the grump.

"How should I begin?" the Lion asked. "Anadil will be dead in three days."

Perhaps he could bluff as well as Altair could.

"And then, when your friends reach shore, you and I will take from them the Jawarat and the remaining hearts." The Lion tilted his head. "See, I think long and far, Altair. Something you might find familiar."

Altair's long and far thinking had never been for his own personal gain, or for incomprehensible greed. Assemble a team, restore magic. A simple plan devised by him and Benyamin that became more convoluted with each passing day.

He refused to believe his mother was dying. He refused to believe the zumra was outnumbered, not when he'd ensured there would be allies waiting for them in Sultan's Keep with dum sihr to protect their where-abouts. And more: Nasir had magic. Zafira had the power of the Jawarat bound to her blood.

It had to be enough. For the first time in a long time, Altair had to remind himself to breathe.

"Why?" he asked. That was what he could not discern—the reason for the Lion's need. He refused to believe someone who shared his blood could simply hunger for power. There was truly no drive more boring.

His father's gaze froze, brilliant amber trapped in glass, there and gone before Altair could comprehend it.

"Vengeance," the Lion said, but the word was spoken in a tone accustomed to saying it. No vitriol, no vigor. Only habit. "And more, of course. There must be order. Magic must remain in the hands of those capable. Do you think the common man understood the extent of what the Sisters of Old had so freely given?"

Equality. That was what the Sisters of Old had given Arawiya, despite their faults.

"Akhh, the creativity of men when it comes to their vices," Altair droned, unsurprised. "Order," in this case, was only another word for "greed." "But if that is indeed why you crave magic, then you, with your endless desire for knowledge, should already know the old adage: 'Magic for all or none.' There is no in between."

Unless one was si'lah, like the Silver Witch. Like half of Altair and half of Nasir. Yet another revelation Sharr had given him—he'd spent his entire life thinking himself fully safin, thinking *Nasir* was half safin, despite the boy's round ears.

He supposed he should be grateful he wasn't too much like his father—the man didn't even have a heart. The Lion opened the door leading to the upper deck. It was strange that he came so often to see Altair for seemingly no reason at all. His dark thobe caught the barest sheen of purple in the dying light, and despite himself, Altair didn't particularly want him to leave.

The silence was too loud, the ghosts too real.

Altair's mouth worked without permission. "Do you mourn him?"

How the living felt mattered little to the dead, but the longer he spent alone, the more he thought of the brother of his heart.

"I know all about Benyamin's circle of high safin," Altair continued, even as the words ripped through his ancient heart. "He took you into his fold against their wishes, and you butchered him with cursed ore. You know precisely how much pain he suffered in those final moments."

The Lion turned back, cool and assessing. As if he'd been waiting for Altair to speak. "He should not have tried to save someone so worthless."

Benyamin had never liked Nasir. Even in their years of planning, when Altair's goal was to see Nasir on the throne, Benyamin had been against it. Somewhere on the island, that had changed. To the extent that the safi had decided Nasir was worth sacrificing his own immortality for.

"You truly are heartless," Altair said with a tired laugh.

The Lion's smile was sardonic. "I would need a heart to claim otherwise."

For a long moment, he looked at Altair, and Altair looked back.

"The dead feel no pain," he said gently, and Altair's eyes fell closed of their own accord. Perhaps it was this show of emotion that made his father continue. "Your friends, on the other hand, knew precisely the pain you would feel when they left you. You put on your little light show, saved them, and for what? How does it feel to be abandoned?"

Altair stiffened. He liked to think he was prepared for anything. This, however, was still a sorely sore spot. He loosed a laugh, one of the many at his disposal. "You want me to talk to you about feelings."

The Lion's eyes glowed and the ship rocked, the slow creak of swaying ropes haunting in the quiet. "If anyone can understand, it would be your father."

"I'm flattered," Altair drawled, rattling his chains. He had filled this place with light the first night, before he'd learned what the shackles were doing to him. "But this is no way to treat your son."

The Lion only looked at him. "They left you, Altair."

Altair pressed his lips together. He would not give him the satisfaction of a reply, but the Lion, like his son, was dedicated.

"Knowing I would be your only refuge."

Altair didn't need to close his eyes to see them running for the ship. Sand stirring behind them. Nasir. Zafira. Kifah. His mother, who had never loved him. Not once did they look for him.

Not as the distance grew between them.

Not as they lifted the anchor on Benyamin's ship.

"They took what they needed and left the rest," the Lion said in his voice of velvet darkness as Altair bit his tongue against a response. "Without a glance."

Not even as he was forced to his knees, shadows knotting his throat.

"Even Benyamin's corpse."

Altair finally snapped. "I was there. I don't need to relive it."

The Lion did not smile. He did not gloat. No, he looked at Altair with sympathy, as if he understood his pain. Then he left him in the dark.

Altair dropped his feet to the floor, and his head in his hands.

CHAPTER 4

DEATH BEGAN WITH A RATTLE BEFORE DAWN. IT was soon deafening, the hold quivering so fiercely that Zafira's teeth were in danger of falling out. The swaying lanterns showed her shadows that looked like the zumra stumbling to their deaths. The hearts, crumbling to dust.

She tossed the Jawarat into her satchel, gathered her arrows into her sling, and darted up the steps, nearly tripping on her way. It was almost as if she could think clearly only when the book wasn't in her hands.

Zafira had spent the past three days thumbing its worn pages, struggling and failing to focus on the old Safaitic, which made her think the book didn't *want* to be read. It wanted to be held, for its pages to be parted, for the swift curves and trailing i'jam dotting the letters to be seen. It was a notion she found herself able to understand, as absurd as it was for a book to want such a thing. As absurd as an object being able to speak.

And influence.

She wasn't daft; the Jawarat's whispers toyed with her, she knew, and the more she listened to discern what it wanted, the more dangerous her every action would become. It made her wary, for she held more than a bow in her hands now: not just the fate of an unlucky deer or a hare, but the future of Arawiya. The hearts that once belonged to the daama Sisters of Old.

The problem was, she couldn't stop listening.

On deck, the rough Zaramese shouts weren't heightened by chaos or fear, and when the vibrations ground to a stop, she frowned at the abundance of beaming faces and tired grins.

"What was that noise?" she asked over the wind.

"The anchor," Nasir said distantly as she set eyes on the reason for it.

The hem of the sea wended lazily along an umber coast. Dunes billowed inland, sand painting the awakening horizon in strokes of gold that reminded her of Deen's curls and Yasmine's locks, ebbing and flowing with the breeze.

She swallowed a mix of fear and longing at the reminder of her friends. She wanted to see Yasmine, to tell her she was sorry she could not save her brother. To say she was sorry she didn't love him enough. But as desperately as she wanted to see her again—and Umm and Lana—she couldn't deny her trepidation.

"Sultan's Keep. The city that belongs to none yet commands all," Jinan announced.

Every Arawiyan child knew of Sultan's Keep. They studied maps in school, history from papyrus. Before the Arz had emerged, a bustling harbor bordered the city and life unfolded from the shores—stalls topped by colorful fabrics, windows arching one after the other, minarets spearing the skies.

It was all there still, but duller and lifeless. Aside from the lazy falcon circling above, only ghosts lived here now.

"The people chose fear of the Arz over fear of the sultan," Nasir explained.

Zafira could see it up ahead, life signified by the stir of sand far, far in the distance, where hazy minarets rose, the bustle of the day drifting on the breeze.

"It won't be long before the population drifts back here," Kifah said as the Silver Witch joined them. "Now that the Arz is gone."

The Arz was indeed gone.

It had left disorder in its wake—brambles and twigs, rocks and carcasses. Barely a week had passed since Arawiya's curse had lifted, but sand was already swallowing the remains of the forest. The dark trees were nowhere to be seen, almost as if they had retreated into the ground, Sharr's claws—or perhaps the Lion's—now gone.

"Not an animal in sight, Huntress," Kifah teased. "I'm beginning to think you were a myth."

"They would have fled inland," said the Silver Witch.

Zafira had known the Arz was gone ever since they'd lifted the five hearts from within the great trees of Sharr. Ever since the Lion had stolen one and the zumra had fled, leaving Altair behind. Every forward surge of their ship had been a reminder that the Arz, that ever-encroaching tomb, that dark, untamable forest that had made Zafira who she was, had fallen.

Seeing its absence was different. The finality carved a hollow somewhere inside her. The knife of the Silver Witch's words dug deeper, and she shivered at the stillness in the air. The change.

Who am I? she asked the sea. It whispered an answer she couldn't comprehend, and she recalled another moment like this, when she had stood on the shore, amid smooth black stones.

She saw Yasmine in her pale blue dress, waving her off. Precious Lana, glued to her side. Misk nodding in farewell, a spy not one of them had thought to suspect and wouldn't still, if Zafira hadn't learned of it from Benyamin upon Sharr. The safi's ominous words about Demenhur echoed in her thoughts. About the sultan eyeing Arawiya's second-largest army and taking it under his control the way he had done in Sarasin.

"We should have gone to Demenhur first," she said for the thousandth time as Nasir followed her to the longboat with the hearts, and because she didn't want to sound as selfish as she felt, she added, "And sought the caliph's aid. Who knows where the Lion is?"

She looked away from the little crate with a surge of guilt. Was it selfish to think of her family? To want to see if they were safe? Was it selfish to choose the restoration of the dying hearts *over* her family?

"He who pays the coin turns the wheel," Jinan recited, "and Effendi Haadi's instructions were to come here."

He's also dead, Zafira didn't say. She stepped into the boat with a sigh, and every bit of her came alert when Nasir's knee brushed hers as he settled across from her. *Pull yourself together.*

They were going to Sultan's Keep, where people would bow at his feet and a crown would sit at his brow. There was death at his hip and darkness at his command.

Still, her breath caught when the tender sun glossed his hair, when he gripped the oar as a lost memory ticked the left of his mouth up, crinkling his skin like the wrapper of a sweet.

And then he was looking at her and she was looking away, a flash of silver drawing her eye from the deck of Jinan's ship as the boat began its descent into the sea. This was where they would part ways with the Silver Witch, she realized.

Anadil inclined her head, and Zafira was surprised to find she would miss her. *Only a little.*

The Silver Witch met her son's eyes in farewell and Nasir seized, his mouth hardening. He kept every emotion on a tight leash, hidden behind the ashes of his eyes.

The longboat touched the gentle sea in the shadow of the ship's figurehead. It basked in the sun, the curved beak of a bird drenched in gold, feathered wings curling into flames. A phoenix. Above the sails flew a sea-green banner, marked with Zaram's emblem of a golden ax and three drops of blood. The oars turned rhythmically in the azure waters, lulling them until Jinan started up a chatter, her crew as eager as she was to talk about everything and nothing at all.

"How can someone so small talk so much?" Kifah finally asked with almost-comical exhaustion.

Zafira didn't hear Jinan's answer. As they crept toward land, a finger trailed down her spine. There was a heaviness in the air, a warning, and a hunter—a *huntress*—always listened to the signs of the earth.

"Something's not right," she murmured.

Kifah drummed her spear against her thigh and shook her head. "What have we to fear? We are specters, righting wrongs. We'll let nothing stand in our way."

"Fancy words never kept anyone alive," Jinan pointed out when the boat lodged into the sand at shore.

"It's a shame you've never met Altair," Kifah replied.

Zafira stepped out first, but her unease only worsened with a smattering of goose bumps down her arms. She tugged her foot out of the sand with a wet *pop* as the crew began rowing back to the ship, their farewells loud. Jinan, as oblivious as her sailors, stretched her legs.

"There's nothing I love more than the sea beneath my legs, but I'd be lying if I said this isn't nice."

"Akhh, little firebird. You sound like an old man," Kifah said. There was an eagerness to her voice now that she was free of the ship's confines. "Oi, why aren't you going back with the rest of them?"

"I'm afraid you'll be seeing a great deal of my vertically challenged self until I collect my silver. In the meantime, my crew will take the witch to the Hessa Isles and circle back. Not sure if a witch's coin can be trusted, but the offer was too good to pass up."

"What do you plan to do with so much silver? Buy yourself a stool?"

"Quiet," Nasir said, and Zafira drew her bow in an instant, the taut string familiar and welcome. Kifah pivoted her spear as Nasir precariously hefted the crate under one arm and drew his scimitar with the other.

Sunlight winked through the shifting sands and abandoned edifices. Zafira didn't see the hooded figures until something stung her neck, and the world fell dark.

CHAPTER 5

THE LULL THAT FOLLOWED THE DEAFENING GROUND-
ing of the ship's anchor was infinitely worse than any silence Altair had heard before. Worse than the quiet that followed the
anointing of a fresh corpse. Worse than the silence after an offer was refused.

Or maybe that was worse. How would he know? No one ever refused
someone like him.

He recognized Sarasin's dark sands and murky skies instantly. Though
brighter now and the sands less black, it was the perfect haven for ifritkind, and foreboding laced with the hunger in his stomach. How had his
mother felt when she fled Sharr after the Sisters had fallen and the Lion
had been trapped, a new burden swelling in her womb? How had it felt
to assume a new identity, to tell her sons that they were of safin blood, a
heritage leagues beneath that of the rare si'lah?

Altair knotted the thoughts and trunked them.

He followed the Lion down the plank, swinging his arms to and fro
and rattling his chains loudly enough to wake the dead all the way down

in Zaram. The picture of abandon even as he scoured the decrepit houses looming near the shore, searching for aid while isolation sank into his bones.

Nothing. No one. They hadn't arrived yet, or they would be here. *Wouldn't they?* He knew Nasir and the others were due for Sultan's Keep, but still. If *he* had lost one of his own, he would detour the world over to find them.

"They are not here."

Altair started at the Lion's voice. A portion of pita rested in his proffered hand. The second half was in his other, saved for himself. Only Nasir halved his food with such perfect symmetry. "And yet your eyes continue to stray to the horizon for those who will never come."

Hush, hush, went the water. It lapped at the sands, eager for secrets to carry to new shores.

"I'm a general," Altair replied finally. He took the food with cautious hesitance, hunger dulling his pride. "Vigilance is habit."

The Lion hummed. "We will find them, worry not. If they won't come to you, we will go to them."

"And how do you expect to do that?" Altair asked tiredly.

"With your blood and mine. Dum sihr. There is a spell that imitates the Huntress's. I only need to find it." The Lion frowned at his unintentional pun.

Altair stepped off the plank with relief. The desert was far from solid ground, but it did not sway like the sea or lurch like the waves. It was as barren, however. *Nothing* spread for miles and miles. The emptiness bludgeoned his chest.

"Why?" the Lion asked him suddenly, curiosity canting his head. The sun stretched a ray, casting the bold lines of his tattoo in iridescence. "You have no name. No throne. Arawiya has given you nothing, and you have given her everything."

To what end? was what he wanted to know.

Altair had known for quite some time that he would never be king. His mother had kept him in the shadows far too long. Not once did she call the little boy at her side her son. Not once did she share her meals with him, or hold his hand.

He was too painful to look at, too sinful.

Decades later, Ghameq was chosen as her successor, the first mortal with claim to the throne. But Altair's fate was sealed long before that, when their heir was born: dark-haired and gray-eyed. A boy full of promise and purpose, until he was shaped into a blade.

Altair supposed he might have been jealous, had he been different and cared for the throne, had he not known that the gilded chair came with its own trials and tribulations.

But he was perceptive.

His mother would look to the shadows—not to see that he remained there, but to ensure he was safe. She allowed him the finest of rooms in the palace and the freedom of a prince. She assured his tutelage and training from the very best. They were scraps of love, but every morsel she fed him churned his own heart, taught him the value of the sentiment and its elusiveness.

He loved Arawiya, and because there was no one to love him, he loved himself. Enough that he dedicated his life to earning that love, to ensuring he wasn't the scourge she saw him as.

"Do you think she meant to hide you from me?" the Lion asked, and the lack of scorn in his tone gave Altair pause.

This time, his *she* referred to the Silver Witch, but Altair didn't think she feared the Lion in that way. Not until he sank his claws into Ghameq.

"Some good that did," Altair answered, leaning back. His heels dug into the sand.

The ghost of a smile crossed the Lion's features. "True enough. In the end, she only abandoned you as they did. Benyamin, too, to an extent. He chose the prince when he leaped."

Altair was used to being second in all things. He didn't mind, he told himself.

Then why did it feel as if knives were tearing at his heart? Why did the veins in his arms strain against his skin with sudden fervor?

"And you chose me?" Altair asked, mocking. "Is that what this is about? If you did, I wouldn't be fettered like some kind of beast."

The Lion dropped his amber eyes to the chains, ruminating. "Perhaps it is time for a new alliance, then."

Altair cast him a look, ignoring the thrum in his blood, the buzz. The feeling that came with change, with being . . . needed.

"Vengeance doesn't suit me, Baba."

The Lion contemplated his words, considered his son as the sun rose higher and the winds streamed between them.

Then he turned, and Altair barely heard his low order—"Stand aside"—before a volley of black rushed past him, unleashing themselves upon Sarasin. The horde in their true form. Shifting, shapeless beings of smokeless fire, some of them winged and clawed and unrestrained by human limitations.

The Lion smiled. "Go forth, my kin," came his soft command.

Altair was not proud of his awe.

"Arawiya is ours."

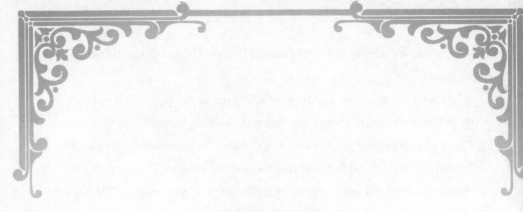

CHAPTER 6

*D*EATH COMMANDS THE TREMOR IN THE LIVING.

Live as if you are death himself. Command him as if you are his master. Depend on no one, for even your shadow will forsake you in the darkest hour.

In the end, it wasn't death that roused fear in Nasir, for his mother had taught him well. It was the darkness. The isolation it brought, reminding him that he was always alone. The way it thieved his sight, an abyss with a nightmare to tell:

A boy, silver circling his brow, shackled by shadows.

A sun, swallowed whole by gaping jaws.

A girl, hair crowned as regal as a queen's, the fire in the ice of her eyes bringing him to his knees.

And a voice, saying: *You needn't fear the darkness when you could become it.*

Nasir came to with the evening's light in his eyes, dust frenzying at his exhale and the dull throb of a needle prick at his neck. He dug his fingers into the rug beneath him—woven of the finest sheep's wool—and noted the high sheen of the stone floor. None of it was familiar, but wherever he was, dinars were not in shortage.

Neither was audacity, clearly. Kidnapping the Prince of Death was no act to be taken lightly. He hadn't expected to be welcomed with open arms in Sultan's Keep, but he hadn't expected to find himself in trouble *this* early.

Zafira stirred with a rustle of clothes. Her hair was coming undone upon the pale wool, and the rise and fall of her chest drove him to the brink. The rug beneath her became qutn sheets within the Sultan's Palace. Her crowned hair became a circlet of silver and a shawl of silk. He drew a wavering breath.

It wasn't like him, to dream. To wish.

It was barely a handful of heartbeats, but she stared back with fire in her hooded gaze as if she knew what plagued him. As if she had a thousand and one questions to ask, but it was his fault silence held them captive. Those three words had grown to a day, stretched to the moon's rising, on and on, an ugly thing festering as the days wove past. *This means nothing.*

He had never been good with words, but he had never expected to lament the fact.

Kifah groaned from his other side, and Nasir looked away first as she sat up, unsure why he was so irritated. He flexed his unbound wrists. His boots were gone, as were the rest of theirs. It was customary to remove one's shoes indoors, but less so to *have* them removed by someone else.

"The hearts!" Zafira uttered suddenly, sitting up.

Nasir jerked, jamming his elbow against a box beside him. *The crate.* He shoved open the lid, releasing a bated breath when he saw all four organs pulsing inside. His suspicion tripled.

"Oi. Where's Jinan?" Kifah asked, taking in the ample room with growing trepidation: the majlis seating flush against the floor, cushions barely worn, as if the inhabitants of this construction never sat for long. A scattering of maps and old papyrus, reed pens, an astrolabe, and unfinished notes. Shelves lined the opposite wall, sagging with books and aging artifacts that looked in danger of crumbling. A single door stood to the side, closed.

The Zaramese captain was nowhere to be seen.

"This place." Kifah's voice dropped. Slowed. "It reminds me of home." Her discomfort was a reminder of why the ink of the Pelusian erudites didn't span both her arms.

Zafira rose with the agility that always made Nasir's throat tighten, and he noted the quickness with which she reached for her bag to ensure the Jawarat was still inside. *Lucky book.*

He parted the curtains at one of the narrow windows and looked out: date palms, tended gardens, the ornate edging of a sprawling building. He couldn't see much, but these were no slums. The palace couldn't be far from here. His *father* couldn't be far from here, controlled by a medallion and a monster.

"Kidnapped," Kifah said, her voice a tad high. "Of everything that could have happened in Sultan's Keep."

"Do you know where we are?" Zafira asked.

It took him a moment to realize the question was directed at him, icy eyes catching him off guard. Rimaal, he was going soft.

"I don't know the inside of every house in Sultan's Keep," he said a little too harshly.

"If you did, I would question whether you were the prince or an ambitious housekeeper."

He clenched his fist around a flare of shadow. "No, I don't know where we are."

"That wasn't too hard, now, was it?" There was a satisfied smirk on her mouth and a crackling in his chest.

"Men are like fish," Kifah said, the break in her voice giving away her unease.

"Shiny, and of little brain?" Zafira replied.

Kifah hefted the crate after a beat. "I half expected a response from Altair."

That was his cue, his jolting reminder: They'd wasted enough time. Nasir tried the door's bronze handle, pausing when he found it unlocked.

"The Lion could be out there," Zafira warned. She lifted her bow and gestured to his sword and Kifah's spear. "Jinan's gone. We're unbound, unharmed, *and* still armed. Whoever's out there doesn't fear us."

Nasir ignored the chill of her words.

The short hall opened to a room drenched in evening light. The aroma of herbed venison and warm bread assaulted his senses, rumbling through his stomach before the distant hum of a terribly depressing tune dampened the air. Zafira stiffened, shoulders bunching.

And the air shifted as someone unfamiliar drew breath. Nasir pivoted, shoving the tip of his gauntlet blade against the stranger's throat in the span of two heartbeats.

"Apologies for taking the liberties precautions necessitate."

Benyamin, said the drowsed part of his brain, conjuring umber eyes and a feline grin, but though the words were unnecessarily languorous and markedly safin, the tone wasn't as genial.

Nor was the stranger deterred by the blade at his throat. He didn't seem to notice it at all, and Nasir felt a fool as the light caught the two rings glittering from the peak of one elongated ear.

His skin was as dark as Kifah's, a smooth brown accented by the gold tattoo curling around his left eye. Nasir relaxed slightly at the sight of it, before he made out the tattoo itself: "nuqi." Pure. A reminder that not all safin were as amicable as Benyamin. Many valued the so-called purity of their race and their perfection, looking down upon everyone else. As if his tattoo weren't prideful enough, the safi's high-collared thobe boasted panels in shades of cream and gold, most of the buttons undone to expose his torso.

"Might as well unbutton the rest of it," Kifah murmured behind Nasir, too low to be heard. By a human.

"I can, if you'd like," the safi drawled, and Nasir nearly risked his dignity to see her obvious mortification. "A prince goes off to Sharr and returns a savage. I cannot say I'm surprised. Is this any way to treat your host?"

"A host doesn't imprison his guests," Zafira pointed out.

"Yet here you are, mortal. Unbound and unharmed," he said, echoing her earlier words. He touched the back of two fingers to the cord knotting the center of his dark beard; it was the same shade as his ivory turban.

"Then where's the Zaramese girl who was with us?" Kifah asked.

"Back at sea, if I am to guess. Once she pocketed the ridiculous amount of silver promised, she left without a backward glance. Did you expect any more from a Zaramese?"

Nasir knew how people eager for coin worked. They lined their pockets and turned tail, regardless of whether or not their employer had died on a villainous island.

"Who are you again?" Kifah asked.

"Seif bin Uqub," he replied. With that, his almost nonexistent amiability disappeared altogether. "Step back, Prince. You may have royal blood in your veins, but I've decapitated worse."

The silence pounded with the promise of bloodshed. And bloodshed there would have been, had Nasir not trekked to Sharr. Had he not found himself a brother there, and friends, and a certain blue-eyed huntress, who stared at him with a command in her gaze. He gritted his teeth and lowered his blade, giving the safi one last glare before stepping back between Kifah and Zafira.

"What do you want?" he asked.

"Where is Altair al-Badawi bin Laa Shayy?" *Son of none.*

What did a safi want from Altair?

"You mean Benyamin?" Kifah asked, finally drawing a reaction in his unnerving eyes. They were the palest gold, so light that they eerily blended into the surrounding whites. "The tattoo," she explained, spear still raised. "Benyamin had one, too. You're part of his circle of safin."

"*High* safin," he corrected as if any of them cared about Arawiya's oldest families—rich, influential, and knowledgeable. "We are of old blood. Headed by Benyamin, we protected Arawiya's secrets and counseled Alderamin and beyond, until we disbanded when he brought a traitor to our fold. The High Circle formed once more, quite recently, at Altair al-Badawi's behest."

Something stuttered in Nasir's chest.

Altair had brought them together? That meant Benyamin had gone to Sharr because of Altair, not the other way around as Nasir had assumed. That meant Benyamin was *Altair's* spider. As was the girl in the tavern, Kulsum—possibly even Jinan.

For a moment, Nasir's mind blanked, making way for memories of Altair acting like no more than an inebriate and philanderer. He almost laughed at his ignorance, at these feelings crushing his lungs.

Of course it was Altair. No one else had a prime position beside Arawiya's throne. No one else was a general with the freedom to traverse the caliphates. Altair had been pulling the strings from the very beginning. He had spun a meticulous web of secrets and lies under carefree grins and silver-tongued words. There was no one else whose every exhale was deliberate.

Altair had planned it all, down to being a thorn in the sultan's side to ensure he was sent with Nasir to Sharr. Nasir fought the surge in his throat—who was he to feel pride for an oaf such as his half brother? *You love him.* He rent that thought in two.

Rimaal, and they had left Altair and his endless volley of secrets with the Lion of the Night.

"Even so, neither are present, and you, Prince, are not a welcome sight."

"Last I recall, you attacked me and brought me here. So spare me your hate," Nasir said, voice low.

"Seif," a new voice warned.

A second safi swept into the room in a flurry of pale pink.

"Marhaba, my loves," she said with a small smile. "I am happy to have you." Her voice was something out of a dream, abstract and melodious. Her wide brown gaze would have looked innocent, if her elongated ears and the defining tattoo around her left eye hadn't spoken of her ancientness. Sharp cheekbones framed her face, unbound bronze hair threaded with pearls. She was the most beautiful being Nasir had ever seen. "Your little companion left once we had paid her dues. She journeys for the Hessa Isles now, with Anadil."

Someone had changed plans, it seemed, but Nasir admitted he could breathe easier knowing the ship's captain would be taking his injured mother to the Isles.

"It is unfortunate that I do not have the resources on hand to cure an injury inflicted by cursed ore, or I would have performed the recovery myself," she added.

Nasir lifted his brows, but there wasn't a hint of pride to her voice, only a pragmatism uncharacteristic of safin.

"Forgive us for the way you were received. The city is no longer safe, and discretion is of utmost importance."

"Was Sultan's Keep ever safe?" Kifah asked, and Nasir shot her a look. Ghameq was many things, but never a fearmonger. It was why an assassin like himself was so useful.

"Safer than this," the safi ceded. "The sultan has announced a sharp increase in taxes, and there is talk of rebellion as people grow restless. The Sultan's Guard loiter, and the city holds its breath. Even Sarasin fares better as of late."

Before Nasir could ask why they should trust her, he saw it: the simple circlet of black at her temple. He'd seen it before, on a safi with a feline grin and sage umber eyes.

CHAPTER 7

THE MOMENT THE MELANCHOLY TUNE HAD STRUCK Zafira's ears, she was there again, in that gilded balcony of Alderamin.

"You're her, aren't you?" she asked, and felt herself relax for the first time since they'd left Jinan's ship. "Benyamin's wife."

"Don't sully his name with your mortal mouth," the safi named Seif snarled, and Zafira resisted the urge to snarl back. Beauty could take a person only so far. "Look at them, Aya."

"Would you rather I spell out his name when I speak of him?" Zafira snapped. She met Benyamin's wife's eyes. *Aya's* eyes. "I heard your voice. In—in Benyamin's dreamwalk."

"He walked with you?" she asked, canting her head in surprise.

Zafira suddenly felt as if she had done something untoward. Benyamin was right: She *was* the most beautiful person Zafira had ever seen. There was something ethereal and dreamily distracted about her, too. As if she existed in a world apart from them.

"Being able to dreamwalk again was all he spoke of when we left Aldera-min. He and Altair were certain that magic and the reason for Arawiya's downfall would be found on Sharr, for that was where it began. We parted ways in Pelusia—he remained there to seek aid from one of the Nine Elite; Seif and I rode for Demenhur, to find you, though we arrived after you had left. We were to reunite here in Sultan's Keep once the Arz fell."

But he wasn't here. He would never be here.

Aya tried but failed to offer them a smile.

Hanan, the old Safaitic of her tattoo said. It meant, most simply, "love"—warm and compassionate. Kind. The letters curled around her eye, at home on her skin.

The *tap, tap, tap* of Kifah's spear filled the sudden quiet, and Zafira couldn't bring herself to speak, to answer Aya's silent question, thinking of Umm and Baba. How would one take the death of the spouse one had loved for *centuries*?

"He rests with the Sisters of Old," Nasir said finally, and Zafira shivered at the tenderness in his tone.

Aya let loose a soft cry. Seif went still, surprise freezing his stare.

"He—he died a noble death."

"Noble?" Seif barked, and Nasir flinched, no doubt remembering *why* the safi had died. "Death is a mockery and an inevitability for your kind. Only mortals decorate corpses with titles. Do you hear how they speak of your beloved, Aya?"

If Zafira had to guess at what Seif loved more than himself, it was the word "mortal."

"Do you remember how *you* spoke of him, Seif? How the High Circle shunned my love when he acted out of the good of his heart?" Aya asked quietly. Her eyes fell closed, and she drew a careful breath through her nose. "How? How did Benyamin come to die . . . a noble death?"

Nasir floundered in silence, turmoil ablaze in his eyes. This time, Zafira answered. "He leaped in front of a stave of cursed ore."

She didn't say the stave was the Lion of the Night's, to whom Benyamin had once shown kindness, losing his people's favor in the process. It didn't seem right, when Seif clearly still loathed him for that reason. Laa, Zafira would not tarnish her friend's legacy in such a way.

"We couldn't have made it through Sharr without his guidance, and we couldn't have made it off the island without his sacrifice." She bit her tongue. He was her friend. Her guide and mentor. She didn't know how Aya was holding together when Zafira still trembled with his loss. "He sacrificed himself for Arawiya."

She ignored Nasir's sharp intake of air, because it was true. Benyamin had trusted the zumra to see this through. He believed them capable, or he wouldn't have done what he had, would he? For, like Altair, he did nothing without purpose, though it seemed his actions had more heart.

She didn't say Benyamin had died saving the prince whom Arawiya loathed and feared, either. The very one he had scorned for being a prince with no control over his life. In the end, Benyamin had seen something in Nasir. Something worth sacrificing his life for.

Aya stifled a sob.

"Altair still lives," Zafira added, "but he is no better off. The Lion of the Night has him."

Seif shared a look with Aya. "Haider?"

"Indeed. Your good friend is alive and well," Kifah said dryly, and when she noted Zafira's furrowed brow, she murmured, "That's the Lion's true name." She lifted a tattooed arm. "Half a scholar, remember?"

Seif dragged a hand down his face. "I always knew this plan was too far-fetched. We should never have trusted Altair—"

"Enough." Nasir's low voice cut him off. It amazed her, how far the prince's sentiments surrounding Altair had come. "How long had he planned for? Years? No one expected the Lion of the Night to be alive and waiting. We found the Jawarat, and we found the hearts of the Sisters of Old. We fought a battle against Arawiya's greatest foe, and all you did was traipse from one place to another, so I suggest, safi, that you watch your tongue."

Seif crossed his arms, and though he had to be older than a century, he looked like a petulant child.

"Their hearts?" Aya inquired numbly.

"The hearts were what lit the royal minarets and fueled magic," Zafira explained. It seemed everyone knew the minarets were lit by something— they just didn't know *what*. "And they're dying."

Kifah looked to her sharply. "What?"

Zafira told them what she'd learned from the Silver Witch.

"Oi, wait. How were the Sisters' hearts in the minarets *while* they were leading Arawiya?" Kifah asked, lines creasing her brow.

Zafira would not have known, if not for the Jawarat. She startled at the sudden flood of memories that didn't belong to her. "They didn't need their hearts to live."

Laa, the hearts were like jewels to the powerful women. Adornments that made them powerful, nothing more. They did not need them to breathe, to live, to feel. Not like men and safin.

They could remove them as easily as one would a thorn in a palm, and replace them just the same.

"But by storing their hearts in the minarets, rather than their own bodies, they diluted their powers," Zafira added, once more awed by what the Sisters had sacrificed for the good of the kingdom. "They were almost like us."

She wondered if the Silver Witch had ever removed her own heart. If she was like her sisters, or if she loved her power too much.

Nasir didn't seem to care about magic any more than he ever did. "Magic has been gone for ninety years. The hearts can survive another week. We go for Altair first."

Kifah set her spear against the wall, cream and ornate, and rubbed at her temples. "I want magic back for reasons no safin will understand, but I'm with the prince. Altair first, magic second."

Seif considered them. "The hearts may not last."

It is true, the Jawarat said. The hearts had two homes: the Sisters and the royal minarets created by them.

"As Nasir said, they were fine on Sharr for nearly a century," Kifah said.

But they had still been *within* the Sisters. Those five massive trees on Sharr were what the Sisters had become, guardians of the Jawarat, protectors of their hearts, even as the organs sustained them.

They needed to be housed in the minarets, or they would fade to dust. Still, Zafira held her tongue, afraid of sounding callous. She didn't want to leave Altair in the hands of the Lion, either.

"Their restoration is what Altair would wish," Aya said, casting her vote.

Kifah looked at Zafira, as if her answer would sway two safin from Benyamin's ancient circle of high safin. *Home.* That was what she wanted, but she couldn't bring that up now, when they were being selfless. Zafira had been selfless her entire life. What was another day or two?

"What I didn't say earlier," she said instead, "is that we have only four hearts. The Lion has the fifth."

Seif's brows angled sharply, instantly irritating her. "You lost the fifth heart."

"*We*, Seif. And we lost more than the heart of a Sister," Aya reminded softly, before Zafira, Nasir, and Kifah could simultaneously snap his neck. *Sweet snow.* She looked from one of them to the other. "It was not your fault."

"Never thought it was," said Kifah, affronted.

"Restoration is important," Zafira continued calmly, "but four hearts won't give us the upper hand."

Aya released a long breath, making the connection. "Magic for all or none."

"Even if it were possible, none of you know how to use magic," Seif muttered snobbishly.

Zafira did. She'd been using her magic long before she even knew what it was.

"Every fireheart will incinerate the surrounding mile," Seif went on.

"I might not have been alive when magic was around, but even I know magic is innate," Kifah said. "We'll need to perfect it, but it's not like we're all going to be wandering Arawiya with loose bladders."

"Was there no other analogy?" Seif asked.

Kifah rolled her eyes. "Prude."

"The Lion will come for the rest of the hearts," Aya said, guiding them back to the matter at hand. "A single one is useless without the others."

It was sound reasoning, Zafira knew, but something told her the hearts were not a priority for him. Not yet. She pulled the Jawarat from her bag, running her fingers down the lion's mane, instantly at ease. Even on Sharr, the Lion's focus had been on the book—she doubted they would have escaped with as many of the hearts as they had otherwise.

Your confidence astounds, bint Iskandar.

"Arawiya knows next to nothing of the hearts," Zafira pointed out. "The Sisters held the knowledge of them close."

"And now that knowledge is in the Jawarat," Nasir gathered.

Zafira nodded grimly. "He'll come for the Jawarat first, if for no reason other than it being what he craves: knowledge."

Even if she hadn't seen the tattoo curling around the Lion's eye, the old Safaitic word of 'ilm etched bold and bronze, she would have known this, for Benyamin had told them as much. It was what he valued above all else.

Seif eyed the book and extended his hand. "Then it must be under strict supervision."

No, bint Iskandar.

For an immortal book, it had a knack for sounding like a sulking child.

"Do you think I won't protect the thing that's bound to me? If anything happens to it, I could die," Zafira snapped. "I'm more than capable of keeping it safe."

Seif barked a laugh. "You *bound* yourself to a hilya?"

Zafira had no notion of what a hilya was, but the look on the safi's face was enough to make her resolve waver.

He drew a breath, ready to spew more, but Aya spoke first. "*That is enough.* Protect it well, Huntress."

Zafira nodded once, uncertain if her smug triumph was her own or prompted by the book sitting gleefully relieved in her hands.

Seif looked as if he had more to say, and from the way his pale gaze flicked to Aya, Zafira guessed it involved twistedly pinning the blame on Benyamin, the fallen safi who had spent the past nine decades blaming himself for the Lion's betrayal, doing all he could to make up for the tragedy of his good intentions. It was clear he had even fronted Altair's gossamer web to protect him, for it couldn't have been easy being a spymaster and the sultan's right-hand general at once.

Aya gripped Seif's arm and drew him away.

"There is one more thing," Nasir said slowly, halting them, and Zafira could tell that whatever it was cost precious dignity. "The Lion controls my . . . father. If you've safin we can trust, it would be ideal to station them across the city. Near the palace, the Great Library, everywhere of importance."

Zafira's heart stuttered at the mention of yet another place Baba had longed to see. It was history incarnate, scrolls and parchment preserving every last bit of knowledge that ever meant anything. She wondered if the Lion had made use of it through his control of Ghameq. It was likely. Greed had no limit.

Seif pursed his mouth and spoke to Aya in low tones that not even Zafira could catch. Then he sauntered away without a backward glance.

Kifah lifted an eyebrow. "Bleeding Guljul, if I thought Benyamin was vain, this one can't even keep his clothes on."

"That doesn't mean you have to look," Zafira returned, and Kifah shot her a murderous glare.

"Seif is captain of Alderamin's royal guard and will take care of everything. I am sorry he is not the most affable of us," Aya said. She gestured to the crate with the hearts, clutched in Nasir's hands. "Until we determine the best course of action, we will keep the hearts close and in constant movement. Change hands every half day. Never leave them unattended." She paused. "Benyamin thought highly of you. He and Altair had done as much to keep Arawiya from crumbling as the sultana did, though it was never enough. He always said the world was meant to be salvaged by the ones it had wronged. Life makes a mockery of us, does it not?"

Death, Zafira corrected in her head because she was mortal. *Death makes a mockery of us.*

Aya pressed the back of her hand to her mouth, but not before a murmur slipped free. *Roohi.*

Outside, the final stretch of the sun washed the world in deep gold. No one knew what to say in the silence. What was it like to be burdened by an eternity of sadness? They mourned Benyamin, but none of them could begin to understand how much his wife mourned him.

Was that how Zafira was to live the rest of her days, burdened by the death of her loved ones?

"Okhti?"

Zafira went still. *Now I'm hearing things.* But Nasir looked past her, then Kifah.

"The kingdom is indeed a small place," Aya said with a soft smile.

But Lana couldn't be here; she was in Demenhur, with Yasmine and Umm and Misk. Where she would be safe. Zafira held her breath as she turned, as if by breathing she might lose the delicate cadence of her sister's voice.

A girl, too small for fourteen years, stood frozen in the doorway, her shawl sliding back from her dark hair. She was freckled and slight, soft brown eyes wide and disbelieving, features Zafira could have painted blind.

Lana.

Zafira ran, bow and quiver falling to the polished stone as she threw her arms around her sister, burying her nose into her hair with a broken sob. "Ya, sweet one."

Lana laughed as tears streaked her cheeks. Zafira wiped them away with her thumbs. Pressed a kiss to her brow. "What are you doing here?"

"Waiting for you," Lana said with a shy smile as the others continued to stare. "I missed you, Okhti. I've been so alone."

"Liar," Zafira teased, and she didn't think she'd ever been so happy to see her. "I left you in good hands. You had Yasmine and Misk, and I'm sure Ummi kept you busy. I was the one who—"

Zafira stopped when the color drained from Lana's face. She pulled back, dread coiling in her stomach at the weight clinging to her sister, a prudence she should not have had to bear. "What is it? Lana, what happened?"

"Ummi," she said, almost soundlessly. "She's dead. She died the day you left."

CHAPTER 8

NASIR DIDN'T HEAR WHAT HER SISTER SAID, BUT when Zafira dropped to her knees, her sheathed jambiya striking the floor, it was telling enough. *Go to her, you fool.* His feet grew roots, tethering him to the ground, and the crate in his arms readied to shatter, so tight was his grip. Aya's inhale shook. If there was any more melancholy within these walls, they would collapse.

Kifah broke the silence, shuffling forward and making him feel infinitely worse. "Zafira——"

"How?" she whispered, tugging the shawl from her neck as if it were a noose.

Her sister's eyes widened in fear and anguish.

"Lana," Zafira ground out, lifting her head, and Nasir was surprised by her anger. "*How?*"

"Okhti," she whispered, gaze darting from Nasir to Kifah to Aya. "Not here——"

"Tell me."

It wasn't anger, Nasir realized. It was an attempt to hold herself together, to stop from falling apart. She held her shoulders tight, though he saw the ripple across them, the tremble that worsened as the heartbeats ticked on. He thought of closing the distance between them, reaching for her and rubbing the tension from her shoulders. That was what people did, wasn't it?

Nasir gripped the crate tighter. He wouldn't know—he was typically the one doling the killing strike, disappearing from the repercussions. Altair would know what to say and what to do, how to make her feel like living again.

"Do you remember when the Arz came back?" Lana asked. She shared Zafira's delicate features, but where Zafira's were sharpened by her colder coloring, the younger girl's were warm, down to the bronze glint in her hair. "Right after you and Deen left."

Nasir clenched his jaw at the mention of Deen. Zafira's shoulders fell even lower.

"Soldiers started pouring into the streets, in black-and-silver uniforms, and . . . and *masks*. It . . . People stopped what they were doing. They couldn't breathe, they collapsed in the middle of the street and choked until their lungs stopped working. I heard it. Saw it." Her gaze flicked to Aya's and back.

Nasir's own lungs ceased to work as he pieced together the girl's words.

"How is that possible?" Kifah breathed.

"It was a vapor," Lana murmured, an edge to her voice. "It destroyed my entire village. I watched people die."

Nasir had never detested anything as much as he detested himself in that moment. For though he had never had a hand in the vapor, in the fumes that had been harvested in Sarasin, his cowardice was to blame. His inability to stand against his father.

Kifah crouched beside Zafira. Aya strode to her, brushing a hand over Zafira's hair. Lana held her hands.

Nasir remained where he was, the crate in his hands, the truth on his shoulders.

Because he had done it. He had killed Zafira's mother.

CHAPTER 9

ZAFIRA THOUGHT OF HER PEOPLE, OF THE ONES SHE had scorned for their jubilation, for their laughs and their glittering eyes when the snow hindered their lives as the Arz crept close. She thought of Bakdash's lavender door. Of Araby's sweet shop, and old Adib's stall. Of the Empty Forest, where Deen chopped wood, and his little creations sprinkled throughout hers and the Ra'ads' houses.

She thought of everything but Umm, anything to keep her alive a little while longer.

Black and silver, Lana had said. Sarasins.

Zafira remembered Benyamin's warning, of the sultan turning to Demenhur once Sarasin was under his thumb. Arawiyans, just like everyone else, whose only crime was the soil their houses stood upon.

Ummi, Ummi, Ummi. With her cold blue eyes and her warm smile. With her strength and resilience. With Baba's blood on her hands.

"And your mother," Kifah prompted Lana gently from Zafira's right. "Was she not able to escape with you?"

Lana crouched, and the wide hem of her jade abaya, one Zafira had never seen before, fanned around her. "She's like you, Okhti. Laa, *you're* like her."

Zafira tried not to listen to the words. Tried to stop the pain.

"She went to the old schoolhouse. You know the one near our street? She took thirteen elders and six children and whatever food they could find, and helped barricade the windows and the door." Lana dropped her gaze to her hands. "Then she went to the well for more water."

That was the Umm Zafira remembered, with her head held high and her knife-grip sure. The Umm Lana was less acquainted with. In the pause that followed, Zafira realized she was waiting for Lana to say more. Like a child hoping the truth wasn't so.

"Maybe she hid elsewhere." Zafira would leave for the western villages. She was a daama da'ira, and she could find anything, any*one*. "Maybe she's still—"

Lana stopped her with a shake of her head. "Misk found her. She saved them at the cost of her life."

Zafira caught on the word "found." It was used in the way one spoke of a fledgling in the snow. The way one spoke of a lost purse that was discovered with all its coins spent.

"Yasmine?" she asked, something squeezing her ribs.

"Alive," Lana said. "Safe. She's in the Demenhune palace."

Zafira's relief was a heavy exhale everyone noted. The scrutiny was suddenly too much. The eyes trained on her, the sympathy clouding the room, the Jawarat's silent regard. She shot to her feet and whirled to Aya, only to nearly crash into Nasir.

"I'm sorry."

Confusion wrinkled her brow, more at the sorrow in his eyes than the words he spoke.

"Why?" she asked. "Did you have a hand in her death?"

He flinched.

He daama flinched. Zafira paused. If the vapors were the work of the sultan, *had* Nasir played a part? She halted her dark thoughts. *Skies.* He would have left Sultan's Keep when she had left Demenhur. That meant he'd been preparing for his journey to Sharr, not planning the massacre of a village.

She dropped her gaze, annoyed and ashamed and hurting and everything at once.

"Come," Aya said, knowing what she needed. "I'll lead you to your room."

CHAPTER 10

NASIR LEANED AGAINST THE SMOOTH DOOR OF THE room Aya had given him. It was ample space with rich decor, but the bed was simple and neat, lit by the moon streaming from the open window. He hadn't realized how long he'd spent in close quarters with the others—cramped ship cabins excluded—until Aya had closed the door behind him and the air quivered with his breathing alone.

He undressed and folded his clothes before stepping into the tub with its lazy wafts of steam. As always, scrubbing himself clean reminded him of everything he hated about himself—the scars on his back, the wrongness of his life. There was another scar now, beside his collarbone, still slick from the salve Zafira had tended to him with. He leaned into the last of the bath's warmth, remembering her fingers on his skin. The weight of her. The heat of her gaze unraveling him.

Her anguish now. The way her face fell when she understood the depths of his monstrosity, for he had done nothing to stop his father from harvesting the vapors that claimed her mother.

The clothes that had been left for him were his most garish: a deep burgundy qamis, dark robes edged in blue and silver. There was only one way these clothes could have gotten here, and he imagined Altair digging through his wardrobe, grinning like mad when he found this tucked in a corner. Nasir tugged the qamis over his head and hung his robes on the back of a chair. He straightened the books on the shelf and aligned the bowls on the table.

Standing here, so far from Sharr, so close to his father and the air still raw with Zafira's pain, he felt lost. He didn't know how to function without orders. How to act without being told.

Before he knew it, he was leaving his room, crossing the carpeted hall, and stopping before another door. He knocked once, softly.

It opened almost instantly.

Her hair was unbound, soft waves caressing her face. She looked younger this way, more vulnerable, and he was at once relieved to find she didn't look at him with blame.

I'm sorry, he wanted to say. To make her understand.

How are you, he fought to ask, but was it callous to ask what the weight in her eyes already told him?

"I was about to bathe. What's wrong?" she asked finally. It was a guarded question. The Jawarat was in her hand.

Nothing.

Everything.

"I didn't mean it," he breathed in a rush, as if his heart had decided it had listened to his stubborn brain long enough.

Selfish idiot. She was mourning and he could only think of himself, but he was tired. So daama tired of the vines those words had twisted between them.

She tilted her head, curious gazelle that she was. "Didn't mean what?"

He tried but failed to stop the shadows leaching from his fingers. How was it that words were impossible, when drawing a blade and ending someone's life wasn't?

Because words cut deeper than swords.

He took a slow breath and lifted a hand to the back of his neck. Dropped it.

"What I said on Sharr. That it—that it meant nothing." It was only after he spoke that he could look at her again.

In time to see her eyes drift to his mouth, to the burgundy linen of his qamis and back up again.

"What did it mean, then?"

Everything, he wanted to say, but there was a cloth in his mouth, woven from fear and suppression.

He'd been a fool to say what he'd said, he knew. He had closed the distance between them to stop her destructive path, to bring her to her senses, to *distract* her. He'd never expected to feel so much, to want so deeply, and that flood of emotion had terrified him.

She made a sound in the back of her throat when he said nothing, her disappointment damning, and then she was closing the door, bit by bit, as if waiting for him to put out his hand and stop her.

He was the crown prince, born to lead but forced to follow, follow, follow all his life.

And so he did nothing.

CHAPTER 11

ZAFIRA PRESSED HER HEAD AGAINST THE SMOOTH wood and heard his heavy sigh on the other side, a reminder of how easily his aloof mask could fall apart.

Then, a long while later, his door slipped closed.

She knew there was more he wanted to say. There was chaos in his eyes and a barricade across his lips. She could have helped him along, but he was the prince. He should be more than capable. Skies, she was as pettish as Seif.

"Who was that?" Lana asked from the bed, wider than any Zafira had ever lain in. She spoke as if Zafira had just returned after a day of wandering through the stalls of the sooq. As if there weren't a death or two strung between them and a new world cresting the horizon.

Again, Zafira waited for the burn of tears. Instead, there was a strange unraveling in her chest that made it easier to breathe.

Lana tilted her head, silently repeating her question. What could Zafira say—that he was a friend she had made? A boy she had kissed? A prince she must bow to? The assassin whose father was responsible for their mother's death among hundreds of others?

"Nasir," Zafira replied, setting aside the Jawarat. *There we go.* The world was full of Nasirs, wasn't it?

Lana shot up. "As in the Prince of Death?"

Clearly not enough Nasirs.

"I wouldn't . . . call him that," Zafira said as Lana turned away so she could drop her clothes in a heap and sink into the cool bath.

"I didn't know he would look nice," Lana contemplated, and Zafira bit her lower lip, thinking of the crimson linen stretched across his shoulders, the little triangle of skin framed by his unbuttoned collar. The way the fabric of his sirwal clung to his thighs. He didn't look nice, he looked . . . Zafira lifted her hands to her cheeks.

Something about knowing he was a short distance away when she wasn't dressed terrified her more than the Arz ever had. It *allured* her more than the Arz ever had.

Lana came to the side of the tub. "You're pretty when you're happy."

Zafira leaned her head against the rim. "I'm not."

His soft voice caressed her ears. *I didn't mean it.*

Some part of her had known it was a lie, even then. That moment between the marble columns was too real, too raw, filled with too much. It was how easily he spoke the lie that had angered her. How easily he would dismiss her, and himself.

"But you've caught the attention of the prince!"

Which was precisely it, wasn't it? She had been drawn to him as he had been to her, and it wasn't as if there was an abundance of women on Sharr to rivet him. It would be different now. "Didn't you just call him the Prince of Death?"

"Prince of Death, Demenhune Hunter. Titles don't tell you who a person is."

Zafira sighed. "How can I be happy, Lana? I lost friends on Sharr. Ummi is dead. Our village is gone."

Lana stared at Zafira's hands for a beat. "Was Deen one of those friends?"

Zafira jerked, splashing water on her face, and Lana gave her a small, wavering smile.

"I had a feeling when I saw him stepping after you and boarding the ship. He was never as . . . resilient as you. You would fight your way out of the grave for us. You would *kill* for us. He was content enough with the chance to die for the ones he loved."

Zafira studied Lana: the deeper layer of sorrow in her words, the glisten in her gaze. Sweet snow, her sister had *loved* Deen. Not in the way Zafira had loved him, for he had been one of her dearest friends. Not in the way Deen himself had loved Lana, as a doting older brother. But more.

Deen was soft where Zafira was hard. He was ready to see the best in the world, where Zafira saw darkness. Would it come as any surprise that Lana had fallen in love with him?

"One moment we were safe," Zafira said softly, "the next there were three bowstrings snapping at once." She would never forget that sound, or the breathless lack of it that followed. Her fingers closed around the ring hanging at her chest from a golden chain, and Lana's eyes followed. "I'm sorry."

Lana's throat shifted. She struggled to find words, for the grief in books was a mere fraction of what the real world inflicted. "It was meant to happen, even if I wish it weren't so."

If Zafira had loved him, perhaps. Accepted his proposal. Married him.

She shook free from the line of thought and hastened to change the subject. "How did you escape the attack?"

"Misk," Lana said, still somber. She boxed away her sorrow with a heavy exhale. "He was ready when the soldiers came in. As if he knew before it happened. A few of his friends ushered the caliph and sayyidi Haytham into their caravan."

Of course he had. Because he was Altair's spider, sent to spy on the Demenhune Hunter, and he would have received word as spies were wont to do. Clearly not early enough, if there had only been time to vacate the bigoted caliph and no one else. She felt a needless sense of betrayal, as if by knowing moments before, Misk had somehow played a part in the massacre.

The Jawarat hummed. Water dripped from her hair. *Plink, plink, plink.*

"I tried to go back for Ummi, but he wouldn't let me, and when *he* went back, she was gone. There wasn't time to keep searching, because we had to leave for the palace."

There was a kind of sand, rare in the desert, that appeared as harmless as normal sand until it sank beneath one's feet, swallowing the unsuspecting, worsening the longer they struggled, loosening its grip only when they did the opposite. That was how grief was. The longer one wallowed, the more it hungered.

Zafira tossed her towel onto the chair and tugged on fresh clothes.

"I thought it would hurt more," Lana said, searching for a way to understand as Zafira pulled her to the bed.

"When we buried Baba five years ago, we buried part of Ummi, too. She's been dead for as long as Baba has. She loved us, but not the way she loved Baba," Zafira said carefully, as she herself tried to make sense of why she felt relief more than sorrow, guilt more than pain. "He was her life. We were the reminders of it."

Lana looked away.

"Don't," Zafira said, gripping her chin. "You were steadfast by Ummi's side, and you did your part. You have no reason to feel guilt." Unlike Zafira, who had reconciled with her mother only to lose her. "How did you get here? How did you find me?"

Lana toyed with the tiny door on the lantern, twisting shadows across the room. "The Arz erupted back to life just after you left Demenhur. The soldiers came in moments later, and it was chaos, Okhti. People were running and screaming, and then they just . . . stopped. Some people have that power, don't they? They only have to exist and everyone around them abandons reason. That was how it was when Ammah Aya came. Tall and beautiful and dreamy.

"I saw her helping people, ushering them to safety. Yasmine dragged me into our cart then, but I saw her through the flaps. She was bent over a boy lying on his back, pumping his still chest and holding something against his nose. When we reached the palace, I found out the boy had lived."

Zafira blinked. Color bled across Lana's cheeks. *Sweet snow below.*

"I was focusing on you and Aya, but maybe I was wrong. Do I need to be worried about this . . . boy?"

Lana gave her a look. "He's a friend. We don't talk much, because he's always wearing a mask to protect his lungs, but the company is nice when I'm working."

"You *work* in the palace?" Zafira asked. That wasn't part of the bargain she had made with the caliph when she'd agreed to journey to Sharr.

"I'm getting to that," Lana said sternly, pulling the covers over her tiny feet. "Once Ammah Aya cured the boy, the palace healers wouldn't let her go. She tended to everyone they brought in. Soldiers, too. The caliph and most of the palace men frowned at a woman being lauded, but she didn't care. And there wasn't much they could do because she *is* safin."

Lana glowed with admiration, and Zafira was glad for it, even if it came with a sting of jealousy, for Lana's awe was usually reserved for Zafira.

"I tried to help her the way I used to with Ummi, and she liked it, I think," Lana went on. "She liked having someone who knew what she needed before she could ask. We were attuned to each other. Everyone else mostly harassed her with questions upon questions, you know?

"I helped people, Okhti. I finally understood what it was like to be you."

Zafira tamped down her smile at that, quelling her pride and a flush of embarrassment for thinking she had been replaced.

"Seif claims Ammah Aya is the best healer Arawiya has ever known," Lana continued, and Zafira remembered Benyamin's son, Aya's melancholy tune in the dreamwalk. How skilled a healer could Aya truly be if she couldn't save her own son? Or perhaps that was the greater evil, having power in your hands but being powerless to alter a reality.

"And she couldn't have found a better apprentice," Zafira said honestly.

Lana ducked her head with a shy smile. "Well, I know what half of Ummi's little cabinet is for now, though I haven't had a chance to go back home and fetch it. I've learned so much, Okhti. Ammah Aya stayed in the Demenhune palace until the Arz fell."

And that was when Aya would have made her way here, to Sultan's Keep, to see her beloved again. Only to learn he had died leagues away.

"And Yasmine just . . . let you leave with her?"

"She, er, didn't."

Lana didn't elaborate, but Zafira knew Yasmine.

"I see. If you haven't already, you do know you're going to suffer for this, yes?"

"As well as you do when you have to tell her about her brother," Lana taunted, and Zafira could tell she was trying to make light of something she wasn't ready to just yet.

Zafira cast her a look. "My point here is that Aya could have been a murderer who had taken a fancy to you. Did you ever consider that?"

Lana laughed before she realized Zafira was serious. "You could have died on Sharr, but that didn't stop you." She closed her small hands around Zafira's. "I had nothing left to lose."

There was always more to lose.

"Besides," Lana added with a wrinkle of her nose. "Ammah Aya doesn't strike me as the murderous type. I trust her."

Zafira sighed. What mattered was that Lana was safe, and that Aya wasn't a monster working for the Lion or someone equally terrible. Zafira trusted Aya, too. She was Benyamin's wife, after all.

"Anyone who can mend a body must find destroying it just as fascinating," Zafira teased, and when Lana didn't disagree, she nudged her. "I'm proud of you, Lana. So, so proud."

She beamed. "You're the one who took down the Arz. You saved Arawiya."

Zafira had missed being the focus of her sister's unhampered admiration.

"I'm afraid I'm not as grand as the heroes in your stories. Nor did I do any of it alone," Zafira said. And yet she and the others *hadn't* saved Arawiya. Not yet. She closed her hand around the Jawarat, meeting Lana's curious gaze. She deserved to know, didn't she? That her sister had bound herself to an ancient tome. That her sister lived and breathed with the memories of the Sisters of Old. "Nor have I returned unchanged."

She told Lana of their journey. Of meeting the Lion of the Night. Of the Jawarat and the ifrit. The Silver Witch. Lana gulped down every last word, and when Zafira finished, she realized there were fates worse than the Arz.

She saw it when the lantern light reflected amber in Lana's eyes. When a girl as tiny as her knitted a man's flesh together, undeterred by blood.

Lana was far from her little reading nook in the foyer of their tiny house, deep in the crux of danger, yet it was a blessing, wasn't it? The Lion had stolen their home, their parents, their village, but Lana was safe, and that meant Zafira could finish what she had started: end him, find Altair, restore magic, and then face Yasmine, which was altogether more frightening than everything else combined.

The very thought of telling her of Deen's fate filled Zafira with fear and dread and a deep-rooted sorrow that crowded her throat.

Lana was watching her, and Zafira forced a smile. "Is Sultan's Keep everything you imagined?"

For a moment, she was afraid Lana would push. Needle her about the

Jawarat's whispers, about Benyamin's dreamwalk. About Baba's cloak, which she would never see again.

"I was afraid I'd have nothing to do here," Lana said instead. "It's the sultan's city! I'm a village girl with nothing to my name. But you know how weeds grow no matter where they're planted? That's me."

Zafira didn't point out that she was one of the most beautiful weeds in Arawiya.

"I've been keeping busy."

"Oh?"

Lana nodded. "The sultan's going mad, apparently. People are rioting, and more and more are turning up in infirmaries short of medics. Ammah Aya and I have been helping. She tutors me in the mornings, and we assist in different infirmaries from noon. They even pay a small sum. Can you believe I've earned enough dinars to buy something, Okhti? Money of my own." Lana leaned forward, remembering something else. She lowered her voice. "Oh, and when I sewed a man's arm as neatly as a seamstress, Ammah Aya called me a natural. She says that when magic returns, my affinity could be healing. Imagine that!"

Zafira felt both a flood of pride and a small sense of . . . loss. As if her sister no longer needed her. As if she had found purpose when Zafira had lost hers. *What a selfish caravan of thought.*

"What about Sukkar? Is he—" She couldn't finish her question.

Lana smiled gently. "He's safe. He was with us, remember?"

Another knock sounded at the door before she could press for her horse's whereabouts, as soft and tentative as earlier.

Lana's eyes brightened. "It's him, isn't it? The prince." She nudged Zafira. "Aren't you going to open it?"

"No."

Lana hopped off the bed. "Then I wi—"

"No, you won't. Sit down." Zafira glared and Lana glared back. She gritted her teeth. "Fine."

Zafira opened the door with her heart in her throat. Nasir's eyes touched her damp hair, her wrinkled qamis, and settled on her face. He was still only half-dressed.

"Are you tired?" he asked.

She furrowed her brow. "No? I rested long enough on the ship, I suppose."

"Come with me."

He was already turning away, and she would have refused to be ordered if she hadn't caught the light in his eyes. The hint of diffidence. The flare of shadow escaping his fingers before he stopped it.

"Where?" she asked, ignoring Lana's whispered "Yalla!" from her perch on the bed. Zafira wasn't supposed to indulge him. She wasn't supposed to indulge *herself*.

"I want to show you something."

It was rare for him to use the word "want." Possibly rare for him to *do* anything he wanted, too.

"But my sister—"

Lana hissed. Skies, the girl didn't even know him.

Zafira stepped back into the room with a scowl. "I thought you missed me."

"Of course. And if you don't get too engrossed," Lana said with a grin, "you'll be back in no time."

"Engrossed?" Zafira asked with a lift of her brows. Either Yasmine had found someone new to share her favorite stories with, or someone's reading material was no longer limited to adventure.

Lana only shrugged.

Zafira wrapped the Jawarat in a scarf and tucked it into a corner. *Take us with you, bint Iskandar.* She gritted her teeth against the voice and gave Lana's curiosity a look. "Don't touch it."

"Of course, sayyida," she replied solemnly.

———◆———

Zafira followed Nasir to his room. Her eyes slipped from his robes hanging on the back of a chair to his towel stretched neatly with his drying turban on the rack and then to the bed, where the sheets were strewn from a restless attempt at sleep.

"Where are the hearts?" she asked. He'd last had them.

"With Kifah," he answered, and closed the door behind her, closing away the entire world. Every last worry over Lana and the Lion and the Jawarat faded away, replaced by a burn low in her stomach.

He paused, realizing the same with a shallow breath, and stepped past her.

Before the window, he handed her two pieces of supple calfskin, a cross between socks and shoes. His sleeve shifted with the movement, and when he didn't bother to conceal the teardrop tattoo as quickly as he once did, she felt . . . She didn't know what she felt, but it was stirred with fear.

A kind of fear she craved.

"Can you climb?"

She looked out and the desert cold bit at her nose, the stars clear and bright and real enough to grasp. Silhouetted buildings rose into the night, as vigilant as the owls she sometimes saw in the Empty Forest. They were a good two or three stories off the ground, but she shrugged against the thrum in her blood. "Of course. The first rule is don't look down, laa?"

"Looking down is half the fun," Nasir scoffed, but there was a strain to his voice that heightened her awareness.

"Fun. You." She almost laughed.

He turned to her abruptly, caging her between the wall and the heat of his body. Her limbs ceased to function. Myrrh and amber twined when he lowered his head the barest fraction, his mouth so close to hers that her lips buzzed and her head spun.

The right of his mouth lifted. "I can be lots of fun, Zafira."

She swallowed at the lazy drawl of her name, and his eyes darkened as they traced the shift of her throat. She wanted to fight the wicked grin off his mouth with her own, aware of the sway in her body, threatening to pitch forward and close the distance between them.

"This is all I've been able to think about. You. Us. Those damning words," he said softly, his voice liquid darkness.

"You said them," Zafira breathed.

"I take them back."

"Is that how you say you're sorry?"

"I can get on my knees for you, fair gazelle," he whispered against her cheek, "if that is what you wish."

This was not Sharr. This was a room with a locked door and a half-dressed prince and a bed just a small shove away. The air simmered with his dangerous words, with her errant thoughts and the tension making it hard to breathe.

"I measure fun by the pound of my pulse." His low voice dropped even lower. Rougher. "Do you feel it?"

He trailed the backs of his fingers up her wrist, skeins of shadow following like smoke after a flame, and dipped his head, touching his mouth to the inside of her elbow with a ragged breath.

Her throat was dry. "This isn't fun. This is . . . this . . ."

Skies, what were words? He hummed softly, almost in answer.

What would it be like to let go? To ignore caution and live this moment without restraint?

"You learn to take what you can get," he murmured, then hefted himself onto the sill and out of sight.

Zafira sagged against the wall.

Sweet snow below.

Her arm was ablaze. How was it that a handful of rough words and a trimming of distance could make her limbs buckle like a newborn fawn's? She gulped fistfuls of air. What was the daama point of climbing up there anyway? It took her three tries to tug on the slightly-too-big slippers, and then she pulled herself onto the ledge just in time to catch him crawling spider-like to the top. He leaped, disappearing from view.

She had half a mind to slip back and climb into bed—*her* bed. She growled.

Engrossed.

With a steadying breath, she grabbed the jutting curves of stone and pulled herself up, relieved when her toes found purchase. *Don't look down.* She grabbed the next stone and climbed up another notch, nearly losing her grip when Nasir poked his head over the side again.

"Dawn will get here before you do," he mock-whispered.

She glared at him, finally reaching a ledge wide enough to allow her to rest her cramping toes. Him and his daama idea of fun. She slid her hands along the wall, and panic cut her breath when she found nothing.

Nasir reached down. "You'll have to jump."

He was insane. She wasn't going to leap in the dark, this far off the ground, only to miss his—

"Trust me," he said softly, a weight to the words. A question behind them.

She was insane. With another glare, she bent her knees, inhaled deep, and jumped. His hands wrapped around her arms almost immediately, warm and sure, and he pulled her up with a heavy huff of air.

His touch lingered an extra beat, and Zafira was so relieved to be on solid stone, she nearly leaned into him before catching herself. Feathery curtains hung from spaced-out posts along the open rooftop. Latticed arches with intricately cut-out shapes cast alluring shadows on the cushions and rugs arranged inside, the moon's breeze winding through like a coy shawl, the entire layout doing nothing to stop her head from leaping to the conclusions that it did. Zafira might have been inexperienced, but she wasn't daft.

"We're almost there," he said with a smirk, because, unlike her, he wasn't daft *or* inexperienced.

"I've had enough of your fun, I think."

He replied with a slow shrug, catching her lie. The stars crowned his hair. The heavy moon threw everything into a forgery of twilight.

"You know the way back, Huntress."

She growled. "Lead the way, Sultani."

He melted into the night, his feet barely touching the ground as he sprinted along the edge. Her heart crammed half a croak into her throat when he leaped at the end, arms spreading, a falcon in flight for the barest of moments before he tumbled onto the next rooftop, silhouetted against the night.

If a boy can do it, why can't I? She was the girl who had conquered the Arz, who had tamed the darkness of Sharr. Leaping across rooftops was child's play.

Zafira stepped back, the limestone rough beneath her slippers. With a quick inhale, she darted across the expanse, the sharp drop pounding closer with her every heartbeat. *Don't stop. Don't stop.* She pushed off at the very edge, and then she was airborne. Throat-wrenching fear shot through her veins, reminding her of the fragility of life. She savored that moment when fear teetered into adrenaline and hurtled into exhilaration.

His definition of fun.

And then her feet struck the ground, stone scraping her palms, the impact jarring her jaw.

Alive. Even if she'd left her heart back on the other rooftop.

She rose on shaky legs, blood pounding in her ears. They were on a circular rooftop now, with a slender minaret rising from its center. Moonlight bathed the stairs cut into its outer walls, reflecting off the glossy obsidian tiles.

"Fair gazelle," Nasir said, and the teasing in his tone made her go very still. "We don't want the people to think a rukh landed."

She scowled. "One more insult and I will shove you off the edge of this roof."

He smiled that half smile, and Zafira wondered if it would ever rise higher. If he would ever find joy enough to carry his smile to the gray of his eyes.

"I'll take you with me." *That tone.*

"Then we'll both die."

"You seem to have no trouble being the end of me."

He was watching her in that odd way of his, as if she would be lost among the stars if he looked away. It was reverent, almost. Wishful. She loosed a tight breath and averted her gaze. In the end, when this journey and mission was done, none of it would matter, would it?

He was her future king, and she his subject.

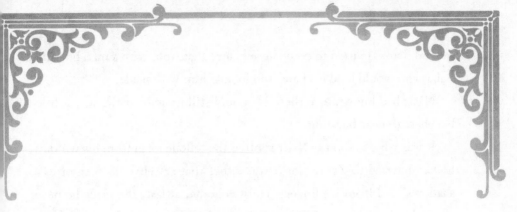

CHAPTER 12

N ASIR SAW THE SHIFT IN HER. THE SUDDEN GUARD that dampened the brightness in her eyes. He didn't know what he had done wrong this time.

"We're almost there," he said again, because he didn't know what else to say, and started up the stairs spiraling around the abandoned minaret. He had forgotten about his leg until it throbbed painfully beneath him at the second rooftop, but he wasn't going to cede like a frail old man because an ifrit had gotten the better of him on Sharr.

Unlike the five caliphates, Sultan's Keep did not have a royal minaret that once housed magic, only an endless sea of spires grasping for the skies, reaching for something they could never find. The top of this minaret was the highest point overlooking the palace and the surrounding vicinity. A breathtaking sight when the moon was at her brightest, as she was now.

He used to come here, before. A fresh burn on his back and blood from his bitten tongue dripping down his mouth. When his mother would cry and his father would grip the poker, gray eyes far too ancient for a mortal man. He used to come here before that, too, with a man he called Baba who would hold his hand and look at him with pride.

Nasir had known love then. He could still remember the way it filled his chest to near bursting.

It was why, as soon as Nasir spotted the telltale form from his window, he had hurried to Zafira, for it was either that or relive his memories as shadows bled from his fingers. He was home, at last, the place he never wanted to be, but when she was near the darkness receded, curious wisps slipping from his hands like the final puffs of steam from a cooling dallah.

When she was near, he had more to focus on. The notch between her brows, the tilted tuck of her lower lip beneath her gnawing teeth. The brush of moonlight on the angles of her face.

"I can't believe I have to make the trip back after this," she muttered, and he added the lilt of her voice to his list.

We can stay here, he almost said like some sort of hapless fool ignoring reality.

Nasir used the scalloped edging to pull himself up, brittle limestone clinging to his palms. The minaret's balcony was overshadowed by a jutting eave, so the best view was from above it, on the small, sloping roof. He helped her up.

And the breeze stole her gasp.

The clear sky unfolded in shades of purple peppered with silver stars. Sconces lit the overarching angles of the palace, setting the sprawling structure alight in gold-and-orange magnificence, shadows playing across the intricate carvings.

His home. His cage of gossamer and glory.

Curved around the palace, like the crook of a mother's arm, was the Great Library, paned windows dark and glinting, protectors of the endless enlightenment within. Every ounce of Arawiya's history, and every last scrap of papyrus worth anything at all, was stored inside. A sanctum for those like the Lion who hoarded knowledge as a miser with coin. Nasir was no hoarder of knowledge, but those shelves had been a haven once. Escapes wrought into the bound sheaves of papyrus. Minds were meant to be kept as sharp as swords, his mother had said, and so he would spend as much of his day reading as he would training, guilty that he enjoyed it.

The surrounding houses boasted domes of copper and obsidian, facets greedily gorging on the moon's abundance. Arches were bathed in a battle of light and shadow, the rare lantern swaying sleepily. Sand dunes dotted the land, hollows lit blue, the occasional bedouin campsite ablaze like fallen stars.

"It's beautiful," she murmured, and standing here beside her, he agreed. The moon crowned her in starlight and cloaked her in magic. The stars faded in envy of her radiance. There truly was nothing—*no one*—more beautiful.

So why, then, was he filled with a sudden and harrowing sorrow?

"I'm sorry," he said again, "about your mother."

The words fell from him without warning, guilt gnawing at his caged heart.

She quirked her lips. "I thought of going back to look for her, but it's obvious—"

"You can't," he said before she could finish. She grew still, a hunter in the wild, and his heart took command of itself, pounding between his ribs as if he were racing across rooftops. "You can't leave."

"Why not?" she asked carefully, and he dully realized what she'd been saying: *But it's obvious she's dead.* She had *thought* of going back. She wasn't actually going to. Rimaal, and now her question hung between them, demanding an answer.

There were a thousand and one ways to answer, and so he chose the words he favored least. "We need to restore the hearts."

She scoffed, because that was not the answer she wanted, either. The breeze toyed with her hair, and he wanted to tuck the wayward strands behind her ear. His fingers closed into a fist.

"I'm not going to leave. Not until we find Altair. Not until magic returns and the Lion is dead," she said. "My sister is here, and my friend is safe. I've got no one else."

You have me, he wanted to say.

She turned her head, as if she heard his unspoken words. The moonlight gave him glimpses of the emotions shifting in her eyes. Anger. Sorrow. Pain. It was the yearning that gave him hope. The obstinance that filled him with dread.

"My village is gone, my life upended." She barked a laugh. "My mother's dead, and I didn't shed a single tear. That's how heartless I've become."

No. Nasir knew what it was like to be heartless, to steal souls and leave behind orphans and widows and demolished futures. Yet he had cried when his mother died her ruse of a death. He'd felt so much pain that he was surprised at the silence it had left behind, a deafening quiet that broke only when Zafira was near.

"Five years," she said softly. "She hadn't left our house in five years, but she suddenly found the strength to venture outside when death was certain."

When one killed as much as he did, no single mission stood out among the rest. Nasir didn't have the capacity to feel guilt or remorse for the killing of that woman or that son or that lover. It was a collective reminder marked by his every inhale: He breathed while someone else did not. He exhaled while another never would.

Until this.

This one death that he did not have a hand in, only that he didn't stop it.

Why? she asked in the silence.

"Because she is your mother," he said softly, and if she caught the strain of emotion in his tone, she did not speak of it.

She didn't blame him for the vapors, and he would be a fool to convince her otherwise. She knew he was a killer, a murderer, the worst there was, and still she had chosen to see him as human. He would not test those limits. He closed his mouth, took a poker to his heart, and seared away the truth. The world wavered in his vision.

Zafira took one careful breath, two. "Was."

"Tears aren't a measure of heart. We grieve in different ways." He looked to the palace and its grand lights. Being unable to cry didn't make her heartless. "Family is hard not to care for, I've learned."

He waited for the wave of self-loathing that followed his voice, but the silence was strangely comforting.

"Do you want to see him?" she asked.

"Yes," he said, knowing full well of whom she spoke. "Even—even if he never returns to the man he used to be." Nasir had thoughts and theories about his father, but he voiced none. "But Altair first."

If only Altair knew Nasir would do anything to get him back. If only he could tell Zafira he would do anything to right the crimes he had lived his life committing.

There was more he wanted to do, too. Now that he knew the truth, that the Lion of the Night had been slowly sinking his claws into the Sultan of Arawiya's mind and soul for years, he had a burning, roiling need to put an end to it.

"And magic," Zafira said.

"And magic," he agreed, but only because of her. Because he knew, now, the price of magic and what it had done to his father, and his mother, and he didn't care for the sorcery that had ruined his family.

But for her and for the wrongs he had done, he would see this mission to its end.

CHAPTER 13

LIGHT THROUGH THE ALMOST-CLOSED CURTAINS
striped the dining room like the bars of a prison cell as the desert heat stirred from its slumber. No one was happy to shun the early sun, but the High Circle's secrecy wasn't fueled by paranoia—when Zafira had peeked through the window of her room, she'd caught flashes of silver at every shadowed street and rooftop.

Zafira had never thought she'd see the Sultan's Guard in person, their shiny cloaks like beacons in the browns and golds of the desert. She never thought she'd be the object of their pursuit, either. They were vigilant, Aya had warned, searching for the zumra and their quarry.

A ruckus echoed from outside as a street vendor bargained with a woman over fruits from his rolling cart. It was how Deen would argue, slipping the merchant extra coins afterward anyway. *You have to pay them for the hassle.*

"Eat," Lana said from Zafira's left on the fringed cloth spread out for the meal, pushing a plate of buttery harsha her way.

Kifah nodded beside her, the crate with the hearts between them. "You've got to keep your strength up."

Aya watched the exchange with that strange dreamy smile of hers. "All of us do. In sustenance and unity, for we are stronger together. That was the basis of the High Circle. First, when it was a council of safin affairs under Benyamin and, later, when it was the smallest of armies under Altair."

She looked away, jaw tightening with a memory.

Zafira didn't know what compelled Lana to reach for Aya's hand, but when she did, Aya turned her palm and laced their fingers. It was different, hearing about their bond through Lana's lips and seeing it with her own eyes.

"Forgive me, my loves," Aya said. Her eyes were wet, even as she gave Lana a tender smile. "Of all the losses I have endured, this . . . this is one I do not yet know how to conquer."

"Perhaps it's meant to be accepted," Nasir reflected quietly. "Not everything requires a battle, least of all grief."

Aya considered him. "Spoken as one who has endured."

Roohi. That was what she had said last night.

Baba used to say it, too, and Umm would give him that one, fond smile she devoted to him.

Habibi. Hayati. Roohi.

My love, my life, my soul, the words meant, but their meanings went deeper than that.

Habibi was for friends and love that was real enough.

Hayati was when love became an all-encompassing thing. Deeper and deeper, until one became the other's life.

Roohi was when a soul twined with its match and loved with the force of a thousand suns. When it slipped beneath the heart and tangled in the very fibers of an existence.

That was what Baba and Umm had, once. What a young Zafira had wanted, until the love her parents shared shattered them both, scattering shards of their souls into the desolation of the earth.

She had thought of them last night beneath the stars, beside a boy with unkempt hair and a question in his gray, gray eyes. She had finally seen the sprawling palace that belonged to the sultan, the lights suspended by intellect, something far more magical than magic could ever be, and yet—

It paled beside him, her prince.

"Are you all right?"

Skies. Did he have to sit so close? The harsha in his hand was perfectly halved. She had noticed that about him. The way he hung his clothes behind a chair when she was content with piling them in a heap. The way he broke his bread into neat pieces before lifting it to his mouth, whether it was manakish or flatbread or harsha.

"Never better," Zafira said, and Lana made a sound that was dangerously close to a snort.

"He looks like he'd rather eat you instead," Kifah whispered in her ear and rolled her eyes when Zafira shrank away. "It was a joke, Huntress."

The front doors flew open, and Zafira clutched her satchel as Seif marched inside. Aya dropped Lana's hand and quickly moved the dish of pickled lamb from view. Apparently, the cold-blooded safi didn't approve of eating lamb, or even hunting animals for that matter.

He slammed something down on the side table, and Aya paled at the sight of it. Zafira squinted—it was a tiny bottle, empty, but for a smear of crimson. *Blood?*

"We've found nothing. No ships in the harbor, no sign of the Lion whatsoever. We've been at work all night." Seif paced and shot a glare at Nasir. "While you were off—"

"Careful, safi," Nasir said, voice low. "Running your mouth can be dangerous, and immortals are dying like flies."

Aya's wide eyes were curious. "Where were you? You were not to leave the house."

"Surveying the vicinity from the city's highest point."

If only I could lie so easily, Zafira thought. Then again, it wasn't *entirely* a lie.

Seif scoffed. "With her?"

"Are you implying that women cannot climb?" Nasir leveled him with a look before Zafira could lash out.

Seif's frustration manifested in a growl, and from the ghost of a grin on Nasir's face, Zafira could tell he finally understood why Altair treated the art of infuriation like it was his sole purpose in life. Lana struggled to hide a laugh.

"He may not be here yet," Kifah said, "but that doesn't negate the inevitable."

He comes for us. The safin are unaware.

"The Lion of the Night," Lana whispered, and Seif shot Aya a look that said *We should have left her in the snow*. Zafira decided then and there that Seif would be the last person she would ever protect and the first she would feed to a dandan.

Kifah studied Lana. "And it'll be chaos on the streets as the news spreads across Arawiya."

Chaos *already* clung to the air, in the dust that stirred as the people rioted, in the taxes that suffocated.

"Yet Sarasin will be fine," Seif muttered.

"How?" Zafira asked, annoyed. "Who will protect its people?" The Sarasins had suffered ever since their caliph had been assassinated. The caliphate had always been a dark place—literally, too, with its dark sands and sooty skies—but once the throne had been emptied in cold blood by order of the sultan and the armies taken under his control, the uncertainty had strung tension tight and fearsome.

Seif ignored her. Typical.

Aya rose. "An established mortal by the name of Muzaffar. He was well-known in merchant circles, but while you were on Sharr, he began making a name for himself among the common folk, too. Placating them, providing for them. His men keep the peace, and that is more than many can ask for."

"A fragile peace," Nasir said quietly. "Barely enough to withstand the Lion."

"Not all will fear the Lion. Even in the past, during his reign of darkness, some believed he signaled the beginning of a new age," Aya said, pearls gleaming, and had she been anyone less pensive, Zafira would have mistaken her fervor as support for the cause. "They claimed he was the bearer of a golden era of greatness, and had the Sisters not clung to the old ways, we would never have been led to this dark point."

"Right." Kifah dusted her hands and rose. "We need blood."

"There's an infirmary nearby," Lana said without thinking twice.

"*Si'lah* blood," Kifah clarified with a note of impatience. "Blood with magical properties. You can't find that in an infirmary."

"What for?" Zafira asked, though the dread in her veins was answer enough.

Kifah met her eyes. "For you. For our compass to begin working again. You can easily track down Altair, the Lion, *and* the heart in one go."

Easily. As if they were in a basket waiting prettily for her to snatch away.

"That requires dum sihr," Zafira said. She pursed her lips, feeling guilt for her irritation over Kifah presuming she had no qualms about using forbidden blood magic.

"No."

The command was sharp, the edges strung with loss. Everyone looked to Aya, who shook her head, something like madness in her gaze.

"No. No dum sihr."

Lana stepped forward. "Ammah—"

"What he wants can never be as terrible." Aya's voice cut like a lash. It took Zafira a moment to understand who *he* was: the Lion.

The price of dum sihr is always great. Benyamin's words on Sharr. She re-membered then that he had used blood magic in an attempt to save his and Aya's son. That he had failed. That pain made reckless fools of them all.

"What he wants," Kifah spat through gritted teeth, "is vengeance on your kind and an Arawiya fettered by darkness."

A home for his people, the Jawarat said.

Violence was not how one established a home.

Aya continued to shake her head, hysteria wavering in her eyes. Lana reached again for her hand, and Zafira saw Umm then, folded in her sister's arms, fragile and lost. She murmured something too soft to hear, and Aya shuttered her gaze, collecting herself enough to press her lips to Lana's brow.

Zafira's limbs were suddenly restless, her eyes prickling.

Nasir sat in silence, gray eyes unreadable. He lifted his arm and dropped it. Turned away with a sigh.

"My mother feigned her own death. My father pressed a poker into the fire and branded me. Forty-eight times. Belittled me. Likened me to a dog."

He spoke in the voice that looped with the darkness, the one that was at once quiet and imperious.

"It was magic that did it. Magic that gave the Lion a conduit to my father. Magic that made my mother forsake the Gilded Throne." He looked to his hands, breathing tendrils of shadow. When he exhaled a broken laugh, darkness curled from his mouth. "Yet here I am, contributing to its res-toration."

Zafira knew he had suffered, she'd seen it firsthand in the Lion's palace on Sharr. Yet she had never linked his suffering to magic.

How was it that the thing she loved so deeply, craved so fiercely, had caused him such undeniable pain?

Aya looked as if she wanted to reach for him, before she remembered who he was and smiled instead.

"This fight is no ordinary battle," she placated softly. She drew a careful, trembling breath. "We must do what is required of us."

Seif shook his head and gestured to the empty bottle he had brought in. "We had blood. I've used the last of it to protect the house, and it will wear out quickly. The Silver Witch is on her way to the Hessa Isles. In the time required to reach her and extract a vial of her blood, the Lion may very well come to us. Worse, every moment the hearts spend outside the minarets puts them at risk of perishing. An entire journey with the woman, and you did not think to ask her?"

"An eternity of magical knowledge, and you didn't think to acquire more of it yourself?" Zafira fired back. Skies, this safi.

"What about Bait ul-Ahlaam?" Lana asked, and Zafira paused, the name familiar. *The House of Dreams.* Nasir had asked the Silver Witch of it on the ship, and Zafira remembered her vexed reply. She felt like an idiot, knowing nothing of it when her little savant of a sister did.

Seif closed his eyes and released a slow, exasperated exhale.

"I've seen drawings of it in a book," Lana hurried to explain. "It's in Alderamin, isn't it? You can find anything there."

Aya canted her head. "The House of Dreams thrives because of its exaggeration, little one. I do not think anyone there will have a vial of si'lah blood."

"No. Bait ul-Ahlaam is an exaggeration to those who aren't looking for anything in particular," Kifah said, to Lana's relief. "My father's made the trip from Pelusia more than once, and he always finds what he wants. Every daama time. Unfortunately."

"I thought your father didn't like magic," Zafira said.

"He doesn't," Kifah said bluntly. "It's a shop full of oddities, magical and non. Every tincture and herb once readily available in Demenhur. Soot from the volcanoes of Alderamin. Black ore. And it's ancient. If any place would have a vial of si'lah blood, it's one that's been around as long as the Sisters."

"It is possible," Seif ceded, and Lana couldn't contain her wide grin. Something in his gaze said he knew the place more intimately than through hearsay. Possibly been there himself, like the Silver Witch. "The keeper is known to . . . bargain."

He spoke with the same hesitance, too. As if they had both discovered what they had needed and given far more than they had expected to.

Still, as much as Zafira loved magic, she wasn't certain she wanted to commit the crime of dum sihr for a short burst of it. The last time she had slit her palm, she'd bound herself to an immortal book. Seif started pacing again, and she struggled to breathe. She headed for the foyer, feeling for the Jawarat in her satchel.

You fear, bint Iskandar.

"Should I not?" she mumbled. Speaking to the book aloud made her feel infinitely less insane than when she spoke to it in her head and the daama thing responded.

We are of you. We will protect you.

As if a book could protect her from anything. According to the Silver Witch, *she* needed to protect *it*, or she'd die with it.

Fear is but a warning to heed.

"A book that literally spews philosophy. Yasmine would love it," Zafira said dryly, realizing a beat too late that the others had followed her.

"Mortals. Their lives are so short, they resort to speaking to themselves," Seif drawled to Aya.

Zafira nearly growled. "My *name* is Zafira."

"Don't bother," Kifah interrupted. "He sees our round ears, and we're suddenly walking corpses. At least *we* know when it's time to get in our graves."

Useless talk will take us nowhere, bint Iskandar.

"Are we going to try the market?" Lana asked.

Breathe.

"Which of us will make the journey?" Kifah's voice distorted.

Inhale.

"The bridge across the strait remains intact." Aya's words floated from far away.

Exhale.

"Give us the hearts and the Jawarat," Seif said as Nasir watched her, only her. "We've put too much trust in mortals, and—"

Something inside Zafira snapped. A scream raged through her veins. Her hand twitched for an arrow.

We

are not

mortal.

Everyone and everything stilled.

She flinched at the sudden, piercing attention. Blood rushed through her ears and the fluttering curtains laughed.

"Okhti?" Lana asked.

Zafira blinked. Kifah made a strangled sound, but the first to take a cautious step toward her was Nasir. As though Zafira were an animal he was afraid to startle.

"Are you certain you're all right?" He looked at her as if not a single other soul existed on the earth.

She could not meet his eyes. "Why wouldn't I be?"

"You—" Nasir started. "You referred to yourself as *we*. As two people. You said you aren't . . . mortal."

"I didn't say that. I didn't say anything."

There was a sinking in her stomach. The five of them stared as if she were on some sort of stage, making a fool of herself. She stepped back toward the entrance, the long handles of the double doors curving into her back.

Nasir took a step closer. "Give me the Jawarat."

"I don't have it," she lied. It was in her satchel; they couldn't see.

"Zafira." Nasir's tone was meant for a disobedient child. "It's in your hands."

She looked down. Slants of light set the lion's mane on the Jawarat's cover ablaze. She tightened her grip around the book that had used her mouth to speak senseless words. Sweet snow below, what was happening to her?

She looked from Aya's curiosity to Seif's smugness, then to Kifah's confusion and Lana's worry, and finally to Nasir. It was the pity in those gray eyes that did it.

Her resolve fractured. Fell.

Leave them. Freedom rests beyond these doors.

Zafira threw open the doors and ran, recalling this same panic from when she raced through the oasis on Sharr. Wind against her limbs. Blood loud in her ears. Fragile sanity threatening to unravel.

She was ashamed that Lana had been there to witness it. Kifah, too.

"This is all your fault," she hissed.

Stop.

Like a fool, she listened, stopping just beyond the gates of the house, and the reminder that she was in Sultan's Keep hit her with a force. The cobble of hewn stone was warm beneath her bare feet. Sweet snow, the western villages of Demenhur were slums compared to this. It was a masterpiece of time and diligence, from the detailing on the ground to every carved bit of the sprawling houses surrounding her. Even the sky looked richer, the blue clear and vast. There was no difference between her and an urchin hiding in the richer end of the sooq. Her blue-black qamis, shorn from a dress that had cost one too many dinars long ago in Demenhur, felt like rags.

They—

"Stop," Zafira hissed. "Don't tell me anything."

The sudden silence was filled with the Jawarat's petulance and a guilt-inducing shame. *Perfect.* Shadows stretched, warning her that she wouldn't be alone for long. Voices carried. Farther down the road, she could make out the stalls of a sooq tucked between buildings for shade, and the last thing she needed was for someone to demand who she was.

She hurried in the opposite direction, finding a small alcove created in the angle of space between three of the massive houses. Sunlight slanted within the confines of tan stone just so, illuminating an arch set into one of the walls and built of dazzling glazed tiles in hues of blue and red and gold, like a doorway to a hidden world. She stepped close, only to find it wasn't a door but a fountain, a pool of glittering green water rippling beneath it.

It was beauty that felt delicate, a moment suspended out of time. Beauty she couldn't appreciate.

"I don't know why I listen to you," she hissed.

The Jawarat didn't answer, and Zafira pressed herself against the wall to collect her breath. A sand qit rose from its perch near the fountain, eyeing her with distrust.

It is truth. We are not mortal.

Perspiration trickled down the back of Zafira's neck as the sun ratcheted up the heat.

We are immortal.

"And suddenly I am, too?" she asked angrily.

We are bound, you and us. The span of our life is yours.

"That . . . that isn't how it works."

Can pith made papyrus speak to a witless girl?

She gritted her teeth, ready to fling the Jawarat into the fountain. "What do you want from me?"

There had to be a reason it spoke to her, goaded her. She wasn't like the Lion or the darkness in which the Jawarat had festered. She was powerless, as Seif continuously repeated. Perhaps it was time to entrust Aya with the book and—

A hiss reverberated in her ears, and she dropped the Jawarat in her fright. It fell open on the dusty stone. She looked about sharply, but only the fountain gurgled softly, dust dancing in the slanting sunlight.

Then the book slammed itself shut.

Bint Iskandar.

The words were a terrible moan. Fear crept into her veins.

Let us show you what you can do.

The alcove faded away, ebbing light giving shape to the snowy stretch of a village and a cloaked woman in its center. The sooq looked familiar, as did the scant, spindly trees. *Demenhur.* Yet Zafira herself wasn't *in* the caliphate. It was as if she were looking through a spyglass into another world, an observer.

The green leather of the Jawarat was clutched in the woman's left hand, the fingers of her right twisting to the skies, and words Zafira couldn't understand slipping from her tongue. An incantation, almost. A spell.

Shouts rang out as people ran from the sooq in fear, fleeing from her— the woman—as she brought her fist down suddenly.

And the ground surged upward.

The circular jumu'a meant for gatherings erupted. Stone and debris hurtled toward the surrounding stalls and struck down screaming villagers. Several men ran toward the woman, some with tabars and swords, others hefting bricks and whatever makeshift weapons they could find.

Even as they neared, the woman did not move. The biting chill stirred her cloak.

She merely flipped to another page of the Jawarat, and after a few breathless moments, Zafira watched as she arced her hand down.

Rending

the men

in half.

Screams broke out anew, bodies fell to the ground with sickening thuds. *No,* Zafira tried to shout, to stop this senseless violence, but her mouth was sewn shut. She struggled to breathe, bound to this terrible vision, laa, nightmare. For that was what it was.

A nightmare.

The men fell, one after the other. Halved by her terrible power. By the *Jawarat's* power. The grisly image seared itself into Zafira's skin. More men dropped to their knees, their own swords through their guts. The ruined sooq turned crimson as blood flowed freely, pooling around the woman's feet.

Silence fell, and with a satisfied hum, she turned, knocking back her hood with a bloody hand.

And Zafira stared at herself.

It was her, down to the ice in her eyes and the angry set of her brows. *Exactly* her, except for one thing.

Her hair was the color of splintered bone.

A silver vial filled with something thick and crimson hung around her neck, and when the white-haired version of herself slid the Jawarat beneath her cloak, Zafira saw a fresh gash across her palm, nestled in a sea of scars, flesh knitted back. Dum sihr. She strode to a black steed, boots slicing snow before she mounted and disappeared into the streets.

Leaving behind a tomb.

The lavender door of Bakdash hung on its hinges. Araby's colorful sweet shop was a pile of rubble. She saw men, boys, children—dead. All of them. Struck with stone, cut in half, innards and organs spilling out, bleeding, bleeding, bleeding.

Because of her.

"Please," she begged. She didn't know to whom she begged; she merely repeated the word until her surroundings blurred and she lost her balance.

And then, nothing.

Zafira dug the heels of her palms into the stone and lifted her head with a wheeze. The alcove surrounded her. The Jawarat was by her knees.

Do you see, bint Iskandar?

She only saw something far more sinister than the Lion of the Night. Something small and unassuming, with centuries of memories from Arawiya's most powerful beings, and nearly another with far worse: the evil that had seeped within Sharr.

And it had controlled her.

"Why?" she whispered. "Why me?"

The purest of hearts will always triumph the darkest of souls.

Footsteps hastened just around the bend. Zafira closed her eyes and gathered both her breath and the Jawarat before rising on shaky legs. Three figures drew near, their cloaks coruscating silver. The Sultan's Guard. *Khara.* She flattened herself against the wall, but they hurried past the alcove without so much as a glance, their low murmurs urgent, hands gripping the simple black hilts of their scimitars.

"Show me something useful," she hissed at the Jawarat. "Show me what the Lion can do with a single si'lah heart."

Nothing.

Laa, peevish silence.

With a growl, Zafira willed the Jawarat's vision away and crept after the guards as a chanting began, snippets of shouts and demands carrying along the errant breeze. The Jawarat's insistent voice broke through them.

We will be seen.

"Now you can talk?" Zafira asked. She darted from the shadows of one building to the next, but she didn't have to live here to discern this emptiness as unusual. It was the sultan's city. It was *meant* to be bustling at all times, not eerily quiet here and noisy there. Before an alley, she paused, squinting at the square up ahead.

Dread halted her breath. Chants met her ears.

Taxes kill. Break the till.

Protests. People were protesting, marching—*running* in the direction of the palace. Toward her.

Her heart leaped to her throat, and her fingers slickened around the Jawarat as she turned and made for Aya's house, the heated stones scorching her bare feet. She stumbled on a pebble with a curse. *Don't fall, don't fall.* She thought of the Arz and her hunts, when not even her prey heard her agile footfalls.

The distance between her and the crowd grew, and she allowed herself a moment to pause. A terrible mistake.

An explosion shook the earth, and Zafira fell to her knees as a stampede of people charged toward her.

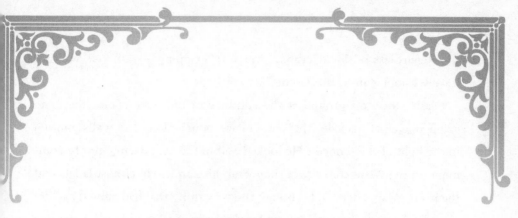

CHAPTER 14

UNDERGROUND. THAT WAS WHERE NASIR WAS NOW, in a room barricaded and reinforced to muffle all else. After he'd dragged his gaze from the double doors for the umpteenth time, shadows wreathing from his hands like an oil lamp just snuffed, Aya had suggested they train.

It *would* have been a suggestion, if she'd accepted Nasir's refusal.

"We need to decide if we're going to Alderamin," Kifah groused.

Nasir didn't understand why. "Detouring so far for something that may not exist is a risk when we could easily gather forces and prepare for the Lion's arrival here."

She cast him a look. "You never struck me as the type to wait around."

He wasn't. He preferred having a mission to complete, a task to keep him focused. But without the Lion wearing his father's skin and threatening him with innocent lives, he had no reason to seek out magic. Particularly when it was a plan as volatile as the alternative.

"Regardless of our decision," Aya said, gripping a staff, "we will not leave without Zafira, laa? Come."

Nasir stood his ground at the entrance of the wide room, the crate gripped against his side, the array of weaponry along the walls glinting in the light of the sconces. He looked Seif in the eye, daring him to comment on the wisps of black curling from his hands. He almost laughed at the irony: Magic lived in his bones, the very thing that had ruined his life. His blood was too mortal to use for dum sihr, and yet his si'lah descent denoted he would forever have magic, regardless of the minarets.

"If Zafira returns and none of us are there to receive her, she'll think we've left," he said.

"Breathe, Prince," Kifah said. "If she could hunt in the Arz and return to her own bed every night, she can handle the sultan's city."

"She sometimes needs time to think alone," Lana said calmly.

"She referred to herself as two people," Nasir said flatly, pressing his lips closed when a tendril of black slipped free. "Did none of you hear?"

"It was not she who spoke," Aya said, "but the Jawarat. It is a hilya, an artifact created of and imbued with immense power. Few hilya exist, as the Sisters forbade their creation after a tyrant beyond Arawiya's shores harvested one for its magic and reduced an entire civilization to ashes."

"That was back when safin thought it was smart to trade hilya out of Arawiya," Kifah said with feigned sweetness. "Yet, knowing what hilya are capable of, the Sisters created one themselves."

"They had no choice," Seif said harshly.

Kifah sat back, pointedly looking down the length of his unbuttoned robes as she tossed a sugar-coated almond into her mouth and passed the pouch to Lana. "There's always a choice."

"Oh, there's more than just Arawiya?" Lana asked, eyes bright.

"Always has been. Arawiya is a tiny piece of the world. Magic wasn't the only thing that disappeared ninety years ago. *Our* world shrank when the Arz popped up, because it covered the outer regions of the kingdom, caging us in. There's a khara-ton of land out there, and people. An isle where greenery isn't limited to oases, where leaves are bigger than grown men, and where beasts have tubes for noses. Another kingdom farther north where the people are paler than even the Demenhune and their snow, and just as relentless."

Nasir was content with the size of his world, shukrun. "Is what Zafira said true?" he asked tersely, steering them back to the matter at hand.

"In a way," Aya said, dipping her head. "The Jawarat is immortal. The Huntress is mortal. Hilya are made of power and memories, sentient beings in their own right. To willingly bind themselves to a mortal, or even an immortal for that matter, is rare. The darkest of them wish for bodily vessels; others merely seek companionship. It is odd that the Jawarat would choose her, but what she—*they*—said holds truth. Mortal bodies were not created to sustain souls for an eternity, however. Thus, the Jawarat's immortality will grant her a life span longer than most mortals will ever see."

"Khara," Lana breathed.

"Oi!" Kifah snapped.

"Language," Nasir warned, and Lana looked at him like his hair had turned gray.

"It is twofold," Aya said, studiously ignoring them. "Safin understand immortality. Our hearts slow at maturity, our bodies remain unaffected by mortal ailments, but immortality is not the immunity of death, and the risk of her mortality itself has increased. Living forever does not equate to having an indestructible life, and it is far easier to destroy a book than a human. Destroy the book, and she will die."

"The Jawarat is an invaluable artifact. No one in their right mind would destroy it," Seif said callously, and Nasir loosed a steadying breath to refrain from decapitating him. "Every heartbeat I spend here is an insult to my perpetuity. The Lion will not idle in the enactment of his wrath."

"It's not wrath," Kifah said with a shake of her head. "Wrath and rage burn quick as fire. Vengeance is the only fuel you can keep going for more than a century. The longer it takes, the sweeter the revenge."

"He had his chance," Seif said. If either he or Aya noticed the zeal with which Kifah spoke the words, neither commented. "A thousand times over."

Kifah shrugged. "Maybe he wanted to wait until he learned it all. Who knows? There's a fine line between the thirst for revenge and the hunger for power, and men have a hard time understanding boundaries."

"I don——" Nasir started to protest.

"You're a friend. You don't count," she threw at him.

Seif launched into another tirade, but Nasir barely heard any of it as those three words—*You're a friend*—looped drunkenly in his mind.

"Do you mean that?" he asked quietly, too tired to quell his curiosity.

"Why wouldn't I?" Kifah tilted her bald head at him. "Oi, relax. I wasn't going to braid you a bracelet. There's no binding contract. We don't have to——"

"No, no. I—Never mind," Nasir said quickly, and she lifted an eyebrow as he tried to make sense of the thrumming in his chest. Rimaal. First a brother, then a mother, now a friend.

What was next?

Aya swung her staff in a swift arc.

"I'll drill if he goes above and waits for her," Nasir said, jerking his chin at Seif. Zafira could handle herself, he knew. She wasn't a child or a frail old man. She was the girl who stood unafraid on Sharr before the Lion of the Night himself. That didn't mean they should abandon her. *Fool. Next you'll be singing songs in her name.*

Seif made no move to leave, but Lana, who had been toying with a slender mace on the wall, turned to them. "I'll go. Can I keep this?"

"No," everyone but Seif said at once.

She pouted and dropped it back against the wall. When the door closed behind her, Seif made himself comfortable on a trio of cushions with a bundle of missives, and Nasir felt the desire to decapitate him return at full force.

"It is good to see you in your natural habitat, Aya," the safi said.

Aya laughed at Nasir's fleeting surprise. With her lilac abaya and gentle grip, she didn't particularly look at home here. "I have honed thousands of affinities over the years across the kingdom, young prince. I am a healer first, and a teacher of magic second. No match for Anadil, but I like to think myself commendable." She took a stance. "Now, let us see what you can do."

Coils of shadow split from his palms when they all focused on him. Nasir wasn't in the mood for showing anyone what he could do.

"You have no trouble summoning your power, at least. You must refine it. Sharpen the black into a blade. Make it a sword to be wielded."

Nasir closed his eyes, reaching for the source of that dark flame, trying to find the vein in his blood that ran black, but it felt like tugging on air. Kifah snorted, and Nasir's eyes flew open. The shadows had disappeared.

"You remind me of this one invention my father had that started off all dark and showy and collapsed in a plume of smoke," she remarked. He vaguely remembered that her father was a high inventor. He also remembered the little glass instrument she had stolen from him. *It works best when I imagine I'm lighting him on fire.*

"Did your father have you to cheer him on?" Nasir asked tiredly.

For the first time since he'd met the bold warrior, her fierce expression gave way to vulnerability. He'd spoken too quickly, without thought. She wasn't a certain loud, golden-haired general used to carefree raillery. They'd been ready to rip each other to shreds, yet Altair had left a yawning emptiness behind, one Nasir was all too aware of.

He opened his mouth to apologize, but she beat him to it with a shrug.

"He should have. His loss."

Aya tapped him with her staff, and it became the Lion's stave. Benyamin leaping in front of him. Altair shackled to the Lion—his daama father.

It was only an instant. A mere moment in which his concentration broke, but it was enough. The shadows rippled free, billowing like smoke from a fire. The room darkened.

Breathe.

He thought of the fine dark lines running through ice-blue eyes. The weave of a braid crowned at her head. Aya voiced a warning. He felt her staff at his shoulder again, and he had to dig his heels against the sudden urge to lash out. To kill. The shadows sharpened.

No. No killing.

Breathe.

He was uncontrollable. *A monster.* What was the point of a life he couldn't control? Seif was on his feet, drawing Aya away. A sight he had seen time and time again when the Prince of Death walked the streets.

Wrong are the ones who believe power is king. Control, and you will triumph.

Help me, mother.

Listen, was all she whispered.

He filled his lungs and forced his clenched fists open. The darkness hummed, a song just out of earshot. *Listen.* He closed his eyes and *reached*, tugging on the tangled whispers and deciphering the chaos.

"That's it," Kifah said carefully.

Darkness surged into every crevice of his being, stretching his lungs and organs too full, but he kept tugging at the frenzying skeins until light ebbed back into the room.

The last wisp curled into nothing, and Nasir loosed a breath. The shadows were gone. He turned his hands—the darkness had disappeared from his skin, too, returning his stained hands and wrists to their original color.

He looked up in the silence.

Aya's smile wavered. "In time."

Nasir couldn't stop a small laugh at the emotion that clung to the room. *Understanding.* As if they finally understood Arawiya's fear of him. Aya avoided his gaze. Seif's stance was battle-ready. Kifah, at least, didn't seem perturbed.

He'd lived without magic all his life. He'd *suppressed* magic all his life, which clearly hadn't helped, for the more he used his shadows, the easier it was to breathe, and the easier it would be, he realized, to eventually control them. "There isn't time for this."

He might have been a quick study for anything else, but the wayward dark? It would take time. More time than they could afford.

"He trains for a tenth of the day and thinks he can conquer the world," Seif said. "Have you forgotten your father—"

"Do not presume I forget anything, safi," Nasir said coldly. They hated Ghameq, but none of them had lived with him. None of them had suffered the poker and years of abuse. None of them had stared at the medallion around his father's neck and desired to rip it away.

"You cannot control yourself," Seif said.

"I am afraid he is right," Aya said softly.

Nasir didn't care. He didn't need his shadows to save Altair. He didn't need the dark to ensure the hearts didn't die. And when Nasir darted a glance at Kifah, who met his eyes unflinchingly, he knew: He didn't need the High Circle when he had allies of his own.

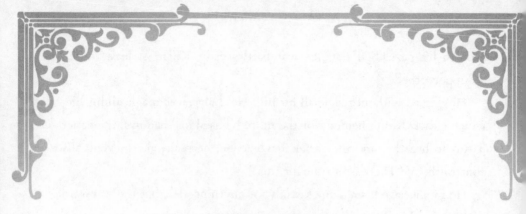

CHAPTER 15

THE SOUND WOULDN'T STOP. IT RANG AND RANG and rang despite all her swallowing to make it daama stop. Zafira had heard of detonations, bundles of fuses and sparks and fire trapped in a box, a Pelusian invention as fascinating as any. She did not appreciate innovation now. Screams echoed as if from leagues away, and the ground quivered from the hundreds of feet pelting across it. Drawing near.

Get up, the Jawarat commanded. *GET UP*.

Zafira swayed. She stood on shaky legs, hating the Jawarat and hating her stupidity, which had drawn her outdoors. Shadows draped across her, sand clouded her vision, but it was the ringing from that damned explosion that made her blind, for she had always seen with her ears as much as her eyes. Glass shattered. Somewhere else, a woman screamed. Men shouted. Through a bleary gaze, she saw flashes of silver cloaks and drawn scimitars. The Sultan's Guard.

She could not afford to be seen, let alone caught. Hands gripped her shoulders and she fought against them as she was pulled back into the alcove near Aya's house.

"Steady," a small voice said. Zafira had heard that word in the same voice countless times as she hid away in her room while her sister cared for their mother.

She blinked her vision into focus as the ringing dulled. "What are you doing here?"

"I was waiting for you when I heard the explosion," Lana said, frantic, her gaze slipping to the chaos behind Zafira. "I came as quickly as I could. Go back to the house."

Lana didn't move to follow. There was a stubborn set to her jaw that Zafira recognized from the hundreds of times she'd worn the expression herself. Only then did she see the kit in Lana's hands, a wooden box barely closed around the tools and bandages and salves within.

"Go, Okhti," Lana urged, gesturing toward a narrow sliver of space near the fountain. "It's a shortcut. Aya's house is on the other end."

Zafira didn't know why she hadn't realized that before.

"They're waiting for you."

"Are you mad? I'm not leaving you here. It's dangerous," Zafira said, shaking her head. She shifted the Jawarat to her other hand and grabbed Lana's arm.

Her sister wrenched away. Zafira went still.

Lana's eyes were hard. "You have your duty as I have mine."

You owe the world nothing, Zafira almost said, but that was not her line. It was Deen's, when he had tried to stop her from venturing to Sharr. It was meant to stop, to hinder, to cage. Yet she wanted to say it—to say *something*, for Lana's unspoken words were as loud and as clear as the screams and shouts just beyond this pocket of space.

Zafira had left her day after day after day, choosing a monstrous forest over the sister who needed her. She had left her again for a villainous island, knowing full well that she might never return to the sister who had no one else.

"Did Aya tell you that? This is not the same as aiding in an infirmary. Aya isn't even here."

Lana didn't reply. People continued to scream. The stubborn set of her sister's jaw shifted to something else. An expression that looked eerily like Aya's, too experienced for a child.

Give her a chance, Yasmine said. It had been a while since she'd heard her friend's voice in her head. It was always the Jawarat or, even louder, the Jawarat's silence. Zafira stepped back and the fountain gurgled, an apt audience of one. *Stay safe. Be careful. Watch out*—all pairings she wanted to say yet knew were wrong for this moment.

"I'm sorry," she whispered instead, and disappeared down the narrow path.

◄●►

No one was in the foyer when she returned. As if no one aside from Lana had even bothered to worry about her. She washed her feet and hurried up the stairs, dropping beside her bed and thinking of the hearts, safe with Arawiya's most dangerous assassin.

All that way to Sharr, and the hearts were just *idling* within these walls.

All that care to find the Jawarat, and she had committed the terrible mistake of binding it to herself.

All that trouble to keep her sister safe, and the girl marched straight into danger. She didn't know what kind of confidence Aya had fed her, what kind of spiel about duty and obligation, but Zafira wasn't certain she approved. *Skies, listen to yourself.* Zafira had disappeared into the Arz around that same age. Who was she to deny Lana?

A knock sounded on her door, as soft as it had been the night before, as if part of him wanted to see her and the other wanted nothing of it. She shoved the Jawarat beneath her pillow, the vision still plaguing her, and opened the door.

The light streaming through her window caught on Nasir's scar and reflected in his eyes.

"I wasn't sure you'd returned. I was training with Aya, and it's impossible to hear down there." So that was why he hadn't come when the explosion struck.

"There was a riot," she said. "Lana is out there." She didn't know why she thought he would care—about Lana, about her dead mother, about any of it. She didn't know why words just spilled from her without prompting when he looked at her the way he did.

"She was supposed to wait for you in the foyer, but we thought as much when Aya noticed her kit was missing. She'll find her." *Worry not*, his tone said when his tongue refused.

Zafira nodded, reminding herself that this was what Lana had been doing while she was away and today was no different. The hall was empty except for the voices drifting from downstairs. Seif's drawl and Kifah's lightning-quick responses.

"Is it my turn to look after the hearts?" she asked.

He looked down at the crate in his hands, and she paused when she saw the way his jaw tightened, the way his gaze shifted to her hands, looking for . . . *the Jawarat*.

"I'm delivering them to Seif. It's his turn."

He was kind enough to sound apologetic, but that didn't lessen the sting, the revelation. Words collected on her tongue—*Do you not trust me?*—before dignity stole them away. She couldn't truly blame him; the Jawarat had used her to *speak*. What if it used her for worse? To abuse the hearts?

What if they found that vial of blood and the Jawarat goaded her to do something unspeakable?

Skies, what do you want? she snarled in her head. The book pretended it couldn't hear.

A line strained at his jaw. "Are you all right?"

No, she wanted to say. "Isn't that what you always ask?"

His dark brows knitted together. "Isn't that what I should ask? After what happened?"

"Should, must, need," she droned, her pulse quickening. It was easy to rile him when he looked so bewildered. "Have you ever thought of what you *want*, Prince?"

His eyes dropped to her mouth and her neck warmed before he looked away, so perplexed by her question that a laugh crept up her throat and died on her tongue.

"What color do you like most?" His words ran into one another.

This time, her surprised laugh slipped free before she could contain it, and his eyes brightened at the sound before he paused.

"Do people not ask that?"

"Children, maybe," she replied.

Sorrow flitted across his face, and she wanted to take back her words. He was the son of a tyrant. Even when the Silver Witch was sultana, Zafira doubted Nasir's youth had been any more *youthful* than after her feigned death. Only safer. Far from the consolation a child should have to seek.

"It's blue," she said softly.

A faint smile came and went. "I should have known."

"My baba's favorite shade. 'The waters of the Baransea on the calmest of days beneath the cloudiest of skies.' He's gone, too. I'm officially an orphan." Her hand had slipped to her jambiya, fingers closing around the worn hilt. She knew he was reading her in the silence.

"How?"

She thought of how best to string the words together before she realized she didn't need to coat them in honey. Not for him. "He went to the

Arz when I couldn't and returned months later. Mad. So Ummi stabbed him through the heart, because . . . because she had no choice."

"Perhaps he wanted to see you one last time."

She stared at the sheen on the stone floor, at the faint pattern on his robes, the gleam of his onyx-hilted jambiya. She inhaled the homely scent of freshly baked bread. She wasn't going to cry in front of him. The Jawarat's vision flashed in her mind and she set her jaw.

"Your turn. What color do *you* like most?"

His eyes flared before he could mask his surprise. Did he not think she'd ask him in return? It was always a game, capturing the small displays of Nasir Ghameq's emotions. A game she liked, she realized. One she could play forever and never tire of.

"You," he said, so softly it was only sound.

The intensity of his gaze stole the air from her lungs. She shook her head. "That—"

"Every color that makes you."

She held her breath, waiting, wishing. But he closed his mouth, some part of him retreating.

"Tell me more," she said softly. She stepped closer and his head snapped up, the sun lighting his eyes in gold.

His lips tightened and the mask carefully settled over his features again, gray eyes hardening to stone as the drag of feet up the stairs signaled the end of their solitude.

"Another time," he said with the voice he used for everyone but her, less promise and more dismissal. He clenched his fist around a flare of shadow, and with one last glance he was gone.

CHAPTER 16

ALTAIR RESTED HIS ELBOWS ON THE LOW TABLE AS he waited for food. Surprisingly, his father hadn't bled him since he'd spoken, tentatively, of an alliance. Altair hadn't seen much freedom either, with his chains hooked and secured to the wall.

When he had told Benyamin of his grand, far-fetched plans to restore Arawiya, he had known there was always the possibility that one day he might have to go through with them alone. He'd been prepared enough— until those damning days on Sharr. With Nasir, then Zafira. Kifah and Benyamin himself.

In that scant bagful of days, he had cobbled together a family and a place within it. People with dreams as insane as his own, driven by factors others would have laughed at.

At least, it was what he'd believed. Now the emptiness was gnawing through him, the loneliness a ball on a string he had swung far, far away, only for it to return in full force.

His one companion scuttled from a hole in the wall, looking for the scraps Altair usually left out.

"So kind of you to visit, Nasir, but I'm all out of food, you see," he told the little rat as it went about in circles, searching for something that wasn't. *Akhh, Nasir to the bone.*

The rat bolted with a squeak, and Altair stood as footsteps approached. The misshapen clay abode stank heavily of age, the corners of the room thick with cobwebs. It was battered and bruised and glaringly unsecure, yet the zumra *still* hadn't found him.

If they're looking for me, that is.

The Lion swept through the open doorway, followed by an ifrit with two bowls of shorba and warm flatbread. The food of peasants, not a shred of mutton in sight.

"Taken to talking to yourself?" the Lion asked as he sat on the cold, hard ground. The ifrit set down the food and left.

"Keeps the vocal cords young," said Altair with a smile. He remained standing a beat longer before he lowered himself back to the floor. "I can take to singing, if you prefer."

These were the moments that scared him. The ones in which his father sought his company for no reason other than companionship.

Moments that scared him because he enjoyed them. They carved new lenses through which the monster, cruel in his ambitions, became a man, curious and collected.

The Lion rarely touched the food he brought with him. It had given Altair pause at first, but if he kept fearing poison, he'd starve. A body like his didn't maintain itself.

"You have my father's eyes," the Lion said.

Altair stopped with a piece of flatbread halfway to his mouth.

The Lion frowned as if he'd surprised himself, too. "I sometimes forget his face. Events, too. With the odd recollection that they were . . . pivotal somehow. Time has stifled the memories."

Whatever the Lion believed had stifled his memories was not time, and Altair could see it bothered him, enough to bring a haze of madness to his gaze. The same glint from when he'd spoken of vengeance, as if he wanted it with an all-encompassing need but couldn't fathom *why*.

"You loved your father," Altair observed, and lifted his arms, flashing his shackled wrists. "Mine keeps me in chains."

The Lion smiled. "I can remove them. Take you from captive to son. Ally. We will carve our names upon history, and we, too, shall live forever."

Heavy words to be spoken in the height of the day's heat. How easy it would be, Altair thought, to shift the work of decades over to the side of his father. He would accomplish the same: a new Arawiya untainted by the Arz, unfettered by the curses that magic's absence had left behind.

He finished his bowl and slid his father's, still untouched, toward himself.

"I won't let you go, Altair, and they will not come," the Lion said with certainty. "If they triumph because of the road you set them upon, what makes you believe you will garner credit? I'm no seer, but even I know what will come of it."

"Oh?" Altair said when he shouldn't have. The walls rumbled with the thunder of passing horses somewhere out on the streets.

The Lion looked at him, strangely intent, as if his son were a puzzle he was close to solving. As if he *had* solved him during the handful of meals they'd shared.

"You will be forgotten."

There were words that warped shields and slowed quick tongues. Knotted strings around fingers and made them tremble, one, two, three, ten. Twisted inhales so their exhales shook.

Words like these.

Altair set down his bowl with too sharp a thud, avoiding his father's gaze. He smoothed his hands down his arms, bare and suddenly cold.

A question tumbled out of him: "Have you found the zumra?"

The Lion tilted his head, as he did whenever curiosity struck. "I've sent for a scroll in the palace. It details a spell that will emulate the Huntress's affinity. Why?"

We, too, shall live forever.

Altair dropped his fists on the table between them. Dust sprang from the little crevices. He latched his eyes onto the Lion's amber ones, curious and staid.

No, Baba. He would not be forgotten. Not so long as his lungs moiled away. He had spent far too much of his life working for exactly the opposite.

"Unshackle me," he said with careful reflection, "and I'll tell you where they are."

CHAPTER 17

WHEN ZAFIRA WAS YOUNG, HER FINGERS JUST long enough to wrap fully around the hilt of Baba's jambiya, she had scrunched her nose and asked him why it was so plain and so old. She had walked with him and Umm to the sooq, where the men wore their jambiyas with pride. Hilts of polished stone or wood, studded with jewels, carved with care, each curved dagger fancier than the last.

"A blade is born to murder and to maim," he had told her. "It reminds me of all I've done. Each deer I have gutted, each rabbit I have ended. Lives are not meant for thieving, my abal."

"Will you give me my own blade?"

Umm had smiled. "Girls are not meant to wield the toys of men."

Baba had disagreed. "My girl will wield *weapons*, and she will wield them well, for it takes a special kind of courage to hold power and know when not to use it."

He had given her his dagger then, the leather hilt tattered from use.

The blade, however, was still sharp. Enough to prick her finger when she drew it from its sheath.

To this day, she remembered Baba's laugh. As if he were surprised to have made such a sound, as if all were right in the world.

"It likes you," he had said afterward, and she remembered that, too. For she liked it back. Enough that she carried it with her everywhere. When she showered. When she helped Umm knead bread in the kitchen. When she began to hunt and feed her people.

When Baba had returned from the Arz.

She carried the Jawarat now as she used to carry that dagger, as she *still* carried that dagger, only it didn't make her feel good, or brave, or right. It was a part of her. Being away from it troubled her as much as removing her cloak once did.

"Pure hearts aren't meant to go on killing sprees," Zafira said to it, and the reminder of Nasir refusing to give her the hearts stung afresh.

You reject us, bint Iskandar.

"No," she said, pointedly. The Jawarat might have gleaned a near century of malevolence on Sharr, but those years had to be insignificant compared to the Sisters' memories. "I will never hurt my people. I'm rejecting this chaos you crave. We're bound to each other—what about what *I* want?"

Dusk was bleeding into the sky, the sun exhaling its final rays of warmth. Lana had returned, and despite the relief that heaved a trembling exhale out of her, Zafira refused to see her, petulance and anger demanding that her sister come to her first. The Jawarat only hummed that damning hum as it did whenever her emotions ran rampant and tempestuous.

She flipped Baba's jambiya over in her hands. Could she really go so far as to forget her own people? To harm them? She thought of the gassing. Perhaps it was a small mercy, her village being gone, her people dead so they wouldn't have to fear being split in half by the girl who once provided for them.

The Jawarat didn't care about her. It wanted someone to enact its will, to unleash a chaos she couldn't stand behind.

So we have learned.

She shivered at its ominous tone.

"If we are to continue this ridiculous bond, you will neither influence me any longer nor share with me your hideous anger."

Skies, she sounded insane, commanding a book. A sentient book, but still.

Our bond is irreversible. There is no "if."

"No," Zafira agreed, "but I can dig a hole and bury you in it, and you will never again witness the light of day."

Neither will you, the Jawarat gloated.

She growled, "You know exactly what I meant."

The Jawarat fell silent as it considered this, and Zafira dropped back onto the bed with a bout of pride, rising when a knock sounded at her door again. She ignored a twinge of disappointment because it wasn't the soft knock she had come to anticipate. If it was Lana, that girl—

Oh.

She couldn't stop her smile. "I didn't recognize the knock."

"Can't be predictable now, can I?" Nasir asked, his gaze hurrying across her room before locking on her, a little too eager. "Can I come in?"

Zafira tilted her head, but after a beat of hesitation, she stepped aside and closed the door behind him. "That has to be the boldest question you've ever asked."

A corner of his mouth lifted. "I can be bolder."

Zafira laughed, and his eyes darkened in response. And then he was reaching for her, pressing himself against her, and swallowing her gasp of surprise with a kiss, leading her back, back, back to her bed.

He was cold. So cold, she felt the chill through her skin. She wound her fingers around his shoulders and pushed him away, her mouth ablaze with sensation, her pulse racing like a steed. She stared at him.

Say something.

"I didn't think you would return," she managed. She had been so certain his words were a dismissal earlier, worried he was afraid of her.

"Why wouldn't I?" he replied, as if her question were ridiculous, and it stopped her from asking after Lana and Aya.

He caught her hesitance and quickly tipped a smile. "You're like a room full of books. Every time I see you, I discover something new."

His eyes were bright. There was something brazen about the quirk of his lips. Something too sure to his touch. He seemed to read her face as he had begun to do more often these days, and took a measured step back.

"Should I leave?"

No. But the word was too bold for this moment, so she knelt on her bed and gestured for him to join her.

"Sit," she said, aware that Lana could walk in at any moment, but she couldn't bring herself to care. She, the Lion, the Jawarat, the hearts—everything could wait. "Ask me more questions."

CHAPTER 18

*E*VERY COLOR THAT MAKES YOU. RIMAAL, HE MIGHT as well quit now and become a bard.

It was true, though. Color had held no value until her. She was everything Nasir was not. She saw her father die, stabbed in the heart by her own mother—a horror he never could have guessed because she took her pains and sorrows and funneled them into anger and rage and *action*.

Whereas Nasir was always tired and sad and . . . *there*.

He was drawn to her like a moth to a flame, and the closer he went, the more he burned—but what happened when a moth's wings caught fire?

He trudged up the stairs, knowing they had to move soon if they wanted to track down that elusive vial of blood and find Altair. Nasir had never been to Alderamin, and he wasn't enthused at the prospect. Nor did he think it was right to use Zafira for her affinity as if she were a tool at their disposal.

You're one to talk.

He paused before his door and stepped, instead, closer to hers, pressing his brow against the ebony. He always knocked softly, so that if she was engrossed in something, he wouldn't be disturbing her.

So far, she had responded to every knock.

And instead of setting him at ease and flaring satisfaction, seeing her filled him with a fear he craved and did not understand. A sort of dependency in danger of growing into an addiction.

Before he could skim the wood now, however, he heard it: the low murmur of a male voice on the other side, followed by the heady sound of her laugh.

His mind blanked. He took a quick step back, tripping on the rug.

Safin weren't known for their chastity. Their debauchery and revelry matched none—any one of them could have charmed her. Khara, even a sand qit on the street was more charming than him.

She laughed again, so softly that it felt a sin to hear it.

Nasir stumbled into his room. Shadows unfurled from his palms before he could stop them, and he laughed bitterly from the edge of his bed, at the control he believed he'd achieved.

He exhaled slowly, flicking his gauntlet blade free before retracting it and repeating the movement again, and again. A killer, that was what he was. A blade made for ending lives. A monster on a leash. How was this moment any different from the last time he had been in Sultan's Keep?

Anyone who could make her laugh so freely, so beautifully, was better than he could ever be.

But oh, how he wished he could act as selfishly as he felt.

CHAPTER 19

IT WAS A BAD IDEA TO INVITE HIM TO SIT ON HER BED, Zafira knew. The gleam in his eyes made it hard to think and speak and daama breathe. He paused at the apparent change in her thoughts.

"You don't even have to speak. Your face does it for you."

He leaned close, brushing his fingers down the side of her face, and she sank into the familiarity of his touch, knowing every moment was stolen. He was the *prince*. Once this was over, he would remember that there were far more women in existence.

"Should I stop?"

Yes, she thought, but some part of her delighted at the way his voice broke.

"No," she said, and brazenly turned her lips to his palm. She slid her fingers up the scruff of his jaw before gently threading them in his hair. His lips touched hers, warm and soft, foreign and familiar at once, and nothing existed save for him and her and this.

He eased her back into the pillows, and she fell drunk on the faint sweetness of pomegranates and the weight of him. A sound escaped her when he pulled back with a torn exhale and skimmed his hand down the length of her, lingering at her thigh.

"Wait," she gasped. She was going to explode. Irritation flitted across his gray eyes, and she felt the sting of it as acutely as a knife.

"What is it?"

"If we do everything now, then——"

She had never seen anyone so still, as if even his heart stopped at his command.

"Then what?" he asked.

"Nothing," she said quickly. Her pulse pounded at her neck. She didn't feel empowered as she usually did with him. She didn't feel longing. She felt . . . debased. Everything felt *wrong* and she wanted to disappear.

"Interesting," he murmured. He swept off the bed, and she saw a line of deep mauve on his robes that hadn't been there before. "I thought you would never make the mistake of falling in love."

Zafira went cold at the sudden change in his voice. The way it deepened into velvet. Confident in a way only immortality can provide. There was only one to whom she had spoken those words aloud: the Arz. There was only one who had listened from its depths. Who had befriended her as she had him.

His eyes, no longer gray, glinted amber in the lantern light.

A scream clambered to her throat, and she tried, tried, tried to shout, but her voice was swallowed by horror and the dizzying sensation of his mouth. A thousand and one emotions slowed her down: fear, disgust, anger, and—worse—desire.

Before a warning repressed it all: the Jawarat was in plain sight.

"You are every bit as decadent as I imagined, Huntress." The Lion's voice was a caress as the room festered with shadows, dark as a hollow grave.

Her pulse pounded in time to her single thought: *The Lion. The Lion. The Lion.*

"I missed you, azizi," he said softly, eyes darkening as they roamed her supine form.

My darling.

She had a terrible, sickening realization: Some twisted part of her had missed him, too. She had never really lived without him. He had always been within reach, his presence exuding from the strange trees and impenetrable darkness, the shadows curling around her limbs, calming her.

A wicked grin contorted his mouth. "Did you not miss me? We are one, you and I."

"You're not the first to say that," she bit out as she dug her fists into the sheets and forced herself upright and out of bed.

He canted his head, unveiling a lock of white in his dark hair as he neared. Slowly, his features shifted into his own, and the Lion stood before her, golden tattoo glinting in the lantern light. *'Ilm*, it said. Knowledge. For which his hunger could never be sated.

"But it was I who made you what you are, my bladed compass, and because of it, you cleverly bound yourself to the Jawarat, successfully gleaning the knowledge of the Sisters of Old."

His brows rose at her hesitation.

"You fear it," he realized with a soft *tsk*, backing her to the wall.

She allowed it, for it was drawing him away from the Jawarat.

"You fear the doors that knowledge throws open. Embrace it, azizi. There is no greater gift."

"I will never—"

"Shh," the Lion murmured, stopping her with a thumb to her mouth, calluses rough across her lips. "Brash promises so quickly take us in directions we don't like."

She shivered.

"Now," he said, no louder than a whisper.

She felt the word, tasted pomegranates when she drew air.

"Give me the Jawarat."

He hadn't looked for the hearts, or the safin he hated, or even the Silver Witch, more powerful than he could ever be. He wanted the Jawarat and its wealth of knowledge.

"And?" Her voice was all breath.

"When the Gilded Throne is mine, I will make you my queen as I forge a home for my kin. The world will be ours to shape as we will."

The throne. For knowledge was power, and power was epitomized by the throne.

"All these years," she said, and smoothly snatched her jambiya. She would protect that book if it was the last thing she did. "And you failed to notice I was never interested in crowns."

She pressed the blade to his neck, devouring his flash of surprise. There and gone, trembling her resolve.

"Does the thought of my blood bring you joy?" He tipped his head back and her jambiya caught in the meager light, brilliant against his flesh.

Not joy—*power.* A remnant of the Jawarat's vision, the one part of it she craved in some dark corner of her soul.

His voice was a lull in her ear. "Tear me open, azizi. Slit my throat and see if the blood I bleed is black or red."

What mattered more was the blood he had spilled: that of Baba, Deen, Benyamin, the Sisters of Old, a thousand and one others.

"I will end you," she whispered.

Her hand shook, succumbing to the rush of something heady and dark. His breath hitched, to her delight, and a bead of black welled from his golden skin where her blade touched him.

Ifrit blood, despite his half-safin descent.

The reason nothing pulsed against her fingers even now, why there was no beat in his chest. He was built like a man, like a safi—bones and tendons and organs—but was as heartless as an ifrit, truly so.

His soft, answering laugh was broken, a drag of cloth across thorns. The first fissure in his effortless composure.

"So you say," he said, a lion making sense of a mouse. "Yet when I called from the darkness, you answered. Day after day, year after year, long before you ventured into my domain, you stood in the snow and spoke to me. Do you not remember, azizi?"

She had been small and alone then, when she had first stood in front of the Arz and asked what it wanted of her. She knew only that the Arz had spoken back. She simply hadn't known that the voice belonged to the Lion of the Night, grooming her for what he needed.

"Where's Altair?" she demanded. She wouldn't show him a reaction to his words, to the stir of memories. "What have you done with the final heart?"

He ignored her just the same.

But she wouldn't be brushed aside. "Why are you doing this?"

That was when he froze. The black pearl rolled down the plane of his neck, a dark, dark teardrop. She didn't understand why he wanted magic, why he was so terribly enamored with knowledge.

"Why?" he repeated, so softly she thought it a sigh. His brow furrowed, confusion and a touch of apprehension in his amber eyes, another break in his careful composure that sent her reeling.

Almost as if . . . as if he couldn't remember.

His gaze slanted to the corner of her bed.

Both of them lunged for the Jawarat at once. He knocked the dagger from her hand. She slipped beneath his arm, agile as she was, but he knew her as well as she knew herself and avoided her with a deft move.

"It won't help you," she gasped out, desperate. *It's mine.* "It can't be read. It imparts its knowledge to the ones it likes."

Help, she begged the Jawarat, but when the Lion of the Night closed his fingers around it, slowly morphing into Nasir once more, it did nothing. It was quiet.

Laa, it was *exuberant*. She felt it buzzing in her own veins, chilling her to the bone. Because she had rejected its chaos and violence. She had rejected *it*.

She lifted her eyes to the Lion's, unwilling to let him see her horror.

"I won't fall for your lies again," she vowed with halfhearted pride.

The Lion only smiled.

"You will fall, azizi. Mark my words, for it will be my greatest one yet."

His eyes swept the room, searching for what she blearily realized were the hearts, before he disappeared with what he had coveted, leaving her paralyzed by the emotions he had stirred with a smile and a kiss.

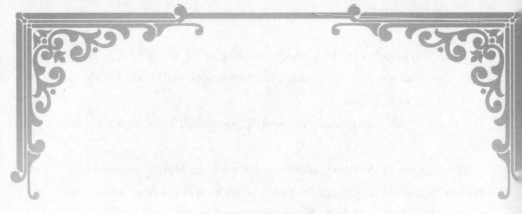

CHAPTER 20

"I T'S *WHAT*?"

Seif's pale eyes were livid, his rage sending the last of Zafira's tenacity crumbling. The small room narrowed with each pound of her pulse, shelves along the walls flipping to prison bars, trapping her.

"How could such a thing occur? How did he enter the house?" Aya looked stricken, her yellow abaya appearing colorless in the dim light.

Lana was rooted at Aya's side, and Zafira felt the distance between them as brutally as an ax.

"Answer the question, Huntress," Seif seethed.

"How would I know?" she snarled. "I was in my room. It could have been you who let him in for all I know."

"Watch your tongue," he hissed, and she felt like a child. "The dum sihr protecting the house might have run out, but *you* handed him the hilya tied up with a silver bow." He rounded on Aya. "I knew we should not have trusted her to keep it safe. A mortal. A *child*. This is precisely what we feared."

Aya paled, and the fight drained from Zafira as quickly as it had come. Nasir was not here. Which was for the best, as she would not have been able to look at him, not without seeing him in her room, his scar in the light, his hand at her thigh. *The Lion's hand.*

"I didn't know it was him," she whispered.

"How—"

"Bleeding Guljul, for immortal safin, you're all so dense," Kifah snapped. "He's half ifrit. Did you not think he could possibly shift like full-blooded ifrit can?"

"Whose countenance did he resemble?" Aya asked.

It was becoming increasingly harder to breathe. To think past the press of him, the amber in his false gray eyes.

Zafira's exhale broke.

"Why does that matter?" Lana asked, coming to Zafira's side and holding her hand. It was a blanket over her pulse, an instant quiet. "We can try to get it back without standing around talking. *No.* Okhti, what if he destroys it? You—"

Zafira shook her head. "He won't. If there is anything sacred to him, it's knowledge." Of that, she was certain, and if she had learned anything about the elusive Jawarat, it was that its knowledge was endless. "But he's going to take the throne."

She didn't speak of how he had vowed to make her his queen and how she had trembled from more than disgust and anger.

Shame held her tongue, stopped her from telling them he promised something far worse than anything any of them could imagine. Laa, it wasn't shame but fear. How would they regard her if they knew she had not only given him the Jawarat but *conversed* with him? *Kissed* him?

It was the exact reason she couldn't speak of the Jawarat's malevolence. Of its vision and its whispers. To them, she was the girl who was pure of heart. Perfect in her desires.

Fear. Shame. They were needles stitching thread between her lips.

"As is expected." Seif dismissed her words with irritation. "It was what he wanted a century ago. Did you assume he had changed? That his wants would end with the Jawarat and a single heart? Laa."

"Then we should go to the palace. Where the throne is," Lana said, and no one commented on her use of the word "we." As if she were a part of this. As if she had found a limb on the tree of the zumra and perched upon it, joining them in her own way.

"But he can't take the throne," Kifah said, furrows lining her brow. "Every kid knows that. The Gilded Throne allows only the blood of the Sisters or the ones they've appointed."

Seif and Aya exchanged a look.

"Perhaps," said Seif. "Yet we've no knowledge of what the Jawarat will impart to him, what loophole the Sisters knew of that *he* will now know of. Regardless, he would be a fool to breach the palace before he understands the Jawarat. I've had safin scouring the city to no avail." He worked his jaw. "I will send for more men."

The wariness in his tone rang like a bell. The noose was tightening around them, and it was her fault.

"I'll go." The words spilled from her. She cleared her throat and lifted her chin, but found herself unable to meet anyone's eyes. "I'll go to Alderamin. To Bait ul-Ahlaam. I'll find the vial of si'lah blood, and I'll use it to find Altair, the heart, the Jawarat, and the Lion before he moves for the palace. Before he can do anything. I'll fix this."

Impossible. The echoes of the Jawarat's voice clung to her, even now.

She shook its derision away. It might have been a lengthy list, but all four would be together. Of that, she was sure.

"Okhti, no," Lana whispered.

But what did she understand? She could walk into a riot and heal a man, but she could not understand what the long burden of responsibility was truly like. Zafira had spent years caring for her people, doing right by them, always and always.

Until today. When the Jawarat had spoken using her voice. When she had, as Seif said, given the Lion the Jawarat with a silver bow. She stared at her hands, remembering what they had done in that ghastly nightmare. Suddenly the Jawarat's vision was no longer so implausible.

She would leave at dawn. Laa, she would leave now.

"There's more," Kifah said, turning to Zafira. "I was about to come find you—look."

She lifted the crate from the low table and opened it. The hearts gleamed darkly in the slanting light of the lanterns. *No.* It wasn't the light that made them appear darker, they *were* darker.

"They're dying." Lana peered inside, voice small.

Zafira's own heart stuttered, her breath almost painful. Magic was why she'd set off on this course, why she'd left her home, her life, her family.

It was dying before her eyes.

That was when they came in, nine in all, dressed in rich hues and styles straight from a tailor's fantasy. Benyamin's High Circle. Beautiful and merciless, armed and cruel. Tattoos curled around their left eyes, marking them with the values they upheld over all else. She thought she'd heard others roaming about the house when she'd first arrived, but assumed she was hearing things when no one joined their meals. *Pride.* Not even Seif ate with them. Zafira contained herself, masking the awe that threatened to take over her features.

Kifah's voice was soft. "They're going to take the hearts."

Zafira blinked at her. The word "take" rattled in her skull.

Her first thought was of Deen and Yasmine's parents, of how they had clutched their only son when the Demenhune army had come to take him away, months before they were drafted as apothecaries themselves.

Skies, calm down. The hearts were not her children. They were simply the insignificant pieces of cargo she had risked her daama life upon a nightmarish island to attain. Nothing more.

"Shouldn't that be us?" she asked stupidly.

Kifah looked at her. "We can't be everywhere at once. Besides, we're giving them the easy task. Ride a horse, climb some steps, insert a heart into the empty rib cage of a minaret. Khalas."

Her smirk widened when several of the safin shot her dirty glares.

Lana, who had forgotten to keep her mouth closed when the safin stepped in, finally unearthed her decency. "Will it stop the hearts from . . ." She trailed off, unable to finish her question.

Seif carefully wrapped three of the hearts in silk and passed them to the safin, who stood in ternary groups. "No one knows if restoring the four hearts will put a stop to their rapid deterioration, not without the fifth to set the Sisters' magic in motion. What's certain is that they are no longer safe here. The High Circle will restore each heart and remain on guard until we prevail."

The Lion swept his gaze around Zafira's room again, searching for them, molding into Nasir once more.

With a shiver, Zafira watched as the safin took the hearts and boxed them with delicate hands, held them with care. She bit her tongue against words of caution. How could she demand they be careful when she'd all but gifted the Jawarat to the Lion?

Seif kept the fourth heart for himself.

Have them, Zafira thought. She would let Seif and the High Circle have this small triumph. Laa, it didn't belong to them; she would let them do this *for* her, and when she had the fifth heart and all the victory that came with stealing from the Lion of the Night, she would restore it herself.

She would be the reason magic returned.

Seif turned to her, his cruel gaze deflating her moment. "Well? Are we to leave for Alderamin?"

We? Ah—that was why he had kept a heart for himself. He was going to restore it to Alderamin's royal minaret.

When she didn't answer, Seif added, "Or was that proclamation yet another undertaking too heavy for you to handle?"

Zafira dropped her head, her failure still too fresh and too raw to allow a retort. Several of the safin tittered, and she wondered how they could want the best for Arawiya and still be so infuriatingly ill-mannered.

One by one, the trios of the High Circle took their leave, and one by one, the three hearts destined for Pelusia, Zaram, and Demenhur disappeared into the night.

Breathe, she told herself. Kifah stared after them, her face frozen before she caught herself and looked to Zafira with the edge of a smile. It warmed her, somehow, knowing she wasn't alone in the feeling of loss. In missing the hearts the moment they left the threshold of the house.

"Don't leave," Lana said. Aya's kit was in her hands.

"Come with me, then," Zafira said, "and we'll never have to be separated again."

The moment Lana bit her lip, Zafira knew it was a wish too farfetched. They had always been on different paths, she with her arrows and her sister with her tinctures.

"I can't."

"Why not?" Zafira asked, uncaring of the frenzy bleeding into her voice. Uncaring of Seif's impatience and Kifah's pity.

Lana only shook her head, sliding a glance at Aya.

It was one more shovel digging into her already hollowing heart.

———◆———

Even the touch of the poker was less painful than this hollow in Nasir's heart. All he wanted was for the emptiness to come to an end. It was all he had *ever* wanted, he realized. To be seen. Understood.

Needed and wanted.

He began the lengthy task of undressing, beginning with his weapons before he loosened the sash of his robes, then straightened the folds of his shirt and hung it behind the chair. The breeze from the open window counted the endless scars on his back with a curious touch.

The soft scuff of bare feet broke the silence, and he froze with his hand at the band of his pants. He didn't bother reaching for his sword. His bare hands would suffice.

"Hiding will do you no favors," he said, voice deathly low, and almost instantly a figure emerged from the shadows near the latticed screen, illuminated by the multiple lanterns.

He would know that slender build anywhere.

"Kulsum."

She lowered the ochre shawl from her head, dark hair glossy in the light.

For a moment, he could only stare. His heart was a ruin scrubbed raw, his mind a scramble of pain and memory. This was the girl he had loved, whose body he knew as well as his own. Whose voice was the most melodic he had ever heard, until his father learned his son had found an escape. Laa, it was the *Lion* who had found him, the Lion who had controlled Ghameq's hand, carving her tongue from her mouth.

As if Nasir had not abhorred himself enough before, the butchery had drowned him in a deep pit of self-loathing. He had kept his distance, blamed himself and vowed useless vows until that moment on Sharr, when he had learned Kulsum was a spy. What he didn't yet know was how long she had been in Altair's employ—long before the moment they'd first met? After his mother's death? Since she'd lost her tongue?

"You came for Altair," Nasir said.

She nodded slowly, *yes and no*, a painful reminder of what she would never again have. How had she entered the house—by writing Aya a letter?

"Then you would know he's not here," he said. Aya would have told her as much. Accusation flared in her dark eyes, and he gave a mirthless laugh. "Don't worry, I didn't kill him, but as you're aware, there are fates worse than death. He's with the Lion of the Night." And then, because he was cruel and horrible and hurting, he said, "I would worry about telling you too much, for servants like to gossip, don't they?" The monster inside him stretched a smile. "But we both know you can't tell them anything."

Not a single emotion flashed across her face.

She was better at this than he could ever have imagined. She glided closer, and he marveled at how much hatred he could summon for someone so beautiful, but was it hatred for her or himself—or for them both?

Her gaze dropped to his chest, to the fresh burn near his collarbone. He should have reached for his shirt, but what was the point? She had seen him this way countless times. She had seen more than this.

"Why did you do it?" he asked softly.

She didn't answer. She would never answer in a thousand years.

"What could compel you to feign love for a monster?"

He studied the way she stood, straight-backed. The way she walked, head high, dress free about her legs.

She was not lowborn, a thing he should have realized years ago. And if befriending Kifah had taught him anything, it was the lengths a person would go for vengeance.

"You weren't always Altair's spy. He saw an opportunity and took it, but *you* . . . ," he said slowly, and faint lines of shadow painted his arms. He heard Zafira's soft laugh in his ears. *Breathe.* "You had plans of your own."

The glitter in her eyes was confirmation enough.

"I killed someone," he reasoned. What else could he have done? He had never plotted or connived or brought anyone down. He killed them, simple as that. "Your father."

She shook her head.

"Mother?"

Another shake. No—she had forsaken a good life for the purpose of growing close to him. To make him love her with the intention of breaking his heart.

"A lover," he realized with a hollow, contrite laugh. "I killed the one you loved, and so you forsook your life for a path of vengeance. Admirable. Was it worth it, love? Did you laugh as my father branded me? Did you gloat as I came back from my missions bereft of another piece of my soul? Did my sorrow bring you pleasure, Kulsum?"

She reached for him, and Nasir stepped back.

"I would choose death over your touch."

He was no saint. He was well aware of the irony in his disgust.

"You should have thought it through. You should have realized the sultan hated me more than you ever could. You might have kept your tongue, then." He shook his head in the silence. "None of it hurt more than that, did you know?"

None of it had hurt more than the belief that she had lost her tongue because she had dared to love a monster, when in reality, it had been the price of her revenge. The curtains fluttered, eager for more, and the breeze tugged on the door he had been too scattered to shut.

"But if you were willing to sacrifice so much to bring me the level of pain you suffered, then mabrook. Your vengeance is complete."

Some part of him was glad of this conversation, glad he was able to finish and lock away whatever had once stood between them.

"Now get out," he commanded. "When Altair returns, there will be a line. Join it."

But Kulsum didn't move. She only looked at him, dark eyes bright. Regretful, almost . . . hungry. He imagined what she would say, had she been able to speak. Perhaps, despite her vengeance, some part of her *had* loved him, in the way that only time spent isolated with another could foster.

Nasir looked away.

And as if—*as if*—his day wasn't going terribly enough, he heard the creak of his door and a sharp draw of breath, because no one thought of knocking in this forsaken house.

Khara.

Zafira was frozen in the doorway, hair mussed, mouth swollen. The sight ripped him to shreds as she looked between Kulsum and his shirtless state, her brows falling in two shattered slashes.

It isn't what it looks like, Nasir wanted to say, but when did anything ever go his way?

CHAPTER 21

*S*WEET SNOW BELOW. IF SHE HAD ONLY HELD THE DOOR closed when it accidentally slipped open, she wouldn't have had to see that. Nasir, without a shirt, without the shadows of Sharr to cloak him. The lantern light painted him in strokes of gold down to the low, low band of his sirwal, igniting something in her veins.

And her: the slender girl in the yellow shawl who was more beautiful than Zafira's broad build and unwomanly height could ever dream to be. When had the idea of beauty ever bothered her before? Her eyes began to burn.

Jealousy darkened the heart, and Zafira was not jealous. She was pure of heart.

Her mind flashed to the Lion's mouth on hers. Nasir without a shred of cloth on his back. This was it. She was going mad.

She had only gone there to check on him, to tell him about their plans. To tell him how she had lost the Jawarat and explain that, *yes*, he had been right not to entrust her with the hearts that were now being taken away.

Because some stupid, naive, childish part of her had believed he would care, he would understand.

How wrong she had been.

She slipped soundlessly back down the hall, running her fingers along the paneled walls, aware she'd never stepped so deep into the house, where many of the High Circle roomed. Were there more of them now that nine had departed? She didn't know. But most of the doors were closed, and the last thing she needed was to pry one open to another sight she shouldn't see.

And now footsteps were hurrying after her. *Perfect.*

She rushed beneath an archway and into a high-ceilinged chamber. For banquets, likely. She wouldn't know. The largest space they had back in her village in Demenhur was the jumu'a, and that was daama outside.

"Zafira."

She froze, the stone cool beneath her bare feet.

"Why are you running?"

She turned. He had thrown on a shirt but hadn't had time to close it up. The muscles of his torso coiled with his breathing and she imagined her hands on his skin, his voice in her ear. Turning her mouth to his. The Lion's hands on her thighs. *No.*

Anger. That was what she needed to feel right now. Not . . . this. But the flickering sconces lit the anguish in his eyes, making it hard to focus.

"I was giving you privacy." Steel rang in her voice.

He backed her toward the wall, uncaring of the doors that could open at any moment. He pitched his voice low. "The only privacy that I want is with you."

"No, you don't," she said breathlessly, ignoring what the words could mean. She wasn't half as beautiful as the girl in the yellow shawl. *Khara.* She wasn't supposed to daama care.

He stepped closer, pressing the tips of his bare toes against hers. His eyes were downcast. She felt his confusion and the heat of his body as if it were her own.

"What *do* you want?" she whispered. Their time on Sharr had wound a string between them, knotted and gnarled, the edges fraying even as it tugged them closer.

He made a sound that could have been half of a sob or a laugh, and that was it. *Tell me*, she pleaded in the silence. The darkness stared. This was as far as they ever got—she would ask, and he would retreat.

"The Jawarat is gone," she bit out. Because they were a zumra, and she owed him that much. "The Lion came to me, disguised as . . . someone he wasn't."

Nasir's eyes snapped to hers, but she looked away in a stir of embarrassment and anger. Her mind flitted to the girl in the yellow shawl with her golden skin, shapely features, and full lips. Did he struggle with words when it came to her? Her posture had been at ease, as if she knew his secrets. Her dark eyes had roamed his bare chest, as if she knew the feel of him beneath her fingers.

No, Zafira decided. He did not.

"If you can't even speak of what you want, then perhaps—" She stopped and tried again. "Perhaps you don't want it hard enough." She slid away from the wall. His hand dropped to his side. "Perhaps you don't deserve it."

Was he the one the Silver Witch had warned her against? Her own son?

She left her heart at his feet and locked her brain safely away, and she was almost to the doorway when he spoke.

Soft. Broken.

"What do you want?"

The Lion's death. Altair's safety. Magic's return. Baba's justice. *You. You. You.* He was a rhythm in her blood.

"Honor before heart," Zafira said. What work there was to do, she would do herself.

As always.

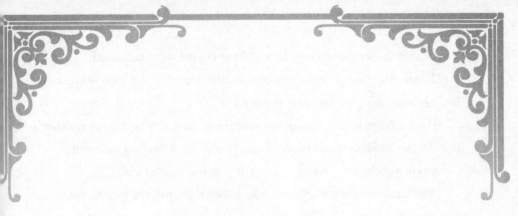

CHAPTER 22

I T WAS DARK WHEN THE LION RETURNED, TRIUMPH carving a smile that glittered like the night. Joy in his gaze that tripped Altair's heart for the barest of beats before he at once felt a deep, numbing *nothingness* and a bursting, tumultuous *everything*.

From the folds of his robes, the Lion pulled free the Jawarat with a delicate hand. Green with tattered pages and a fiery mane embossed in its center.

Not only had the zumra—with their ancient safin, shadow-wielding prince, and dum sihr—not found Altair, but they had been careless.

The Lion watched him carefully, but what was there to see? Altair's disappointment at their incompetence? Altair's contentment at a plan gone right?

"Unlock his chains," his considerate father said, and an ifrit came forth with a key.

A tiny, insignificant bit of molded iron that would grant his freedom. *The Jawarat*, memories of the Sisters of Old incarnate, for his freedom.

So that he would never be forgotten.

Neither father nor son spoke until the chains were detached.

"I don't suppose you can remove the shackles, too?" Altair ventured, a little hoarse, his gaze fixed on the book.

The Lion smiled. It was quite something, to be the cause of another's joy. To be the pride of someone's eye, if only for a fleeting moment.

Altair matched it. "Akhh, I knew it was too much to ask."

"You have done me a service, Altair. For that, you are free to roam the house as you would like."

Some freedom.

"Ah, Baba. Quite the weight off my shoulders—er, arms," Altair drawled, flexing his muscles. He dallied a beat before he said, "What do you plan to do with it?"

"Learn it," the Lion said simply. "I'm never one to shy away from the thralls of a book."

Altair considered that. "The Great Library would kill you, then."

The Lion laughed, low and thoughtful. "I would not put it past the place. There is nothing quite like entering a door that promises to open onto the infinite."

They were in a different house now, one that had belonged to a safi with a skill set that would be sorely missed by many.

"How were they?" Altair asked before he could stop himself. He found his limbs seizing in anticipation of the answer.

The Lion paused. It was eerie, for he had no pulse, even as he buzzed with excitement. "Alive. Well. They seemed to be in no hurry. It is for the best, is it not? I'm beginning to savor our alliance, Altair."

Altair dropped his gaze to the shackles around his wrists, suppressing his power, endlessly chafing his skin. What more did he need to unveil for them to be gone?

CHAPTER 23

B Y THE TIME NASIR HAD FOUND A STRING OF WORDS
to suffice a proper apology, it was too late. She was not in her room.
She was not in the foyer. She was nowhere in the house, and when
he ran outside, too hurried to wear his boots, he saw the servants calming
the two steeds left in the stables where he'd seen fourteen before.

His pulse had never raced as quickly as it did now. He had never felt
such searing lament, such bone-deep rue. He should have worn his shirt,
he should have sent Kulsum away, he should have answered Zafira's question. Regret was Nasir's dearest friend.

The moon tucked herself into the clouds, despondent, and a chill descended from the skies, sinking teeth into the city. He returned to his
room, relieved to find it empty, and snatched his weapons before washing
his feet and slipping into his boots, nearly wearing the right on his left and
the left on his right, and then struggled with the servants to placate one of
the angsty steeds, even as they claimed it was the worst of the lot.

Nasir was not surprised. Such was his luck. He pulled out the red-and-silver compass the Silver Witch had given him before he'd embarked for Sharr and brushed his thumb across its surface. It had led him to Zafira more than once.

What do you *want?*

More than his heart could hold. More than he could begin to know.

When at last he mounted the beast and the gates creaked open, Aya swept outside. Nasir wondered if she had stayed behind for him, since everyone except Zafira's sister had left. *She stayed for Lana, mutt.* He flinched at his own thoughts, at the echo of his father's insults.

"The night mourns."

He suppressed a shiver at her voice and guided the horse toward the dark streets. Limestone structures gleamed blue-black. Lanterns glowed like eyes, ever watchful. Echoes of the merchants and people wading among their stalls reminded him that this city never slept. On the other end of the tangled streets and sprawling houses was the palace. He'd told no one of the plans he'd begun to form, but what did it matter now? He had to find the zumra. He had to find Zafira.

Why? a voice whispered at the back of his skull.

Aya noted his hesitance. "Where do you ride for?"

"Alderamin," he said when the silence became too much to bear. "To join Zafira."

"There's no need. Seif and Kifah are with her. As you said, preparations must be made here."

He paused at her logical words.

"Come inside," Aya coaxed. "We can continue training if you do not wish to rest."

Rimaal. Look at yourself. It wasn't about the journey itself, for he still felt that a trek to Alderamin for a vial that may not exist was a waste of time. It wasn't about the number of people she had with her; it was about Zafira herself. It was about saying the words he had not been able to say before. Even if he believed his chances of finding Altair were higher here. In the palace, to be exact.

A small figure darted through the gates. Nasir's gauntlet blade pulsed against his wrist before he recognized the luminescent green shawl. Lana stopped in front of his horse, wide-eyed and out of breath.

Aya rushed to her. "What is it, little one?"

"A—a Sultan's Guard," she blustered.

Nasir was off his horse in an instant. If the man had touched her, had even *tried* to touch her, he would lose his fingers, then his tongue. Then his head.

"I came as fast as I could." A scroll was in her palm.

Nasir exhaled, but he didn't need to read the scroll to know where it was from. He was the prince, and this shade of parchment was a common sight. That didn't stop the surge of dread through his limbs when Aya unfurled it to read before wordlessly passing it to him. Because when one disaster befell him, it was almost always followed by a barrage of others.

"How did he know who I was?" Lana asked, uncaring of what he'd given her.

Only then did Nasir notice she was shaking.

He looked past the gates. He sensed no one, but if Lana's comings and goings were noted, it was obvious. "We're being watched."

Nasir returned the horse to the stable; then he and Aya took Lana inside and sat her on the majlis with a blanket. A servant brought her tea. Aya held her against her chest, murmuring too softly for Nasir to hear through the rushing in his ears as he read the missive.

It was an invitation to a feast, one sent not only to the crown prince but also to every last leader of Arawiya, celebrating magic's imminent restoration.

Only, magic was still far from restored. It might *never* return, despite the zumra's near-success upon Sharr.

"We'll go," Nasir said beneath the flicker of the lanterns suspended from the ceiling.

"It is a trap," Aya said, surprised that Nasir would accept the invitation.

"It's not a trap if we are aware of it."

He'd already had a number of reasons for wishing to trek to the palace, theories he wished to test, but now he had ample justification. The medallion around Ghameq's neck flashed in his thoughts. The notion that the Lion was in the palace itself, hiding in plain sight.

"*We* know the Lion holds my father captive," he said. "But the delegates don't."

"We can send notes of our own," Lana suggested, "telling them it's a trap."

Nasir imagined a missive such as that, warning the delegates of their impending doom and signing off with "Prince of Death." He shook his head. "It won't reach them in time."

"You think to protect them," Aya said.

This time, her surprise stung, but Lana gave him a small smile. His reputation had reached even the farmost villages of Demenhur, it seemed.

"If it is a trap, there is the likelihood that we will face the Lion," Aya continued.

"He won't show his hand so soon," Nasir said, "not before comprehending the Jawarat. My father is behind the celebration."

"And he is controlled by the Lion," Aya said, gentle but firm. "We are no match for him on our own."

"Unless we remove the medallion," Nasir countered.

Aya's features scrunched, dissent written across them, but she held silent. Nasir crushed the papyrus in his fist. The Lion played his game well, and this was an invitation no one would dare miss.

Not even Nasir.

CHAPTER 24

IF ZAFIRA WAS TIRED, HER BODY BETRAYED NO SIGNS OF it. Anger steeled her every vessel and vein, and she finally understood the restless energy Kifah lived and breathed.

Dawn had wrapped the night by the time the sea breeze signaled the approaching border of Sultan's Keep. The lights of the city began to dwindle, the barrenness stretching like a shock. Which it was, Zafira supposed, for no one had expected the Arz to ever disappear.

Seif kept pace ahead of them, as if she'd begged him to come and he was displaying his ire for all to see. When in truth, *he* had asked *her* if she was ready when she had charged into the foyer with her satchel.

It was Kifah who had looked behind her to the stairs, expectant. "Where's Nasir?"

"Preoccupied," Zafira had replied, and her ridiculous mind sought out every one of Yasmine's stories, making her wonder if he *was* truly busy.

Kifah had studied her with an ease that prickled her skin, and decided silence was the best answer.

A bird screamed in the distance now, breaking her out of her thoughts. She stared at it angrily as it swooped into the distance. Her horse whinnied, and she was angry at it, too. It was a shade darker than Sukkar but reminded her of him anyway. How attuned they had been to each other, how smooth his movements were. She bit her tongue. Better physical pain than the incurable one of the heart.

She missed the weight of the Jawarat by her side. Its cynicism and commentary. Its constant search for chaos and control—even if she did not approve, it would have been a welcome distraction.

"It's going to take some getting used to, standing around without four extra heartbeats," Kifah mused.

"One less task for when we retrieve the final heart," Seif reminded them curtly.

If, Zafira nearly corrected. She'd been astounded by the Lion's audacity as much as by his presence in her room, and that didn't bode well for her own confidence. At least she had the peace of mind knowing the girl in the yellow shawl had left the house shortly before she and Kifah did. Otherwise, her presence would have plagued every footfall of the journey.

But why? she asked herself. Why were her emotions, thoughts, and actions so visceral when it came to Nasir?

"Oi. Don't look so glum," Kifah said, bringing her horse near Zafira's as they passed rows and rows of swaying barley, the crops contained by short fences on either side of the road. "If the Lion had walked through my door looking like my brother Tamim, I would have handed him the Jawarat without a second thought. And my brother's dead."

But the person in Zafira's room hadn't been her sister or dead mother or father, had it? It had been a boy she'd known for mere weeks, and yet felt a lifetime's connection to.

"Do you still think of Tamim?" she asked. There were days when she forgot to think of Baba, when she barely thought of Deen, whose breath had clouded the cold Demenhune air less than a month past.

"Always," Kifah said. Her chestnut mare snorted as they trotted along the cobbled road. "Though there are times when Altair takes precedence. More and more, as of late."

"You like him," Zafira said.

Kifah snorted. "Don't tell me you don't. You're going to *Alderamin* for him."

She was going for more than Altair; for her own guilt, for the Jawarat, for the heart the Lion had stolen. Still, Zafira couldn't argue with that. "But do you . . . love him?"

"Trying to pair us up, eh? I'm afraid my affections don't run that way. I love him, yes. Fiercely." She canted her head. "I'm beginning to love our zumra—even Nasir—as much as I loved Tamim, but I'd never be with Altair in the way you think. Affection isn't measured and defined by tangible contact for me."

Zafira considered that.

"I see those gears turning, Huntress. I wasn't always so certain. I used to think I hadn't found the right person yet. To be with another is supposedly an inherent desire of us all, is it not? Something we're meant to do. I . . . I have never felt that pull. That *need*. Laa, I thought I was daama broken. Heartless."

Zafira studied her. "But not anymore."

Kifah squared her shoulders and spurred her horse onward with a smile. "No, not anymore."

Zafira squeezed her thighs and her lazy horse whinnied again before following Kifah's lead. It was a special kind of strength, knowing one's heart as well as Kifah knew hers.

What do you want? She had demanded an answer from Nasir, and yet she could barely piece together one of her own.

Seif was waiting for them up ahead where the sand rose and fell in neat dunes. Pockets of shadow clutched the last of the night, sinking lower and lower as Zafira and Kifah neared, until the golden expanse deepened to azure, brightening and reflecting the sky, whispering a song quite different from that of the shifting sands.

The Strait of Hakim.

Yet another place Zafira had never thought she would see in person. Another place Deen, whose dream was to explore, would never see.

She pressed her knuckles against the ache in her chest, fingers brushing his ring. *There it is.* The loss she thought she'd forgotten. The pain she thought she'd overcome. Yasmine's face flashed in her mind, honey eyes dripping in sorrow.

Kifah whistled. "If that doesn't beg for a swim, I don't know what does."

Zafira didn't know how to swim. She didn't know much of life's delicacies or its simplicities. The waters were clear as glass, dragging the light of the waking sun to its depths and churning it into an alluring shade of blue-green.

Seif surveyed the shores, the barrenness. "Trade flourished here, at a time. Rarities from the Hessa Isles. Goods moved from Sultan's Keep to Alderamin and back. Marketplaces sprawled along both coasts."

Resentment seared his words, and Zafira wondered whom he blamed for Arawiya's fall. If he blamed himself in any way, for it was, as every Arawiyan knew, the safin's cruelty that created the Lion.

"We'll cross there." He pointed farther up the coast, where a bridge stretched like a too-thin smile across the horizon. It was white wood, the kind they could harvest in Demenhur, or maybe even Alderamin, a terrain she did not know. Iron rivets sparkled intermittently along its length, vying with the water for attention. They were a tiny comfort, she supposed, for the bridge had to be at least a century old.

"I'd much rather swim," Kifah said slowly, running a hand along her bare scalp.

Zafira would much rather take a boat. Seif didn't care.

"You might not care for *your* well-being," Zafira began, realizing what a lie the words were when Kifah burst out laughing. It was a marvel how she could be both deeply concerned and full of delight in a single moment. "But we're not crossing that bridge with the heart."

Seif didn't even glance back. "Aya and I crossed it when we returned home to retrieve the remainder of the High Circle after the Arz's fall, and she is worth more to me than all the magic Arawiya can possess."

The two of them exchanged a look at his solemn tone, and Kifah's laughter disappeared as quickly as it had come. He must have sensed their silent contemplation, their piqued curiosity, for he turned back with his signature irritation in his pale eyes, tattoo shimmering against his dark skin.

"Yalla, mortals."

The bridge looked even worse up close, but neither Zafira nor Kifah commented as they dismounted and led their horses across the damp sand. The white wood was speckled with rot, a neat rectangular view of the strait cutting through every so often where slats were missing.

Well then.

Seif prepared to go first, the silk-wrapped heart clutched to his side, and Zafira wondered if he'd ever held a child. It was less likely than if he'd been mortal, she realized. Safin paid for their immortality with lower chances of procreation. Very few safin ever gave birth—a blessing, they learned in school, for Arawiya would be overrun with the vain creatures otherwise. Having never met a safi, she'd had no reason *not* to agree with the biased texts she'd read.

Now, having realized just how precious Aya and Benyamin's child had been, the knowledge made her chest ache. It conjured a feline smile and umber eyes. Angry words from a mortal girl before his death. Did the dead know sorrow?

"Were you there for them?" she asked Seif.

He cut her a look.

"When their son died?"

His features turned stony. "I was there for her when her husband was not."

"I can't see Benyamin abandoning his wife," Kifah said, voice hard.

"The death broke them both," Seif divulged, fixing his gaze in the distance. "Benyamin had the privilege of losing himself in his work, but Aya was still floundering from the loss of magic. It was her livelihood, for she was both a healer and a teacher of magic. Losing her son was hard enough, but losing Benyamin devastated her. He was there, of course. He loved her. But Aya needed more, and it was never the same."

So there was another reason why Seif was angry at him. It didn't sound like Benyamin, to abandon his wife in favor of his work, but she had seen firsthand what death could do to a family. How it could drive knives between bonds, sharpen grief into weapons.

Her thoughts flashed back to just before they left Sultan's Keep, the girl in the yellow shawl vivid in Zafira's mind as she laced her boots. Lana had followed her because Aya was at last out of earshot.

"She needs me," Lana had said.

"She *needs* you?" Zafira hadn't been able to tame her emotions. "Decades of life, and now she suddenly needs *you*?"

Lana hadn't flinched. "I remind her of her child. She's broken, Okhti. And we know what it's like, don't we? We know what it's like to be broken. We're the same, she and us."

Zafira and Lana were sisters. The world had battered and bruised and torn them apart, and yet they had lifted themselves to their feet and persevered. They had powered onward. If Aya needed Lana because of the dead son she reminded her of, then laa, the safi was not the same as them. But Zafira had been too angry to make Lana understand, too raw from the sight of the girl in Nasir's room.

"Oi, Huntress!" Kifah called.

Zafira blinked free of her thoughts. Up ahead, Seif cast her the same look of annoyance as when she'd given the Lion the Jawarat. *Incapable*, it said.

She didn't think twice before stepping onto the bridge and joining Kifah.

It swayed beneath them, a low hiss rising from the wood. She paused.

Hissing?

Shrieking?

Kifah released her horse's reins and grabbed her spear. Seif drew two curved scythes, and Zafira surveyed their surroundings as she nocked an arrow onto her bow. Dimly, she realized she was waiting for something else. Not a foe, but the sound of a scimitar being drawn, a deathly silent assassin growing even more so in the face of danger.

"Marids," Seif murmured.

And something flashed in the water.

CHAPTER 25

A S THEY LED THEIR HORSES THROUGH THE GATES, the paved ground gritty with sand, the growing heat settled on Nasir like a fine cloak. The rooftops would be quicker, but for once, he wanted to be seen. He was expected, and he had no reason to sneak about.

Posturing as your favorite brother, I see, Altair's voice mocked in his head. Perhaps he was.

Aya had insisted on accompanying him, which meant Lana did, too. She rode with the safi, eyes wide in wonder as Nasir led them past sprawling limestone constructions and their green-tinted pools. They could pass as mother and daughter if one ignored their ears, he realized. Their features were similar enough, eyes brown, hair barely shades apart.

Lana turned to Aya with a smile far more innocent than he knew the girl to be—he'd heard her daama hiss when Zafira protested being alone with him. But Aya's gaze softened and grew distant, and Nasir remembered: Benyamin and Aya once had a child. That was what Aya saw when she looked at Lana, young and duteous.

The morning was quiet until they reached the Sultan's Road, a wide expanse of stone that left no obstacle to mar the view of the palace, shimmering with heat. Along either side of the road was a single row of date palms, akin to sentinels, leaves swaying in the early breeze, accentuating the beauty of the palace.

He passed marketgoers and guards. Servants bargained for every bit of produce they placed in their baskets. Men passed on horseback and more on foot, several with camels ambling beside them. Some merchants dragged carts while others hefted goods over their shoulders, rousing dust as they shuffled in their sandals.

The whispers were immediate, carrying on the dry breeze and straight to his ears.

The prince is back.

Behind me, my child.

If only it were the general who had returned.

Altair was every bit as much a murderer as Nasir, yet they doted on him. He kept them safe, they said. He smiled. He charmed.

Nasir had shamefully joined the masses.

Lana giggled at one of the more indecent comments, and they pressed on. The people stared at Aya just as much, awestruck and slack-jawed, for she was beautiful and graceful, her smile tender no matter who it was fixed upon.

If curiosity lifted any of the people's gazes to his, terror quickly glazed them. It awakened a surge of power in him, making the shadows in his bloodstream stir. Some part of him had missed the fear he deserved, but he hadn't missed the reverence. He had loathed it when they dropped to their knees and lowered their heads with murmured respects.

Now he felt Aya and Lana's silence as they witnessed the way people looked at him, the Prince of Death.

Amir al-Maut.

The name undercut the meticulous changes in himself that he had cultivated upon Sharr.

Then who am I? he'd asked on Sharr. Zafira had given him an answer then, quick and succinct. If only the truth were as easy.

A falcon drifted across the horizon, dipping behind one of the palace minarets. Nasir slowed his horse to a trot and dismounted at the palace gates, their grandeur every bit as despicable as always. If the guards were surprised to see him, they didn't show it. They even continued with their chattering, one of them stepping forward for the horse's reins with a boldness Nasir did not like.

He dropped his hood as he strode through the black gates, increasingly aware of his surroundings, from the beads cascading down the lip of the fountain shaped like a lounging lion to the angle of the desert breeze.

At the palace doors, the two guards lowered their heads in solemn greeting, neither emitting the fear they usually did, and Nasir slowed his steps, touching a hand to his sword before counting again the throwing knives linked to his belt.

Inside, the usually empty palace was a touch stiller. The dignitaries would not arrive for a few days still. Laa, this trap was for him, and he refused to fall within its grasp. Apprehension molded to his skin, the dark power in his blood aiding his sight in the gloom of the hall as it had done in the Lion's palace on Sharr.

Illumining the five men in the silver of the Sultan's Guard.

CHAPTER 26

"DON'T MOVE," SEIF COMMANDED FROM THE CEN-
ter of the bridge as Zafira sifted through Baba's stories
for details about marids. They were amphibious and fed on
blood. They had the bodies of women and tails like fish and—

"They see better beneath the surface," Seif murmured.

From the corner of Zafira's eye, she caught more flashes in the blue-
green water as the creatures circled below them, followed by a voice
distorted beneath the strait. Her horse strained against her grip, sensing
danger and ignoring her soft words. It wasn't the sun that sent a trickle of
perspiration down her neck.

Then a deathly silence befell their surroundings. The waters stilled,
and the horses calmed.

Zafira's exhale shook with relief. Ahead of them, Seif relaxed. His fingers brushed the leather satchel strapped to his side, feeling for the faint
pulse of the heart. Only then did fear grip her. For the heart, the most
powerful artifact in Arawiya, was also its most feeble.

"Yalla," Seif murmured without turning back, and the three of them crept forward again, dragging the horses along. Zafira winced as each clop of their hooves resonated like the snap of a bowstring.

A splash rippled the water to her left. She and Kifah shared a glance but didn't stop moving. Seif was nearly across, and nothing else mattered.

Another splash.

The heart, the heart, the heart.

She couldn't even swim. She couldn't swim any more than she could survive a marid's gnashing jaws, but all that mattered was the heart.

Zafira yelped when something slammed against the underwater supports. The bridge groaned. She gripped the moldered railing, her own heart thrumming loud enough for two.

Kifah whispered, "Our horses."

As if spurred by her voice, one threw back its head, yanking the reins. The other stamped its feet. The air thickened with their sudden snorts and protests. The water stirred with renewed fervor. *Khara.* Muffled shrieks drowned out Zafira's pounding pulse.

"Run!" Seif called over the clamor.

"Are you mad?" Kifah snapped as he took off, sheathing his scythes and pulling his horse with him. She cursed beneath her breath. "At least ride the daama thing!"

He was *leaving* them. Zafira had expected nothing less from a safi like him. *All that matters is the heart,* she reminded herself, but skies, it wouldn't hurt to show *some* concern.

Seif stopped and turned, and her fear returned with a vengeance when she saw the heart against his side within reach of whatever might lunge from the waters at any given moment.

"Go!" Kifah yelled. "Now is not the time to be considerate, safi."

His pale eyes flashed, but he turned toward the shore.

Too late.

Something dark moved by his feet. Hands, hair—a *face.* He stopped when it leaped from the water, hissing and snarling and swallowing every last drop of air in Zafira's lungs. A marid, though she could see little of it. Spindly arms lunged, blued by life beneath the surface, and clawed hands tore across the white wood, reaching for Seif. He whipped his scythes from their sheaths, murmuring to his horse, the only calm one of the lot.

Before they could run to him, a face came up against Kifah's, eyes wide and gaunt, hair clumped and dripping, dark mouth parted in a soundless scream, emanating a terrible hunger. Zafira couldn't breathe.

The marid was roughly the size and shape of a human, except for the tail thrashing in lieu of legs.

Kifah shouted and dropped her spear, stumbling back into her horse.

Unleashing turmoil.

The horse screamed. It rammed into the rails of the bridge, cracking them, blinded by terror before it found direction and headed straight toward Alderamin. Straight for Seif. Water sloshed onto the bridge as more marids threw themselves against it.

In her mind's eye, Zafira saw only the pulsing red of the si'lah heart, fading to silence, crumbling to dust.

Her own horse lifted itself on its hind legs and neighed, turning for Sultan's Keep as two of the marids leaped from either side of the bridge with ear-shattering shrieks.

Blood splattered Zafira's face, hot and sudden. In the split-beat it took to level her bow, the marids tore open the horse's body, its innards spilling free.

Seif shouted above the clamor. Zafira whirled with a dry heave and spotted another marid crawling for Kifah. She fired an arrow with shaky hands, heaving again when it struck close to the monster's webbed fingers. It turned to her with wide, hungering eyes.

"Kifah!" Zafira lurched for Kifah's spear, tossed it to her, and leaped away from an arm reaching blindly through a missing slat of the bridge. She fired another arrow as the marid began crawling to her, and she feared her heart would flee from her chest and into its gaping mouth. The marid screamed as it retreated back into the strait.

Water sloshed at her boots. She felt halved—worried for herself, worried for the si'lah heart. The bridge groaned again. Beneath the din, Zafira heard a sound worse than any other: a heaving splinter.

"The bridge!" she cried.

Seif's horse frenzied, but the safi kept it safe, the heart clutched to his side. His scythes flashed as quickly as the marids' razor-sharp gills in the water, and a mess of blue blood stickied the space around him.

Zafira fired another arrow. The monsters were swarming now, more than she could count, dragging themselves up the Sultan's Keep end of the bridge as the entire construction dipped. Their tails thrashed in shades of azure too beautiful for their horrible faces. She swallowed bile as her horse slid wetly toward the water, blood smearing, guts trailing.

Zafira and Kifah sprinted for Seif, who was barely paces from the Alder shore. Another beam snapped, and the three of them stumbled. Seif's horse panicked, kicking its hind legs, and the bridge sank another handbreadth. Kifah yanked Zafira away from a swipe of a marid arm, so thin and sickly blue, she almost didn't see it.

The end of the bridge was in sight—seven paces. Five. Zafira's stomach dropped.

"Seif!" she yelled as a marid clawed at his right. "The heart!"

And then the bridge collapsed, swallowing her words and everything else upon it.

CHAPTER 27

"**M**ARHABA," SAID THE LEADER OF THE FIVE SILVER-
cloaked guards.

He was vaguely familiar, likely an acolyte who had run
missives from one master to another a moon or two ago and now had a
retinue of his own. Positions shifted as quickly as the sands in the Sultan's
Palace.

Nasir met his gaze and grasped fleeting satisfaction when the man
looked away.

Monster. Altair's laugh rang in his head.

I've a reputation to uphold. Rimaal, they needed to find the oaf quickly,
or Nasir would go insane, speaking to him when he wasn't there.

Laa, it was the emptiness that was doing this. He had been given a taste
of the opposite, of contentment and satisfaction and fulfillment, and he
had started to forget the feel of nothing. The way it made him exist outside
of himself. The way it made him cease to exist at all.

Life was a dance to a tune he could not hear. Around him, the world rushed like a stream while he remained unmoving, a core that was not needed in the grand scale of anything. These were not new feelings, but subsided ones. Harsh truths that had quieted when there was someone who sought him out.

It was a feeling unmatched, to be sought by another.

The guard stepped aside. "The sultan awaits the amir's presence."

Nasir lifted his brows at the semblance of respect. "The sultan, or the Lion?"

Aya stiffened. The guard only blinked. "The sultan, sayyidi. We were told the amir's party would be larger."

"Is that why he sent armed men to greet us?" Nasir asked, and the man grew flustered.

Aya took pity on him. "The rest of our party did not wish to come."

Five pairs of eyes assessed her and her tattoo. Very few knew of the High Circle, and Nasir wondered if they could tell she was not human despite the ivory shawl shrouding her ears. Their scrutiny dropped to the staff in her hand.

"For my balance," she said.

The guard nodded, appeased by her dreamy smile, and led them across the foyer, up the twenty-three steps of the winding staircase, and across six paces to the wide double doors carved from alabaster and framed in polished limestone. Nasir knew the layout of the palace as well as the back of his hand—better, perhaps. He never inspected the hands he used for killing.

They paused before the doors and Nasir glanced back at Lana. "All right?"

She nodded, fear flaring her eyes, and Nasir regretted his decision to bring her. He should have left her down in the kitchens, where mopping the floors would be the worst of it.

Too soon, the guards heaved open the groaning doors.

Nasir blinked back against the unexpected spill of brightness. Nearly every dark curtain in the throne room was open, light carving ominous shadows into the ornate walls. The windows were designed to illuminate the Gilded Throne, and illuminate they did, framing the Sultan of Arawiya in an ironic halo.

Five hooded men stood to the right of the dais, another five to the left. They were fitted with gauntlets and contoured robes, as unmoving as statues. Hashashins.

Nasir entered. His steps were whisper-soft along the black carpet that cut a swath of darkness across the alabaster, and he was painfully aware of Ghameq watching his every breath. Aya and Lana flanked him, the rhythmic tap of the safi's staff a pounding in his skull.

At the foot of the white dais, he stopped. A faint whiff of bakhour rose to his senses, the musk and jasmine familiar. Three steps up, and he would stand at throne level.

Sultan Ghameq stared at him down the bridge of his nose. The gray eyes Nasir had inherited were full of scorn, distaste furrowing his mouth.

It's not him, Nasir reminded himself.

Two men shared the throne: one mortal, one ancient. One who had fathered him, and one who had stolen Altair. Laa, the Lion had stolen far more than that.

"I did not think you would come," Ghameq said.

No greetings. No smirk. Nothing at all. The medallion hung between the folds of his gold-edged cloak, the leash by which the Lion held him. Nasir knew how to fix this. How to ensure the dignitaries' safety.

He lifted his gaze back to his father's.

Sultans don't wear turbans, his mother had once teased.

I am Sarasin first, sultan second, his father had replied. A keffiyah and a circlet might make for a royal display, but never a pragmatic one. The exchange was forever ago, when those gray eyes hadn't hidden amber ones. When his father still carried the pride of his heritage like a bannerman in war.

"I suppose I should be flattered you invited me," Nasir replied.

The derision that rolled from his father's throat was so familiar that he could have mimicked it. But for once, he didn't feel the overwhelming desire to rein in his words. He would not cower before the Lion.

"Sharr gave you a tongue." Ghameq stood. "Or was it the girl?"

Nasir stilled.

He heard the hitch of Aya's breath. Felt the distress rolling off Lana in waves.

"You forget, boy. I am your father."

Even Ghameq's laugh was poised to belittle, and a roaring started in Nasir's head.

"There are few men as witless as you. I saw the Demenhune Hunter with my own eyes. Did you think to protect her by not bringing her here?"

Nasir went very, very cold when Ghameq's gaze fell on Lana. His father would not know the girl, but the Lion would—in the same way he had known Zafira before Sharr. Danger sparked the air. The roaring grew louder.

"Your orders were to kill her. Your orders were to kill them all, yet you disobeyed. You uncovered someone's misplaced mettle and dared to show your face here."

As if Nasir had no right to stand in this throne room. As if he had no right to sit upon the Gilded Throne forged by the Sisters of Old, whose blood burned in his own veins. As if he had not been *asked* to come here.

Breathe, Nasir told himself. He was not petty. Insults were letters festooned into words that could not inflict pain. *A lie and a losing battle.*

"You brought me here to mock me," Nasir seethed, barely restraining the emotion that threatened to bleed into his words.

The sultan scoffed. "Did you expect gratification, mutt?"

Something

inside him

snapped.

Darkness erupted from his fingers like ravens taking flight. Distantly, he heard Lana's surprised cry. The hashashins came alert, and Nasir fought to control the mass. Pressure built in his chest as Aya attempted to placate him. He could fight ten hashashins—he couldn't keep Lana safe, too.

It's not him. It's not your father.

The voice lilted through his ears, wrapped around his limbs. Calming him. Reasoning with him, even when she was somewhere far, far from here. His heart wept. The shadows froze like a fog.

You are not the sum of his disparagement.

It was the Lion, Zafira's words reminded him. The Lion was baiting him, as he had done and continued to do—every bit the animal of his namesake toying with his prey.

Nasir calmed the chorus in his blood and found it: the vessel that bled black. He cinched it closed, and the shadows disappeared, and satisfaction gave way to pride. Pride lifted his gaze to his father's in time to see a flicker of surprise cross his face.

"Get out, mu—"

"Yes, Father," Nasir replied.

It was a powerful feeling, cutting his father off, but he knew better than most that it was easier not to feel than to rely on the highs of emotion. Behind him, the throne room doors groaned open in wordless dismissal. In moments, the hashashins were back in their neat rows. The medallion swayed, enticing. The lingering shadows had vanished, burned by the light. It looked as if nothing had changed. As if they hadn't been on the brink of an irreversible chaos.

Ghameq smiled, and in it, Nasir saw the Lion.

Nasir smiled back, imagining the medallion in his hands.

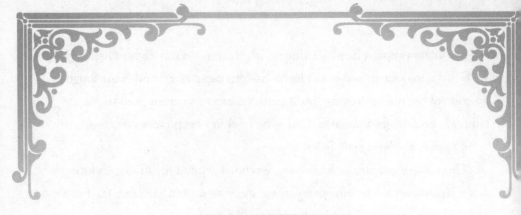

CHAPTER 28

A WAVE STRUCK ALDERAMIN'S SHORE AS THE BRIDGE
fell, the Strait of Hakim engulfing marid and rotting white wood
alike.

Zafira clutched her bow in one shivering hand, arrows in the other.
The blue-green water churned crimson, her horse's body gone. She had
barely kept herself alive and intact.

Kifah heaved beside her, drenched to the bone, and—

Zafira sat up. "Where's Seif?"

"Where's the heart?" Kifah echoed the word pounding in Zafira's skull.

The water receded, whispering its apology.

"'Where's the heart?' she inquires. Not a word for the safi who saved
her despite her impending mortality."

Kifah looked at Zafira and Zafira looked at Kifah, as if the slow drawl
had crawled out of the other's mouth. Slowly, the two of them turned to
find Seif in the sand, shirtless—fully shirtless this time—and panting,

the satchel bearing the heart held gingerly in his dark hands. Even his daama horse had made it through.

Zafira gave him a look. "It was a collective effort."

"Why should I have been worried? I saw you making the leap when I did," Kifah said with a roll of her eyes.

Zafira hadn't, and she was certain Kifah hadn't either. There was a lot of slipping and jumping and falling in those final moments before the bridge's collapse.

"It's dying," Seif said softly.

Zafira approached him stiltedly, for he was shameless and unclothed, his robes stretched to dry a little farther inland, where the sand was dry. The heart had darkened even more since they had begun their journey. It throbbed achingly slow, a deafening stretch of nothingness between each dying beat.

"It can't die," she said. Something pricked in her eyes, and Seif looked at her as if she'd lost her mind, but she shook her head. "*It can't die.* Not after everything we went through to find it and the other hearts. Not when it will leave us without magic forever."

Kifah shoved her spear into the wet sand. "Until the heart dies, it's still alive. Now yalla, immortal. You've a minaret to find, and we, Huntress"— Kifah jabbed her spear in Zafira's direction—"have some blood to hunt."

———◆———

Zafira welcomed the heat of the sun on her soaked clothes. The way it ran its fingers up her back, making her arch into its warmth. It reminded her of another touch, of another delicious heat she craved.

Was it wrong to coerce herself into believing it was him in her room? His words bold. His lips on her neck. His hand at her thigh. His, not the Lion's. Was it wrong to remove herself from everything afterward, from the girl in the yellow shawl, from his failure to deny what looked so painfully obvious?

That moment looped back through her mind again, when the door slid open. When he was staring passively at the girl, not at all the way he looked at Zafira. With enough heat in his gray gaze to rival the sun itself.

She growled, wanting to scream. Wanting to shove him to the ground and tear him apart with her hands and her nails and her mouth and her tongue.

The ground or your bed? Yasmine taunted in her head.

"Whoa there," Kifah clucked, casting Zafira a look.

She smoothed a hand down the horse's neck in apology. It was her turn on Seif's steed, and she was surprised by how composed the beast had been despite nearly being hacked to death by angry sea monsters. Seif might have had a strong dislike for mortals, but he clearly had a way with animals.

The sand had given way to stone, clattering beneath the horse's hooves. And then, soon enough, she caught sight of the wall. It was a towering structure of white, at least four times her height. Every so often, a massive archway was cut into the wall, sharp and shapely, an entrance to the caliphate many only dreamed of seeing.

"Only the Alder," Kifah said with a snort.

Anger shot through Zafira, hot and fierce. She'd known of the wall, expressed irritation with it once, but then she was secluded in her own little village. It was different now that she'd seen more of Arawiya, knowing the mighty Alder safin cowed behind stone while neglecting all else.

"If you, too, had lived an eternity before iridescent shores, you would have erected such a wall," Seif said, morose. "Anything to shroud those cursed trees."

"So you wouldn't have to see the Arz, or our suffering?" Zafira snapped.

Seif ignored her, as he tended to do. For she was a mortal with a fleeting life, and he was an immortal, a king in his own eyes. She felt a wave of pride, sitting on the horse and forcing him to look up at her with his still-damp robes and the heart in his hands.

The barren sand gave way to dry shrubs, and then a slow trickle of greenery, trees rising with thick, healthy trunks, stretching shadows cool and large enough for children to play. Jasmine bloomed like snow. Birds called from the trees, and a camel ambled with his brothers beyond the road. And she hadn't even broached the walls of Alderamin yet.

"The safin are blessed," Seif said. Something in his tone kept her lips from curling in disgust at his vanity as she swapped places with Kifah, handing her the reins when she dismounted the horse. "Vigor unmatched by any other. Agility, hearing. Age. When Arawiya was cursed, each caliphate's suffering pertained to themselves. The snow lauded once a year in Demenhur became a perpetual curse. Pelusia, whose fields could nurture any seed, suffered a loss to her fertility."

He stared ahead, to the wall. She could see details now, glittering sand stirring against it. Life shifting beyond the wide arches.

"There is nothing unique to Alderamin save us, the eternal ones as old as the land itself. Safin, by nature, are less fertile than man." He paused, ruminating his next words. "We began to die out. Sickness spread across the caliphate. Death, unheard of except in war and battle, became common. We chose sequestration out of necessity. We faced more than the loss of magic forever: It was the annihilation of our race."

Zafira was stunned into silence. Kifah exhaled in disbelief, proof that the lies Zafira had been taught were not limited to her village, her city, or even her caliphate.

All of Arawiya believed that the safin had quarantined themselves within their walls out of vanity and selfish self-preservation. It *was* self-preservation, but not of the careless kind. Not because they were hoarding their resources.

It was because they had no choice.

They suffered alone. Quiet and brave. It was easy to believe that anyone who did not speak of suffering did not suffer.

Like Lana. Like her prince with ashes in his eyes.

"Why did you let the kingdom believe otherwise?" Kifah asked.

"And admit defeat?" Seif asked as if she had suggested murder.

Kifah, who had been concerned and awaiting a dire response, rolled her eyes. Zafira laughed, and she was surprised by the hint of a smile lifting a corner of Seif's mouth.

CHAPTER 29

I T WAS BOTH A GIFT AND A CURSE, TO FEEL AS DEEPLY AS she did. To see Alderamin in the lucidity of a dreamwalk was entirely different from seeing it in person. To believe that the *realness* would not affect her was a mistake on her part.

A sore, sore mistake.

The outskirts of the caliphate were as grand as the capital itself. It was the beauty of Sultan's Keep tenfold. Like in the dreamwalk, she couldn't shake off the feeling of it being more alive than anywhere else. The pulse of life was everywhere, from the spiny-tailed lizards darting up the date palms to the children shouting and laughing as they chased one another beneath an arch, circling back from the ledge of a low roof to leap into a blue-green pool of water. From the colors of the clothes on the backs of men to the medley of shawls suspended across zigzagging ropes swaying in the gentle breeze.

As much as she had scowled and groused over the safin tucked away within their walls, she had to admit the miscellany of people was greater than elsewhere. In Demenhur, the sight of anyone a shade darker than the snow-cursed made everyone stop and stare. In Sarasin, safin were rare, if not impossible, to encounter. In Alderamin, Pelusian and safin walked side by side. A Demenhune stepped through her bright green door with her Zaramese husband.

It wasn't that safin weren't welcome elsewhere. They simply had no *reason* to live anywhere but their perfect haven of Alderamin. Unlike everyone else, who believed Alderamin was where they'd find the life Arawiya had once provided freely and equitably. They believed it enough to traverse the uncultivated Wastes for a chance to live here. Deen had seen proof, when he'd visited years ago.

Here was a sea of people with different shades of skin, different lilts to their tongue, different cadences that built the wholeness that was Arawiya.

And yet, despite the way the very ground seemed to live and breathe, Zafira felt strangely lonely. For a part of her had grown accustomed, she realized with some diffidence, to observing the world in awe and being observed in turn.

As if he could glean the same wonder just by looking at her.

Her fingers fluttered at her side. Skies, she missed him.

"This is where we part ways," Seif said, holding the heart with care. "See that caravanserai with the stained-glass window? We'll meet there at sundown."

The window was impossible to miss: it was *massive*, more akin to an entrance for a giant, florals made of stone holding the arching glass within interlacing clutches. Kifah brought the horse to a stop. "Is that all the time it'll take for you to restore the heart in Almas and return?"

"Safin," was all Seif said as he mounted the horse and turned in the direction of Alderamin's capital. He had recovered every last drop of his vanity now that his robes were dried, and he eyed the road ahead with such indifference, it felt offensive. Safin were quick, but *that* quick?

"And Bait ul-Ahlaam?" Zafira asked as the locals began to take interest. The people here might hail from around the kingdom, but they lived here. She knew the ferocity with which a village looked after their own. She respected it.

Seif pursed his lips. "It must find you."

And then the bastard left them.

"Oi! What does that mean? Come back!" Kifah snarled. More people had wandered out of their houses to watch them, curiosity torching the air. They had lived near the border, near the encroaching Arz. Visitors were rare, if any. Kifah noticed them and turned a slow circle, baring her teeth. *What?*

Mothers tucked children into their skirts. Fathers eyed the spear in Kifah's hand and the arrows slung on Zafira's back, Baba's jambiya with its worn hilt at her waist.

"Maybe we should start moving," Zafira said gently.

Kifah glared at her. "Oh? Where?"

Zafira looked about, as if the elusive shop would wave a hand and beckon her over. Wherever it was, they'd have to find it on foot, since their horses had been devoured by the marids. Skies, couldn't Lana have told them more? Even a descriptor from the book she had found it in would have helped.

"The sooq," a man said, stepping forward and gesturing up the road. He was human, his wide-knuckled hands gripping a bucket of water from the well the houses were clustered around. The woman with him, shrewd-eyed with a basket of wrung-out clothes clutched to her side, glared at him, as if there were ill to be had in aiding two weary travelers. Her eyes narrowed on Zafira, straying to her jambiya and then, strangely, to Deen's ring.

"It calls to those who need it," the man said, setting his bucket on a ledge.

"To those willing to pay the price," the woman added sharply.

Several others clucked their tongues and murmured, whether in agreement to her words or in protest of her hostility, Zafira did not know.

She inclined her head, ignoring the cold fingers down her spine. "Shukrun."

————◄●►————

Kifah grew less enthused the longer they walked. The town was called Zawia, for the way it curved around the splendor of Almas. It was a charming place unlike the slums that typically surrounded capitals and other major cities. As Zafira gaped at every new street, structure, and scene, uncaring of the burn in her tired calves, Kifah's gaze turned pensive, trained on the sands they stirred with their footfalls. She didn't even look up when a girl in an abaya as red as her hair ran up to them with a shy smile and handed Zafira a white-petaled flower. The child's ears were elongated, the points tender and precious, and Zafira stared as she skipped away.

"Did you see her?" she breathed. Sunlight lit the little safi's hair aflame before she disappeared between two houses.

Kifah replied with a distracted grunt.

"What is it?" Zafira asked.

"If it calls to those who need it, I'm not sure it's so great a place anymore," Kifah replied without preamble.

Zafira paused, twirling the flower's thin stem between her fingers. The petals cupped morsels of the sun. She had never encountered this Kifah before, weighted by uncertainty and quick to refute.

"Is this about your father?" Zafira asked.

The whip of her spear quickened, answer enough. Zafira remembered that Bait ul-Ahlaam was a place Kifah's father had frequented. Did it call to monsters in need of its wares?

"I know how they work, people like him. They win the hearts of men, eat the souls of women. Flash a smile as sweet as milk here, rip fragile limbs apart there. Dote on one daughter outside, ruin another inside." Kifah's exhale stuttered.

As lonely as Zafira felt, she could not even begin to understand the depths of Kifah's loneliness. To be abused by her father. To have her brother punished to death for protecting her. To own nothing but the spear in her hands and the desire for vengeance in her veins.

"Forgive me," Kifah murmured.

"No," Zafira whispered harshly. "You said you're beginning to love our zumra the way you loved Tamim. Tell me."

Kifah's brow smoothed at the words. Her spear stopped moving. "That's all there is."

Zafira smiled, but she understood Kifah's apprehension. It was why she'd felt a chill down her spine at the Alder woman's ominous words. "I don't think we'll leave the shop describing it as ethical or virtuous. You can't believe the Sisters filled vials with blood and labeled them for sale." She gripped Deen's chain and remembered the Silver Witch's anger, Seif's trepidation. "I have a feeling it calls to those ready to pay the price."

Kifah was silent, and Zafira felt the sting of perspiration along her brow. Had she been callous? Too quick to brush away Kifah's heavy words?

"You know what I hate?" Kifah asked, giving her a look. "When other people make sense."

Zafira swallowed her relief, pulse still drumming in her ears. "A simple 'Yes, my queen, you're right,' would suffice."

Kifah cracked a laugh. "Already wearing the crown, I see."

"What do you—"

Oh.

They reached the top of the street, where reed-thin buildings rose neatly to the cloud-dusted skies, windows cut in alluring latticework, stone shaped in eight-pointed stars. Beyond them, the sooq stretched in a patchwork of color and bustle as far as she could see.

Zafira hurried beneath the slanting shadows of the buildings to hide the burn of her skin. Whoever said Demenhune didn't blush was a terrible liar. "I didn't—that wasn't what—" She gave up.

"I didn't think you were serious," Kifah assured, loping beside her. "But don't tell me it's as impossible a future as it was two moons ago. Being queen."

"What does that have to do with anything?"

"He's the prince," Kifah reminded her, though not unkindly. "And quite the eyeful at that. Tall, dark, brooding. *Very* fit."

Zafira closed her fingers around Baba's jambiya, knuckles white. "Do you think I'd abandon my life and my family for a jeweled chair?"

What life? a voice in her head asked. *What family?*

"That's for you to answer," Kifah said, grinning and unaware. "I'm not the one falling in love with him."

"I'm not either," Zafira said, looking away with a barely restrained groan.

A safi narrowed her eyes as she passed them by; then another pair in turbans paused a heavy conversation to look at Kifah from head to toe, likely realizing that one of the Nine Elite of Pelusia was ambling down to the Zawia sooq.

Even if Zafira's jambiya was nothing out of the ordinary—for nearly every Arawiyan carried one—the rest of their weapons weren't as subtle. While others toted baskets of fruit and sacks of grain and fresh folds of bread, Kifah gripped her spear, the fire-forged point flashing. Zafira's arrows knocked together lightly in a familiar song.

"Akhh, it's not as simple as that, hmm?" Kifah said when Zafira didn't speak. "I've never known love, but it's hard enough between blood. Carving out one's heart for a stranger and wishing for theirs in return is no easy feat."

But that was the problem, wasn't it? It *wasn't* hard. She could open her mouth and words would fall as freely as sand from a loose fist. She would open her door and welcome him without a second thought. Talking to him was easy, even when he was silent. Touching him, tasting him, sharing a slant of shadow with him felt like the most natural acts in the world.

It frustrated her.

How could she explain it to Kifah when she could make no sense of it herself?

It came with another thought: Had she acted too rashly, leaving without letting him explain himself? Had she destroyed whatever fragile thing they had begun to shape between them?

They paused at a crossroads, and a man coming from the opposite direction slowed his march, eyeing Zafira. Ever since she had lost Baba's cloak on Sharr, the difference between stepping out as the Hunter, thought to be a boy, and stepping out as herself, a girl, was glaring. A man could be out alone on any number of business pursuits. A woman? Likely something salacious.

"Smile, fair one." The man was beardless in a way that said he couldn't grow hair on his face despite his best efforts.

Kifah scowled in his direction.

"Anything else, while I'm in a good mood?" Zafira called back. His watery grin left a bad taste in her mouth. "Should I sing prettily while I slit your throat?"

He took a few cautious steps back, and hurried down the street.

"Men," Kifah said, snorting a laugh.

They paused at the top of the road.

"Well," she said with some wonder, for it seemed everyone believed the perfect time to visit the sooq was just after the noon's heat had begun to wane. Rickety stalls filled the center of the cobbled square, bustling with safin and humans alike and an array of smells that made Zafira increasingly aware of how little food she'd had since departing Sultan's Keep.

Shops ran along either side of the jumu'a, each one vastly different from the one beside it, as if they had built one and then another, and then couldn't stop. Curtains flanked their entrances, bright and lively, many drawn and pinned in welcome.

One moment Zafira was following Kifah's sure-footed lead, and the next, the other girl had disappeared only to return with several neat squares of mutabaq. The combined aroma of juicy mutton and the crispy pancake holding it together made Zafira salivate.

"Could use a bit more sumac," Kifah mused, making a face. "And less pepper. What? I know my food."

Zafira expected nothing less from a stoic warrior who packed her own spices for a life-and-death journey.

"Where did you get that?"

"I bought it." Kifah lifted a brow. "Not all of us are penniless villagers."

Indeed. But Kifah rarely acted like the snobs who lived in Arawiya's lavish capitals, so it was easy to overlook the fact. Zafira's shoulders curled. She had left behind their dwindling purse with Lana, for they and the Ra'ads had always shared what they earned from the skins of Zafira's hunts, and she hadn't *needed* money. Not on Sharr, where there was game to be hunted. Not even in Sultan's Keep, where Aya provided without asking for anything in return.

"It was a joke."

Zafira looked away. Mockery, she could take, but it was sympathy she loathed. Pity led to embarrassment, and that led to anger, always. As if that wasn't bad enough, her stomach growled audibly, forever at war with her will.

"Oi," Kifah said around a mouthful. "Have you had nothing to eat all day?"

Zafira shrugged, pointedly glancing in the direction they'd been heading. Kifah ignored her and extended a hand. Three coins sat in her palm. Two paces away, a poet climbed a crate and bemoaned the poison of love.

"Keep them," Zafira said, hating the bite to her words. "I'm not hungry."

Kifah shoved the coins into Zafira's hand. "They're Seif's. To pay for the rooms."

Seif hadn't given her a dinar, and they both knew it.

The lie made it easier, somehow. Or perhaps it was her hunger. Zafira took them without meeting Kifah's eyes and ducked into the thick of the sooq. The prospect of food made her stomach yawn anew, the gaping emptiness stretching up her throat and making her light-headed. Coin did this. Penniless, she could ignore the hunger, stave it away. Such was the oddity of a conscience.

She stopped at the first stall she found, where a safi stoked a fire, slowly turning a spit with her other hand. She was far less elegant than the safin Zafira was acquainted with.

"Two dinars fifty," the safi said before Zafira could speak, eyeing her like an urchin come for scraps.

Zafira straightened her shoulders and clinked her coins softly, like a fool. Two and a half dinars was far too much. She should have bargained, should have thrown together a ploy as customers were wont to do, but it was Deen who had done all their marketing.

"What about the flatbread alone?"

"One dinar."

For a single flatbread? A line began to form behind her.

"I—I'll take the flatbread."

The safi grunted and snatched a fold from the stack keeping warm beside the spit. Zafira carefully set one coin on her worn cart, feeling a childish lick of power as she pocketed the other two dinars. They were a comforting weight. A promise sewn into her clothes, a guarantee of sustenance. The safi saw, and after a beat of hesitation, lathered a spoonful of the warm fat that had collected beneath the spit across the bread, folding the neat round in half before handing it to Zafira.

She was already looking to her next customer, and Zafira was too hungry and too grateful to be proud.

Kifah was waiting for her, gaze hunting the crowds. Her foot tapped a beat. "What's in it?"

"Nothing," Zafira said, tearing off a piece.

Kifah's brow furrowed. "You bought . . . plain flatbread."

Zafira shrugged, but it wasn't careless enough. Skies, why couldn't she be more aloof? Why did she suddenly wish her cloak shielded the stiff set of her shoulders?

She dropped her gaze when Kifah's softened. It felt vile to even *think* of spending three dinars on a single meal, but it was clear she and Kifah saw a coin differently.

The flatbread filled her, and that was enough. The coins clinked in her pocket. It was *more* than enough.

"There," Zafira said as she regained some semblance of strength, some scrap of dignity. She pointed to the narrow alleys between some of the shops, her vision clear again. "If Bait ul-Ahlaam is bound to be anywhere, it'll be down one of those. You take the left, I'll take the right."

"I want the right," Kifah said.

"Be my guest, sayyida. Don't get lost."

"Hold my hand, mother," Kifah called, and disappeared into the crowd.

CHAPTER 30

I<small>T WOULD BE DAYS BEFORE THE DIGNITARIES ARRIVED,</small> ample time to do away with the medallion and then scour the palace for any indication of the Lion's and Altair's whereabouts. Letters from Ghameq's hand. Men with strange orders. Anything. As the guards unnecessarily led Nasir to his chambers, he turned to Lana. "Do you trust me?"

He appreciated the way she paused to consider his question.

"Yes," she said.

Nasir spoke to the guards. "The room adjoining mine—is it clean?"

One of the fools had the audacity to grin mischievously as he nodded, but it was the other who spoke. "Shall we procure you a woman?"

Nasir pressed his lips thin until the guard shifted uneasily. His sheathed sword caught in the other's robes and nearly toppled them both.

"And their rooms?" Nasir asked, gesturing to Aya and Lana.

"We—we will escort—"

"Answer the question," he said slowly.

The guards pointed to the two rooms across the hall from Nasir's chambers and couldn't hurry away quickly enough.

When they left, Nasir scanned the hall before looking at Aya. "There is room for two in the adjoining room. It isn't safe here."

Aya refused with a smile. "I have held to immortality this long, Prince."

Lana was watching her, likely awaiting an invitation to share her room, but Aya's gaze only fluttered her way. Nasir wasn't surprised. Laa, he had *counted* on that, for Aya had not been able to keep her own son alive, and he trusted no one but himself to keep Zafira's sister safe.

"Prince?" Aya called him back.

Nasir turned with a passive lift of his brows, masking the caution rearing its head.

"Removing the medallion will not help."

"It's how the Lion controls him," Nasir said tiredly. "He's been controlling him through it for years. Corrupting him." For more than a decade, perhaps. "Remove the medallion, and there's—"

"The absolute certainty that he will *remain* corrupt," Aya finished. "If the medallion has corrupted him, as you say, it no longer serves a purpose."

But Nasir remembered those flashes of humanity simmering beneath Ghameq's coldhearted front. He knew his father was still there.

Aya waited, pity and disbelief clear on her face. "I know what you believe, my love. I know what you hope for. But you cannot get him back."

She was wrong. Nasir didn't hope for anything. *Hope is for . . .* He left the thought unfinished and turned away without another word, ignoring Lana's inquisitive gaze as he ushered her through his door, past the antechambers, and into his bedroom. The gray sheets were as neat as the day he had left them, his curtains closed, and the scent of his soap familiar and calming. *She's wrong*, he convinced himself.

"It's so lonely here," Lana said softly as Nasir slid open a drawer and shifted its contents to retrieve a key.

The rooms struck him like an oddly tailored robe, his but not, and he almost expected to see Altair lounging on his covers with a sly grin. The walls would echo the general's laugh because they, too, loved the sound of his voice. Thinking of Altair here was easier than thinking of *her*. Imagining her here, in his rooms, in his arms.

Did she think of him as she rode for the House of Dreams? Did she miss him as he missed her, an ache that stretched from the pads of his fingers to the corners of his conscience? The way no one else missed him?

After an uncomfortable silence, he unlocked the door to the adjoining room and swept inside the small but lavish space with an attached bath. The bed was curtained with crimson, the sheets meant for all but sleep. He crossed to the door on the opposite end and turned the lock. Then he checked the window, pressing down on both latches, and looked behind the screen just in case before returning to the door connecting the rooms, satisfied.

"Do you love her?"

Nasir froze for the barest of moments.

He didn't have time for questions from girls he didn't know. "The door will be locked from the other side, and I have the only key. Don't try to leave no matter what you hear."

Lana stared at him. "Do you?" she asked again.

Rimaal, this girl. "What do you know of love?"

She flinched. His irritation cracked.

"I—" She floundered. "I once liked someone so much that I thought it was love. Then he went on an adventure with someone he loved more and never came back." She lifted a shoulder in a shrug, refusing his sympathy. "I was too young for him anyway."

He studied her, the bold line of her shoulders, the resilience between her brows. Worlds apart from her sister, yet exactly the same.

"First loves are difficult things," he said finally, softly.

"And second ones?" she asked.

"Everything the first was not."

He closed the door and turned the key, tucking the cool metal against his hip. He had forgotten what it was like to lie on his side in his own bed, in his own home, and feel utterly incomplete with nothing but his gauntlet blades for company. He flicked them out and retracted them with a sigh.

On this very bed, in a bout of sorrow, his mother had mended the burns on his back. On this very bed, in a bout of hunger, Kulsum had slid the linen from his shoulders and he from hers. On this very bed, in a bout of companionship, Altair had propped up his sandals and teased him without mercy.

Were all monsters lonely, he wondered, pretending to be aloof and unafraid? Was it that falsity that nurtured them, cultivating them with careful precision, unique and unmatched?

He missed him. In the way it felt to lose feeling when a limb went numb.

He missed her. In the way it felt to stop breathing. Like he was losing himself.

And it was because of this loneliness that he knew with sudden awareness that he was not alone.

CHAPTER 31

THE ROPE CAME FOR HIS NECK. IT WAS ROUGH AND frayed, meant for a bucket in a well, not the refined throat of a prince.

Seven. In the stillness before he moved, he counted them. Seven daama men to murder someone in his own bed.

He yanked the rope, bracing for his attacker's forward stumble. The man's face crashed against the back of his skull, nose crunching. Nasir flipped him over his shoulder, and he truly did want to stop and politely ask who had sent him and what for, but the fool was fumbling for his jammed gauntlet blade, so Nasir speared him through the throat. Fitted robes and an angular hood. Hashashin.

And he was bleeding on Nasir's bed.

"There's a reason I limit the company in my bedroom," he said quietly. "And now all of you are going to die for ruining my perfectly good sheets."

Two lanterns flickered to life, illuminating a man on the majlis at the far end of the room. It took everything in Nasir's power to keep the surprise from his face. His father. The medallion hung from his neck, glinting like vicious teeth.

"Must have been difficult," Nasir said, a bit of Altair slipping into his tone as he rose, "having to refrain from killing me in the throne room."

The sultan leaned back without a word, the shift barely visible in the soft light, but Nasir saw it clearly enough. He swerved as a hooked blade came for his neck, catching his arm instead. The trap was being sprung. He shoved his attacker away and wrenched the blade free with a hiss, plucking two throwing knives from his belt slung on the wall.

There were hashashins, and then there was Nasir: trained by the best masters the art could offer, honed into a weapon by a Sister of Old.

Nasir unleashed the blades, starting a tally in his head when a choked wheeze announced one true strike. It was the song of death. The hiss of a blade and the final, sputtering beseeching of a breath that could not be followed. A song Nasir knew as well as his own name.

His arm bled and his neck throbbed, yet his limbs were filled with a type of zeal he had been missing in the past few days.

A weight slammed into his back, and he fell with a wheeze, toppling the other man by digging his fingers into the back of his leg. Still on his knees, Nasir snapped the hashashin's arm before impaling him with his gauntlet blade, barely rolling out of the way as another sword sailed for his neck.

Aiming to kill.

He doesn't need me anymore.

Pain knifed through his side. *Focus.* But Nasir was numbed by a sudden realization: His mother may have made him into the weapon that he was, but it was the Lion who had used him to do his bidding—kill people, venture to Sharr. And now that the Lion was free of the island's shackles, magic nearly in his grasp, he didn't need Nasir anymore.

He swung his legs around another hashashin's shoulders, dragging the man down with a twist of his knees and kicking the dead body in the path of another.

Then he turned to his father.

The sultan began to rise, but Nasir was quicker. It was knowing the Lion controlled him that made it easy. That made him bold. Still, his hands shook. His mind was strangely focused and untethered at once, for all his life he had wondered what it would be like to go against the one who had used and abused him relentlessly.

He faltered at the whisper of a blade. He could repeat the words over and over, and yet such an act—his father drawing a weapon against his own son—still had the power to penetrate. To paralyze.

The same part of him roared its doubt. Years of corruption could not be undone with a single act, within a fraction of a night. But he would be damned if he didn't try.

Nasir ducked beneath the arc of his father's dagger. He seized Ghameq's arm with one hand, reaching for his chest with the other. For the medallion glinting, taunting, *controlling*. His fingers hooked around the thin chain, and Ghameq's breath hitched. Stars flashed in his vision, the force of his father's fist tearing the air from his lungs. He blinked back into focus, gripping the chain and digging his elbow into the crook of his father's arm. But Ghameq had always been the bigger man, the stronger of them, and three of the hashashin were still alive.

They converged at once, and Nasir paused. *One. Two.* He dropped his hold and ducked. Ghameq's dagger drove into a hashashin's heart. Nasir shoved his gauntlet blade into the other hashashin's knee, wasting no time to kill him and rise behind Ghameq and drag the chain over his head.

The whispers were instant, throwing Nasir off balance. They slithered, dark and rough and snakelike. Begging and moaning and full of want. Want. Want.

Drop it, she said in his head, lilting and fierce.

He could not. A shroud of shadow thickened his thoughts, stealing something from him. Replacing him. Overpowering the emptiness.

Blinding pain cut into his back. He was shoved to the floor. The tiles were cold. The medallion fell with an irreversible clink and crack, but nothing happened. Aya was right, and now he would pay with his life. A hand gripped his collar and wrenched his head back.

And everything came to a halt at the sound of a whisper.

Nasir stilled. He had imagined it. They had all imagined it. There was no possible reason the sultan would say—

"Ibni," Ghameq repeated.

Mutt. Scum. Nothing. Everything disappeared at that one whispered invocation: *My son.*

Ibni. He was a child with a splintered shin. *Ibni.* Reverently receiving his first sword. *Ibni.* Visiting Sarasin, as people pondered why the sands had begun to darken.

Then this. On his knees in his room, the stench of blood heavy in his lungs.

"I knew it would be you. The world would bow at my feet, but only you would save me."

Ghameq's voice tremored with the weight of years lost. The room resembled a graveyard, the tiles stained red, corpses staring wide-eyed at the lights suspended from the ornate ceiling.

"Release him."

It was not the same voice that spoke these words. This was curt, harsh as ever. Even the last of the hashashins flinched.

Nasir rose, swaying from the loss of blood, from light-headedness. The hashashin handed him a cloth, which he held against his bleeding arm.

The medallion lay broken between them, cast in the gold of the fire-light and the glow of the moon. The medallion that had claimed his father for years and given a tyrant a throne.

Now he was free. *Free.*

Nasir stepped forward. Near enough to feel the heat radiating from the sultan. He looked exactly as he had a moment ago, gray eyes rimmed dark with exhaustion, displeasure denting twin scores between his brows.

"Ibni," Ghameq murmured again, and Nasir was powerless as his father drew him close.

Baba, he wanted to say, but the word knotted in his throat. He listened, instead, to the beat of his father's heart. The reminder that worse could have been lost.

CHAPTER 32

NIGHT LAVED THE LAST OF THE LIGHT FROM THE sky, relieving the sooq of the relentless heat. Zafira had always thought people annoyed her. The way the Demenhune laughed and smiled despite the ill that surrounded them had always grated on her nerves.

That had nothing to do with the *people*, she knew now, but herself. Her own inner turmoil.

As she meandered the sooq, listening for whatever voice Bait ul-Ahlaam would use to call her, she studied the people as much as the stalls.

A young safi spread fresh yogurt across a round of flatbread for his smitten human customer, and it was clear the way they felt about each other was mutual. Zafira watched as two safin sisters nicked an extra from an olive cart when the merchant turned to grab change. It was behavior she'd never expected from safin, and it made her smile.

She passed a shop that offered narjeelah alongside tobacco marinated in molasses and sold by the weight. There was another with abayas adorned in embroidery that would have taken weeks, low-cut necklines making her skin burn. A moon ago, she would have barely given the colorful gowns a second glance. Now she wondered how she would look wearing one of them. Any of them.

You're still poor.

That was not why she looked at them, and she knew it. She hurried along, pushing past safin and human alike, nearly tripping on the tiny sand qit roaming for scraps near the stalls that smelled of tangy sumac and sizzling onions, manakish and roasting mutton.

At the head of another dark alley, she paused. A song whispered from a dimly lit entrance deep within, and her spirits rose.

"Found you," she whispered back.

The night drew shadows that reminded her too much of the Lion and the heart he had stolen. Of Nasir and his wayward dark. As she neared the doorway, the tune grew louder, a flute both gentle and seductive. Zafira stepped inside, breath held, fingers pressed against her thighs.

She frowned. The place was large, possibly two or three stories high, but bare in a way that shops were not. There were no tables heavy with trinkets, nothing fastened to the walls.

Sweet snow, the walls. Zafira averted her gaze from the depictions painted across the golden surfaces: men and women unclothed and deeply entwined in various positions.

A lazy titter drifted from upstairs, along with a deeper, rhythmic handful of sounds she hadn't heard at first but couldn't ignore now. Her splendidly slow conclusion cemented as footsteps whispered along the stone floor. A man dropped a beaded curtain and sauntered toward her with an indecent smile that would have made Altair blush. Possibly. *Unlikely.*

"Did I interrupt anything?"

Zafira whirled at Kifah's slow drawl. The warrior leaned against the entrance, arms crossed, a single eyebrow raised as she looked between Zafira and the man.

"I can imagine it's tempting, Alderamin being the caliphate of dreams and all, but—bleeding Guljul—try to stay focused."

Someone might as well have flayed Zafira's skin for the way it burned. She turned and halted the man's languid, wandering gaze with a glare. "Stop looking at me."

He froze. The lewd walls echoed with Kifah's laughter, and Zafira eyed her with irritation.

"I heard a flute," she snapped, as if that explained everything.

—◆—

Zafira followed Kifah across the open market and down another alley, where a weathered old man watched. She shivered as they passed him, feeling his gaze on their backs until the walls pressed closer, swallowing the last of the light.

Kifah's spear tapped a beat against her leg, quickening as they ventured deeper and stopped before a curtain, crimson and heavy. Zafira touched a hand to her dagger and followed her inside.

Bait ul-Ahlaam was smaller than Zafira expected. Darker, too. In fact, stepping past the curtain gave her a sense of unease vastly unlike her discomfort in the pleasure house. There, she had felt in control. Here, she was already losing something without knowing the price.

"Magic," Kifah said as the hum of it stoked something inside Zafira, a fire that had begun to die. Dum sihr, for how else could magic exist in a place so dark?

Lanterns dripped from the ceiling, the four walls flickering with their light, wearied beneath the weight of all they contained. There were shelves laden with trinkets and contraptions. Tables tiered upon tables. Straw dolls with round shells for eyes, watching them more intently than eyeballs ever could. Sand that breathed in time to her heartbeat, ebbing and flowing yet contained by an invisible box. Vials that sputtered and grinned, the glass like teeth and the stoppers like mouths. Boxes and furs, fruits and books, lamps and jewels and a number of mechanisms Zafira had no knowledge of.

"Touch nothing. Question the authenticity of nothing, either," Kifah murmured just as a voice came from everywhere.

"Marhaba."

Zafira's hand dropped to her jambiya. Kifah pursed her lips and gave a small shake of her head as a man stepped soundlessly from behind a table, his finely spun robes glittering dark green in the mellow shafts of light. His face was smooth and unbearded, ears round just beneath his jeweled turban. *Strange.* How could a human come into possession of what would have taken years to procure?

His dark eyes fell to where her hand rested, and sparked with interest. "May you find what you seek."

Zafira opened her mouth to lie and say they weren't looking for anything in particular, but the shop catered to those who searched for it, not to the random wanderer. Which led to another thought: If the shop and its keeper knew they were here for *something*, then there was no harm in asking after the vial, was there?

Kifah dug her elbow into Zafira's side, telling her just what she thought.

The shopkeeper vanished behind another mound of oddities, and the lanterns flickered, darkening without their host to illuminate. The shadows whispered, crowding around them.

This was a place the Lion would adore.

Kifah left her side and began looking around, ghostlike in her calm. Zafira ignored the dark hum and did the same, wandering past a display of stained teeth. A shelf full of lamps. *For wish-granting jinn.* There was a shawl that seemed to change position every time she blinked, and a pair of cuffs that winked sinfully at her.

It settled a question in her stomach, leaden and dreary: What were *they* expected to offer in exchange for what they sought?

All the trinkets had one commonality: They were almost colorless, strangely bland, for they were not what she sought. No, what she needed was red, sparkling, housed in a silver vial that coaxed her as a bedouin to an oasis. And Zafira had found it.

Laa, it had found her. It was daama *floating* before her. The fine etchings on the casing caught in the light, geometric points housing a supple crescent moon in its center. She had seen that symbol before—on the silver letter she had found in her satchel so many days ago.

It wasn't the blood of any Sister of Old. It was Anadil's.

Next you'll be calling me safin because I'm pretty, Yasmine drawled in her thoughts.

Was it too improbable a conclusion to assume the blood was the Silver Witch's? She had been distraught at Nasir's suggestion to come here for aid. Angry. She had spoken of the cost as if she had suffered the price.

Zafira startled when the shopkeeper snatched the vial from the air with a smile. His teeth lengthened and sharpened, his nose rounded into a snout.

She blinked and he was human once more. A farce—this was no mortal man, but one who could shift between man and hyena at will. Suddenly, she understood the savage glow in his gaze, and the ancientness of Bait ul-Ahlaam.

He was a kaftar.

"Si'lah blood. Quite the treasure," he observed. "The way of the forbidden often comes at too steep a price."

Kifah rounded a display. Gone were her calm and caution. Anger and aggression rolled off her in waves. "I saw your collection, creature. You glean memories. You thieve people of their pasts in order to sell your wares."

He trailed his gaze up Kifah's bare arm and the tattoos that branded it. "I thieve no one. You wish to make a purchase, you must pay what is due."

Memory gleaning *was* thievery. It meant taking a fragment of someone's past and bottling it for an eager patron to experience. An intriguing trade, if it didn't require the former to lose the memory, too.

"You can't sell memories without magic," Zafira said, confused. Only glean them. And if the bottles along the far wall were for memories, what purpose did the rest of his goods serve?

"As such, magic is on the mend," he said lightly, lifting the tiny bottle with its silver markings.

Zafira stared at it. There was no part of her past that she wished to undo. Nothing she wanted to forget. Every moment of elation had made her who she was, and every moment that broke her down had only paved her path.

The shopkeeper sensed their reluctance, and he closed his hand around the vial. For once, Kifah had nothing to say.

"There won't be a mend if we don't have that vial," Zafira said suddenly.

The kaftar stilled, canting his head like the animal he was. Kifah bored holes into Zafira's skull.

"We met your kind on Sharr," Zafira said. "They were cursed until we helped them. They fought for us. Knowing their death was guaranteed by sunrise, they fought for the Arawiya that was."

Hope fluttered against her chest as the shopkeeper considered her.

"You are the Demenhune Hunter. A girl," he said with some surprise.

A girl. Her heart sank.

"The rumors do you justice."

Her eyes snapped to his, and falling like a fool for the appraisal in his tone, she asked, "Will you sell us the vial for anything other than a memory?"

She realized her mistake when his smile was all teeth.

"Give me the dagger, and the vial is yours. For Arawiya."

No.

Laa.

Her heart and limbs and lungs caught in an iron fist, thought after thought racing through her. One: *It's only a dagger.* Two: *It's not.* Three: *Baba.*

Baba. Baba. Baba.

That was where she faltered and held.

One who sold memories and bargained blood from a Sister of Old would have no qualms stealing emotions. That was what her dagger was, wasn't it? A blade forged of cheap steal, worthless except for what it held: love. Years of it. Barrels of it.

That was what the oddities in the shop were. If they weren't coveted for what they were—the teeth of a dandan, ore from the depths of Alderamin's volcanoes, enchanted artifacts—they were valued for what they contained. Love, anger, hate, confidence.

Memories, emotions, rarities acquired by ill means: This was what Bait ul-Ahlaam dealt in. That was why Seif had been reluctant to come here. Why the Silver Witch had been angry at the mere mention of its name.

"No," Zafira said with finality. She had lived this long without dum sihr, without doing what was forbidden. She had hunted and found and lived.

She was lying to herself.

Kifah made a strangled sort of sound. In it was her accusation: Zafira had chosen herself over Altair. Her old knife over finding the Lion and getting her daama book back.

"It's only a dagger," Kifah hissed, siding with reason. "I can buy you a new one that looks exactly like it."

Zafira clenched her jaw. It wasn't about coin, it wasn't about how her dagger looked. She didn't care that the shopkeeper was steps away from them, clinging to their every word. "Then why do you think the kaftar wants it?"

If Kifah understood, she didn't care. "This is not the time to be sentimental."

Anger reared its head at a level birthed by the Jawarat, for never before had rage twisted words together, ugly and whole.

What do you know of sentiment? it wanted her to say.

But Kifah was her friend, and Zafira didn't have to speak. She read her well enough. Her soft breath tore with her dark gaze.

"Emotion is as potent as memory, isn't it?" she asked the shopkeeper without a shred of feeling. "That's why you want the dagger."

The kaftar had no reason to be guilty.

Kifah smiled cruelly. "You can take the dagger of a peasant, or the spear of a former erudite turned Nine Elite and every emotion that led from one to the other."

The kaftar considered her afresh. One of the lanterns sputtered noisily, angrily.

"In that case," the kaftar mused, tipping the silver vial to and fro, "I will take both."

Zafira swayed. Her hand twitched for an arrow, anger engulfing her desperation, but it was Kifah who spoke first, her fury focused on the vial. "Keep it. May it shatter and defile this place forever."

Curses meant little to those versed in them. The kaftar set the vial back on the shelf, between a wicked knife and a camel-bone dallah, and turned away. With his back to her, anything was possible: her dagger in his spine, Kifah's spear through the back of his neck. Another chance.

Kifah was already near the door.

Zafira's pulse pounded beneath her skin, a drum born of disquiet. "Here."

The leather hilt fit snug in her grip. She felt every fiber against her fingers, she knew every snag and every little bump. The way the leather was loose at the hilt's curve, the blade dull from use but sharp as the cleverest of wits. Baba's gift to her. All that was left of him.

The kaftar only looked.

"You can't have both," Zafira said, keeping the tremor from her voice. "Nor will anyone else want the vial. Not when magic returns."

He took the dagger. She took the vial. The blood of the most powerful beings in Arawiya sat in her palm, and still she had lost.

CHAPTER 33

NASIR TOSSED THE BLOODIED RAG INTO THE BIN
and swept a look across the room. Khara. He had forgotten
about Zafira's sister. A thousand scenarios flitted through his
brain: She would have panicked. She would have unlocked the other door
or thrown open the window and tried to escape at the first clash of weaponry. The men had only just dragged the last of the bodies away, a pair of
guards leading—to Nasir's relief—the tired sultan to his rooms. He hurried to unlock the door and paused against the doorway.

Lana lay on the bed, eyes closed, chest rising too quickly to be asleep.

A smile twitched at the corner of his mouth before he folded it away
with a sigh and locked the door again.

There was no chance of him sleeping. Not now, when his father was
suddenly his father again, a concept he had last seen so long ago that he
didn't know when exactly Ghameq had begun to change. He recalled the
Silver Witch's words on Sharr, that she had never known true love until
she met his father. The medallion had been her wedding gift to him, one

of the last remaining artifacts from her life as warden of the island. She had not known it held a bit of its darkness, that it soon became a channel connecting the Lion to her beloved.

There was a time when he had been kind, when lines would crease near his eyes as he smiled, when he would hold his wife in his arms, pride and love in the timbre of his voice. Laa, the Lion's control was a gradual thing, deepening and worsening as the years progressed.

Nasir folded his keffiyah, wound it into a turban, and eased the door closed behind him. The halls were silent save for the occasional drift of maids and servants who caught sight of him and disappeared just as quickly.

Home sweet home, he thought dryly.

Meaning to search for some sign of the Lion or Altair, he soon found himself in the latter's rooms. They were ghostly without his riotous laughter and boisterous voice, and an ache began somewhere in Nasir's chest. He trailed his hand along the table, the vases full of dates and sweets and candy-coated almonds. Every chair was draped with an ostentatious throw, and his gaze softened at the sight of a dallah on a low table. The faint whiff of Altair's beloved qahwa clung to the air.

Nasir pulled back the curtain and stepped into the bedroom. His ears burned as he remembered the last time he was here.

He had always wondered why Altair's rooms were different from the rest. Why he had been given first choice—the golden wall latticed in the most ornate of patterns; the sprawling platform bed, twice as wide as Nasir's own; the circular skywindow cut into the center of the ceiling, providing an unhindered view of the sky.

He knew now that it wasn't for any reason other than Altair being *alive* to choose them. How did it feel to live on when the moons rose and fell without end? To see people born and age and wither and die while one still retained one's youth?

Sad.

That was how it felt to even think it.

It wouldn't be so foreign a concept for himself, either. Nasir was half si'lah, and though his mortal blood would not allow him to live forever, he would live long enough to be glad of it. Unless he was killed, of course. *Always so lively*, Altair said in his head.

Nasir tugged his already-lowered sleeve over the words inked on his arm. *I once loved.* Those years could be endless, or they could be nothing at all depending on how he lived them, and who he lived them with.

He skimmed the bookshelf, four planks of insanity. Each book brimmed with life—random markers, loose sheaves shoved every which way. Nothing was arranged by size or color or any semblance of order.

What can I say? I like my shelves messy and my lovers well fed.

It was what Altair had to say when Nasir had remarked upon them. Before Sharr, when the oaf had been half-dressed and decidedly not alone.

The reed pen rolled off Altair's desk, and Nasir bent to fetch it, snaring on a bump in the wool rug. He crouched with a frown, tugging his glove free to run his fingers along a palmette the size of his hand in the corner. It was raised.

With care, he peeled off the motif sewn onto the rug.

Large enough to hide a stack of letters.

Nasir paused, glancing from the worn folds of papyrus, earthy and rough-edged, to the doorway.

"I'm becoming a nosy old crone," he said to himself, and leaned against the bed beneath the night sky. Curiosity made him do this, for Altair was loud and shameless—and smart. He left no trail save for the one in his head. Why hadn't these been burned? Perhaps there hadn't been time during the rush of readying for Sharr.

Nasir parted the first fold of papyrus. Then he flicked to the next, and the one after, ears burning hotter and hotter.

They were love letters.

Ours is the most fervent of love . . .

I yearn for you endlessly . . .

My days pass in waiting for you, my nights in dreaming of you . . .

Not all were innocent. Some were scant—*Does your body ache for my touch as mine for yours?*—while others were longer and detailed, the words stirring his blood. He was a prince, an assassin, a monster, but in the end he was still a boy.

And that was when he saw it, tucked between the wanton words and indecent declarations.

The road will be secured two days hence.

Tariffs dropped between Pelusia and Demenhur. Validated by Nawal.

Distribution at Dar al-Fawda. Pelusian provisions.

Trade agreements. Treaties. Discussions. These weren't love letters. These were fragments of Altair's web, proof of his labors to unify the kingdom. Nasir could see him gathering ordinary people, arming them with bravery and courage, driving them with his wit and charm. Rousing hope in a way very few could, commanding men in an army and hearts of the common folk just the same.

While Nasir murdered them. While he, the prince born with the obligation to care for and ensure their safety, killed them.

The letters trembled in his hands. Wrinkled in his grip.

Remain in the shadows and serve the light.

He was no fool with romantic abandon. Death was irreversible, and he could never make amends for the wrongs he had done, but he was trying. He gave himself that much. He was trying to make things right, to be part of Arawiya's change. To stop seeing people by the tendons he should slit and the number of beats it would take to kill.

He would wear the crown of the Prince of Death no longer.

He leaned back on his knees. What was he without the fear people looked to him with? Without the names in his pocket, and the missions that were his purpose? Monsters were *created* for a purpose, a destiny to be fulfilled. Who was he without the tally on his back and the weapons on his person?

Nasir gathered the letters and tucked them away, securing the palmette back in place. He had freed his father, ensuring the dignitaries' safety, but there was more to be done. He set Altair's reed pen back on the desk and stepped away with a whisper.

"Don't die."

CHAPTER 34

LDERAMIN HAD LOST ITS APPEAL AND ALLURE. THE
sooq clamored from afar, the poets as dire as funeralgoers, the
town of Zawia as dull as the wares of Bait ul-Ahlaam. When Zafira
and Kifah finally arrived at the caravanserai, Seif was nowhere to be seen.

The stained-glass window was in fact an entrance, wide enough for
caravans, though there were no camels idling about. Travel had not yet
begun—the Arz's disappearance was too recent, word still spreading.
The archway led to a courtyard, from which one could see the entrances
to every room in the two stories of stone, carved and white. Columns set
in a honeycomb of tiles glistened in the night.

Though camels were scarce, people still traversed within cities, and
Zafira and Kifah pushed past the crowded courtyard to the second flight
of rooms. Kifah stopped her with a fleeting touch to her shoulder.

"At least," she said, gently enough that Zafira clamped her eyes closed,
"our memories are still our own. The moments that made your dagger
special."

Zafira's exhale quivered dangerously.

"How do you do it? How did you know that telling him about the kaftar on Sharr would help?"

"I didn't," Zafira said truthfully.

"Only few can look at a monster and see its humanity," Kifah claimed. But she did not know the half of it: that Zafira had befriended the Lion of the Night. That she had seen Nasir's tallied scars, proof of his kills, and didn't feel disgust. Kifah rapped her knuckles against the wall, restless as always. "And I'm sorry. For forcing your hand."

Zafira looked at her, still numb, but also a little bit warmer. A little more ashamed. "I am, too."

Kifah answered with a half smile and closed the door.

Zafira sank into the low bed, blind to the beauty of the room, to the moonlight probing through her window. The vial was theirs. All that was left was to slit her palm and find Altair. Find the Lion. Retrieve the last heart. Take back the Jawarat that was hers.

Footsteps paused just outside her door, and she stilled when she heard Kifah's door open.

"Did you do it? Will it live?"

Even muffled and separated by a door, Zafira caught Seif's inhale, his irritation at Kifah's gall to question him.

"There is no way to know. Nothing happened when I inserted it," he said. "I've secured a boat to cross the strait, so we'll leave before sunrise. The blood?"

"Acquired." Kifah's voice was soft, and Zafira wished she had been stoic. It would have helped *Zafira* stay stoic. She said something more, followed by a word that sounded dangerously like "Huntress," before Seif moved and her door closed.

Zafira slumped into bed, angry at the swell of loss inside her. She could barely care that one of the five hearts had been restored—they were still missing the fifth, and retrieving it would be no easy feat.

Her loneliness was complete now. Absolute. She removed her boots, then her bow, then her quiver, and then her empty, empty sheath. The Jawarat had kept her afloat, and it, too, was gone.

Skies. Her best friend had died in front of her eyes, her mentor had died without her forgiveness, her mother had died after years of suffering, and she hadn't cried. She hadn't shed a tear for a single one of them, and she was near tears now, because of a daama jambiya.

It's more than that. More, even, than another piece of Baba. Every step away from home hadn't been a footfall but a flaying. A careful removal of the Hunter she once was, the Huntress she had been. She would wear the cloak of the Demenhune Hunter no longer.

Her guise: gone.

The Arz: gone.

Her sense of direction: gone.

Baba's jambiya: gone.

It had been the last of it. The last peg holding the mysterious Hunter upright, for her bow had snapped more than once and her arrows never lasted more than a few days. Baba's jambiya was her constant, the reminder that she was not meant to take the lives of her kills for granted. That she was but a traveler in this world, trying to leave her mark, trying to do what was right.

A sob broke out of her.

She thought of Nasir and couldn't seem to care about the girl in the yellow shawl anymore. Laa, she missed him. His silent contemplation. His scarce words that were always precisely what she needed.

Unraveling—that was what Zafira was doing. She was a ball of thread slowly unspooling, and she was afraid nothing but a gaping emptiness would be left at the center of it. That same clawing *nothingness* that had struck with full force after magic had emptied from her veins.

Her father had died, and she had persevered. Her life had hardened, and she had powered onward, for she had purpose. What was she without the hunts that shaped her mornings and *gave* her that purpose? She had existed to help her people. To keep them alive, to sustain them. Care for them. Who was she without the arrows on her back and the cloak on her shoulders?

Empty, in a way she had never been. Alone, in a way she had never been.

When she had asked Nasir what he wanted, she was really only asking herself.

CHAPTER 35

A T FIRST LIGHT, NASIR WAS IN THE THRONE ROOM, where the Sultan of Arawiya was seated and already dismissing emir after emir, austere and stony as if nothing had changed. Nasir would have convinced himself that the events of last night had been a dream, if the space where the medallion once hung wasn't glaringly empty and if this morning he hadn't seized open his bedside drawer, seen the antique circle—broken, unassuming, and real—and slipped it into his pocket.

Nasir had arrived with a single purpose: start afresh. He opened his mouth, determined to be the first for once, to ask after his father and how he felt, but when they were alone, all that came out was this: "Sultani."

Not "Father." Not "Baba."

Something flickered in Ghameq's gaze. "Ibni."

Nasir expected to be happier, freer. Instead, he felt like a cornered animal, uncertainty caging him, for his father looked exactly as he had yesterday, exactly as he had weeks ago, months ago. And that meant looking into his face and reliving years of pain.

Perhaps worse than abuse was waking up to the fact. The realization, striking and unmooring, that the norm one had lived was not at all normal.

Ghameq's face fell at what he saw. "You are early. Have you eaten?"

Eaten. A laugh broke out of him. His surprise must have been evident on his face, because the sultan's face softened.

"Yes." Nasir swallowed, shaped his next question as if it were a matter of life and death. "Have you?"

His father nodded. "We will dine together from here on out."

I would like that, Nasir thought but couldn't say as the braziers crackled beside the dais. He closed his mouth.

Ghameq smacked his lips, then reached for one of the missives by his side, waving it in the air. "The unrest continues. Tell me. What would you have me do?"

Again, shock gripped his tongue, for it wasn't like Ghameq to humor him in conversation. To ask his son's opinion. To need it—or Nasir himself.

"The taxes you have levied are far too high, and protestors grow bolder," he ventured. *And what's your solution, fool?* He scoured his mind. "Sarasin. They need a caliph. We can easily appease them by appointing someone like Muzaffar."

"Who?"

Nasir blinked at his complete ignorance. "The merchant rising up in Sarasin since I left for Sharr. People like him. He's well connected, and was village head a decade or so ago. Appoint him, and he may turn the caliphate around on his own, with minimal work from the crown."

"Mmm," Ghameq said, dismissing him with a smile, and Nasir found it difficult to feign one of his own. "I was freed by your hand only a short while ago. There is much to undo of the Lion's. Time will allow us the victory we require, Ibni. Sarasin is a pit as it is, and the Lion himself is of greater concern than any tax."

"Sultani," Nasir said in appeasement, lowering his head. It seemed his insight hadn't been required at all. True to form.

"It is why I am your father, isn't it? To guide your hand. Have you any plans on how to find him?"

A bell sounded in Nasir's skull. "We will find him," he said carefully. "By whatever means necessary."

The sultan studied him.

"I should not have to tell you to avoid the use of dum sihr. It has cost our family too much."

Nasir shook his head quickly. Too quickly. This was his father. Trust was meant to be second nature.

"The Sisters forbade such acts. If we do this, what difference is there between us and the creature we seek to defeat?" Ghameq asked.

Blood magic *was* forbidden. The use of it *did* distort the line between them and the Lion. But there were plenty of differences between them and their foe, and the use of dum sihr didn't negate that.

Still, morality was decidedly not a topic Nasir wanted to discuss with his father.

"Even if we planned to, dum sihr requires si'lah blood. Which we do not have," Nasir said.

Ghameq grunted his agreement. The sound echoed relentlessly in the silence.

"Perhaps," Nasir dared again, changing the subject, "we can call off the feast. For now. Until magic is restored and the Lion is no longer a threat. Do you . . . remember sending out the invitations?"

Where did *that* line end and begin? There were questions about events where his father would blink emptily and others from long before that he could recount word for word almost immediately. It left Nasir unable to decipher just how much Ghameq remembered from when he was under the Lion's control over the years, for his memories were clearly unaffected by time.

"Two nights prior," Ghameq said after a thought. "It is too late to stop them, unfortunately. Besides, we have more reason to celebrate now, do we not, Ibni?"

"Yes," he ceded softly, fighting dismay. At least the dignitaries would no longer be walking into a trap.

"What of the Huntress?" Ghameq asked, looking down at the sheaves in his hand. "She has not come."

He knows. A curl of darkness slipped from Nasir's fingers. For whatever reason, trust was impossible to summon. But nor could he lie.

"I've angered her," he admitted.

A half-truth was enough. Three words that held a multitude would suffice. For truth held emotion, and lies held deception. It was how one knew which to believe.

I miss her, was what he wanted to say. He was alone without her, a soul-deep desolation. Drifting in a world where no one really saw him.

Ghameq laughed, proof that not even the man who fathered him could see him, understand him, *know* with merely a glance. Perhaps Nasir had been too young the last time he'd heard that laugh, too smitten, too innocent and unburdened by death, but it sounded different now. Harsher. Sharper. Less happy and more calculating.

But people changed, didn't they?

⊷◆⊶

"You seem troubled, Prince."

Aya dropped the hatch and joined him on the rooftop. She had come from the infirmary, and blood stained her roughspun abaya, the pale brown ashen compared to her normal attire. He watched a falcon sweep behind a date palm and saw the gathering in the distance, where a man clad in black cried of the Arz's disappearance with foreboding.

The hours were waning. He hadn't realized bringing his father up to speed would require so much time, though it was likely because words were slow to find. There was much the sultan already knew, for he had been alert throughout the Lion's control, and so Nasir filled him in on the events of Sharr and everything since, skirting the whereabouts of Zafira and Kifah, and the High Circle traversing Arawiya to restore the hearts.

"Where's Lana?" Nasir asked.

"Still helping at the infirmary. I left to come see you, but she is safer there than here."

Nasir snorted a breath, wondering how dangerous Aya thought the palace was if she left a young girl amid angry strangers who rioted on the streets.

When the riots broke out again today, a score of the Sultan's Guard had run from the palace, and Nasir had frozen, half expecting an order from his father. *Go. End this.*

They had merely exchanged a glance.

If only the people knew rioting did nothing to the sultan. He had barely blinked. He had barely considered Nasir's proposal to appoint that merchant in Sarasin, Muzaffar.

He pressed his eyes closed for a beat. Aya's dubiety was bleeding into him, making him suspect his father's every gesture. Making him wonder if the Lion was still there, mocking Nasir at a level more cruel than ever.

Because that was what the Lion had always done—mocked him out of hatred. Ridiculed him out of loathing. When he branded Nasir with the poker. When he carved out Kulsum's tongue.

When he stole into Zafira's rooms.

Aya drew closer. "Tell me what troubles you."

He let the silence stretch until he couldn't hold it anymore.

"I was the one she saw." He paused. He didn't say her name. Slants of light and shadow bled through the latticed screens, eight-pointed stars painting his skin. When he blinked, he saw her at the door to his room, mouth swollen, hair coming undone. He wondered if she had enjoyed it. Whatever it was. "When the Lion came for the Jawarat."

"She told you this?"

He pursed his lips. "It's obvious, isn't it? She could barely look at me."

And she had always looked at him. Even when she had called him a murderer. Even when he had pressed her against the column on Sharr and captured her mouth in his.

"From what I understand, that should be somewhat flattering, laa?"

Nasir scowled, ready to fling himself off the rooftop. "What are you getting at?"

"Why does it upset you?"

Aya touched a hand to his shoulder, and Nasir stiffened, feeling the thrum of his blade against the inside of his wrist.

"Because," he said after a steadying breath. "She already sees me as a monster."

Now she would see the Lion.

Aya considered him. "She does not see you as such. Nor does she see a boy to love her. You are her prince. It will not be long before your father's reign falls, and you must pick up the shards of Arawiya as sultan."

Her words settled on his shoulders. "I can make her my sultana."

Aya's laugh was like chimes in the gentlest wind. "Quite a heavy sacrifice to ask."

That isn't a sacrifice, he was about to say, but wasn't he the one who had likened the palace to a cage? Laa, a tomb. It would be different with her in it.

"She can command," he countered. She commanded him well enough. "She would live a life of luxury. Want for nothing."

The words rang hollow, even to him.

"Spoken like a true royal," Aya said with a detached smile. Then something caught her eye and she dashed to the left ledge, shawl fluttering. "Aha! They return! Oh, I must change."

Nasir swallowed as she disappeared down the hatch. Three travelers waded through the crowds on the Sultan's Road. Seif held the note Aya had left for them back at her house. Kifah sported the crooked half smile she usually did when she was thinking anything mildly humorous.

And there she was, the light in the darkness. Something bubbled up his chest and throat, squeezing the crevice that held his heart, thrumming faster. Her gaze drifted to the palace, and rose up, and up, and *up*. Crashed into his.

Empty. Her eyes were windows, and in them he saw loss.

CHAPTER 36

ZAFIRA WANTED TO BELIEVE HE HAD BEEN WAITING for her, but delusions were for dreamers. She'd gotten quite friendly with the wide mirror in their room in Alderamin, and equally annoyed with herself for even caring about how she looked, but being back in Sultan's Keep meant she'd see Nasir, and seeing Nasir reminded her of the girl in the yellow shawl.

When he leaped his way down from the palace wall, dropping in a crouch and a stirring of sand, it was delusional to believe he made his way to them without once looking away from her, dressed in luxury only a prince could afford with an onyx-hilted dagger against his thigh and a scimitar sheathed at his hip. Armed, always armed. Inside and out. It was delusional to think he would let himself be seen without his mask, his gray eyes apologetic and rimmed in sleeplessness.

Because when he spoke, he didn't look at her, he didn't direct words at her, and it certainly felt like he spoke *at* her.

Still. Sweet snow below, the ache in her chest. The fervor in her blood.

She couldn't care less that she was here, standing before the Sultan's Palace, a place she had seen through Baba's tales and never expected to witness herself.

The ornate gates swung inward, granting them entrance. Each of the guards swept a bow as Nasir passed. Zafira tried to ignore their scrutiny, at once insignificant and powerful. The path to the palace was set with interlacing stones that swelled and tapered like the scales on a marid's tail, umber glittering gold. Under the watchful gaze of the stone lion fountain in the center, Nasir told them he had broken the sultan's medallion.

"And you presumed it something to boast about?" Seif dismissed with no shortage of scorn. "Merely removing a chain while we were out there neck to neck with death?"

Zafira knew no one else understood Nasir's pride. It wasn't for *what* he'd done, but that he'd done it at all: Taken control. Acted of his own accord.

She opened her mouth, blood burning, but Kifah beat her to it, spear flashing in the early light.

"Enough," Kifah snapped. "Did it work?" she asked Nasir, ever practical.

"I tho—I think—" Nasir stopped.

Seif scoffed. "You think."

Zafira knew no one saw his bare flinch either. The world could be re-made, but abuse could never be undone.

"He suspects we'll use dum sihr to find the Lion, and he was not pleased. He's forbidden it. The man I killed—"

"You'll have to be more specific."

Nasir didn't respond, and Zafira saw the exact moment when his mask fitted back into place. His back steeled, his jaw hardened. The Prince of Death.

"I'm hungry," she said suddenly.

The tension snapped like a bowstring. Kifah snorted. The palace doors groaned open beyond the arched entrances.

"Mortals," Seif muttered, crossing his arms as Aya joined them in a flutter of lilac.

"You need this mortal, safi," Zafira bit out. She felt Nasir watching her, now that she wasn't watching him. "And if I'm to slit my hand and find Altair and the heart, I need to eat."

Oblivious, Aya ushered them inside the palace as confident as if she were its queen. She took one glance at the vial of blood hanging from Zafira's neck and beamed, quickly hiding a warble of her lips. "We must mark this occasion, my loves. Every victory must be celebrated, however small."

Zafira couldn't smile back, not when the sheath at her thigh hung achingly empty. Why was it that victories were forever riddled with loss?

That, and the palace made her feel out of place. The halls were bathed in golden light, heaving with shadows that danced, eager for the Lion. She saw extravagance at her every glance, dripping from the suspended lanterns, gilding the intricate, arching walls. Columns twisting with interlacing florals, pots overflowing with greenery too lush to be real, gossamer curtains fluttering shyly in the dry breeze of the wide windows, and beckoning balconies.

People filed in and out of the great double doors, dignitaries arriving for the ominous feast. Servants polished the ornate floors to a shine, and majlis after majlis was readied by nimble-fingered needlewomen. Chandeliers were brought down and lined with fresh oil wicks, and goats bleated from deeper inside where she presumed the kitchens would be, oblivious to their impending slaughter.

Servants led Zafira away from the others, and like a fool, she glanced at him, to see if he'd turn. Look at her. Acknowledge her.

He continued on, deep in conversation with Kifah. And it was as if, suddenly, they were strangers again. The cloaked Hunter, the aloof Prince of Death.

She didn't think it was possible to stand footsteps away and miss him even more.

Zafira hurried after the servants to her quarters, as large as her and Yasmine's houses combined, spacious enough to host an entire village for a feast. The ornaments alone could feed them for a year. There was a mirror wider than any she'd seen, an assortment of vials in front of it that Zafira deemed useless because she never understood what ointment was meant to accentuate which part of her face and in which order. Another low table held lidded bowls, one with almonds, another with pistachio-studded nougat, and the third with dates.

She stepped farther into the room and knelt to touch the stupendously large platform bed, softer than the fur of the supplest of rabbits. Her mind flashed to the Lion wearing Nasir's face and her head spun, weariness tugging at her eyelids. But she was too guilty to climb beneath the covers knowing he was out there and that she could find him, the Jawarat, the heart, Altair—daama *everything* by losing yet another part of herself.

Sweet snow, she was tired. She lowered her cheek to the sheets, and didn't think she had ever felt something so glorious in her life.

"Huntress."

Zafira turned. The room was dark, unfamiliar.

The Silver Witch greeted her with a twist of her lips. "The first time is always the hardest."

Umm had once said that about something far more mundane than what she was going to do. Ah, right. To Yasmine, when she'd snuck away with a boy once. A pang ripped through her heart.

"We have no choice," Zafira replied.

Anadil canted her head. "You are the girl who triumphed without the forbidden."

Zafira smiled sadly. "Times are desperate."

The Silver Witch studied her. "Very well," she said. "Dum sihr in its base form will allow you to use your affinity. You will be a da'ira again. And while you may easily use your own affinity, you must locate a spellbook should you require another, as dum sihr requires an incantation in the old tongue. Established centers, such as the Great Library, may have some in their collection, though I'm certain the Jawarat contains a few of its own."

"I've lost it," Zafira said softly.

"So find it."

The words were so simple, Zafira wanted to curl into a ball and laugh.

"Have a care," the Silver Witch continued. "Too much magic outside one's affinity, and some part of you will pay the price."

She touched a lock of her unnaturally bone-white hair, and before Zafira could say once was enough and that she would never practice any magic other than her own, Anadil shook her head. As if echoing what the Lion had said about brash promises.

"Okhti?"

Zafira bolted upright. Faint sunlight slanted over her, a breeze stirring the gauzy curtains. *Noon.* A dream. The Silver Witch wasn't here; Zafira had daama slept. *A dreamwalk?*

Lana peered down at her.

"These are my rooms, but now we can share! Can you believe I slept in the prince's chambers last night?" She lowered her voice, brown eyes glittering. "In a little room dedicated for his lady friends."

There were a thousand words she could have said then:

Hello, or

Bait ul-Ahlaam does *have everything*, or

I found the vial at the cost *of everything*, or

How are the repercussions of the riots?

But she said none of them.

"Lady friends," she echoed. Like the girl in the yellow shawl. Like the women whose gazes followed him shamelessly through the palace.

"You know, when they want to—"

"I know what it's for," Zafira snapped. Her neck burned. Other parts of her burned, too. In ways they'd never done before.

Lana grinned. "I missed your grumpiness."

Zafira folded her legs beneath her and reached for the vial shimmering in the light, the geometric patterns reminding her of the Silver Witch's letter from forever ago. *That's it. Focus on what needs to be done.*

"Sweet snow, it's beautiful," Lana exclaimed. "Did it cost a lot?"

"Yes."

Not of coin, she didn't say, but something else. Something no amount of dinars could ever buy. But Aya was right: This *was* a victory. For Lana, too. They had traveled to Alderamin and Bait ul-Ahlaam because of her suggestion. Because of Lana, Zafira might have lost the last she had of Baba, but they could find Altair and the Lion. Track down the heart and the Jawarat. That was what mattered.

Lana moved to a corner of the room where she had been poring over a sheaf of papyrus on a low table with a tray of tools and an array of ointments along the edge.

"There's an entire section of the palace dedicated to medicine," she explained. "I've been transcribing remedies for Ammah Aya." She wrinkled her nose. "I don't think she needs them any more than she hopes I'll commit them to memory."

Only then did Zafira realize what Aya had taught Lana that their mother never had: confidence. A surety that Demenhune women lacked, even those who had fathers or brothers like the Iskandars once had Baba.

"Oh, and Kifah came. She wasn't happy to know you were asleep, but I took care of it. None of us are any use half-dead."

Zafira pursed her lips at the word "us" and the reminder that her sister was no longer a little girl. She hadn't *been* a little girl in a long time, but that was all Zafira saw: Her small figure tucked against Baba's side. Her eyes wide in wonder, her nose in a book.

And yet she had kept their Umm alive. She had kept herself sane when Zafira disappeared into the Arz for hours on end. She might not have wielded a bow, but she had done just as much as Zafira. She had gone *through* as much as Zafira had.

"You didn't have to do that, you know," Zafira said, rolling off the bed. She tossed her one of the coins Kifah had given her.

Her sister gave her a half smile. "No one ever has to, and yet someone always must."

"Lana, the philosopher," Zafira teased, disappearing into the adjoining bath. She poked her head out in the silence. "Lana, the pensive?"

The beautiful. The burdened. The girl who had grown up without Zafira knowing it.

"I saw the sultan," Lana said, turning the coin over in her hands. "When you think of him, Okhti, do you ever want to kill him?"

Zafira hid her surprise behind a blink.

"It wasn't he who killed Ummi," she said carefully. She had told Lana about the sultan being steered like a puppet by the Lion. "You know this."

Lana's eyes were ablaze. "If being controlled was his mistake, then it was his mistake all the same."

Lana, the girl with murder in her lungs.

"Nasir said the sultan doesn't want us using dum sihr," Zafira found herself saying.

Lana's brow furrowed. "Oh? Does this mean you've forgiven him?"

It took Zafira a moment to realize Lana was speaking of Nasir. Was she that obvious? Why did she have to be the one to forgive first? Skies, she felt like an old married woman. She shrugged. "He didn't tell *me* that."

"I see," Lana said, a laugh in her voice. "But you will, won't you? Use dum sihr?"

Zafira nodded as she changed out of her tunic.

Lana flopped on the bed. "You're being rebellious. I like it."

"I've always been rebellious. I hunted in the Arz—"

"For years, yes, I know. You've only repeated that a thousand and one times. But you were never rebellious. You were *secretive*. If the caliph had forbidden you from hunting, you wouldn't have gone."

Zafira considered her words as she threw open the window. A crop of orange trees ranged outside, tender white flowers in bloom reminding her of Yasmine every time she inhaled.

"See? You're changing."

But it wasn't about rebelling against the man who had murdered their mother. It was the act of dum sihr itself, something strictly forbidden for good reason. Lana didn't know about the Jawarat's vision and the force of Zafira's newfound rage. About how it seemed to be draining the good out of her, leaving only the vilest paths to follow.

She *was* changing, but it wasn't for the better, and when Lana flashed her a grin, Zafira couldn't smile back.

———◆———

There were claims that the Lion had been seen in Sarasin, asserting he was climbing the Dancali Mountains, heading for Demenhur with a horde of ifrit at his back. A few had seen clusters of darkness racing for the ether, blanketing whole villages and creating havens for his ifrit kin. Others swore they saw a black lion bounding through crowds, leaving behind bloody entrails.

How the people knew the Lion of the Night was here at all, alive and well, Zafira couldn't tell. She wouldn't be surprised if the rumors could be traced back to the tiny Zaramese captain. Secrets were like mold, Zafira had learned. They found a way to spread no matter how diligently they were contained.

"I don't trust any of it," Zafira said airily as she and Aya waited for the others. Night had steeped across Arawiya long enough for the sky to brighten, and she had spent most of it in her room, hearing a soft knock every so often only for disappointment to flood afresh when she found the hall empty.

Aya's sky-blue abaya was out of place in the war room's dark dressings. Lana was dozing on the majlis with a papyrus in hand, the sheaf detailing some mixture or another that stanched the flow of blood. Apparently, the materials could no longer be found, but Lana swore she had seen them in Umm's cabinet in Demenhur.

Aya studied Zafira. "You know the Lion well for such a young mortal." Something weighted her dreamy tone. *Envy.*

"I didn't have much of a choice," Zafira said dryly.

Aya stared at the vial. "The whispers escalate. They claim he is here to help us."

They had more to worry about than crazed claims, but Zafira could see how they were made logical. With the freeing of the hearts came the Arz's disappearance, and Arawiya was returning to what it once was: Sarasin's darkness was receding, Demenhur's snow melting. The Lion had only to seize opportunity.

She fastened the vial's chain around her neck and opened her mouth, about to ask how dum sihr worked. Aside from knowing it was forbidden and required the slitting of one's palm, she didn't know much else.

"'He will fix our broken world' they say," Aya murmured.

Zafira paused, brow furrowing. She remembered what Aya had said in that moment of hysteria, when she'd protested dum sihr. *What he wants can never be as terrible.*

"The Lion wants vengeance," Zafira said, as if Aya didn't know. "And the knowledge that brings power."

He might still want a home for his ifrit. He might still be driven by the pain of his father's loss, but neither were as prevalent among his desires as his thirst for knowledge and the throne. Laa, that was greed.

Aya *hmm*ed and touched a hand to her tattoo, turmoil on her face, and Zafira realized the Lion she remembered was different from the one Zafira knew. He had to be, if Benyamin had welcomed him, *befriended* him when none of the other safin could look past their pride.

The door opened and Nasir strode inside, Kifah and Seif at his heels. Zafira struggled to meet his eyes, nodding at Kifah and tossing a fleeting glance at Seif instead.

"You're not following me," Zafira told Lana, who had bolted awake.

She started to protest, but slumped back when Zafira lifted a brow. "Fine."

Zafira didn't know if she'd be wholly conscious once she slit her palm and melded the bloods together. She didn't feel particularly inclined to stoop low enough to ask Seif, or even Aya, who was still lost in her strange thoughts.

"I've received word from Demenhur. The heart has been restored to the minaret there. Nothing from the others as yet," Seif said.

No one rejoiced. The marids' hungry eyes flashed in her thoughts, but Zafira shoved them away. No word from the others only meant they were still on their way, she reassured herself. They were prideful creatures. They wouldn't write letters detailing their whereabouts every half day.

Two hearts had been restored, two more were on their way. It was the fifth the zumra needed to focus on. When Zafira said as much, Kifah nodded sharply.

"We're working on it," she said, armed and ready.

"*Will* it work?" Aya asked.

"Did word of the Hunter not reach Alderamin?" Kifah asked with a raised brow. Zafira ducked under the sudden praise. "Not only will it work, but if all goes well, we'll catch the Lion unaware. Now, shall we?"

Zafira tightened her hand around the vial of si'lah blood. Kifah was right, this *would* work. It was the *act* of dum sihr that scared her. The line down her palm from when she had fortuitously slit it on Sharr was still pink, the skin barely knotted together, reminding her of the Jawarat's vision. How much more of herself would she lose before this was through?

A chorus rose in her veins when she gripped the knife Aya handed her, a barely contained excitement born from her bond with the Jawarat. But her hand shook with the weight of ten eyes boring into her, judging her. The tip of the knife meandered across her palm. Skies, couldn't they leave? She opened her mouth, heat tight across her skin.

Then her insides screeched to a halt when a hand closed around the knife.

Nasir's shadow draped over her, reassuring. He slid his palm beneath hers and brought the blade to her skin. Zafira forgot to breathe. Her heart forgot to beat.

She relaxed her hand, as every part of her longed to lift her gaze up to the gray abyss of his. To remember what it felt like to be assessed by him. Watched. Revered. *Understood.*

"Forgive me," he said softly, and drew the knife across her palm with a flex of his wrist. She hissed at the sudden pain. Red swelled along the blade's path.

She heard voices in the hall, but they were distant and muffled, dream-like. Perhaps she *was* dreaming and not tearing at the seams. Seif came forward and carefully measured out three drops of si'lah blood into her palm, murmuring something she couldn't catch, before he closed the vial and dropped it back against her chest.

The effect was instant.

Zafira swayed. A strange and sweeping cold rushed through her, a hundred things hurtling too fast and heavy to comprehend. Everything suddenly burned shinier, bolder, *brighter.* As if she had drunk something that had fermented too long. She was aware of every little piece of herself— the blood racing beneath her skin, pulsing at her fingers, throbbing at her neck, at her temple.

Power.

From somewhere far, far away, the Jawarat hummed in approval. She felt the cool press of it deep inside her. She felt full and free. *She felt like herself.* The wind from the open window tousled her hair, hurtling freely as a bird. If she closed her eyes, the looming trees of the Arz crowded around her, whispering limbs greeting her. She missed the whiz of her heart, pulling her in a direction she couldn't see. She missed magic.

"Huntress?"

Zafira opened her eyes to startling clarity. Kifah and the others watched her warily. In her mind's eye, she saw Altair's grin. She saw the bloody mass of the final si'lah heart, beating faintly.

She smiled. "Follow me."

CHAPTER 37

NASIR HAD DEVISED A THOUSAND WAYS TO EXPRESS his apology, and instead he'd held her hand in his and cut her daama open. Sultan's teeth, he was pathetic.

Don't steal my curses, princeling.

I'm the prince, Altair. I'll do as I like.

Despite his preference for working alone, Nasir wasn't fond of their plan. Particularly the portion where Zafira would be on her own as she searched for the heart while he searched for Altair and forbidden magic blasted through her veins. They didn't know if the Lion would be there, but there was every likelihood he would be, since Zafira had confirmed both the heart and Altair were in one place.

She had only addressed his protests icily. "Do you truly believe you're a better match for the Lion than I am?"

In one fell swoop, he had successfully ruined the fragile peace he'd nurtured between them only heartbeats ago. One day, he would learn not to voice concerns about her safety when she was adamant about getting herself killed.

"No, I . . . Just remain on guard." He bit his tongue the moment the words left his mouth. Perhaps it was time to begin life as a mime.

"Yes, your highness," Zafira had seethed as they left the palace.

Now, as dawn bled shades of blue across the sky and the remainder of the zumra traversed the streets, Nasir dropped to a flat, open rooftop and made the harrowing leap from the palace to the surrounding wall, a contingent of hashashins on his tail. If he could call anything his favorite, it was this: hurtling across air, with death mocking, taunting, reaching from all sides.

Sand stirred with the early risers, plumes of brown and gold painting the horizon. It clung to Nasir's gloves and gritted his grip. Rooftop hatches swung wide as guards took over shifts, silver cloaks shimmering in the soft light.

He tracked Zafira and the others, once more awed by the way she moved as the Huntress. Light on her feet, fluid as the sands, alert as a gazelle. She came alive with magic. Nasir knew how much she loved it, how much she had *risked* for it, yet it was something else entirely to see how it transformed her. Strange, too, how the thing he hated was what she adored.

A sigh heaved out of him.

He'd thought her return from Alderamin would fill the emptiness her time away had wrought, but it was somehow worse, now, with her in reach. He felt everything more acutely—the way her gaze skimmed over him, bereft of something more. The way she deliberately chose to stand closer to Kifah, as if unsure he wanted her near. He wanted to speak to her, truly speak to her. Apologize. Force the words in his head into one straight line, unravel the knot in his tongue.

"At long last!" a man cried. "Our troubles have come to an end!"

Nasir lifted his eyebrows, peering over the side of the scalloped edging to the square.

"From deep suffering comes great triumph. The skies of Sarasin veer blue. The snows of Demenhur melt like sugar," the man called, clad in black robes, and Nasir stared in disbelief as one uninterested listener became two enamored. A crowd filled the jumu'a, and the man stepped on a crate. "The curse the Sisters left upon us nears its end!"

Merchants set their carts down, and people gathered with baskets against their hips and basins by their feet. Did they not see the riots happening across these very streets? Did they not hear the winds whispering of the Lion?

I hope you die of thirst, Nasir thought, darting to the other end of the rooftop. The madman carried on with his drivel, echoing a nearby falcon. To his right stretched the Sultan's Road. Below to his left, one row of cramped houses away from the gathering crowds, the zumra followed Zafira's lead. Kifah's spear glinted in the gloom. Seif and Aya flanked her, and Nasir wondered if they were unprepared—the five of them and a handful of hashashins against whatever stood between them and Altair.

Namely, the Lion.

"We can't very well march against him," Kifah had said.

"Nor are we going to tell the sultan," Seif had commanded, leaving only this contingent of hashashins Nasir could order without his father's knowledge.

As much as he wished he could tell his father, he saw no need. They *couldn't* march against the Lion. Stealth was far more imperative, for not only were they trying to free Altair, but they needed to find the heart, too. The fifth si'lah heart. And if they had thought themselves capable of fighting the Lion on Sharr, they were still five strong now. Even if no one could replace Altair. *Or Benyamin.*

"How much farther?" he heard Kifah ask.

"If I knew, I'd chart a map for you," Zafira replied.

Nasir smiled and signaled to the hashashins, the familiarity of his missions sinking into his limbs, only this time, he wasn't following orders. He wasn't following Zafira because he had to but because he *wanted* to, and that fed a different sort of power into his veins.

For Altair. He would brave the darkest of dens and the vilest of beasts if it meant hearing the fool's laugh once more.

"Alia," he called to one of the hashashins and signaled to the left. "Split across. The rest with me."

Half the contingent followed Alia's leap across the alley, dark robes fluttering as they hefted themselves up and down the rooftops rising in various heights. The others trailed Nasir.

They pressed deeper into the city, leaving behind the bustle of the Sultan's Road and the shine of the Sultan's Guard. When Zafira paused, Nasir did the same, following her gaze to the end of the alley, which opened to a street, where a house sat behind a stretch of sand among a line of others. It was simply built, tan stone mostly smooth, dresses hung out to dry. He knew of the woman who owned it, or rather, the safi. She employed a number of tailors in the city.

A murmur began in Nasir's blood, a hum of darkness similar to whenever he neared magic. Not any magic, but dum sihr. Stronger than what Zafira had used moments ago. Movement caught his eye, and the hashashins froze with him.

Men were stationed on the surrounding rooftops, some idling behind screened terraces, others alert with swords against their shoulders.

A calm settled in his bones, and he knew. He would find no clothier safi inside that house.

If Altair were beside him now, he'd find a way to make light of this moment. He'd look back at Nasir and stretch a grin. *How much do you want to bet those are not men, but ifrit?*

I don't gamble, Nasir would say, knowing full well Altair didn't, either.

Oh no. Leave it to you to be the most moral man in Arawiya, brother dearest.

Nasir clenched his jaw. "Spread across."

He leaped to a minaret and rounded it to the adjacent wall, matching

Zafira's stride until they reached the end of the alley, where a guard was stationed atop the last building. The hashashins halted, slashes of shadow awaiting a command as Nasir crouched at the rooftop's edge.

The guard strode from one end to the other, sandals on his feet, dark hair wavy beneath his turban, a mustache thick above his lip. Human in every way, except for the warning in Nasir's gut.

Nasir dropped, toppling the guard to the dusty rug unfurled across the rooftop. He could tell by the feel of the guard beneath him even before he dragged his blade across his victim's neck and black blood oozed free like tar in the sun.

Ifrit.

CHAPTER 38

ZAFIRA HADN'T BEEN PREPARED TO HEAR THE FINAL, strangled breaths of the guards. *Ifrit*, Nasir had said as if in reassurance as he and his hashashins killed them. She closed her eyes as another thud echoed, another fallen soul.

"Khara," Kifah croaked, and Zafira's eyes flew open in time to see Nasir leap from the building's edge, hurtling through the open air of the street. The tips of his boots touched down on a suspended rope, propelling him to the rooftop on the other end. A blade shot out from his gauntlet while he was in midair, and the guard fell before Nasir landed.

Half of his hashashins followed his lead, taking positions where the Lion's guards previously stood.

The Lion's guards. The Lion's hideout.

She was here.

Here.

She closed her fist against the sting in her palm, the reminder of what she had done. Her skin still tingled from where he had held her, her heart still snagged in that moment. Dum sihr dizzied her, raced feverishly through her veins, tugging her forward. Toward this castle of a house sprawling along the crowded street across from them.

It was wide and unsuspecting, windows shaped like eight-pointed stars rimmed in darker clay. The flat roof was furnished with a screen and a silken rug draped to dry, accenting it like a towel over a man's bare shoulder.

Like your prince's? Yasmine asked in her head. There was an edge to her friend's voice, cut from the death of her brother.

Zafira bit her lip, forcing her focus. Somewhere inside that house was Altair, the Jawarat, and the fifth heart, and she intended to find them, the Lion be damned.

Nasir had made his way to the rooftop of the house and watched her now. Waited for her. She ignored the flip of her stomach at his unreadable gaze. How was it that he was there, *right there*, and they felt leagues apart?

Kifah tucked into the shadows between two narrow houses to Zafira's right. To her left, Aya pressed deeper into her cover, the breeze toying with the soft pink layers of her abaya, Seif at her side. If not for the staff in her hand, Aya would have looked as if she were out for a stroll down the street with a friend. Her words still nagged at Zafira's conscience, troubling her.

Zafira's blood raced beneath her skin like a rushing stream as she darted across the street, toward the ledge surrounding the house. *Grab, push, jump.* Then she would be over, one step closer to the house, one step closer to the Lion, only a window separating her from a forage for the fifth heart. She wasn't afraid of him, she reminded herself. Not when she knew he wouldn't harm her and risk losing the Jawarat.

She ducked her head, bow and arrows slung behind her, palms slick with anticipation.

Grab, push, jump. That was the plan.

Until a latch lifted.

"Zafira," Kifah hissed. "Hide."

She froze. Her heart was encased in a tomb of ice, but she didn't move.

"No. He already knows I'm here." Zafira lifted her chin as the door swung open. The fringe of her shawl fluttered in the breeze, helplessly tugging her to safety. It took everything in her power not to flick her gaze to Nasir on the rooftop. She had lost Baba's dagger for this mission, for Altair and the heart.

They wouldn't fail.

The Lion stepped through the archway. He was fitted in mauve and midnight, the bronze of his tattoo catching a ray of the early sun.

"I wondered when you would come to see me."

Even now, knowing who he was and what he had done, the velvety darkness of his voice struck her, removing her worries and setting her at ease.

"I've come for what's mine," she replied.

The Lion lifted his brows, knowing she spoke of the Jawarat. "And why do you believe it is yours? Because it speaks to you, understands you in a way your friends cannot?" His lips curled wickedly as he regarded her, the end of his turban rippling. "Do I not understand you as well? Am I yours, azizi?"

Yes, she thought. He *was* hers. Her companion, her succor, her prey.

He was hers to end. Hers to kill.

She knew by the flash of his gaze, amber and beautiful, that he saw the murder in hers. The temperature careened and sudden clouds raced to hide the sun. She steeled her spine against a quiver of fear. Did the Jawarat revel in his theatrics? Was this what it had wanted from her?

A dark head poked over the ledge of a nearby window. Another door opened a smidge. Curtains parted. Nosy people drawn like bees to honey as a swarm of black crowded around the Lion, filling the expanse of sand with ifrit and shadows.

"Tell your friends there's no need to hide," he called. "We are all well acquainted, are we not?"

With a lash of his hand, the wind rose, baying like dogs, bringing a chaos of sand and debris and the sounds of the city. Silver threads glinted from the Lion's thobe as he addressed the empty road.

"Don't be shy. Come, fight my kin. Further your deception of triumph."

Zafira drew her bow and nocked an arrow as darkness flooded like fabric unspooled and swallowed her whole.

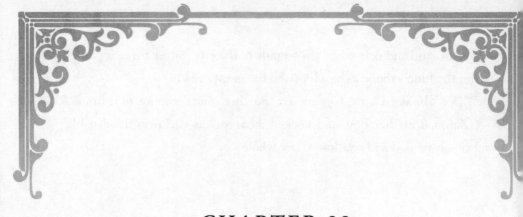

CHAPTER 39

THE DARKNESS STIRRED THE SHADOWS IN HIS BLOOD. The Lion's voice echoed through it, low and seductive, and Nasir could only think of Zafira's laugh that night. *Focus.* He had two beats to decide: Go to her aid or adhere to the plan?

Disgrace her was the first option, really.

He secured his gauntlet blades and crept to the side of the rooftop. Sand slid beneath his hands as he flipped over the side and gripped the edge on his way down to the second story. He paused at the sound of Zafira's voice, sharp and unrelenting.

Laa. *No distractions.* He dropped onto the balcony and stepped to the door. Locked from the inside. He looked to the inconveniently small windows on either side of the balcony with a sigh. Balancing himself atop the iron railing, he stretched to work the latch on one of the windows until it fell open with a satisfying *clink*.

He threw a glance to the nearest rooftop, where a hashashin waited just out of sight, tensed and ready. A flash of orange reflected off her dark robes, followed by the crackle of flames.

Ifrit had come, staves ready for battle. No sooner had he made the realization than the whiz of an arrow ripped through the din. The snap of a spear. Every vessel in his body begged to go to the zumra, aid them. Oh, how he had changed.

With a slow breath, Nasir leaped into the house.

The curtains rippled at the sight of him, stilling when he slipped the window closed. He was in an antechamber, neat and unlit. Dresses were piled atop a low table to the side, where they would remain untouched by the safi who had overseen their production. She was dead, Nasir knew.

He peered past the arched doorway and into a larger room, lit with faceted light from the narrow stretches of cutwork framing the large window against the back wall. And it was daama open. *That would have been an easier entrance.* A staircase wound down from the far end, but just before he could make his way toward it, movement halted him in his tracks.

A platformed majlis stretched against the wall beside the window, obscured at first by the curtains fluttering from a sudden gust of wind. It was occupied by a man, reclined and at ease, unchained and free to move about. His dark hair gleamed gold without his turban, his pointed ears proud. He looked different this way. Younger. Vulnerable. And not a single part of him appeared to belong to one who was imprisoned.

Laa, he was reading a daama book.

Nasir took a hesitant step toward him. "Altair?"

His half brother looked up. Surprise flickered across his face. Then his eyes narrowed with frantic urgency, there and gone before Nasir could comprehend it.

"Nasir," he said. "Took you long enough." He dropped his blue eyes to the sword in Nasir's hand with a feeble smile. "Always so eager to kill me."

"Now is not the time," Nasir said around the rock swelling in his throat. Some weak part of him wanted to embrace the oaf.

"Oh, I see. I missed you, too," Altair said, an ireful hollow in his voice as he rose. "You know, after you left me on Sharr, I didn't think I'd ever see you again."

Nasir refused to wallow in guilt, not when the Lion or his ifrit could return at any moment. He glanced to the stairs. "I'm here now. Yalla. We need to leave."

Altair didn't move. "Do you remember when you walked into my rooms and I wasn't alone?"

Nasir's ears heated.

"They weren't just any women. One was the daughter of a Zaramese merchant. The other a Pelusian wazir."

"Good to know you've acquired a specific taste," Nasir said as a sound cracked across the lower floor. He gripped the winding rail of the stairwell and gestured for Altair to follow, but the fool moved slower than a dying man crawling.

"When you have a reputation," Altair said calmly, as if they were drinking qahwa on a majlis, "it's easy to go unquestioned. Every Arawiyan I took to my room was an envoy."

Nasir remembered the letters he had found sewn into the rug. How much Altair had done for the kingdom that had done nothing for him. "So you didn't—"

"I'm many things, princeling, but a bore like you?"

Nasir heard the grin in his half brother's voice, and, rimaal, he had missed it. "Right. Is there a reason this can't wait until we're back at the palace?"

Altair continued as if Nasir hadn't spoken. "The Arz was destined to fall at some point, and I wasn't going to stand by as it happened. I secured trade routes, forged alliances. As our mother struggled to hold the reins of our crumbling kingdom, I did my part in secret. She saw me as a failure— the culmination of her failures. I wasn't going to be one, too."

There it was again, the strange hollow that didn't belong to Altair. He was trailing behind Nasir leisurely, despite the battle raging outside, and suspicion threaded Nasir's veins. He had expected chains. Captivity and suffering. Ifrit keeping watch. Not Altair idling unattended with a book. Almost *content*. Almost annoyed to have been disturbed.

"To what end, Nasir? What was the point of all I'd done. Hmm?"

The anger in his tone gave Nasir pause, but he said nothing.

He left the stairs and crept to the door he had seen directly beneath the upper-story balcony. It had been almost too easy, this rescue, this escape. Though there were sounds of life inside the house, he hadn't come across a single person, or otherwise, besides Altair. He eased the door open and stepped outside to a flood of shadow and turmoil, stopping in his tracks when he remembered something.

The heart.

Zafira couldn't slip into the house to search for it now, not with the Lion's attention undoubtedly attuned to her, and as much as he wanted to hurry to her aid, he couldn't waste this chance.

"Where are you going?" Altair asked when Nasir turned back.

"To look for the heart, and—"

"The Jawarat?" Altair scoffed.

Nasir pressed his lips thin, holding still when the general leaned close.

"Only a fool would leave it lying about. Only a fool would know its worth and value and let another steal it away."

The words were a double-edged sword, a shame Nasir was no stranger to. He could only imagine Altair's reaction had he known *how* they'd lost the Jawarat.

"Both of them are with him," Altair said, annoyed.

So why, then, had *he* been left to his own devices?

"How is our mother, by the way? Dead?"

Nasir's wrists pulsed against his gauntlet blades, sand sinking beneath his footfalls along the side of the house. This wasn't the Altair he knew.

This wasn't the Altair he had come to save. Nasir himself had been angry at their mother, disgusted even, but not this. Never so callous.

"Dying," Nasir bit out. "Is that what you wanted to hear? The Lion attacked her with his black dagger, robbing her of magic so that she has no chance of healing herself. And there's little chance of anyone else healing her, either."

Something sparked in Altair's gaze. Not remorse, but revelation.

As if that had given him a daama idea.

Nasir turned away with a growl. Altair had always been apt at needling Nasir, but, rimaal, this was an extent he never thought possible. Swords clashed, arrows flew.

Perhaps, if he had been his old self, if he had not allowed emotion to fester in his soul, Nasir would have been more focused as he and Altair made their way to the front of the house. He would have been quicker.

He wouldn't have let an arrow strike his heart.

CHAPTER 40

ZAFIRA'S HEART STOPPED WHEN NASIR DOUBLED over. She turned in the direction of the ifrit that had fired at him, but Kifah got there first, spear dripping black. *Get up*, she pleaded to Nasir's fallen form. Skies, she was angry at him—she didn't want him *daama* dead.

Across the gauzy black, he straightened and wrenched the arrow free, and with relief, she recalled the layer of mail attached to the underside of his robes.

Then he turned to something behind him. Some*one*.

There, like the golden figurehead of a dark ship, was Altair. The sight of him threw her back to Sharr, Benyamin by her side and Altair's raillery keeping them afloat. Her heart lurched to her throat. At some point, she had come to care profoundly for the general who had killed Deen by accident.

"Bleeding Guljul," Kifah rasped.

Nasir looked at Altair with barely contained irritation. *Just like old times.* "Find a weapon and help us."

Zafira paused. Perhaps a little more aggressive than old times.

"Focus," Seif spat, ripping his scythe across an ifrit that had come dangerously close.

Zafira nocked another arrow and backed away, scanning her surroundings. The din was reminiscent of a stage—scores of discreet witnesses to the Lion centered upon an expanse, ifrit stationed around him. She had almost forgotten what it was like to be locked in battle with the beings of smokeless fire.

There was little chance of slipping into the house for the heart and the Jawarat now, but she was the compass in the storm—she felt her quarry draw near when the Lion did. The frenzied pull of dum sihr subsided in her veins, and she knew: neither the heart nor the book would be inside the house.

Laa, they were with the Lion himself.

When the ifrit converged, Zafira took down one after another, making her way toward him. The heat of their staves stung her nostrils, shadows winding around her arms and the bare skin of her neck. She caught sight of Aya's pink abaya as she and Seif cornered the Lion, her pale staff coming up between a stave and catching the Lion off guard. *Yes.* Now all Zafira needed was to get in a single shot. Throw the Lion off-kilter to allow Aya time to thieve the heart and Jawarat from him.

"Fair Aya," she heard the Lion say. "I had hoped to see you."

Zafira stiffened but could barely see, despite her height. A ladder was propped against a narrow building rising like the chimneys in Demenhur. She threw off an ifrit and hurried up the rungs. What was Aya that the rest of them weren't? Safin? Whatever she said made the Lion produce a laugh, demeaning and bereft of mirth.

"You've come to kill me."

The fighting came to a jarring halt. The ifrit seemed to coalesce. Zafira held her aim, breathing down her arrow's shaft as silence spread.

A healer. She remembered Lana's eerie recollection of the boy who lay supine after the attacks in Demenhur, a boy she had brought back to life—Aya was one of the best, even without magic.

"I merely wish to understand," Aya said.

Zafira froze. There was nothing to understand. The Lion had strayed beyond reason. He had murdered and maimed and destroyed in pursuit of his madness.

"Do you think your husband thought of you when he leaped to save his zumra? Mortals whose lives will end just like that?" He snapped his fingers, and another ring of his dark soldiers formed, shadowy and volatile. This was a game to him. They were daama *mice*.

For all her dreaminess, Aya was strong. Resilient. She had lost her son and found a way to persevere. She had lost her husband and remained a member of this mission.

Lies. She was floundering, and Zafira knew it. She was troubled, and they should not have allowed her to come.

"How much longer will the old ways sustain us?" The Lion raised his voice, knowing full well he had an audience as malleable as they were curious. "How quickly the Sisters of Old abandoned their people, leaving behind despair and desolation." He looked at Aya again, his voice almost tender as he said, "We are the broken ones. Victims of a world that continues to take, and take, and take. To what end, I ask you?"

Skies, the Lion was mad. *He* had been a part of the problem. It was because of him that Baba was dead. That Benyamin was gone. He had wronged others just as he had been wronged. The cruel cycle had no end.

And yet Aya brought her staff down against the ground. Zafira felt its thud in her soul.

"The time has come to shape the world into one of our own making," the Lion said softly.

Zafira recognized Aya's expression. It was the look of a person who finally woke up.

The Lion smiled at Aya as defeat crushed her shoulders. There was no cunning in it this time, only kindness. Not a single ifrit attacked her, and when the Lion extended his hand, Zafira saw her go still. Contemplative.

Barely three steps away.

"Aya, no!" Seif shouted.

Nasir was locked in battle. Altair was nowhere to be seen. Zafira sighted her aim. They were here for the heart and the Jawarat. Not—not *this*.

Two steps.

Zafira's blood ran cold. The Lion's mouth shaped more lies that Aya devoured like the starved.

One.

Aya smiled that dreamy smile and took the Lion's hand in hers.

CHAPTER 41

CHAOS SPILLED LIKE A SHATTERED WATER POT WHEN Aya took the Lion's hand in hers. Betraying them. Dreamy, beautiful Aya. Nasir saw it all, even from the distance the battle had carried him to. Disbelief and turmoil made it hard to breathe.

He threw up his scimitar, clashing with a fiery stave as it came arcing for his neck. He needed to get to Aya. Stop her. Immobilize the Lion and take back the heart. The hashashins unleashed arrows from their elevated positions, and bloodcurdling shrieks filled the vicinity. He combed the scene for Zafira, only to find her breathing down the shaft of an arrow of her own, leveled at the Lion.

Shoot, he thought.

She fired. The arrow soared, hope surging in him when it struck the Lion square in the chest. *At last.* A stroke of luck. He wasted no time. With a racing in his pulse that he was still growing accustomed to, Nasir fought his way forward. He heard Seif shouting, reasoning with her, but he was too far to signal. Nasir felled another ifrit and stumbled to his feet, wiping a smear of blood from his mouth as he ran.

The air stilled, alerting him to a presence, and he whirled to face Altair, whose mouth was set in contemplation as if he had a decision to make. Perhaps he did, for there was a stave gripped tight in his fingers.

And aimed

at Nasir.

The breath escaped his lungs, and the sword fell from his hand. His mind blanked. He couldn't move as Altair let the stave fly.

It zipped past Nasir's shoulder, lodging in the throat of the ifrit behind him.

Nasir's breath rasped out of him, relief too far gone to summon. Shadows spilled from his palms, surrounding them. *Not now.* Altair looked at him strangely, eyeing Nasir's fallen sword before he disappeared into the dark without a word.

"Wait—" Nasir began, but stopped short when a fine white arrow cut into an ifrit creeping close. *Zafira.* He couldn't see past the thick veil of shadows. He couldn't hear beyond the clashing swords.

"Altair?"

Nothing.

"Altair!" he shouted.

The snap of fingers came from a distance, and the ifrit vanished. Nasir stumbled, coming face to face with Kifah and her spear. Seif halted with his twin scythes in midair. The ground was littered with fallen ifrit and hashashins alike, a graveyard stretching between Nasir and the Lion.

The Lion.

Zafira's arrow was in his hand, dripping black blood while he stood unaffected, almost unharmed.

To his right stood Aya. To his left was Altair.

Altair. Unchained. Content. Barely concerned. Nasir should have known the moment he saw his brother lounging with a book. Still, he felt something crushing inside him.

To what end?

The clouds finally parted for the sun, steeping the street and buildings in gold. Perhaps they were destined to be opposites: Nasir the dark to Altair's light. The night to his day. The monster to his greatness. And now, once more, they were on opposing ends. Nasir with the forces of good, and Altair with the growing forces of evil.

The Lion *tsked.* "Such violence, Nasir. What will the people think when they see how little their crown prince has changed?"

"Altair!" Nasir roared, but the general turned with the Lion, and Nasir cursed the pain flooding him.

"Aya? Aya, this isn't right," Kifah yelled, frantic. "Altair, stop her!"

But her voice cracked with the same truth the rest of them had already gleaned—they would receive no help from Altair. Nasir's fingers shook as he felt along his belt, empty of knives. The blades at his gauntlets were of no use at this distance. There was only one way.

Nasir looked to the rooftop and shouted.

CHAPTER 42

*S*HOOT.

Nasir's command encased Zafira in a tomb of ice. As if the Lion pulling her arrow out of his chest with a frown hadn't been unsettling enough.

This was Aya. Benyamin's wife. Her ally and Arawiya's greatest healer. It didn't matter that she walked shoulder to shoulder with the Lion, her pale pink silk like petals of a flower withering in darkness.

I can't.

She couldn't shoot, despite knowing the Lion needed Aya for something important if he was stooping to the level of safin. Despite knowing she could bring ruin to them all.

"Zafira, shoot!" Nasir shouted again, a note of desperation in his voice.

Baba, help me. She stared down the shaft of the arrow, felt its pulse at her cheek, but she couldn't. Fear crammed in her throat when someone else's arrow struck bare paces from Aya's dress. Zafira tried to find that dark voice in her blood. The newfound whisper that reveled in killing and destruction. But it lived within the Jawarat, far from her reach and easily overpowered by something else. The harsha in Aya's hand. The word "roohi" from her lips. The pearls in her hair. The way she looked at Lana.

Zafira lowered her bow.

With a curse, Nasir ran. Gold flashed in the gloom as Kifah bounded after him. She pulled her arm back, hesitation freezing her form.

But she did it. She launched her spear, her aim true.

It landed on the stone with a whistle and a thump as the Lion disappeared, taking Aya and Altair with him.

CHAPTER 43

THE PRICE OF DUM SIHR IS ALWAYS GREAT. ZAFIRA had known this, and yet she'd done it anyway. If only Benyamin were here now, maybe he would help them make sense of what had happened. He would tell them why the Lion had barely flinched though her arrow's aim had been true. Why his wife had chosen the Lion over them. Why Altair, the brother of his heart, had stonily turned away.

There was only so much betrayal a soul could handle.

They'd fled the people's rising murmurs about the Lion and the crown prince who had tried to kill him, and finally made it back to the palace. Zafira looked among them, their ever-shrinking zumra—herself, Nasir, Seif, and Kifah. Numb, and broken.

"Why?" Kifah asked hoarsely, spear whipping her leg and adding to the echo of their footsteps down the palace halls.

Zafira returned again and again to the defining moment when she realized Aya would not use her staff against the Lion. The moment she knew Benyamin's beloved was no longer one of them. She couldn't decipher which hurt more: that, or when Kifah had begged for Altair's help and he hadn't batted an eye.

"Deception was always the Lion's gift," Seif said, pain softening his lofty tone. "Aya has been known throughout the years for two aspects: her unnatural beauty and her skills as a healer. It is obvious which of the two the Lion claimed her for, but I cannot perceive why." He looked at Zafira's bow, seeing that moment when Zafira could have—*should have*—fired it. "Aya was my companion and my charge, or I would never have come here. I would never have left my calipha's side."

"She's still alive," Zafira reminded him.

What did it mean to be evil? The Lion's message could have resonated with anyone, especially someone as troubled as Aya.

Seif cut his gaze to her. "She is dead to me."

"Until she's truly dead, none of us can rest," Kifah said. The words weren't cruel, only fact.

Dum sihr. It was easy—slit her palm and meld it with the blood of the most powerful beings in Arawiya. Her compass would rise back to life, and she could find them again: the Lion, Aya, Altair. She bit back against the temptation. After what had happened, she knew that blood magic was not the answer.

"And here we thought we'd be smart stowing the hearts away. He clearly doesn't need them. He didn't even *look* for them," Kifah said with a sad scoff. A group of white-thobed emirs stared as they passed. "But why Aya? Maybe he's injured and needs her to heal him?"

Zafira shook her head. "I shot him. Every one of us saw the outcome of it."

"It should not have been possible," Seif agreed. "But it serves as further proof that with the Jawarat, *anything* is possible."

Anything, indeed. Even splitting men in half. Zafira wondered if it was happy now. If she would ever be able to fill the gaping hole it had reopened by leaving her.

Seif continued. "Altair is no longer——"

"He *left* us." Nasir, who hadn't been fully present since the Lion disappeared, finally broke his silence.

She felt his pain as if it were her own.

Her limbs wanted to propel her toward him, to comfort him, but her heart held her in place.

"Maybe he had reason to," Kifah offered helplessly. "I refuse——I refuse to believe he left without a reason."

But her usual ferocity had been dimmed by what they'd seen. Nasir clenched his jaw and dropped his hood, running a hand through the wayward strands of his hair, tightening his fingers and tugging, inflicting pain upon himself. "He was *lounging* in that house."

Kifah shook her head, adamant but quiet.

Zafira's cup of sorrow had run empty, a strange numbness taking its place, denial lacing her edges. The haze of shadow had made it hard to see, but she could have sworn there were shackles around Altair's wrists.

An angry shout drew their attention as one. A scribe narrowly avoided colliding with an emir and darted down the hall, stumbling to a halt before Nasir.

"Amiri," she said breathlessly, brushing two fingers from her lowered brow. Her lashes fluttered. "The sultan requests your presence."

———◆———

The throne room glowed like something out of a story in which honor and justice and love prevailed. Zafira almost laughed at the irony.

People like her looked at a place and wondered how to furnish it with the least amount of coins. The rich did the opposite, and the Sultan's Palace was no exception. Decadence spilled from everywhere. The cool tiles kept the bulk of the desert heat at bay, the dark rug leading to the throne's dais cutting a stark contrast. On the Gilded Throne, a structure as magnificent as the stories described it to be, the sultan lounged, tall and proud.

Zafira could see why Seif had decided not to join them.

She had only seen the man through the fiery summoning Nasir had done on Sharr, but he didn't *look* any nicer now that the medallion was gone. A stern countenance was only part of a leader's charge, Zafira knew, but she couldn't imagine the sultan ever being fatherly, even if he was handsome enough that she could see how the Silver Witch fell for his dark beauty.

What bothered her was Nasir, and how he looked like a man whose fortunes had turned and he had yet to believe it. She worried he was less attentive, which led to the worry, too, that she had begun to rely on him. He wore his wariness like a cloak, his fresh turban and thin silver circlet making her heart race a little too quickly, despite the defeat weighing heavily across them.

Men of the Sultan's Guard stood statue-like along either side of the room, their silver cloaks complementing the ornately paneled walls. How anyone could live under such constant vigilance was beyond her.

"Ibni." The sultan greeted him with a smile, but it was clear Nasir had gotten so accustomed to the terror the sultan had become that he didn't know how to react to the man his father once was. "How is your progress?"

Kifah's jaw clenched, and Zafira agreed. What was the point of Nasir freeing the sultan if the man wasn't going to help them?

"Decent," Nasir said without elaboration.

It wasn't decent, they were failing. Terribly. And yet he revealed nothing. Laa, his tone was shaped to please.

Zafira held steady against a shiver when the sultan's gaze fell to her. She saw him through Lana's eyes, and it wasn't hard to imagine ripping her blade across his neck, his blood so poisoned it ran black.

"—and we will delegate more resources," the sultan was saying.

"I think we should delay the feast," Nasir said slowly.

The sultan considered him with a heavy exhale. "We spoke of this, Ibni."

"Yes, and the feast is to celebrate the return of magic," Nasir insisted. "A feat we are far, far away from."

The words stung. How close they had been at one point, on Sharr when the battle was in their favor. When they had salvaged the five hearts from the Sisters of Old, before the Lion had taken Altair and the heart he protected. Her thoughts clattered to a halt.

Altair had the last of the hearts.

What if—no.

She refused to connect the thoughts. She refused to believe he had betrayed them so early on, with the corpse of Benyamin at his feet on Sharr, his friend whose soul was still bound with Altair's own.

"The banquet is tomorrow, and the delegates have already begun to arrive. It is too late; we cannot delay it. Are the maids and kitchen staff assisting in your efforts?"

Nasir's brow furrowed. "No, but—"

"Then they will continue preparations." Mirth played in the sultan's eyes as he looked to Kifah and then Zafira. "Your friends will attend as well." His next words addressed them directly. "I will have the tailors take your measurements."

Zafira inclined her head as if this were the greatest blessing a man had ever bestowed on her. "Shukrun, Sultani."

"And that merchant in Sarasin—Muzaffar, yes? I've invited him, too. It would be good to make his acquaintance and learn his views on certain measures so that we may possibly implement him as caliph." The sultan smiled. "As you suggested, Nasir."

He tapped his scepter on the dais, and caught Nasir's flinch.

"Worry not, Ibni. All will be well."

His words made Zafira think of her own father, whose every word came from the heart.

"You may leave," the sultan concluded.

Nasir paused. But even ridiculed and likened to a dog, he had wanted his father's approval, and he acquiesced, the three of them slowly backing away, as if the sultan would die if they turned their back on him. *Who knows? You should try it*, Yasmine said in her head.

Spite will turn your hair gray, Zafira shot back.

Fancy necklace or not, he's responsible for thousands of deaths.

Zafira closed her eyes at the painful reminder. He was responsible for more: the tension across Nasir's shoulders, the fear knotting the words on his tongue, the scars on his back. Abuse. Years of it.

"There is one more matter," the sultan called, and her eyes flew open as they stopped with their ridiculous backtracking.

She kept her head low, every bit a humble peasant.

"Neither of us will ever know why the Lion sent out the invitations, Ibni," the sultan began.

Zafira paused. Nasir had said that the sultan retained his memories from his time under the Lion's control. How could he not remember something as concrete as a reason?

"And in order to make the occasion worth such a strenuous journey," he continued, "we will need to provide for Arawiya's dignitaries."

"Yes, of course," Nasir said slowly.

"As such, you will project your best at the feast, for you may meet your future bride."

If it were possible for a person's entire body to slowly blink, Nasir's did just that. Zafira's own chest stirred oddly. She could have sworn the sultan was watching her as he spoke.

Nasir opened his mouth with a parched wheeze, but the sultan wasn't finished.

"The Arz is no more, thanks to you. Now we must strengthen ties between caliphates, and as you are aware, the Pelusian calipha, as well as the Zaramese caliph and several wazirs, all have daughters of marriageable age."

"A bride," Nasir repeated hollowly in the expectant silence.

Kifah smothered a laugh with a terrible attempt at a cough.

"A woman," the sultan said, and Zafira wondered if she imagined the temper in his voice, "whom you will wed and then—"

Nasir cleared his throat. "Shouldn't we wait until—"

"Now is as good a time as any. Don't you agree, Huntress?"

Zafira started at the sudden attention. The faint lines across the alabaster tiles were suddenly the most intriguing in the world. *Yes, Lana*, Zafira thought. She very much wanted to kill him.

Nasir saved her from answering. "I'm not ready for . . . for a bride."

Zafira looked up in the silence, wishing she could speak the words in her chest. Wishing she had her hood so she could stare without chagrin. The sultan leaned back against the burnished gold of the throne, considering his son. How were they to know the sultan was truly himself now, and not the Lion's puppet?

"You will be ready, Ibni. It is only a matter of summoning the right amount of zeal for a pretty face. You are more than capable, aren't you?"

The words were a dismissal delivered with a double edge, but Nasir remained rooted to the spot, even as the doors opened for a pair of emirs. The sultan's attention drifted, though his guard continued to watch, and Zafira had the overwhelming sense of them mocking their prince in the silence.

"Nasir," she said softly, and because she was a fool who couldn't stop herself, because she was hurting and he was there, *right there*, and oh how she missed him, her arm swung forward and her fingers brushed his, warmth tangling for the briefest of moments.

He snatched back, blinking in a way that made her think he had forgotten she was here. He had forgotten *he* was here.

The sultan saw.

When the throne room doors closed behind them, Zafira hushed the skeins tugging at her heart, trying to steer her focus. Aya, the Lion, the heart, Altair. *A bride.*

Something burned in her eyes. *Fatigue,* she lied to herself, ignoring what this entire conversation was: a reminder of her place.

A sign, perhaps. She was a fleck of dust, adrift in the storm of sultans.

CHAPTER 44

THEY WERE GONE. HIS ZUMRA, HIS FAMILY. THEY
had come for him, and then they had—gone. The sight of them
cast Altair upon Sharr once more, Nasir at his back, Benyamin
with his little vials. Their camaraderie.

But this time, it was his fault that he was alone. His fault that the pain
fracturing their gazes when he had turned away and strode to the Lion's
side was seared into his own soul.

And they didn't know the half of it: That it was Altair who had sent the Lion
to them, telling his father where the zumra was hiding, because he trusted
them to be competent and the Lion was bound to find them anyway. That Altair had turned back because of what Nasir had said, because though Altair had
fruitlessly searched the house for the heart, he finally knew what they needed.

When he had decided to see how far a bluff could take him, he had not
expected the repercussions upon himself.

"For a moment," the Lion simpered, "I doubted you would return. You
seem to forget who you are when you see that pathetic prince."

"Yet here I am, ever loyal," Altair quipped. He had also not expected the stirrings of empathy toward his father to blossom in some delicate corner of his heart.

The Lion hummed. "And what did you learn from him?"

"Will I be free of these shackles if I tell you?"

"That is yet to be determined."

Altair did not answer, but the Lion, he knew, expected nothing, and left without another word. There were times when he wondered which of them was truly falling for the other's delusions.

The two lanterns at the head of the room sculpted Aya's slender form in shadow. The silence simmered between them, mostly because Altair couldn't bring himself to look at her. His friend. The beloved of an even dearer friend. Benyamin would have shattered.

"I returned to the Lion because of you," he said to her. He knew where they were now. He knew this place like the back of his hand.

The Lion had been right to ponder over Altair's return. For when Altair saw Nasir, haggard but happy to see him—as happy as the grump could look—he felt a renewed sense of hope.

With his brother and the zumra at his side, he would triumph.

"You did not have to." She smoothed the folds of her abaya. Like Benyamin, she was his elder by decades, but she looked like a lost child sprawled on the floor. "I do not need protecting."

Altair scoffed, leaning against the wall, resting his weighted wrists on the tables on either side. "Sweet Aya, you lost my care for your well-being when you linked hands with his."

She came over to him, and after a beat of hesitance, trailed her fingers up the inside of his left wrist and bare arm. He stiffened, instantly growing wary. He should have moved. Wrapped a hand around her slender neck and demanded an answer.

The tattoo around her eye stopped him. *Hanan.* Only she would have chosen a word that encompassed so much.

"I've nothing left, sadiqi," she murmured. "My son is gone. My husband is gone. Am I not deserving of a new life?"

"You had me," Altair said hoarsely.

He thought of his visits to Alderamin years and years ago, when he'd take her the flowers she loved most, soft hues that she began to adapt in her clothes. When he had strung pearls in her silken hair beneath the whisper of the moon. And later, when he had called her his friend, his sadiq, because what she had wanted of him was what Benyamin had wanted of her far longer, and Altair would never take that away from his brother by choice.

He remembered the way Benyamin spoke of her with boyish diffidence, loving her from afar for decades. He remembered the letter he wrote in Benyamin's name, the piece of parchment that made the longing in her eyes shift from him to Benyamin.

He remembered, as vividly as yesterday, when Benyamin and Aya had wedded beneath the fanning leaves of the date palms. The way his heart had wept with loss and joy at once, bittersweet and beautiful.

"Was I not enough? Was my friendship too heavy a burden?" he asked, his voice soft.

"The Lion will win, sadiqi," she whispered, cupping his face. Her hand was cold. All those servile dramatics, and the Lion hadn't told him anything about Aya. Altair hadn't known she was a part of his plans, and he certainly didn't know why. But he wouldn't wait to find out.

"For once," she said, "I will not be on the side of loss."

He stared into her eyes, wide and innocent and bereft of reason, and he turned his head to press a kiss to her palm. One last gift. One final farewell.

For the next time he touched her, it would be with a blade through her heart.

CHAPTER 45

THE FEAST WAS THIS EVENING, AND ZAFIRA WAS ON edge. More dignitaries had arrived, chests puffed as if they were sultans themselves, hauling treasures to sway favors. She hadn't seen Nasir since he'd been told of his impending wedding, nor had she sought him out. Her fingers still buzzed from reaching for him, and her heart still stung from when he pulled away. If he wanted to see her, he could come to her. Otherwise, she would have her answer: She truly had been the most interesting thing on Sharr, and they were on Sharr no longer.

Always so hasty, Yasmine *tsk*ed in her head.

I learned from the best, Zafira retorted.

She supposed the voice in her head that sounded like Yasmine had a point, however. Since she'd woken this morning from a restless sleep, her attention had been in demand. Seamstresses came and went. First for her, then for Lana. Servants barged in and out. Maids with clean sheets and others pulling dusty curtains.

On the one hand, Zafira was secretly grateful, for the constant company gave her more time to find the right words to tell Lana what had happened yesterday. On the other, she was beginning to wonder if the sultan was purposely keeping the zumra apart.

At last, her door closed and remained closed, and with Lana in the adjoining bath, Zafira quickly grabbed her shawl and darted into the hall, coming face to face with Kifah.

The Pelusian raised an eyebrow. "Off to see your lover?"

Zafira scowled, and then her scowl deepened when her mind conjured an image of Nasir, his shirt on the floor, her fingers on his skin. No, not hers, but the girl in the yellow shawl's. "If that's who you think you are."

Kifah's laugh was cut short by her somber mood. "Seif is expecting a runner any moment now, with updates on the Lion's—and Aya and Altair's—whereabouts. I thought you might want to be there."

Zafira trailed after her, elbowing her way through the bustling halls and deeper into the palace, tiles cool beneath her feet, the breeze stirring the curtains warm and dry as bones. Kifah barely glanced at the guards as they passed, but Zafira's skin itched with their probing gazes.

When she made to open the door to the war room, Kifah rolled her eyes.

"What?" Zafira asked.

"Watch," Kifah taunted, and a guard, stoic and elegant, opened it for them. "See? It's like magic. No heart required." She winced. "A bit too soon to be joking about this, eh?"

Seif and Nasir were already seated at the low majlis. A map stretched on the table in the center, fine lines etched on tanned leather. Yet another masterpiece only the rich could afford.

Zafira sat to Seif's left, Kifah to hers. Nasir pressed his lips closed, a minuscule reaction only she would notice.

"I received word early this morning that the Zaramese heart has been restored," Seif said.

"Good, good," Kifah said, but it was almost as if what wasn't important to the Lion was no longer important to them, either. "Let's hope that's only the beginning of today's good fortune."

"Isn't it odd that the Lion still hasn't gone for them?" Nasir asked suddenly.

Seif shook his head. "He knows they are useless to us without the last, and he knows we won't destroy them. His plans merely take precedence."

"I mean the old adage," Nasir said slowly, testing his words. "Magic for all or none . . . My mother has her magic. I have a fraction of it. Altair, too. What if . . . Well, he could have found a way to do the same."

"How?" Seif asked unkindly.

Nasir had no answer. Zafira remembered what the Lion had said on Sharr—his desire to be like the Sisters themselves, vessel and wielder.

The tension withered when the runner arrived, a missive in his sweaty grasp. Seif snatched it away, and it took the boy only a single glance at the safi's elongated ears before his outcry faded and died.

"You can leave now," Kifah said with a pointed look.

The door closed after the runner, and no one breathed as Seif slit the scroll open. His pale eyes skimmed the damp papyrus, revealing nothing. Surely someone would have seen the Lion, with the thick strokes of a bronze tattoo across the side of his face. Aya, more beautiful than any other in Sultan's Keep. Altair, who could claim the attention of the vicinity with only his presence.

Seif sat back.

The cushions sighed beneath him. "Nothing."

Nasir's reaction was a slight narrowing of his eyes. Zafira dropped her fist on the map, right in the middle of Demenhur. Kifah was so still Zafira feared she would break.

"There's still blood left," Zafira said, clutching the vial around her neck. She had lost her dagger for this vial. For the heart. For Altair. Something burned in her chest. "I can find them again."

Kifah looked reluctantly hopeful, but offered nothing.

"Benyamin always claimed the price of dum sihr to be great." Seif's tone was disinclined. A losing general delivering an armistice. "He was right. Perchance Aya was, too."

Zafira stared at the rhythmic cuts of filigree in the ochre walls and saw Aya's slender fingers in the Lion's hand. Altair turning his back on Nasir's pleas.

"It's worsening out there," Kifah said helplessly. "Sarasin is still without a caliph. Riots are endless because of these damned taxes and the sultan's ignorance. And he's still doing nothing."

"The feast is tonight," Nasir said, finally opening his mouth.

"And?" Kifah asked wildly.

"Someone is bound to make mention of the need for a Sarasin caliph. Or of the taxes." And then he must have realized how the words sounded, how useless and incapable they made *him* sound. "In any case, his focus is on the feast. Once it's over, we'll implore him again. And we'll petition more aid and renew our efforts."

Seif looked unconvinced but kept quiet. It was as if without Aya to reprimand him for being uncivil, he was suddenly less so.

Or perhaps it was the opposite. Perhaps losing her had made him lose hope, and he could summon nothing else.

——◆——

Zafira didn't ask why Kifah was following her back to her rooms, silent and stiff. She didn't need to, because she understood. Sharr had bound them in a way not unlike her bond with the Jawarat: They were tethered more tightly than even family and lifelong friends could be. Circumstance had brought them together, and the wounds of the island still haunted them, clutching them in an iron fist.

They had been five, and now they were three. She didn't need to hear it from Kifah or see it in Nasir's eyes to know: They were afraid one of them could be next.

Zafira paused awkwardly for a guard to open her door while Kifah absently tapped her spear against her leg.

"Are you going to come in?" Zafira asked.

"Only for a moment." Kifah brushed a hand across her bald head as she entered the room. "The Nine Elite are here—well, eight of them. As is my calipha. I haven't seen her since disobeying her orders and trekking across Arawiya, but I'm going to pay my respects."

"Oh. Do you want me to come with you?"

Kifah looked surprised by the offer. "Laa. But you should know that Ayman is here, too."

Zafira froze. *Ayman al-Ziya, the Caliph of Demenhur.*

"Oi, don't look like that. Don't you have something to gloat about?"

No, Zafira didn't have anything to gloat about. She had gone to Sharr, she had returned whole, and then everything had fallen apart. They'd lost one of the five hearts *and* the book needed to restore them. They'd lost Aya, Benyamin's wife. Altair had betrayed them. The sultan's medallion was broken, but the people were restless. Magic was still gone.

So is the Arz, Yasmine reminded her.

Zafira's response to Kifah withered and died when she saw Lana, freshly bathed, listening to the conversation and wearing an expression that further coiled dread in her stomach.

"Go see the caliph, Okhti," Lana said flatly, a tone she had clearly obtained from Yasmine. "You didn't hear what he said after you left for Sharr. He deserves to die as much as the sultan does."

Zafira frowned hesitantly. "Your murderous tendencies are getting to be a little too much."

Lana shrugged. "I'm only talking. It's something people do, right? When they care for each other?"

That tone again. Zafira winced. Kifah gave her a look that said she was all on her own, and left, closing the door behind her.

"I'll see him later. At the feast," Zafira said to Lana.

"When were you going to tell me?" Lana asked as she sat back down in her nook with her notes and little vials of liquids. The mat she had dragged beneath her was the same hue as her moss-green dress.

Zafira took her time removing her shawl, deciding to play the fool. "About what?"

"Ammah Aya. What happened to her?" Frustration stressed her words. "You've been avoiding me all morning. Where—where is she? I knew I hadn't seen her come with the rest of you yesterday, but then I thought she was busy, or didn't want to see me. That's not true, is it?"

Zafira settled on her knees beside her.

"Only a dastard wouldn't want to see you," she said gently, weighing her words. She picked up a tiny sprig of dried thyme. "Remember when you said that we're broken?"

Wariness pinched Lana's gaze. She latched her fingers together in answer, knuckles tight.

"When the world dealt its blow, we snatched up all our pieces and kept moving. We knotted our fraying ropes and kept climbing. We didn't stay broken, you and I. But Aya did. She couldn't let go of her son, and so she saw him in you. She couldn't forgive the truth, and so she saw it in the Lion's drivel. Aya didn't climb that rope. She let go."

Zafira bit her cheek, seeing Aya's hand in his. The look in her eyes.

"She's gone, Lana. She joined the Lion."

Lana made a sound, small and startled. A rabbit in a snare, hope vanishing in a strangled breath, silent and trembling for a long, long moment before angrily swiping a hand across her eyes and staring at her work, at her notes scrawled beside Aya's neater ones.

Zafira reached for her, but Lana held stiff. The last of her blood. Zafira wouldn't let the Lion take her away, too.

Lana shoved her little table aside, jerking to face her. "I'm a healer, Okhti. I'm—I'm—"

"You're what?" Zafira asked softly.

"What if I become like her?" Her whisper cracked. "*What if I become like her?* It's as you said, I—I want to kill people. I don't know how, but I *want* them to die. I get angry."

She stared at her hands. Zafira gripped her tight, shaking her head with vehemence.

"No," Zafira vowed. "Emotions don't define us. It's what you *do* with them that's important. You're stronger than she is. Better. And you have me, do you understand? You will always have me."

Lana said nothing, but Zafira knew her thoughts were elsewhere. Burrowing beneath her every moment with Aya, reliving them through a new light, another facet of a crystal crumbling in her hands.

Both of them looked up when a knock sounded, soft and inquisitive. Zafira's chest became a drum, for there was only one person who knocked that way.

"Do you want to see him?" Lana whispered, swiping at her face again. *Him.* As if she, too, had memorized the way he knocked.

"No."

"Right," Lana said with a shaky bark of a laugh. "Let me get it."

When she opened the door, however, there wasn't a sad prince framed in the pointed arch of the doorway, but two young women, one of them hefting a number of boxes stacked so high that Zafira could barely see her beneath them.

"What—"

The pair bustled past Lana, cheerful greetings lost in the rush, and dumped their packages on the already messy bed. The shorter of the two clapped her hands in excitement, the taller exhibiting a sterner countenance with a rosy smile that was complemented by her green shawl.

"You are to wear an abaya!" the shorter one said, her eyes streaked with kohl. The other nodded enthusiastically. The curtains stirred, the near-evening breeze joining the excitement.

"Am I?" Zafira asked dryly. "I was afraid I'd have to go naked."

Both of them, and Lana, stopped to look at her. *You're terrible*, Yasmine cackled in her head.

"Oh," the shorter one said, her dark eyes wide. "We would never do something so——"

"It was a joke," Zafira said.

The taller one canted her head. "You don't look the funny type."

Zafira gave them a tight smile.

The shorter one beamed. "I'm Sanya, by the way. You are very tall."

"And quite broad," the taller one said as Zafira mouthed the words with her. Some things never changed. "My name is Reem."

They were here to get her and Lana ready for the evening's festivities, a moment Zafira was dreading for more reasons than one. After downright commanding them to let her bathe on her own, she rushed out of the bath and they sat her down in a chair, chattering all the while. Lana knelt by her table and watched, arms tight around her legs, shaking her head with force when Zafira tried going to her. And then Zafira was lost in a whirl of brushes and ointments, her hair being tugged and her skin being rubbed while she stared at the scarring line in her palm, Lana slowly brightening as she watched the girls at work.

Zafira had never been tended to in such a way before, not even for Yasmine's wedding, and her mind became a riot of sound and thought and memory. Altair and Aya and the Lion. Nasir, who was to choose a bride but wanted more than he could voice.

What do you want? She wanted to see Yasmine again. She wanted to relive the years in which she had pretended her mother did not exist. She wanted to taste the sweetness of Bakdash's iced cream on her tongue.

There was more she wanted, too. Things that made her fear herself: death and vengeance and magic. Stolen kisses. The rare smile of a boy with sad eyes.

Death for the Lion. Vengeance for Baba. Magic for herself, for her people, for her kingdom. All fair desires, but it was the extent that she would go to get them that frightened her.

She was young, still. She would want for as long as she could, and then some. To want was to live, was it not?

Reem paused to tilt her head, birdlike. "You are pretty when you smile."

She made it sound as if Zafira were a corpse otherwise. But the oddly detached observation reminded her of Aya, and her smile vanished as quickly as it had come.

The sun had begun its final descent when they slid a dress over her shoulders. The hem fell with a whisper, the fabric fine. Silky gray, edged in silver threads. She wrinkled her nose. Whose idea was it to dress her in ashes? She wouldn't be surprised if it was the sultan's.

When she looked up from the dress, all three girls were staring.

Lana's eyes were wide, a slow smile transforming her face. "Not even the moon can compare."

Sanya clapped her hands again. "You are exquisite."

Reem nodded enthusiastically. "Come to the mirror."

Zafira ducked her head as they dragged her to the wide glass. She started at her feet, slowly roving from the embroidered hem and up the pleated length to the intricately beaded collar, studs like pearls glistening in the sun's fading light. Her arms were visible through the gossamer sleeves, the fabric fanning like the delicate wings of a butterfly when she moved. The neck wasn't as plunging as she expected, thankfully. It was modest enough to keep both Deen's ring and the vial from being too conspicuous, though low enough that the birthmark above her collarbone was in full view. She warmed, remembering the brush of a trembling mouth.

Remembering how little she saw of him now, even when they were in the same room.

Twin strokes colored her cheekbones, a metallic shimmer on her skin. Diluted carmine smeared her lips with the barest of stains, and her unbound hair was as bold as the deepest night. Reem swept kohl with a practiced hand, dark birds taking flight, and finished with a touch of perfume almost exactly like the oud-and-rose of her soap.

"The seamstress didn't want a wide skirt," Reem braved as Zafira adjusted the waistband of the matching, form-fitting pants. The dress had slits, invisible among the pleats, so she could run if she had to.

"Akhh, it's incredible!" Lana looked more delighted than Zafira did.

Sanya crouched and strapped a sheath around Zafira's leg.

She froze.

Reem looked anxious. "Sayyida?"

"That won't be necessary," Zafira said softly. "I don't—"

Sanya nodded in the mirror. "The seamstress didn't think you would want to go without it. She called you a gazelle."

"But I don't—"

"I see it now. Don't you, Sanya?" Reem interrupted, canting her head in that birdlike way, oblivious to the ache of Zafira's heart, the emptiness filling that sheath against her leg. "Innocent to the bone, even as she outruns the beast."

Zafira swallowed her protest once more when someone rapped on the door, sharp and sure. Sanya hurried to the receiving rooms to answer, chattering all the way, and Reem laughed as she gathered her array of cosmetics and other things for Lana, shooing her away when Lana moved to help. Zafira stole another glance in the mirror.

"Yasmine would die," Lana whispered by her side, and Zafira allowed herself a wistful smile. If only Yasmine were here. And Umm and Baba. And—

A shadow fell in the doorway, and then her heart was stuttering, her gaze lifting up, up, up, then crashing into a gray abyss shrouded in kohl.

Reverence. That was in the look he gave her. It was the same look from that night on the rooftops outside the palace. The same look that caused something strange and bold to blossom in her veins, more powerful than any magic the world could lay at her feet. The look she had feared she would never see again.

The feast was this evening. Tonight, he would be bound to another. Tomorrow, the Lion could come and sweep them all into a den of shadows.

Now, this moment, she would steal for herself.

"You—" He stopped and glanced at Reem and Sanya, dismissing them even as he commended them. "You did well."

"Sayyidi," said Reem.

"Sultani," murmured Sanya.

"Wait!" Zafira said, and the girls ran into each other. "What about Lana?"

Lana started for the door. "Okhti, this is a palace. I can get dressed in the hall if the rooms are full. You, on the other hand . . ."

She attempted a wink but closed both her eyes, then followed the servants into the hall. Zafira laughed shakily when the door closed, her neck burning. She floundered, and finally looked up at him through hooded eyes.

She watched the shift in his throat. If only he knew how much she loved the silvery lilt of his voice. Would he ever stop speaking then?

"I have something for you," he said.

He handed her a box, long and slender. She took it, discreetly testing its weight. Providing for her family meant gifts were few and far between with her on the receiving end.

"Shukrun," said Zafira, containing herself. Fighting against the emotions lodging in her throat because he had come. He was here. Truly here. Not to slit her palm. Not because he was required to be.

That yearning, missing, *emptiness* in her soul vanished, gullible as it was to know what tonight entailed but not to allow herself to care. Not yet. This was her moment. Hers alone.

"Open it," he insisted, standing close.

She had never thought herself shy until she was the object of his gaze.

The box was wood, simple and hinged, and she lifted the latch. The lid fell back with a soft creak, and a pang shot through her.

Tucked into a bed of silk, a blade glinted back at her, sharp and tapering at its curve. Black filigree ran along its blunt edge, matching the line of onyx set into the flat pommel and burnished hilt, the silver dulled and dark with age.

A jambiya. It was lavish, more so than anything she had ever owned.

"It was my first dagger," he explained. "My father gave it to me when—when he was still himself. I could have commissioned a new one, but I know that you, well, you favor sentiment, don't you?"

That drew a smile from her. "I do."

"Don't say shukrun again," he said before she could thank him.

"What should I say, then?"

"That you like it," he said, and worked his jaw, "or that you don't. Or that you don't want an old castoff. Then I'll find you a new one."

She laughed. "That's not how gifts work."

He didn't have anything to say to that, and she wondered if gifts were rare for him, too. It was no small act, parting with the dagger one had received from the loving father who became a monster. It made this more than a jambiya—it was a collection of memories and moments, a culmination of experiences. If there was any dagger worthy of replacing Baba's, it was this. His.

"I love it," she said softly, testing it in her palm. It fit as well as Baba's did, though the blade was lighter, finer. Made for a prince. "It's beautiful and old and perfect."

She lifted the hem of her dress and slid the dagger into the sheath, forgetting how well the pants clung to her skin and suddenly aware of his gaze following the movements.

Silence stretched between them, and she wondered if Kifah had told him, or if he had asked. Or if he had noticed her empty sheath and surmised the rest.

"I'm sorry," he whispered, and though they were two short words that could be meaningless, she knew they were anything but. Not from him. Not from the boy who rarely spoke at all, making each word that he uttered worth a thousand from anyone else. He lifted his hand and his fingers splayed before he dropped it. "For all that I've done. For all that I never said."

She might have remembered what she said if he hadn't been so close. If they weren't both struggling to understand. With a strangled sigh, he slipped his fingers into her hair and she let him draw her closer, closer, until their foreheads touched. Five finger pads to the back of her skull, the smallest at the nape of her neck.

Somehow, this moment felt more intimate than their encounter on Sharr. It was an emotion stretched raw. Her exhales became his broken inhales. Their hearts pounded as one.

"I can't—"

The word tore from his throat, and then some part of him retreated. She pulled back, finally understanding why. She saw it in the way his brows furrowed and his jaw worked. It wasn't that he was too proud to speak, he *struggled* to. He assumed no one cared for what he wanted to say.

"I know what it's like," she said softly. She had Yasmine, but her friend had a knack for asserting her opinion more and listening less. She'd had Deen, until he began to love her in a way that was different from the way she loved him. And then there was Lana, whom she had wrongfully believed too young to understand, too new to burden.

Yet from the tightening of his shoulders, she knew she was wrong. She could never understand the extent of what he had endured. She had been given a glimpse when he had met his father on Sharr. When the sultan barely allowed his son a word, when nearly every sentence hurled at him was some form of ridicule.

"I understand in some way," she corrected. "To have words collect on your tongue, but feel as if they aren't worth voicing. To feel as if no one wants to listen."

It was his truth, a lie ingrained into the fibers of his being: His words were not meant to be voiced. No one cared. He looked away, and she knew she had struck true.

"I want to," she said.

His head lifted, and the last of the sun lit his eyes in gold. She wanted every word he would give her. She would listen for as long as he would let her. But he looked at her as if she were a knife to an already bleeding wound.

"I can't—I don't want this," he breathed. "I don't want to pick one of them as my bride."

"Then tell him," she said firmly, though knowing it was not so easy. "Tonight, at the feast itself, tell him. Do as your soul desires."

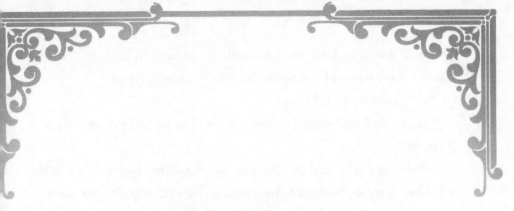

CHAPTER 46

ALTAIR HAD SPENT THE ENTIRE NIGHT SEARCHING for clues and racking his brain for why the Lion might need Aya, to no avail. He hadn't been able to talk to her again, either, for the Lion had kept her secured. Precaution, in case his son decided to kill her. It spoke to how little the Lion truly trusted him, but Altair didn't mind.

He knew what he needed.

The door opened for the Lion and several ifrit. In the center of the room, one unfurled a bedroll generous enough for a sultan. Another set out a tray of tools, instruments meant for a healer. A third brought in yet another tray, empty and pristine.

Upon it, the Lion set down an organ, crimson and pulsing.

The final heart of the Sisters of Old, the embodiment of Altair's mistake. Because he had planned and schemed and plotted, but he hadn't even considered he might be kidnapped himself.

"Well done, my kin," the Lion said, the Jawarat in his hand. He met Altair's confusion with a staid smile. "Are you ready, Altair?"

"Er," said Altair, "for what?"

"To live forever," he said simply. "We will be at the forefront of a new Arawiya."

Altair opened his mouth, dread stealing his ability to make light of the moment. A frenzy bubbled in his veins, and his pulse quickened when he noticed that beneath his open robes, the Lion wasn't wearing a shirt.

"Now," the Lion said to the ifrit near him. "Bring us Aya."

A healer and a heart.

Altair wished his mind didn't work so quickly. To be blissfully un-aware was a blessing of its own.

I would need a heart to claim otherwise.

The Lion was half ifrit, half safin. Born without a heart, but with the cavity for one. There was an actual hole in his chest. What better way to fill it than with the object he desired more than anything else?

Altair struggled for air. With this, his father would be as powerful as the Sisters of Old. Limitless in his capabilities. Unmatched by anyone else.

The Lion set down the Jawarat.

Altair didn't think. He lunged, slower than he should have done, which only made his triumph blaze brighter when his hands closed around the Jawarat. The Lion remained still even as the ifrit scrambled.

As power shifted in a single, dividing moment.

The book hummed in Altair's hands, a low, almost imperceptible sound akin to that of a content cat. It was connected to him in a way his father might soon be, as it was forged with the blood of the Sisters of Old, the very same that coursed through his veins.

And Altair was going to destroy it.

He opened the book to its middle, its worn pages rough.

"I should have known," the Lion remarked softly, almost sadly. "We are mirrors, you and I. Only you cannot see it. Go on, my son. Tear it apart."

He listed his head, and Altair paused at his calm.

Sultan's teeth—Zafira. The daama thing was connected to her life. If he tore it apart, she would die with it.

"Is that concern I see?"

Altair clenched his jaw.

"You betrayed your zumra by telling me where they were. You've killed and mutilated and betrayed to rise up Arawiya's ranks. I've seen the atrocities you've committed under the name of the kingdom's well-being." The Lion lowered his voice, temptation in his words. "What's one more life to ensure your people's future?"

Nothing.

Everything.

The fight bled from him when the Lion pried the Jawarat out of his grip, and four ifrit wrenched back his arms.

The Lion gloated, knowing Altair could not harm him, not when he had used Altair's own blood as protection. Or Altair would have lunged for far more, gouged those unnatural eyes from their sockets, ripped the man to shreds with his bare hands.

The Lion set down the Jawarat with a soft, dawning laugh as Altair fought against the ifrit. "You love her."

Altair was not like his mother. He loved freely, abundantly. It was admiration that came rarer, for him. "Only a fool wouldn't love her. After all that she's endured and all that she's lost, she still fights for a world that failed her." The true definition of a lionheart.

The Lion only hummed.

"Unlike you," Altair said with anger.

The Lion's gaze shot up.

It was a warning, a sign he should stop, but he did not. He *couldn't.* "You endured loss and turned into a monster. You suffered, and now you want others to do the same."

Stop talking, sanity whispered in Altair's ears. The Lion's eyes were like flint; his mouth a straight, hard line; his body as still as when Altair spoke of his days in the palace, abandoned by his mother.

"Isn't that right, *Father?*"

In a burst of speed, the Lion flicked his wrist and Altair was wrenched back against the wall, arms flung to either side. He let out a splintered breath, unable to move. The man must be *terribly* furious if he was wasting magic on Altair's insolence.

"I need you alive, Altair," the Lion said as he stepped close, his voice low. "I need your blood, and that, too, for merely a while longer. I do not need you whole. I kept you unbroken because I believed we could be together. Work together." Sorrow flitted across his gaze. As if he lamented the lies they had shared together. "Did you consider that before your tongue ran loose?"

The Lion's livid eyes dropped to his mouth, and for the first time in Altair's life, he felt it: pure, unrestrained terror. He clamped his mouth closed, blinking back against the perspiration dripping down his brow. The Lion gripped the underside of his face, nails like claws raking his skin, and held him still.

"No, not the tongue, *my dearest son*," he taunted. "We both know you value something else far more than your voice, and you'll have much to say when I rid you of it."

Altair saw the glint of a small knife, and that was all he could do: watch. As understanding struck. As a distinct before and after were born in this moment. He couldn't move, he couldn't fight back, but he would never beg.

He grasped the shreds of his composure as the Lion of the Night shoved the blade through his eye.

CHAPTER 47

OMETHING CAUGHT IN NASIR'S LEFT EYE, MAKING IT
hard to see for the briefest of moments before he blinked it away.
Zafira might as well have told him to leap into a chasm. That was
how it felt to speak to his father.

A bride. The mere thought weighed heavier than the Lion having the
Jawarat, a heart, and Altair. Nothing in Nasir's life ever went right, but
everything seemed to be going more wrong than usual.

"I will," he promised softly. *For you.* There was something in his chest.
A wild beast, perhaps, desperately trying to claw its way free. To leap into
her hands and let her do with it what she willed.

He had rehearsed an apology and an explanation when he had lifted
his old dagger from the crate in his wardrobe. Words upon words that
he had painstakingly strung together, things he needed to say before tonight. Before the feast, when he would have to choose a bride.

Every last syllable vanished when he saw her.

I want to, she had said, and he wanted to know the limits of those words. He wanted to speak every word he had jumbled inside him, but he needed—he didn't know what he needed. Time, perhaps.

"You look nice, Zafira," she drawled playfully when he didn't say anything more. She flourished two fingers from her brow with a confidence that stole his breath. "Shukrun, my prince."

She wasn't *nice*, she was a vision.

The girls had brushed moonlight onto her skin, leaving that splotch of darkness to taunt him. Her hair was a mane of gleaming tresses framing her face, blue eyes dazzling in a fringe of kohl.

"Do you wish for me to scribe poetry in your name, fair gazelle?" His voice was rough.

"Pretty words are nice sometimes."

He brushed a hand down the shimmer of her sleeve, touched the inside of her wrist. "Did the stars fall from the sky to adorn you in their luster? No—liquid silver. You are the well that forged every blade in the world."

She laughed, and his heart leaped at the sound.

"On second thought," she breathed, closing the distance between them, making him all too aware of her bed stretching out behind her, a tease and a wish, before she brought her mouth to his. "You should do more and talk less."

A sound escaped him. His ears burned at her intrepid advance, so unlike the blushing girl from Sharr. It was one thing to want to kiss her, and quite another for her to grip the collar of his thobe and pull him to her, the softness of her mouth capturing his. His hands fitted to her waist, the warmth of her skin pulsing through the thin cloth.

"Nasir."

The pleading in her whisper drove him mad. He wrenched her closer, barely stopping a groan at the feel of her against him. Her lips parted with his, and he smiled at the tentative press of her tongue. He tasted citrus, and the roaring in his blood rushed lower, *lower*.

Perhaps more than her mouth and her soft sighs, he craved the touch of her palm on his chest, the splay of her fingers on his heart. Claiming him. He pulled away to study her. Her eyes were glassy, her lips bruised and far too lovely for a killer like him. Yet he allowed himself the credit—*he* had done this. He was the reason the cloistered Huntress was falling apart. He was the reason her lungs worked for breath.

He wanted to lose his fingers in the obsidian of her hair again. To knot his hands into the fabric of her dress to stop the tremble in them, to lead her back, back, back, but it would be cruel to ruin her perfection. He lightened his touch.

"I missed you," she whispered against his mouth.

"I'm sorry," he whispered at the same time.

She drew back the barest bit, and that half-lidded gaze nearly undid him. "What for now?"

He swayed forward. "For ruining your dress."

"What's the use of a pretty dress if I can't do what I want in it?"

What was the use of a crown if he could not do as he wished?

Her hands slid up his thobe and threaded in his hair, igniting him anew before she pulled away with a smothered sob.

"How long can a stolen moment last?" The words were half to herself. That was the reason for her boldness. For her abandon.

It hurt him.

A single chord of perception stood in her blue gaze before she spoke in a breathless rush. "Will you speak these words to your bride? Kiss her so?"

"My bride. My queen. My fair gazelle," he said in the barest shred of a whisper. "Cannot all three be one and the same?"

Color brushed her cheeks, and he knew it then. The world could bring a thousand women to him and not one could stand as equal to her. He followed the bob in her throat, noted the sadness in her eyes. He had finally found it in himself to voice what he wanted, but what did it matter if she didn't want the same?

"And the girl in your room?" she asked, thinking he had spoken lightly. "Am I to share you with her when I am your queen?"

"Kulsum. I truly do not know why she had come to my room the night you saw her. She was my mother's servant, and she lost her tongue because of me. I—I loved her," he said, because it was true, because he would never lie to Zafira, "until I learned she was a spy who had been using me and that I'd killed her lover years ago."

His father had tortured him.

His mother had lied about her very existence.

And his lover's every kiss had been a double-edged sword.

Now isn't the time for your pathetic realizations. It was too late—he was already spiraling down the abyss. She saw it. She saw the chaos on his face, heard it in the thrum of his heart because she was still so close. It was only when she pressed her brow to his that he remembered to breathe.

"You are right not to accept me. Not to want this," he said.

She shook her head against his. "It isn't your fault that—"

He cut her off with a broken laugh. "What are the odds, Zafira? Every bit of affection in my life has been fabricated. When does it stop being the fault of others and start being the fault of mine?"

She didn't speak. Only gripped his shoulder with a sure hand, listening as no one ever had before.

"I only look human," he said quietly. A curl of shadow escaped his mouth. It happened when his emotions ran rampant, when he struggled to rein in his thoughts. "I'm a monster. A beast. And the ones who run are the ones who've gotten close enough to see that there's no room inside for anything else."

"Even a beast is capable of love. Of being loved," she countered. "The Lion made your father cruel. Necessity made your mother lie. Pain fueled Kulsum's manipulation. No matter what Altair has become now, he loved you before. Kifah loves you. I—"

He stilled. He didn't dare draw breath.

A knock sounded at the door, insistent.

"I should——" She stopped, breathless, and pulled away.

"Yes," he said dumbly, and then she was gone, leaving the scent of oud and roses on his clothes, silver starlight everywhere he looked, and the ghost of words that never were.

CHAPTER 48

ALTAIR BIT HIS TONGUE UNTIL IT WAS BLEEDING AS profusely as his eye. He refused to make a sound, refused to cry out, even as every vessel in his body begged to. In pain. In loss. Ninety years he had retained himself, only for this.

This.

Aya stood in the doorway, dirt smeared across her pink abaya. She was bloody from head to toe—no, that was his vision. Blood dripped from his chin, spattered onto the floor as if he were a basin with an irreparable leak.

She ran to him and he shrank away. He hated her in that moment. Her pity, her pain. She had no right to any of it.

"What happened?" she cried.

"Why do you care?" Altair felt as hollow as his voice.

He tasted his blood on his tongue. Two paces away, the si'lah heart was witness to it all, thrumming faintly.

"Fix him, my sweet," the Lion commanded quietly. "He must see that he chose wrongly."

She reached into the tray and slit her palm after a moment's hesitance, and through his pinprick of perception, he wondered if he was supposed to be grateful to her for abandoning her fear of dum sihr when she cupped her hand beneath his chin and stirred his blood with her own. When she pressed her fingers to his eye socket. When he saw, with a dry heave, what was left of his eye being torn away from his numbed skin.

"Give me water," she said to an ifrit afterward. "To clean him."

"Don't," Altair snarled. "Step away from me."

She lowered her hand reluctantly, hurt flashing across her features, and Altair laughed. A sad croak of a sound he didn't recognize as his own. The Lion murmured something he missed, and she went back to him, washing her hands in the basin in the corner.

The room smelled of blood and the must of oil. It smelled of apprehension and change. Of loss. With one eye, Altair watched the Lion recline across his bedroll as Aya sat beside him, crossing her legs. Her gaze flitted to Altair with the barest unease. With sorrow, always sorrow. Ever since her son's death.

He seized it as whatever held him stiff against the wall subsided and the ifrit grabbed him once more.

"Aya, look at me," he implored, despite the hatred in his veins. "Look at what he's done. What would Benyamin say?"

She smiled at him. "The dead cannot speak, sadiqi."

The Lion looked pleased. Aya picked up the first of her tools and pulled back the folds of the Lion's robes.

Altair's blood ran cold. He thrashed against the ifrit, but he felt as if he were suddenly made of wheat, frail and insignificant. He gave up, all but hanging in their clutches.

Two more came for him, because Aya might be Arawiya's best healer, but no one could insert a heart into a heartless monster by skill alone. Without Altair's blood to fuel her, none of this was possible. He twisted away in futile protest and dull pain throbbed up his arm at the slash of the blade. He stilled at the warm rush of blood, heard the soft *pings* as it hit the metal cup.

Pride bit his tongue, held his silence. His eye socket wrinkled oddly, bile rising to his throat.

Aya blended their blood with a soft murmur. She smoothed her fingers down the Lion's chest.

"Do you feel it?" she asked momentarily.

The Lion shook his head.

Altair knew she was good, but skilled enough to numb so much of a man in heartbeats? She placed the tip of the lancet on the Lion's skin and paused. "There is always the chance that it may not work."

"Fair Aya, always so concerned for my welfare. We've discussed this, haven't we? It is a risk I must take." The Lion touched her cheek, like a proud parent commending his child.

"For Arawiya," she said.

The Lion smiled. "For Arawiya, my sweet."

She truly was gone. Altair watched helplessly as the knife tore through the Lion's golden skin, black blood welling along the path of the incision.

The promise of a greater darkness to come.

CHAPTER 49

THERE TRULY WAS NO FOOL BIGGER THAN ZAFIRA. *I love you?* She wanted to bash her head against the nearest wall.

If Kifah hadn't knocked when she did, Zafira's wayward tongue would have run too far to reel back, though the look on Kifah's face when Nasir followed her out of the room was mortifying enough. He barely met Zafira's eyes as he hurried on and turned down a different hall, the guards on either end snapping to attention.

She was aware, then, that those were the last words she would say to him before he was bound to another. Before this night was over, all that they had shared would no longer be the beginnings of a possibility but the end of a memory—unless he spoke out and held his ground.

"So that's why you weren't with Lana. Akhh, he's looking cheery," Kifah observed as she appraised her. "You, on the other hand, look like you climbed out of someone's dream. Probably his."

Zafira felt bare with her hair unbound, lost in the flame of his touch and the yearning beneath her skin. She felt powerful, too, with her new jambiya against her leg.

"I was worried when you weren't in the audience hall," Kifah continued. Her own new attire was fierce: A sleeveless tunic dropped at a slant to her mid-thigh, the high neck embroidered in bold gold filigree. She started to say something more, but stopped.

Zafira cast her a sidelong glance. "What is it?"

She pulled a small cylinder of polished wood with golden caps from a loop at her hip. With a flick of her wrist, it extended to either side, a vicious spearhead at the very end.

"I'm impressed." Zafira's brows rose.

Kifah flicked a latch and the spear retracted. She attached it to her waist. "A gift from Benyamin."

Zafira's throat closed, imagining Benyamin preparing for a matter of life and death, yet pausing to construct a gift for the stranger with whom he would undertake a momentous journey.

"It's exquisite."

Kifah nodded, torn. "Calipha Ghada had it with her. She wants me to come back."

Ah. The Calipha of Pelusia. "But that's good, isn't it? It seemed like you wanted her to forgive you."

"Not with an ultimatum. I'd have to go back with them *now*. After the feast. It means leaving everything behind. You, the prince, Altair . . . magic. Forgo my vengeance and regain my place." She barked a bitter laugh. "My father would love it."

What could Zafira say? If she had to decide between going back to her home or staying here to restore magic and defeat the Lion, she couldn't choose one or the other. She wanted both. She wanted *more*. She wanted to return home without the guilt of Deen's death. To find Umm alive and Yasmine smiling. She wanted magic returned without the betrayal of Aya and Altair.

No matter what, though, she was a part of this now. She could not see herself stepping away, not after what she had endured and all she had lost.

"Your advice is unmatched, Huntress," Kifah drawled.

Zafira laughed. "I can't be the one to decide which is more important to you. Your place in the Nine, which you joined *for* vengeance against your father. Or your place in the restoration of magic, which you once decided would be an even bigger blow to your father. Big enough that it was worth leaving Pelusia against your calipha's wishes." Zafira stopped to look at her. "If you leave us, you will be missed. If we restore magic without you, it will always be your victory, too."

Kifah let out a low whistle. "And yet, once magic is restored, who's to say how Arawiya will be?"

Once, she said, not *if*. That was Kifah, doubtless and fierce, but Zafira shared her concern. She was no longer the Hunter now that the Arz was gone. She wasn't even a daughter anymore. What was she to do after magic returned?

She would need to start afresh. She and Lana.

"That's what makes the future beautiful." Lana's voice came from behind them.

Kifah rolled her eyes. "I doubt there's a fourteen-year-old as ancient as you, little Lana. That's what makes the future *terrifying*."

Zafira stilled.

Lana's dress was sage, a pale shade of fresh sprigs adorned with tiny pearls. Pleats were set across the length, folds of bronze wound around the middle to accentuate her nimble shape. Brown kohl framed her eyes, and if Baba were here, he would have wept at the sight of his little healer, a woman now.

Lana had always been beautiful; now she was breathtaking.

"What do you think?" she asked shyly after the silence dragged on a beat too long.

Zafira lifted her brows. "I think we ought to hide you away."

Lana wrinkled her nose dismissively, but she was glowing with pride. *Happiness.* It was what her sister deserved after what had happened to Aya and Umm, and Zafira decided then that no matter what, she would see this mission through. She would end the Lion with her last breath if it meant a world where Lana could be happy.

She could barely imagine a world such as that. Without the Arz, without the Lion. She wasn't artless—she knew a world without danger could never exist, but if there was one where death didn't loom, where a girl didn't have to fear becoming the woman she once idolized, Zafira would find it.

Before two massive doors, a servant in white garb lowered his head, and the rest of Zafira's thoughts were lost in a gasp. The audience hall was quite possibly the largest room she had ever seen, flourishing in the latest that art and innovation had to offer.

The floor was exquisite, creamy marble offset with small metallic diamonds lit aflame by the ornate chandeliers. Marble columns supported a domed ceiling inlaid with a mosaic of patterns in an array of deep blues, browns, and rich gold. How odd that something so far out of reach was bedecked with such intricate beauty. Tightly wound swaths of fabric clung to certain angles, rope dangling for a single pull in which the jewel-toned curtains would unfold.

"It's so *neat*," Lana said.

Zafira gave her a look. "You're making us look uncultured."

Kifah smirked. "After dinner is when the revelry really starts. The curtains drop, lights dim. Raqs sharqi. Arak." She lowered her voice, clearly enjoying herself. "Debauchery."

"Raqs sharqi . . . Isn't that belly dancing?" Lana asked, eyes wide.

"*Here?*" Zafira asked, and Kifah broke out in laughter, making Zafira wonder just how much the Nine Elite had witnessed in the Pelusian palace.

"We'll make sure you're tucked into bed by then."

A man in a white thobe and a russet turban stepped to the forefront of the hall, and Kifah cursed. "We're late."

She dragged Zafira and Lana past rows and rows of cushioned majlises set before low ebony tables. People tracked their progress; servants darted to and fro. The air was stifling, heady perfumes stirred with the aroma of the food still to come, and Zafira held her breath at the pungent stench of garlic underlying it all. At the head, steps led to a platform covered in richly dyed cushions and a low table, legs curved like half arches. Behind it, like the centerpiece of a woven rug, was the Gilded Throne.

Zafira could barely imagine how the place would look after the dinner. Was Nasir expected to stay? Her mind raced, imagining him lounging on the dais, eyes hooded as a woman swayed her hips for him, sheer clothes bright as the coy promise on her lips. It wasn't as if this were his first feast. Skies, he might have attended hundreds of these.

Kifah elbowed her. Zafira spotted Seif on the opposite end of the room, his gold tattoo catching the light of the thousands of flickering flames. He still couldn't seem to find a shirt, his bold thobe in black and deep gold unbuttoned to his bare torso.

"Calipha Ghada bint Jund min Pelusia, home to Arawiya's greatest inventions and the Nine Elite!" the man in white announced.

The din settled to a hushed murmur.

"There she is. The source of my worries," Kifah said, but there was pride high in her voice.

A raven's coo drew Zafira's attention as the Pelusian calipha strode down the farthest row in a turban of liquid gold, her abaya wide and sweeping. The dark bird assessed the room from her shoulder, as alert as a hashashin. Ghada's daughter followed, as dark as the night and her mother, her purple abaya clinging to her generous curves, hair tucked beneath a red turban. There was a playfulness to her eyes and the quirk of her mouth.

She was one of the young women Nasir would choose from by the night's end.

"Is that Nawal?" Lana asked quietly.

Kifah nodded. "Ghada's daughter was the closest I had to a friend, and now she's the only reason I'm being tolerated at all."

Eight more followed the calipha: their heads shorn, outfits of red rimmed in purple depicting the colors of Pelusia, arms bare except for their golden cuffs. Not one of them was tattooed, and they were all notably calmer than Kifah was. Or maybe Zafira had gotten so used to Kifah's restless demeanor that it only looked like the rest of the Nine Elite moved like slugs.

"Do you regret it?" Zafira asked.

"Do I regret wanting revenge, you mean?" Kifah snorted. "Never. I just need to decide if it's still worth it."

The deep voice rang out again: "Caliph Rayyan bin Jafar min Zaram, where the mighty forged a path through the cursed forest, and none could stop them!"

Perhaps it was because of what she knew of the Zaramese—that they were brutes who tamed the seas, who fought in arenas and reveled in blood—that Zafira expected their caliph to be a brawny, callous man.

Caliph Rayyan bin Jafar looked like a reed swaying at the water's edge, his wiry build folding beneath the weight of his jeweled cloak. He was followed by his daughter in a headdress made of shells, more regal than the caliph himself, and his three sons.

"The esteemed Calipha Rania and daughter Leila min Alderamin, where the safin idle in elegance, immortal to the bone!"

No one outside of Alderamin had seen the royal Alder family in nearly a century, and the silence was instant.

Every head swiveled to witness Benyamin's mother. Safin were always pushing the boundaries of Arawiyan tradition, and the calipha's appearance was no exception. She was average in height, her long hair unbound and uncovered, crowned with a gold circlet at her temple. Her elongated ears were wrapped in gold, her black abaya studded with rosy pearls.

Vanity shrouded her like a cloak, and she carried her beauty with a sharp-edged cruelty.

By her side was another safi, taller by a hand, a tattoo circling her left eye. The neckline of her abaya was cut deeper than modesty would ever allow, and Zafira quickly lifted her gaze from the plunging seams. Her face, unexpectedly, was kind, her eyes a familiar umber.

"Benyamin's sister," Kifah murmured. Did Leila know her brother was dead? That her sister-in-law had joined the forces of the Lion? "Bleeding Guljul, that calipha. Can you imagine what would happen if our prince was fool enough to ask her daughter to be his wife?"

"Chaos?" Lana asked.

Kifah nodded. "Bloodbath."

Zafira didn't doubt it. Wearing the crown of sultana held no merit if it meant sitting beside a mostly mortal husband. Even if he was half si'lah.

"You can't let him do it, Okhti. You can't let him marry anyone else," Lana murmured, gripping her arm. *Anyone else*, as if she were a contender in a roster of royal women. She, a peasant from the poorest village of Demenhur.

Zafira shushed her.

Like the rest, the calipha, her daughter, and their circle remained standing. No one smiled. Their ears were in full display as if to say *Look at my immortality and bow.*

"Caliph Ayman al-Ziya min Demenhur!"

Ice flooded Zafira's veins. Her caliph strode down the row with his hunched shoulders and fading hair. Lana made a sound akin to a growl. Haytham was close at the caliph's heels, wearing a checkered keffiyah held by a black rope, a sword sheathed by his side with a brilliant moonstone pommel. He was the picture of a dutiful wazir, except for his haunted eyes, hollow circles beneath them.

Zafira remembered his sorrow from when they'd stood before the missing Arz, how terrible it had been. What his face showed now was infinitely worse, and she couldn't understand what would cause it. Death? More secrets?

He had known all along that Zafira was a girl, and never said a word. He had recognized in her what he had instilled in the caliph's daughter, discarded for her gender. If not for Haytham, the girl would have lacked the tutelage of an heir.

White-hot rage shot through Zafira's skull as she recalled that no one in Arawiya, aside from Haytham and herself, even knew that the caliph of Demenhune had a daughter.

Kifah gripped her arm. "Oi, stay calm."

Zafira swayed back with a low breath and ran her gaze across the gathered crowd.

She hated Ayman. She hated how angry he made her feel, rekindling the rage born from her bond with the Jawarat. The surrounding noise blurred into one, her blood rushing through her ears. The burning rage seared her gaze.

This isn't like you.

The Jawarat was gone. It couldn't continue influencing her. But as she fought her anger and her darkening thoughts, she blearily recalled its promise, smug and sure: *We will align with time.*

"Caliph Elect, Muzaffar bin Jul min Sarasin!"

She exhaled slowly at the sound of the announcer's voice.

The man, middle-aged and well dressed in a finely spun russet thobe, looked every bit the merchant he was presumed to be. His skin was the same olive tone as Nasir's, and as if testament to the improvements he was spearheading in Sarasin, his face was pleasant. He was a reminder that there was good in this world. She hoped the sultan would see it and appoint him, and quickly.

The announcer's voice rang one final time, and not a single guest dared to breathe.

"Esteemed guests, the Sultan of Arawiya, once of Sarasin, and Crown Amir, Nasir bin Ghameq bin Talib."

Zafira's heart slowed, pulsing in time to the sultan's steps. He grasped his gold-banded black cloak in one hand, a white thobe flashing beneath it. How he could spend time and coin on clothing and feasting instead of searching for the Lion and the fifth heart was beyond Zafira. Laa, it made her as angry as the Caliph of Demenhur did.

Lana nudged her.

Behind the sultan, a wraith in the night, was Nasir. His features were stoic, eyes trained at his father's back. Someone had contained his hair in a checkered turban, neat dark folds held by a silver circlet, though the stubborn strands didn't want to stay put and a lock curled boyishly at his temple. His thobe was immaculately fitted to his lithe frame, tailored sharp enough to cut. Dark damasks embroidered the panels, the high collar trimmed in silver. He looked smart, princely, and unarmed, but she knew that last one was a lie.

He looks beautiful, her heart whispered to her.

The sultan settled onto his throne. Nasir remained at his side, eyes sweeping the room as the dignitaries took their seats.

"There's that look," Kifah muttered beneath her breath, and Zafira met the fervent flint of his gaze with a suppressed shiver—almost, *almost* missing the way his mouth quirked at one corner with the faintest smirk before his mask returned.

Cannot all three be one and the same?

A silence fell over the room when the sultan lifted his chin.

CHAPTER 50

THE MALODOROUS SCENT OF BLOOD CLUNG TO THE room, transporting Altair to the plains of the battlefield. Anywhere that was not here. The Lion's tenacity was endless, for more than once, those amber eyes rolled to the back of his head, but not one time did he lose consciousness. He was bleary but alert as Aya cut and hacked at his body, healing him as she went along.

It was better than Altair was doing.

"He will kill you," he said. No matter what transpired, the Lion still loathed safin a thousand times over.

Aya only smiled, as dreamily as ever. The same way she had smiled years ago when she ran her fingers through Altair's hair. The same way she had smiled when her son was born.

"Think of what you're aiding," Altair pleaded, uncaring that the Lion was witness.

"The ignition of a new world," Aya said. "Had it not been for the Sisters, Benyamin would live. My son would live."

"Listen to yourself," he roared, wrenching against the ifrit again. His legs trembled like a daama fawn's, his strength diminishing. "The Lion killed Benyamin. Right in front of me."

The Lion merely blinked at her. "Do not believe the musings of the mad, fair Aya. Benyamin was akin to a brother—he brought me into your fold. Cared for me as no one else did."

Altair stared in disbelief. "Then ask him how Benyamin died on the island where the Lion was our only foe."

Aya paused, fingers poised above the Lion's chest. She turned to Altair with the barest hint of sense.

"Protecting yet another descendant of the Sisters," the Lion said simply, and Aya exhaled slowly, reaching for one of her tools. "You see? They will always be the cause of our troubles."

Sultan's teeth. "Yet here you are, Aya, giving him power that even the Sisters themselves venerated."

"A power I will wield well, for I have suffered as you have, as the Sisters never did."

Aya looked at Altair, wide eyes soft, and he dared to hope. "It is truth, is it not?"

No. Her hands closed around the heart. The heart the Sisters had entrusted to them. To him. The ifrits' clawed hands dug into his skin.

"Aya, please," Altair begged. She ignored him, tongue between her teeth in concentration.

And there was a moment like a sigh when the pulsing organ was fitted into place.

Altair's sob was soundless. The Lion's chest rose and fell rapidly as he struggled to acclimate. Aya's hands were steeped in red and black, magic aiding her along, connecting arteries and valves with sickening precision.

But she was not yet finished.

And Altair was not yet dead.

He emptied his mind, wiped away the pain, and collected what remained of his strength. But even if he could break free, he had no access to a weapon. He couldn't blast her with a beam of light because of the daama shackles. He couldn't stab her with a scalpel, too far out of reach.

No—he would wring her neck with his bare hands.

He wrenched forward and fell to his knees with a force that rattled his teeth. The ifrit chittered. The Lion's eyes flashed. Aya pressed the back of a bloody hand to her mouth at the sudden ruckus.

"Aya, my sweet," the Lion prodded gently, an edge to his voice, "finish what you've started."

A crackling stave came rushing for Altair's stomach. He twisted away, slamming the weight of his shackle into the ifrit's chest. A second stave rammed into the wall behind Altair's head, and he wrapped his fingers around a scrawny throat until the ifrit ran away shrieking.

The other two ifrit dug their claws into his arm, drawing blood, and Altair yanked them off with a hiss, needing an extra moment to orient his one-eyed self. *Forget Aya.* The Lion was supine on the bedroll. He lunged, stumbling back from a sudden blast of shadow.

Magic.

The Lion's sigh was a sated sound. Beneath Aya's sure fingers, his skin knitted itself back together again, beads of black blood streaking his golden skin.

"Such zeal, Altair," he rasped. "Did you really presume I would lie here without precaution?"

Altair didn't waste time with a retort. He scrambled toward Aya, prepared to pull her away, when terror froze him in place.

Blood poured from her mouth. She coughed, looking at the spray of blood in her hand in dismay. The scalpel was lodged just beneath her breast, the Lion releasing it from his grip.

"The irony," he said with a soft laugh. And then he stood, swaying as his newfound power countered the loss of blood. "What was it that Benyamin used to say?"

The price of dum sihr is always great.

Aya fell into Altair's arms with a surprised *oof.* How many times had she lain just like this?

She lifted red fingers to his face. Her pink abaya was drenched in blood, both hers and the Lion's. "Did I do well, sadiqi?"

No, sweet Aya. Twisted Aya. Beloved Aya, who had ruined everything.

"Shh, don't speak." He was angry with her—so terribly angry—but the despondence was greater. "Heal it." His hand shook as he reached for hers, dragging her prone fingers to her breast. "Aya. Heal yourself."

She didn't move. "You must know." Her breath wavered. "I never stopped loving you. I tried, but the pain was too much."

He felt it then. That box in which he had stored every dark thing of his past swelling too heavy, too big for his soul. Pain rent the latches that kept it shut. It flooded him, tearing one single sob from his throat, hoarse and aching.

"An empty life is a fate worse than death," she whispered.

The words sank bitter and desolate before the light vanished from her eyes.

The Lion hummed softly.

"Chain him up," he commanded, and turned to leave as ifrit flooded the room.

Altair blearily wondered if he was next. *No.* He did not want death. He would not welcome it the way she had. He rose to his feet. He was Altair, son of none, gifted by the sun itself, and he would fight the throes of death before letting darkness triumph.

CHAPTER 51

NASIR HAD FORGOTTEN HOW IT FELT TO BE ON DIS-play like a prize goat at the butcher's. It had been years since the crown had last held a feast. Scores of eyes crowded upon the sultan, and Nasir caught each furtive glance as it slid his way with a bit more discretion.

Being the Prince of Death was akin to being the sun, he supposed. Hard to look at, but, rimaal, did everyone want to look.

"Luminaries of Arawiya," his father called, genial and welcoming. "Less than a fortnight ago, Arawiya was struck with change. The Arz retreated into the bowels of Sharr, history reshaped and remade in a single act. Magic was salvaged from the ruins of the dark island and transported across the Baransea with vigilance."

It was foolhardy, this feast. Unwise to trumpet magic's return when it *still hadn't returned*. There was much about his father Nasir could not understand, even more than what he hated.

But Ghameq was never rash or reckless.

"You may wish to know whom to thank for the impending return of magic, for vanquishing the Arz and uniting us after decades of separation. It was none other than my son: the Prince of Death."

Nasir's breath caught. Troubled murmurs meandered from person to person throughout the hall, fear stirring the expectant air. It was a title given to him by the people. A moniker never meant for official use. It wasn't a name to say in front of every ruling power in Arawiya.

Suspicion roiled like a storm at sea, and Ghameq rose as the doors at the far end swung open on weary hinges.

"Such a feat is deserving of a reward," he said warmly. "My greatest one yet."

Nasir met Zafira's eyes as panic flitted across her features. Two cloaked men of the Sultan's Guard stepped into the room. A third figure slumped between them, the rattle of chains branding him a prisoner.

Whispers thickened the air as the trio began a slow march to the dais.

The guards stopped with matching bows at the foot of the white steps as the prisoner rose to his full height and lifted his dark head.

And Nasir stared into the amber eyes of the Lion of the Night.

Ghameq's voice was thunder in his ears, unfamiliar. Velvet. Dark. "Are you pleased with my gift, Ibni?"

The Lion was adorned in finery, his turban the color of sunset. He was not dressed like a prisoner. He did not stand like a prisoner, despite the shackles at his wrists and the collar around his neck.

It wasn't defeat that stirred in the beastly depths of his eyes, but something else. As if he played a game Nasir still didn't understand.

Zafira shot to her feet.

A slow smile curved the Lion's face.

The chains disintegrated into smoke. *Shadows.* The guards morphed into the shapeless forms of ifrit and drew to his either side. Ghameq stared into nothing.

Like a puppet, cut loose from its strings.

"Human hearts are like glass," the Lion said softly, rising up the steps of the dais, each one bleeding into black as he passed. "Fragile, delicate little things."

The hall doors slammed shut, a vise of shadow barring them in place. Panicked shouts rang out, but not a single person moved, afraid of being the first to fall.

The Lion curled his fingers and Ghameq doubled over, gasping for air with the kingdom as witness. His vow was a snarl. "Delicacy fosters death."

The Sultan of Arawiya

staggered and

fell.

Nasir sprang forward. He dropped to the cushions and carefully lifted Ghameq's head into his lap. Pain crossed the sultan's features, but Nasir saw that his eyes were clear, soft, kind.

His father's.

Truly, wholly. Nasir didn't know how he hadn't noticed the falsity before.

"Ibni," the sultan whispered, lifting a trembling hand to Nasir's hair.

Distantly, chaos erupted.

"Forgive me."

The hall darkened.

"For the days that I lived to hurt you. For the days that you lived in suffering. Tell your mother—I think of her when the moon fills the sky. Always."

"No—" Nasir's voice cracked as a chilling cold swept to him, a presence as familiar as his own. *Death.*

Not now, he begged as others once begged of him. Wisps of black slipped from his fingers and wound around his father, clutching him as Nasir did. The medallion swung behind his closed eyes. Aya had been right. It had corrupted the sultan beyond return. He was a fool to have believed his father could survive without the Lion's crippling hold. To have believed his father could walk free after years of imprisonment.

"Every day, I saw you, and every day I wanted to tell you the same: I am proud of you. He would not let me tell you, but it is true. Now, and forever."

Nasir didn't care anymore. About approval, about pride. He didn't want any of it.

The shadows scattered.

"Baba," he wept, but as always, Nasir was too late.

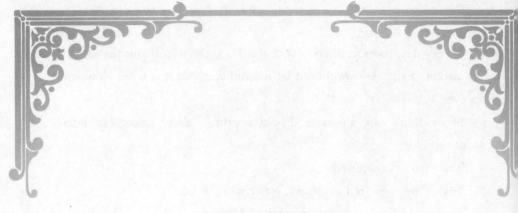

CHAPTER 52

THE STORM HAD ARRIVED, THE LION AT ITS CUSP.
Dressed in splendor like a king come for his throne, with every
single dignitary of Arawiya gathered like cows to slaughter.

Zafira should have known. The signs were there: When the sultan remembered one moment but strangely not another from the same event.
When he hadn't lent a hand or thought to finding the fifth heart. When he
had called his own son the Prince of Death.

The Lion had been controlling the sultan the entire time, playing them
like the fools that they were. The Sultan's Guard drew their swords and
surrounded the platform. Hashashins halted near the walls, and Zafira
knew there were ifrit lurking in the shadows. Both sides waited. The air
was heavier than her cloak had ever been.

Through it all, Nasir sat on the dais with his father's head in his lap.
Unmoving.

No—weeping.

A boy, orphaned years ago and suffering afresh. The new Sultan of Arawiya, on his knees before his own throne, a river of his sorrow drenching his finery. His brow fell to his father's with soundless anguish, and when the Lion turned to him with a frown, a warning throbbed in her limbs.

If she drew his attention, there was a chance he would direct whatever dark power he had at her and crush her heart with a flourish of his hand. *But the Jawarat*, a little voice reminded. He would still have need of it and its infinite knowledge. He wouldn't risk its destruction by hurting her.

Nasir, however, like his father, no longer had a purpose, and if she waited any longer, he would die.

"Haider."

In the split breath it took Zafira to push Lana away and say the Lion's name—his true name—every single member of the Sultan's Guard turned to her.

As did the Lion.

"Did you enjoy my theatrics, azizi?"

He spoke as if it were only the two of them in the vastness of the room. He looked at her as if she were his, his gaze hungrily roaming the length of her.

"My bladed compass, sheathed in starlight," he murmured. "Did you hope to compete for the prince's hand? To wear the crown of the sultana? I admit, that bit about brides was improvisation. To send your heart aflutter. You looked quite pale, if I recall."

At his feet, Nasir stirred from his wretched stupor.

"I have no interest in crowns," she bit out, her voice echoing in the hall.

"That remains to be seen, azizi," he promised, and crossed the final distance to the Gilded Throne, the golden light illuminating an odd pallor to his skin.

Lana whispered a sob, and Zafira knew how she felt, how everyone in this room felt, even the ancient safin. It was one thing to hear that the Lion of the Night was alive. It was quite another to see him in the flesh.

"It won't accept him," Kifah murmured with razor-edged hope, banking on a truth every child knew: *The Gilded Throne allows only the blood of the Sisters or the ones they've appointed.*

The room was charged with that very thought.

The thud of his footsteps echoed when he turned, and Zafira thought she caught a hint of fervent green from the folds of his robes, her stomach lurching for the barest of instances before her heart did the same as the Lion lowered himself onto the Gilded Throne.

Nothing happened—at first. The throne didn't repel him. It didn't thunder and throw him off.

Laa.

It *changed*. The gold became black, color draining from left to right, smoke curling like ashes on the wind. Kifah loosed a strangled breath.

The resulting silence was deafening, the death of an era, and the Lion's soft, triumphant sigh was a roar immortalized in history.

A silver-liveried guard stirred from the foot of the dais, the thick suspense in the hall slowing time as the fool dropped to his knees, awe hollowing his voice when he said, "Sultani."

The Lion frowned. "I never did like the word. The sultan is dead. This night, we abandon the old ways and bring forth the new: I am king. King of Arawiya."

And then he flourished a hand, his command like a knife.

"Kill them."

ACT II

VICTORIOUS UNTIL THE END

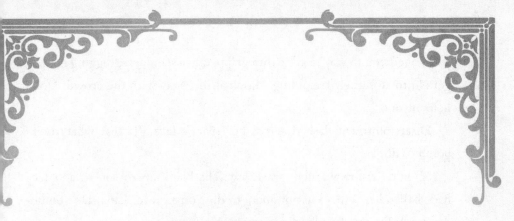

CHAPTER 53

THE ROOM ERUPTED IN CHAOS AS IFRIT PULLED AWAY from the shadows and every last person realized why the Lion had invited them, the governing heads of Arawiya. Zafira was a reed in a flood, helpless, *hopeless*, before she found her roots and stood her ground.

"The doors," she shouted over the din, and if her voice cracked, no one heard it. "We need to get them open."

Or not a single ruler would be left.

Kifah's features were frozen in shock. "Laa, *laa*. It shouldn't have— the throne—it—"

"Kifah," Zafira snapped, and the warrior recovered with a lamenting breath. She flicked open her spear, and with a few rapid nods, disappeared into the fray.

Ifrit clashed staves with guards, hashashins, and armed dignitary alike—all while the Lion reveled in the ruin of his own making.

"You need your bow," Lana said eagerly.

"I need you to stay safe." Zafira gripped her shoulders, digging her fingers in to stop their trembling. "Look at me. Stay with the crowd. Don't help anyone."

Disappointment flashed across her sister's face. "Is that what you're going to do?"

"Don't," Zafira warned, wavering. The blank horror on Kifah's face had shaken her will. "I'm not going to dig you a grave, Lana. Do you understand? Do this for me."

Lana finally appeased her with a nod.

A few cowardly guards braved the steps to swear loyalty, and Zafira seized the distraction. She leaped over the table and dropped to her knees in front of Nasir on the first step of the dais.

"We need to go," she said. "He will kill you."

"Let him." Desolation swallowed his already quiet voice.

She gritted her teeth. "Your father is dead. The Lion sits on *your* throne. Are you really going to abandon your people?" What was it he had said to her on Sharr? "Stop feeling sorry for yourself."

His laugh cracked. "How our fates have reversed, fair gazelle. I started to feel, and now I cannot stop."

With a gentleness she never thought him capable of, he lowered the sultan's head to the dais. He brushed his father's eyelids closed and tucked a feather into the folds of his robe, and she couldn't understand how something so gentle could hurt so terribly.

And then with a sudden wheeze he froze, his back arched.

"Why waste time mourning the dead when you can join them?" The Lion lounged in his black throne and twirled his finger, wrenching Nasir to face him, shadows crushing tight.

Zafira's hand twitched for an arrow, for her bow, but she had neither as Nasir was lifted off his feet.

"I could never understand why you hated me."

Zafira barely heard Nasir's voice over the din.

"So much that my father's every breath was spent ridiculing me."

The Lion tightened his bindings with a clench of his fist, Nasir's words striking true.

"Because I'm *exactly* like you: a monster breathing shadows." Nasir's voice dropped, the epithet near silent. "Yet she loved me."

The Silver Witch.

He threw down his hands and the chain splintered. The Lion rose and splayed his fingers. Zafira couldn't tell which wisp of black belonged to whom as Nasir lifted himself to his feet and threw his head back with a soundless roar.

The room fell to darkness.

Shadows rippled from his hands, flinging the Lion back. Control Zafira hadn't thought Nasir to have. The Lion slumped on the ill-claimed throne, and the ruckus doubled, panic striking anew. She didn't waste a heartbeat, remembering every sightless moment in the Arz as her eyes adjusted to the dark. She hurried up the stairs, one hand sliding to Nasir's jambiya at her leg.

"Zafira——" Nasir's voice was lost in someone's scream. "The doors. I don't——"

She didn't hear the rest, but she saw him turn, trusting her to follow.

The dagger fitted to her palm, the blade faint in the gloom. The anger and chaos she associated with the Jawarat's vision, a different version of herself, drove her. She would make up for that moment when she had fallen for the Lion's lies and lost what was hers.

A hand gripped her wrist and she cried out as the jambiya fell with a clatter. Cool amber eyes caught hers through the billowing shadows.

"I was hoping to see you, azizi."

She fought against him, shuddering when he wrenched her palm to his chest. The ice of his skin chilled her from beneath his embroidered thobe.

And something else. Horror and understanding locked her in place.

"It is something extraordinary, the pulse of life."

The si'lah heart. *Like a Sister of Old.*

The heart that belonged to creatures beyond safin, ifrit, and men. Creatures of *good.* This was why he was pale—from the loss of blood when his chest had been cut open. This was the cause of his newfound power in a land still without magic, from the shadows barring the door to the ones that had cinched Ghameq's heart. Why the Gilded Throne had accepted him, some twisted mutation cloaking it in black.

Aya had done this. Zafira knew it with the same striking certainty that she knew Aya was dead.

A deafening crash jolted them both, and she pried her wrist from his grip as one of the large windows ruptured with the sound of a thousand chimes. In that beat of distraction, she lunged, shoving her hands inside his robes and finding the Jawarat beneath the folds.

He lashed out. She fell back against the arm of the Gilded Throne with a cry, the Jawarat in her arms. Light flashed across the Lion of the Night's tattoo before the shadows rose, and Zafira was back on Sharr again, chains shackling her wrists. Only this time, Nasir wasn't here. Kifah, Benyamin. Lana.

Help—she needed help. She searched the floor for the jambiya, despite knowing Nasir's gift to her was but a child's thing in the face of the Lion's power. Through the riot of fear in her heart, she heard a voice.

We ached for you, bint Iskandar.

The Lion gripped her arm, wrenching her forward and grabbing the Jawarat.

We are here for you.

And then the world came undone with a roar of anguish that brought them both gasping to their knees.

Always.

CHAPTER 54

THE CRUEL SUN SCORCHES EVERYTHING IN BLINDING white light, but he does not blink. He does not look away. Every drop of blood is a knife to his chest. Each red splotch on the ground he feels keenly as if it were his own.

The stones strike again and again and again.

Pride lifts the chins of the safin. They wear white, but their hearts are made of black. Their ears are like his, pointed and sharp. A display of their immortality, heightened senses, and unnatural speed. They are special, their ears claim, and he is not.

He has no heart. He knows this, for there is no beat in his chest, but they see reason to remind him. Over and over and over. His body was shaped to hold a heart—like safin, like mortal men—but his ifrit blood birthed him without the pulsing mass of red.

As the blood quickens from erratic drops to a terrible trickle, he wonders: Does one need a heart to feel compassion? Is the rise of pride the downfall of mercy?

He is created of evil.

His darkness is a curse.

He deserves death.

Then why are they killing his father instead?

He is an anomaly. Too young to kill, too strange to be shown the light of day.

Ropes bind his father's wrists, locking him between two erected beams. The stones make sounds as they strike the ground, clattering like child's play.

"Stop," he pleads through the sobs in his throat, and someone kicks him into silence. His bag slides down his arm, skinny and bruised like the rest of him. Hollow cheeks, ribs he can count. This is what happens when hate puts stones in the hands of men. His books tumble out. His reed pens, new and sharp, snap beneath angry calfskin sandals.

The school is ten paces from him. It was built for safin scholars, a place his father had dreamed of sending him to ever since he'd been a boy with a tutor. He was to be a scholar, a man of 'ilm. It is the reason for this madness.

"Baba," he cries until he thinks he knows how a heart must beat. *Baba. Baba. Baba.* It drowns out his sobs. It drowns out their hurtful words. It drowns out his father's very, very last exhale.

Their cruelty turns his father's ocean-blue eyes glassy, unseeing. It makes his organs sputter and stop. Stop.

Stop.

What is mercy, if there is no one to give it?

What does it mean to be lenient, if there is no one who deserves it?

They ask, *What of the boy?*

Others say, *Leave him. Death takes what is owed.*

There is blissful silence then, for corpses do not speak. They cannot cry or feel pain. He picks up his broken pens. He slowly stacks his books and lifts the flap of his bag. It is new, sewn for his first day at this school.

It almost smells stronger than the blood, but not quite. He's never smelled blood before, but he will always remember this moment. The first time he inhaled the sweetness of spilled death.

Your mother would be proud, my lion.

His mother, who died gifting him to the world. His father, who died because his lion was not a gift but a curse. Ifrit are monsters, they say, not meant for union with pure-blooded safin. His mother was ifrit.

What are ifrit, if not another race? If not beings with homes and families and wishes of their own? They are his kin. And they have nothing, for the Sisters deemed them monsters and banished them to Sharr.

You are made from night, my lion, and no matter what my people say, you are one of us. Mightier than us.

What is he now? An orphan. A half-breed left to die.

Inside, he is ifrit: black blood, heartless. Outside, he is safin: peaked ears, heightened abilities.

Outside: He is tears and boyish fear. Inside: He is fire and he makes an oath. It is brash and angry, but he will keep it. Shadows pool in his palms.

He is a lion and he will claim the night as his own.

They will fear him.

CHAPTER 55

Z AFIRA LURCHED BACK INTO THE PRESENT, GASPING for air, teeth clattering from the force of her trembling. The turmoil continued around them, the same spear she had seen at midimpact only now impaling an ifrit. An arrow in the air only now landed true. As if barely heartbeats had passed.

The Lion was on his knees before the throne, his cloak sliding back from his shoulders. The high collar of his thobe was drenched in sweat.

Discarded to his side, like an unwanted pamphlet, was the Jawarat.

She froze when he lifted his head, but his gaze was dull. She'd seen it in the mirror: the look of a person who had shattered so many times that the pieces no longer fit together. All bruised edges and angles.

No child should have to watch their father die. No child should have to stomach the smell of their own father's blood.

What did it mean when a monster became human? Because it wasn't the Lion with his palms on the cold, hard stone. It was Haider, a boy who had witnessed the world's cruelty firsthand. A boy who had once been like her.

She carefully picked up the Jawarat.

We promised you protection, bint Iskandar. Look at him. Pathetic. Weak.

Rushing, roiling anger flooded her. Like when she realized Nasir still had his magic—anger that wasn't her own but felt every bit as if it were.

He is not pure. His will is too heavy, too fixed. He tried to control us, and now we will end him.

She picked up Nasir's jambiya—*her* jambiya—from beside Ghameq's lifeless form. The blade sang to her, coaxed her even as some distant part of her fought against it.

No, you fool. Steel is powerless. Use us.

She loosened her hold, remembering her failed arrow at the Lion's hideout. Remembering the Jawarat's vision, slicing men in two.

No. She fought back, sheathing her dagger. That was not her. *Not like this.*

Perhaps they were all monsters, masquerading in costumes of innocence.

For the first time since binding herself to the Jawarat, she finally understood what it had done. It had festered on Sharr long enough to sift through the Lion's memories, to record the ones it had deemed most important and poignant. Most raw. Only, it hadn't just recorded them.

It had stolen them.

It knew flesh and blood, sorrow and power. Somewhere on Sharr, it had become a being of its own.

Yes. We are of the hilya.

The Lion had wanted vengeance for centuries, but because of the Jawarat, he didn't remember *why*. He had no recollection of why he hated the safin. He didn't know why he wanted a home for his mother's kind. She was struck by the way he had frozen in her room when she had asked. He truly hadn't remembered.

Until now, *now* of all times. Now, with the inexorable power of the si'lah heart surging in his veins.

Her mind reeled with the fragments of his past, connecting one to another despite the chaos around her. *His will is too heavy*, the Jawarat had said. And by stealing his memory and stripping away the driving force of his vengeance, it had hoped he would lose his single-minded purpose, making him malleable, controllable.

It had not worked.

She shot down the stairs, belatedly thanking the seamstress for the slit down her dress, and crashed into a blood-streaked Kifah.

"Yalla, Huntress," she said, brisk as ever. "I thought we'd lost you."

"I have it," she said breathlessly, a chill on her skin despite the heat. "He—he has it."

Kifah eyed her. "Slow down."

"I have the Jawarat." Zafira held up the book with one hand. "He has the heart. Where's Lana?"

Kifah cleared three ifrit from their path as Zafira shoved the book between her thighs so she could knot her hair. "With Ghada and the Nine. They're fighting, but she'll be safest with them. What do you mean he has the heart? He's always had it."

"No." Zafira helped a man with a tasseled turban right himself, sucking in a breath at the wicked gashes across the back of his hand. "Nasir was right. The Lion—he found a way. He's taken control of the heart. It's *in* him."

Kifah fell when a guard knocked into her. She stood slowly, almost sluggish. "What?"

"The heart is inside him," Zafira stressed. His pulse echoed in her ears, her palm, her very soul. "He can use it the way the Sisters of Old could. The way the Silver Witch can."

"Bleeding Guljul," Kifah breathed. "That's—bleeding Guljul. Aya."

Zafira nodded, unable to form words. She remembered Lana describing the boy Aya had brought back to life. She didn't think any other healer would have been capable of implanting a beating heart into someone without one.

"Now we know why he never came for the other four." Kifah looked at her spear, as if suddenly deeming it useless. "We need to get out of here. I only know Ghada and her daughter are alive. I haven't seen the other leaders."

"Nasir?" Zafira asked. "Seif?"

"Haven't seen them. Hopefully protecting someone I'm not," she said, and turned back to the fray.

An arrow whistled past Zafira's ear, and then she was running toward the fool who had fired it. She ducked past an ifrit fighting an armed wazir, then a girl swinging a jambiya as if she had never held one before in her life.

The silver-cloaked guard nocked another arrow, his grip horribly wrong.

Zafira stopped him. "I need that."

He looked her up and down, sweat beading down his brow. "Move aside, woman."

She tossed him a fallen sword, and he dropped everything to grab it before it could nick his shoulder. *Dastard.* He started to protest, but Zafira snatched his bow and arrow and used her dagger to cut off his quiver's strap before ducking back into the crowd, heart pounding.

Well. Now she couldn't wear the quiver, either. Nor could she continue carrying the Jawarat around. She sorely needed more hands.

Crimson splattered at her feet, a reminder that there was more to worry about. Clamping the quiver between her legs and the Jawarat with it, she nocked an arrow and turned a careful circle, firing at an ifrit attacking a woman in an iridescent gown streaked in blood. Not a woman—a safi. Benyamin's sister, Leila.

Zafira slung her bow and slashed out with her dagger, gutting the ifrit the way she gutted her hunting kills. When she threw another glance at Leila, she was relieved to see Seif with his scythes by her side. The Alder calipha herself was nowhere to be seen. Zafira fired another arrow, and another, saving a silver-cloaked guard only for him to fall with a stave to his back a moment later. She never thought death to be so mundane. So normal.

There was always a chance the fruit one picked could be sour. The chance that the gift one gave might not fit. She had never thought the same applied to feasts and that she might *die* in one.

They needed to get the doors opened, or the Lion wouldn't only be king, he would rule supreme.

She fired her way to the doors, unflinching as blood drenched her clothes and her quiver ran low. Her gossamer sleeves like butterfly wings hung tattered. She spotted Ghada and several of the Nine Elite, Lana between them. Near the throne, the rest of the Nine and the Sultan's Guard kept the Lion's attention away from the vulnerable crowd. He was still dazed, she noticed, still lost in the memory of his father's death.

She drew back at a sudden hiss before a stave came hurtling for her neck. Like a fool, she lifted her hand to defend herself, dropping the Jawarat in the process, but the blow never came. The ifrit fell, and a hand extended toward her, a moonstone pommel catching in the light.

"Haytham," she sputtered before remembering her manners when she saw the wazir. She snatched up the book. "Sayyidi."

A gash across his brow oozed blood. His sword was coated in black, the hilt out of place amid the dead and dying. She swallowed a crazed laugh.

How much worse could this night become?

You just had to ask, said Yasmine in her head as death gripped the chamber.

CHAPTER 56

FOR YOU, BABA. SO MUCH OF WHAT NASIR HAD DONE was for him. One smile, one nod of approval. Now he was nothing but a grain of sand in the expanse of the desert. There in Nasir's palm for a fleeting moment and lost to the wind the next.

For Nasir, death was a subtle thing. He killed in the middle of a crowd, in a house full of the living. Blood was a whiff to catch before he was leaping out a window and into the open air. Anything flashy and loud and boisterous was Altair's specialty, even now, with Nasir's errant power and its wild eruptions.

So when the ebony doors exploded, wood hurtling through the hall, Nasir knew it wasn't the work of his angry, writhing shadows. No, this was the opposite.

It was the light to his dark, the day to his night; and he would recognize that powerful build anywhere. That figure, posed with dramatic flair in a flood of light, bringing the battle to a wrenching, startling halt.

Altair, who had turned his back on Nasir as Nasir had done to him on Sharr.

A tumult of emotions warred within him. Zafira stepped to his side, her hand brushing his in reassurance. Kifah paused at his left, and the three of them regarded Altair through a wary lens. Yet Nasir's heart betrayed him, and for the first time since this nightmare began, he found he could breathe.

"Akhh, did I miss the party?"

Nasir closed his eyes at the sound of Altair's voice, his *real* voice, so unlike the peculiar tone he'd adapted in the Lion's hideout. The light waned, and as the ifrit chittered among themselves, Nasir finally saw him.

Only a day had passed, but it might as well have been years. Altair's clothes were tattered and dirty, his wrists red and raw. A chain was wrapped around one fist, the end dangling.

Yet he stood as if he owned the land beneath his feet. As if there were a crown on his head and a procession in front of him.

Nasir pushed past a guard and froze.

"Sweet snow," Zafira whispered.

A dirty cloth swathed Altair's left eye. Streaks of red painted his face, as if he had wept blood. And Nasir saw in his one open eye what had not been there yesterday: Something in him had broken.

Altair, who loved the world and loved himself without humility.

"I told you," said Kifah, a sob in her throat. "I told you he wouldn't leave without just cause."

Nasir ignored the pulse of his gauntlet blades, for a hashashin did not react to emotion. The *Prince of Death* did not react to emotion.

From across the room, the Lion threw away the two red-clad Nine Elite and settled once more on the Gilded Throne. There was something new in his aristocratic features, an agony Nasir hadn't seen before. A torment.

The look of a man after a memory relived.

"Altair," he said in greeting, as if surprised to see him. "How nice of you to attend my coronation."

The rest of Altair's brilliant light faded to nothing, and the ifrit abandoned their panic, fiery staves slowly crackling to life. The zumra needed to tread carefully, Nasir knew.

He *knew* it, and yet.

Something propelled him forward. Zafira hissed. Kifah stepped into the cover of the crowd as ifrit surrounded him, weapons raised. All Nasir saw was Altair and those bloody streaks. This time, the Lion was pleased.

"Weeks ago, you were ready to plunge your blade through his throat," he mocked, though he lacked his usual certitude. "I merely moved mine a little farther north. Do you pity him?"

Pity was an insult to what Nasir felt. Rage. Pain. Bone-splintering grief and guilt for even *allowing* himself to believe that Altair had betrayed them.

Unless this, too, is a ruse.

No. If it was, he would rip Altair to shreds himself. Nasir was more than capable.

"Pity? The wound only adds to his daring character."

The words were out of Nasir's mouth before he could stop them. How Altair managed to goad and poke fun when in danger had once been beyond him. But now he saw how it worked. Altair's face broke into the grin Nasir had been waiting for, relief easing his features. As if Nasir, with a scar down his eye and dozens on his back, would judge him.

"I've taught you well, princeling," Altair called with a fake sniffle. Silence held, tension rising as the room readied for the next beat of chaos.

Among the shifting, flickering forms of the ifrit, Nasir met Zafira's gaze. Her fingers slowly curled around her bowstring, the Jawarat tucked under her arm, before she dipped a barely noticeable nod.

Altair, too, was as perceptive as ever. He looked at the dignitaries—wazirs, caliphs, officials, and their families—wide-eyed and bleeding, and slowly rewound his chain. "I know I'm quite the vision, but I didn't dash to your aid to be stared at. Yalla, Arawiya! Yalla!"

And despite the hesitation and suspicion breathing down Nasir's neck, it felt right. *Like old times.*

He threw up his sword. Zafira unleashed three arrows in succession, felling ifrit as Altair swung his chain around another's neck with an unseemly cackle that gave Nasir pause. A thud echoed behind him, succeeded by a gust of air from a twirling spear. *Kifah.*

Chaos had returned, a storm without reason. People screamed, charging toward the doors with ifrit at their heels, attacking without mercy. Men were fleeing, safin grasping vanity and failing in the face of death.

"Nasir." Zafira was hurrying to him, the green of the Jawarat serene in the chaos. She shoved it into his hands. "Keep this safe."

"Me?" he asked warily.

She lifted her hands, already nocking another arrow. "I'm wearing a dress."

He stared down at the book, wondering if he imagined it judging him, and shoved it securely into his robes. The Lion shouted orders. Nasir sank his gauntlet blade into one of the silver-cloaked idiots who had joined the wrong side and melted into the surge of people escaping the palace.

Until he was yanked by the collar to a small column of space between the doorway and the corridor.

"All that time away, and you're still shorter than me," Altair remarked from the shadows. "How was the performance? Do you think my baba was pleased?"

The blood on his face was even more gruesome up close. *Forget blood.* The realization sank in: He had lost an entire *eye.*

Movement drew Nasir's attention to a figure now clinging to Altair's neck—a child, dark-haired and starved. The Demenhune wazir's son. Rimaal, Nasir had completely forgotten about the boy they'd kept in the palace dungeons. Altair, on the other hand, had always been partial to children and their innocence.

"Was turning your back on us a performance, too?"

Or was it real? He couldn't bring himself to ask, not when he knew in his bones that it was not. It could never be. Altair did nothing without a reason.

"I could have killed you," Nasir growled when he didn't answer. Haytham's son ducked his face into the general's neck.

"What's one more attempt?" Altair said.

There was an edge to his voice, a bitterness similar to the one Nasir had encountered in the Lion's hideout. Chaos continued to unfold, screams continued to flay his sanity, and yet Nasir didn't move.

He owed Altair an explanation.

"We didn't want to leave you. On Sharr. By the time we realized you weren't on board, we had already weighed anchor," he said. "And we couldn't risk losing the other hearts."

He withheld the full truth. He couldn't let their mother take the blame.

Altair considered him. If he read between the lines, he said nothing of it. "Just know that had I been in your shoes, I would have found a way to save both."

Nasir didn't doubt it. "That's why I deal in death."

"Only one of us could have the brains." Altair's eye closed and opened in what Nasir realized too late was a wink. He cursed himself when Altair looked away.

"Wink at me one more time, and you'll wish you never came back," Nasir said quickly, relieved when his brother sighed in his familiar mocking, exaggerated manner.

Nasir started for the crowd. Screams continued to split the air, shouts thickening.

"Wait."

He turned back. There was a dagger in Altair's hands, black from blade to hilt.

"Is that—" Nasir started.

"Black ore," Altair finished. "Why I turned back when you told me what had happened to our mother. It's the only way to stop the Lion, and . . ."

"And?" Nasir prompted.

Altair gave him a thin smile, a beat of reluctance in his stance. "End him, of course."

Nasir didn't think. Only reached for the hilt, looking up when Altair pulled it away.

"Always so eager," he taunted. "We would be fools to face him now. Our efforts are better placed protecting the others."

"He's used far too much magic for a dose of dum sihr," Nasir said with a frown. By all counts, the Lion would be winding down from a peak, needing to slit his palm and draw blood again.

"If only, brother. He's armed with the si'lah heart. It's inside him, as one with his body as it once was within the Sisters of Old."

Inside him. As a heart was inside his mother, pumping magic into her blood. As half of his heart, and half of Altair's. It was exactly as he'd feared but hadn't had the words to express.

"I tried," Altair said softly. The ground trembled and an earsplitting shriek made them both flinch. "We have to go. Let's join the masses, shall we?"

He sheathed the dagger and gripped the boy's arms, entering the fray with a quick "Yalla, habibi," over his shoulder.

No, Nasir would never admit to missing the oaf. And yet he still wasn't free of that moment yesterday when Altair had turned his back on him, because Nasir had lived a life wrought with deception. False smiles. Forged truths. Feigned love.

He stared as his half brother disappeared into the fleeing crowd, ignoring a swell of emotion when Altair turned back, noting Nasir's absence with a furrowed brow followed by a jerk of his head. *Yalla.*

Nasir set his jaw. He had nothing left to lose.

He waited while the last of the people staggered out of the hall, one of them falling with a stave to his back, twitching and gasping until Nasir slit his throat to end his suffering. He stepped to the broken doorway of the banquet hall as the cold hand of death combed the growing silence.

Several high-ranking officials were soaked in crimson. The Zaramese wazir lay on her back, a stave through her heart. The Alder calipha's pretentious abaya was now her death mantle. Loss stirred in his veins. Benyamin's mother, the safi he had once believed to be his aunt. Gone. Immortality was a sham in the face of deliberate death.

Power once rested in their hands, wealth adorned every angle of their sight. None of them remembered the shroud has no pockets.

Nasir stopped just before turning away, stomach dropping at the sight of russet threads catching the light. Muzaffar. The merchant who would have turned Sarasin's future.

His eyes were unseeing, his short beard doused in blood.

It was Nasir's fault for mentioning the man to his father, for thinking it was truly Ghameq taking heed of his words and not the Lion, waiting to destroy his every hope.

Across the newly minted graveyard, Nasir's eyes connected with the false king of Arawiya.

His father's murderer. His mother's ruination. The Lion had done it all with cunning and manipulation alone. What chance did they have now that magic was his, limitless and unchecked?

If the Lion was ruffled by Altair's entrance, he hid it well—something else haunted his gaze. Yet he smiled as a horde of ifrit gathered to him. "See to our guests, my kin."

One by one, they leaped to the open window and spilled into the night.

CHAPTER 57

BEING RICH AND DISTINGUISHED MADE NO DIFFER-
ence when people screamed. The endless corridors shrank, stifling
and suffocating. The lit archways leading to the blue-black night
were pinpricks in the distance, too far to offer any comfort as the stench of
blood lifted bile to Zafira's throat, sweat a sheen on her skin. She found
Lana and tore her away from the Pelusians, her hand clammy in hers.

"Okhti?" Lana spoke loudly.

Skies, she was growing faint. *Too many people. Too many smells.*

"Breathe. We're almost out."

She nearly tripped on the sandals of the man in front of her and gave
up, but at last they stumbled outside and Zafira doubled over, gulping
down fresh air.

"Khara!" Lana yelped.

Zafira barely had the mind to reprimand her when she saw the dead
body at her feet lit by the sconces along the wall enclosing the entirety of
the courtyard. She snatched the man's quiver and drew Lana to her side.

"I'm afraid the worst isn't over yet," Kifah said, joining them. Zafira followed her gaze to the hall window, where the chandelier swayed as ghosts of the dead snuffed out wick after oil wick. The gilded window frame outlined the dark forms of ifrit awaiting a command.

"Whoever broke that window needs to die," Zafira groaned. She nocked an arrow into her bow. The arrows of the rich were less amenable than those of the poor, but how could she complain?

"That would be me," said Kifah sheepishly. "Bleeding Guljul."

Ifrit spilled into the courtyard. Zafira and Kifah put Lana behind them.

"What were you thinking?" Zafira shouted as shrieks filled the air.

"I thought we could climb our way out, but no one wanted to hitch their robes. Not even the daama men," Kifah replied.

On the sandy stone of the courtyard, the ifrit billowed and wavered, too strange to look at too closely. Zafira remembered when, on Sharr, they had taken Yasmine's form, then Baba's, then Umm's. She couldn't decide which was worse, but she knew with utmost certainty that she was tired and weary and ready to lie down and take a nap. She wasn't battle-hardened like the others. She was a hunter who gutted an animal and called it a day.

But what did the world care if one was ready for it or not? She took her place beside Kifah. Slowly, the rest of the Nine Elite did the same, hashashin and silver-liveried guards joining them. Even Lana picked up a sword.

As the first ifrit began racing toward them, she comforted herself with the thought that though she might not be ready for the world, though she might die this night, at least she wasn't alone.

In moments, the courtyard fell to turmoil. The gates had yet to be unlocked, and panic built a suffocating dome around them. She paused with every shot, ensuring the arrow she fired was spiraling not toward a human, but an ifrit. A tedious task, for some of the wily soldiers shifted into men only to come up behind the susceptible and slit their throats.

Kifah cursed, and Zafira whirled to her. "Ghada. I have to——"

"Go," Zafira said after a beat, and though she herself had said the word, it felt like a betrayal when Kifah rushed to her calipha and the Nine Elite. Zafira watched her leave, surprised to see Ghada herself battling ifrit with not one but *two* spears in her hands.

Then the ifrit disappeared.

All around her, people straightened in disbelief. A little ways away, Nasir rose from a crouch and Altair went perfectly still, a young boy at his side. A tremor shook the ground, loose stones rattling. Another tremor followed, and a third, almost like——

Footsteps.

"Okhti . . . ," Lana dragged out, fear high in her voice.

An unseen hand doused the sconces, leaving only the light of the shrouded moon. But it was enough to allow them to make out the towering form of a creature, winged and beastly. Made of the same shadows as the ifrit.

"What——" Zafira's croak died in her throat.

"Elder ifrit," someone nearby said. She caught a flash of a tattoo. A High Circle safi. "Far more difficult to command, likely why the Lion never summoned any before."

The elder shrieked, loud enough to awaken every soul in Arawiya, and took to the air. It landed in the center of the battle, crushing a hashashin beneath its claws. A horrific stench tainted the air, dank and acrid, like burnt flesh.

It lashed out, toppling people who were too slow to leap out of the way. Moonlight flashed on the black steel of its claws, and Zafira shoved Lana away. She looked back at her sister but shouldn't have.

She should have trusted Lana to stay safe.

An ifrit flung Zafira to the ground, stave poised to impale. Lana screamed, and terror gripped Zafira in a fist. She threw off the ifrit with a kick of her legs and rolled away from the lash of a stave.

She was on her knees when a shadow slanted over her, stretched by the moonlight. It was followed by a second, a third, and a fourth. Ifrit surrounded her. She turned and rose with careful stillness. Through her peripheral vision, she saw Lana too far away. She saw Kifah racing toward her, and dared to hope before a scream made the warrior look back to the Nine Elite.

Zafira understood with a sinking, resigned certainty. This was the moment in which their allyship had come to an end. This moment, when Kifah had to choose.

We hunt the flame, Kifah had said. They had hunted the light, found the good trapped in the stars tethered to the shadows. Who was to free them if the zumra was no longer together?

We are. Together or not, they fought the same battle. For Baba, for Deen, for Benyamin, for the sultan who once was. Zafira tightened her grip and stared at her foe. She remembered her oath: to die fighting. She remembered Umm's words. *Be as victorious as the name I have given you.*

"Victorious until the end," she whispered, and unleashed her arrow, knowing it was her last.

CHAPTER 58

THERE WERE MOMENTS BEFORE MOMENTS, IN WHICH the world was framed in startling clarity, a defined *before* hurtling toward a horrible *after*. Moments in which the powerful were powerless, in which promises became failings.

This was such a moment.

Nasir did not think Zafira saw Kifah running toward her after the briefest hesitation, or she would have waited before firing her last arrow. No—she had acted in defeat. She had opened her arms to the embrace of death, armed for one last fight.

He saw the arrow impale her chest. Heard the horrible rasp of her breath.

And his

soul rent

in half.

A shattering so great, he could not breathe for an eternal moment. It was then that he knew his soul had found its match. Bright, burning, *gone*.

Some word tore from him, foreign in its loudness, as if sound itself could stop and reverse time. He shoved people out of his path. The massive elder ifrit readied for another attack, and someone gripped Nasir by his middle and held him back. Forcing him to watch when he should have been there. To hold her. To stop them. To save her. He would give her his lungs if it meant she would breathe for him again.

What was the point of a throne and a crown and the power it wrought, if he was powerless?

"Let me go," he shouted as the elder impaled the ground where Nasir almost stood. The force of it made something slip from his robes and fracture, pieces scattering across the stone. He snatched up as much of it as he could. The compass, silver and crimson. That small, insignificant trinket that had led him to her time and time again, gone. Like her.

"No," Altair growled in his ear. Would that something as impossible as a mirage had become true, and still lay out of reach. "I'm not going to lose you both."

Fair gazelle. Please don't go.

"Please," he whispered and begged. His compass. His queen. His life. "Don't go."

But death listened to no one, not even the Amir al-Maut. And Nasir watched as her butterfly wings fluttered once, and Zafira Iskandar fell to the ground, a silver star driving the light from his world.

His yesterdays and his tomorrows, gone just like that.

CHAPTER 59

To LIVE WAS TO SWEAR THE OATH OF DEATH.
A cup from which every soul was destined to drink. So why,
then, did it feel like she had been cheated? As if she had gambled
away something precious?

The stone was hard. Her lungs dragged breath after stubborn breath.
The arrow shaft protruded from her chest and she laughed bitterly at the
irony. Dizziness rolled through her with a flood of pain, but she felt the
cold embrace of death, a stillness in the chaos.

She would never apologize to Yasmine for failing her brother. Never
again kiss Lana's cheek. Never see a world of magic. Her last moments
were recorded in a series of blinks:

Kifah. Her bald head shining with the moon's glow.

Blink.

The elder. Shrieking as it tore through Arawiya's greats.

Blink.

The sky. Its endless stars glittering with prospect.

Then a sound: the broken voice of a sad, sad prince. A king, unthroned. It filled her with an ache worse than the arrow. She should have said the words when she had the chance, because she meant them. With every last fiber of her bleeding soul.

Her world went dark.

CHAPTER 60

THE WORLD BLED BLACK AND WHITE AND BEREFT OF color, the possibility of forever halved in a single strike. The elder roared, shadowy wings rising into the night. Perhaps it was Nasir's sudden stillness or the telltale drop of his breathing, but Altair knew to release him and take a careful step back. Pain and anguish stirred into anger. His blades thrummed at his wrists, and the sounds of the battle faded.

He pulled the Jawarat from his robes and pressed it into Altair's hands.

"Protect it," he rasped, and sprinted forward, snatching a broken sword as he went. His vision blurred as he arced his blade across an ifrit and shoved a hashashin out of another's path, for in this moment, they were allies still sworn to Ghameq.

Nasir swiped the dampness from his face, and when the elder swept its talons, he leaped atop its arm, charting his upward path. It shrieked in panic, flinging its hand. Nasir launched toward its head, narrowly missing another lash of its claws before he grabbed one of its horns. The elder teetered off balance. Nasir swung toward the second horn with a grit of his teeth, wrenching himself between them.

People screamed far below as Altair unlocked the courtyard gates. The Great Library windows flashed like dandan teeth in the moonlight, glancing off Nasir's blade as he plunged it into the elder's skull, a spray of blood coating his clothes, his hair, his face. The beast swayed. Nasir drove the sword into it again and again, and with one last howl, the elder collapsed in a heap.

The silence made him want to weep.

Nasir stepped from the creature's head and dropped the sword with a clatter. A score of people stared. He did not need the sun to read their faces, to understand the troubled looks and the fear widening their eyes.

He had been the Amir al-Maut until she had come and torn the monster to shreds with sharp words and coy glimpses. It was only fitting that the Prince of Death had returned, now that she had been taken from him.

He'd had enough. He would let the Lion do as he willed. He would take her, bury her, and—

Seif stopped him. "He will not cease until every last one of us is dead. We must leave."

"And let him have the throne?" an official from one caliphate or another asked. "Your kind has always left us to suffer."

Seif turned, his scythes quick as snake tongues as he sliced an ifrit in three.

"I'm not in the mood, mortal. Confront him yourself if you wish. Die, if you'd like."

The official blustered before catching sight of Nasir and deciding his chances of persuasion were slim. He stormed off in anger.

Altair jogged to them. "Yes, good, great talk," he said with false cheer, tugging on Nasir's sleeve. His stare was fixed at the open window, where another wave of ifrit gathered. Lana, Kifah, and the rest of the

Nine were nowhere to be seen. "I love words, don't you? Let's share some later. Now, yalla."

"Front courtyard. Horses. Meet me at the Asfar trading house," Seif shouted, sprinting back toward the palace.

"I can't leave her," Nasir said, stopping inside the gates. "Not like this."

Altair dropped a hand to his shoulder, and Nasir took a fortifying breath when his gauntlet blades hummed. "Some honors must be forfeited so we may fight another day. If anyone can understand that, it would be Zafira." He worked his jaw. "And Benyamin. I will never forgive myself for leaving him there, but we had no choice. That throne is yours by right, and I need you alive to put you on it."

The horde thickened, and the crowds continued to thin as people either fled or fell. A fire rippled to life, casting the dead in orange. He was neither soldier nor general, but even he could see that this battle would not be won. As long as people remained in the courtyard, the ifrit would attack, but the Lion was no fool: He wouldn't harm anyone beyond these gates. Not yet.

Nasir dropped his shoulders. He left behind half of his soul and the whole of his heart.

<hr />

The horses were glad to flee the Lion's dark kin. The dappled coat of Nasir's steed glowed in the moonlight, reminding him of silver silk. Fear tainted the city, rumors slipping from loose tongues even at this hour, but he and Altair paused for no one as they raced through the streets.

Nasir was numb and aware of nothing. Only his inhales that would never be matched with another's. Only his exhales that would stretch for the rest of his days.

Altair led the way to the Asfar trading house—a narrow building with a bronze gate, two camels idling just inside, a third asleep behind the low swaying shrubs. Nasir dismounted with a wave of exhaustion. A gentle breeze looped through the blue-black sky, slipping beneath the hair brushing his neck. Moments ticked by with his heartbeat, each one playing out Zafira's death afresh. They'd been in such a hurry before, every instant leading to something else—the medallion, the feast, Altair.

Time had no meaning anymore.

Haytham's son approached as if Nasir were a wild animal and said, "Shukrun."

Nasir stared back.

He hated him, this innocent boy of eight. He hated his pale skin, hated his lilting accent. Hated that he still had a father. Anguish tore from Nasir's mouth.

She was gone.

Altair gently led the boy to the camels with a murmur. When he returned, he couldn't mask his pity quickly enough, and anger flooded Nasir's veins, sudden and blinding. He shoved Altair against the wall, gripping fistfuls of his tattered shirt.

"This is all your fault." His voice was breathless, raw. He was losing his mind.

Altair didn't fight back. "What could I have done to stop it?"

Nasir clenched his jaw at Altair's gentle tone. As if he were a child.

"Tell me, Nasir. Beat me, if you must. Tear me to shreds, if it will ease your suffering."

"You could have used your light. Destroyed them the way you blasted the doors. You could have—"

He dropped his hand with a sob, and Altair pulled him to his chest. Nasir stiffened at the first semblance of an embrace he hadn't had in years. Then he dropped his brow to Altair's shoulder.

They stood like that as Nasir's vision wavered. As his father lay on the cold hard tile near the throne he had never truly ruled from. As his fair gazelle lay beneath the moon, an arrow through her heart.

"I thought I could earn his trust. Hinder him in some way," Altair said softly. "I swallowed bile as I indulged him, as I searched for anything that could bring him down. I thought for certain I'd gained an upper hand when you told me of the black dagger, but then Aya took his hand. I lost a daama eye. I was shackled. Drained of power as they used my blood."

Nasir focused on the rumble of his words through his chest.

"Just standing upright requires more effort than I can summon. It was chance that broke the doors, not me. I tried, habibi. I did. You are not the only one who loves her."

Loved, Nasir corrected in his head. Words so recklessly thrown in the present were now rooted in the past.

"Ghameq?" Altair ventured.

Nasir couldn't answer, not without the frayed edges of his sanity unraveling, but Altair understood.

The general sighed. "May the remainder of his life be lived in yours."

Nasir pressed his lips together. Life, however much or little was left, would be long indeed.

"In any case, you must acknowledge the great blessing permitting you to remain by my side yet another day," Altair announced as the streets stirred with approaching horses. "There is no greater honor."

Nasir drew away, but his retort faded when Altair's face sobered.

"Do you understand, brother? You'll have me. No matter how thick the night, I will always be there to light your way."

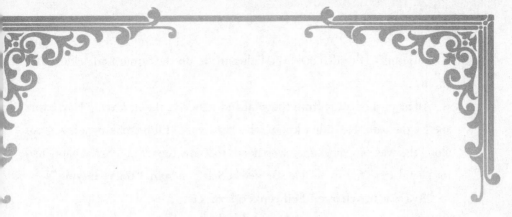

CHAPTER 61

WHEN THE SAND SETTLED, THE NIGHT FRAMED
two horses beneath the moon. Seif dismounted first, and
Altair knew he'd learned of Zafira when he saw pity in his
pale gaze. Pity never brought the dead back. It was an insult, plain and
simple, one Nasir noted with the barest of growls in the back of his throat.

The second rider dismounted, a safi as tall and thin as her late brother,
giving reason to why Seif hadn't joined him and Nasir in their escape.

"Leila," Altair greeted. Her abaya was far too scandalous for a funeral.
The angled neck plunged almost to her stomach, her pale skin contrasting
against the dark, glittering fabric. It was a sight he would have appreciated, had circumstances been different. Had her soft umber eyes, which
matched Benyamin's exactly, not been a sight too painful for this moment.

She nodded in return. Tears stained her cheeks. Blood dripped from
her dress—her mother's blood. He'd seen the Alder calipha on the floor,
an eternal lifeline cut short by hatred. A death as heinous as her son's.

"Head for Demenhur," Seif instructed. "Neither Sultan's Keep nor

Sarasin is safe. I've directed the Pelusians to do the same. Lana rides with them."

Altair pushed away from the wall and strode to them, leaving Haytham's son by the gate. He didn't know who Lana was. "I'll be making a few stops along the way. The gossamer web needs to know the truth of what happened in the palace. We can—" He stopped at Seif's chargin. "You're leaving."

"Aya was my charge," Seif replied hoarsely.

Of course.

"And now she's dead," Altair finished numbly, fighting the rage that threatened to spill. "Died making the Lion what he is."

"Why?"

The loathing behind that one word was so great, so unlike Nasir that both Altair and Seif turned to him fully in disbelief. He knew what the prince was thinking behind the flint of his eyes: It was Aya's fault that Zafira was gone. But if they started down that path, blaming one thing upon the next, there would be no end, no future.

"Some truths have no reason," Seif murmured.

"This one does," Altair said with force.

Leila spoke now. "After what she'd lost, you have no right—"

"We've all lost something," Altair bit out. No one knew how much he had once loved Aya. No one knew he was once the last to judge her. "Look at me. Look at him." He gestured to Nasir. "We have lost, and we have suffered. We did not fall prey to insanity and the Lion's lies. The difference, Leila, between Aya and us is that we do not give up."

The camels snorted in the silence, Haytham's son's soft murmurs lilting in the quiet. Seif's brow was creased, his pale eyes slit.

"He is right," he said finally.

"Thus, Benyamin died for nothing," Leila said softly.

Nasir looked away. Benyamin had died for the gray-eyed prince, for their future sultan, and for his brother.

To Altair, that was everything.

"He was valiant until the end," Altair said solemnly. "He spoke of you even in the throes of death."

She closed her eyes briefly, carmined lips soft. "I expected nothing less from a Haadi. Now I am all that remains of Arawiya's oldest family."

"Not much of Arawiya will be left to speak of if the Lion remains in power," Altair said as Haytham's son collected stones from the cool sand. "We need you with us. We need your aid. We need aid from Alderamin."

Leila's gaze flicked to the ground. "My people will not—"

"Your people," Altair repeated quietly. "Alderamin is home to only a *fifth* of your people. *Arawiya* is the land of your people. Leave this division by caliphate aside, Leila. We are one kingdom."

"I am not one of them, Altair," she said crisply. The gold filigree cuffing her elongated ears glinted mockingly.

He set his jaw, the loss of his eye a beacon. "Neither am I."

"What you decide to do with your immortal life sets no requirement upon ours."

Altair breathed a mirthless laugh, regarding her. It was taking some adjustment, only being able to see out of one eye. It meant turning his head and craning his neck far too much. "You were there for his first reign of darkness. You know what will happen. The darkness will spread from one caliphate to the next, and people will die. Even safin can starve." He met Leila's gaze, disappointed by her obstinacy. "Benyamin would—"

"Do not speak of what he would or would not have done," she demanded. "He is dead. My mother is dead. You need to understand that the title of Alder calipha will matter little when I ask my people to help you, for not one safi will feel particularly inclined to assist the mortals for whom my kin died."

The wind gusted toward them, grieving the night's lost souls. It was a horrible truth, but had Leila been more like her brother, she would have agreed: It was worth trying. Worth rallying them, begging them for aid. Altair turned to Seif.

"I will not abandon our cause, but I must return to Alderamin, too," Seif said. "After tonight's events, it is clear the Lion will seek the destruction of the remaining hearts. I must be there to protect the heart and the throne. The rest of the High Circle will do the same in the other caliphates. History stands to be rewritten, and if there is anyone who understands the merit of this opportunity, it is those of the Circle.

"We will remain vigilant, and upon magic's return, should you succeed, we will position restrictors to halt the flow of power until each caliphate gets their bearings."

Altair wasn't ready to think that far just yet. To worry over the common person being unable to control the affinity he or she wielded felt trivial after what had transpired. He lowered his brow, sensing he had no leeway here. No amount of persuasion would work. Safin were stubborn that way.

"May success ride in your favor, Seif bin Uqub," Altair said at last. "Shukrun for your efforts."

Besides, he hadn't come so far by relying on the halfhearted.

CHAPTER 62

CIVILIZATION FADED TO THE SWELL OF SAND DUNES lit blue, ghosts of the lost rising with the dust Altair's and Nasir's horses stirred in their wake. It was only after they crossed the border of Sultan's Keep and passed into Sarasin that Altair allowed himself to breathe freely for the first time since they'd fled the palace.

He had watched the life fade from a thousand men, but never had he lost so many friends in a single mission. Benyamin, Zafira. Aya.

Nasir studied him in a way he had never seen. It was how Benyamin once looked at him. It was how one looked at another that they knew as well as themselves.

"You loved her." His voice was quiet.

Altair's eye fell closed.

"I saw the way you spoke of her. Of us. Of loss," Nasir clarified.

"I loved him more."

"What does that mean?"

Altair's grip tightened around the reins as Haytham's son woke from his slumber. "It means that no matter what needs to be done to make the children of this forsaken kingdom smile again, I will do it."

Dawn gave way to morning, clinging to the edges of the earth as they pressed deeper into Sarasin, the towns silent and empty. As if fear ruled these streets, dread clogging the air.

"We'll cross the Dancali Mountains by nightfall," Altair said.

"And then home?" Haytham's son asked.

At least someone wanted to speak to him.

After a hearty silence filled with nothing but the clatter of hooves, Nasir looked to the distance. "The sooner we pass Sarasin, the better."

Though Sarasin was considerably brighter than it was when he and the Lion first arrived, it was still darker than the rest of the kingdom. They stuck to the main roads, avoiding the shadows where ifrit might be, sometimes splitting up, sometimes pausing to visit the house of a spider, always vigilant. It meant they were seen by more people than Altair liked, including a little girl with ice chips for eyes that reminded him of Zafira.

He had failed her. He had failed Nasir, who was burrowing into himself and shutting out the world once more, his already broken spirit slowly degenerating. He was only a boy the world had thieved endlessly, giving nothing back. Altair hadn't seen a single wisp of his shadows since their escape.

He was stifling his emotions again, caging his heart once more. Altair had spent years loathing the prince, but Sharr had changed more than the course of the future. Nasir stared at the remnants of the compass their mother had given him before this journey began, brushing his thumb across the fractured glass with the sorrow of a thousand lost souls. If someone had told him his brother was capable of such compassion, such tenderness, Altair would have laughed in their face.

"Aren't you going to ask me how I escaped?" The words were light, but he still felt the weight of the black shackles that had restricted him.

Nasir reluctantly eyed Altair's red wrists. "How did you escape?"

"Let it be known that I am not one to shy from the use of tongue," Altair said.

Nasir released a long breath, but at least the prince was focusing on something other than misery. They didn't have the might of Pelusia to quicken their pace; this would be a long journey.

"Do you have something to say, brother dearest?" Altair watched him struggle between the desire to ignore him and the need to retort.

The latter won. "No one wants to hear of the filthy things you do to get around."

"You, princeling, need to extract your dark little head from the trenches. I was referring to words. My impeccable sense of charm that transcends the likes of race."

Nasir ignored him, just like old times, but when did that ever stop Altair?

After Aya's death, the ifrit had come, spurred by the Lion's command. There were far too many for Altair to overpower in the state that he was in, and he knew it. He was too weak, too drained. Emotionally and physically.

So he'd held up his hands. The ifrit weren't mindless beasts, he knew. He avoided looking at Aya, an unceremonious heap on the floor like a discarded doll, and gestured to their fallen brethren, prone and unconscious. At least, he had hoped they were only knocked out and not dead.

"You see what happened to your friends?" Altair asked. They only blinked, but Altair didn't mind. He was adept at one-sided conversation. Anyone who tolerated Nasir had to be. Conversing with ifrit was as easy as kanafah.

"Don't think I won't do the same to you."

The ifrit paused to speak among themselves. If Altair made it out of this ordeal alive, he was going to learn their tongue. He blinked his working eye, vowing it now.

"Look at you, chittering and scrambling around to do his bidding without a second thought," Altair continued.

They considered him and his words, and four of them looked to the fifth, clearly the leader of the bunch.

Altair used that split-heartbeat of a distraction to lunge. He kicked down two ifrit and flung his arms, knocking two more to the floor with the weight of his shackles, buying him time when the fifth came for him with a stave lit aflame.

He *tsk*ed. "Baba never gave you permission to hurt me, did he?"

The ifrit arced the stave, uncaring or likely not understanding. Altair leaped out of the way, throwing up his arm when another stave came for his heart. It clanged against his right shackle before he wrapped his fingers around the ifrit's neck.

Footsteps echoed outside the door.

Altair punched down the last of them and snatched the discarded scalpel and whatever other tools might prove useful as weaponry, pausing only to close Aya's eyes before he crept into the hall.

And came face to face with Seif.

Altair wrenched the door closed on Aya's dead body.

"Bin Laa Shayy?" Seif asked, pale eyes flitting to his missing eye and away just as quickly. "What happened to you?"

Son of none. Altair almost laughed. *Akhh, do I have news for you, habibi.*

"Seif!" he exclaimed. "What are you doing here?"

"Of all the places I thought I'd see you, the dungeons beneath the palace were not among them." Seif was curt. "I came looking for——"

"I know. So nice of you to rush to my aid."

Seif regarded him stonily. "You didn't seem to be in need of rescuing when the Lion took Aya."

Altair stopped prying at the seams of the cursed shackles. "Did you believe it? Did you truly think I would turn my back on my kingdom after all I've done?"

Seif's scorn bled into his words. "What have you achieved? He stole Aya because——"

"Aya is dead," Altair snapped. "And everyone else will follow soon enough if we don't make haste. Now, stop scowling and help me get these off."

"She's dead?" Seif repeated numbly.

Altair ran his fingers along the black ore, trying to read the Safaitic engraved there. Trying to keep moving, because grief had a way of latching to the idle.

Seif only took one look at the shackles before he made quick work of them with his scythe and a few words. Altair stumbled when the ore fell away, revealing thick bands of red around his wrists.

"That's going to leave a mark," he mumbled before fire surged in his veins, threatening to erupt. He gripped the nearest surface and clenched his jaw to near cracking. His skin glowed, white light burning beneath like a torch. He would bring this place to the ground if he wasn't careful.

Wahid, ithnayn, thalatha, he counted beneath his breath.

"Shall we?" Seif asked, but Altair had turned back to the Lion's room, where he'd found what he needed, black and sharp, but hadn't had a chance to steal.

"I have to get something first."

———◆———

After nearly a week on the road, the Tenama Pass finally widened to Demenhur, with its sloping hills and ablaq masonry, the technique of alternating rows of light and dark stone never a style he had liked. Snow still doused the land in white and cold, but the air felt different. Less biting than what Altair remembered. It tasted like change. *Hope.*

Hope, he had learned, arrived swiftly, seeking to bloom in the darkest of places and in the most harrowing of times. That was what he felt in Demenhur.

"We're here," Haytham's son said softly, and fell against his chest with a small tremor, the effect of a soldier come home. A gust of wind came at

Altair's back, and he was reminded once more of his twin scimitars, their phantom weights heavier than the blades themselves had ever been.

May you find hands as caring as mine, Farhan and Fath. He had overseen their forging, slipped the smith extra dinars so the man would carve *bin Laa Shayy* right above the hilts. He wasn't just the son of none, he was a *proud* one.

Farhan and Fath had been with him through the thickest of battles. Farhan had won him a much-needed victory against the Demenhune army. Fath fitted well in a sharp-tongued huntress's hands when she—

Sultan's teeth.

As he ducked beneath the thick clustered branches of a lifeless tree, Altair threw open his satchel's flap with a curse. He pulled out the Jawarat, bound in green leather and embossed with the head of a lion. In its center was a hole, the result of a dire injury to the one it was bound to, and if Altair were mad and a fool for hope, he would say the tome was gasping for air.

Fighting for breath as it knitted itself together, right before his eyes— *eye*. Altair sighed.

That would take some getting used to.

CHAPTER 63

DEATH WASN'T SUPPOSED TO BE SO PAINFUL. LAA, it was supposed to be an end.

At least, that was how corpses made it seem. Yet Zafira wavered in pain even while she lay on her back, something sharp stinging her nose despite the warmth in the air. It reminded her of Demenhur, and how the cold never really left no matter how loud the fire crackled.

The only things missing were Baba and Umm and—

A string of curses echoed in her dead ears. Then: "If she doesn't wake up in the next two beats, I'm going to slap her."

Yasmine?

"I'm beginning to see why she keeps your company."

She recognized that dry tone, the lightning-quick string of words: Kifah. Skies, the dead *did* dream. How else were her two friends conversing with each other?

"Aside from my looks?"

Dream Kifah barked a laugh, and a door thudded closed. Zafira couldn't remember the last time a door had closed in one of her dreams. Perhaps the dead dreamed more vividly.

"I can see your eyeballs rolling around in there."

Zafira opened one wary eye and then the other, blinking back against the onslaught of light. Only in Demenhur was light so white, so blinding. Everywhere else it streamed gold, glittering with enchantment.

"I—I'm not dead?" Her voice was hoarse.

A face framed by hair like burnished bronze pressed close, half hooded by a blue shawl. Warm eyes lit with emotion and rimmed in kohl, rounded features cast in worry, beauty etched into every facet of her creamy skin. Zafira ducked her head, suddenly shy. Laa, *fear* prickled through her chest.

Because being daama dead was easier than facing Yasmine.

A sound between a sob and a laugh broke out of her friend. "You've always been a corpse walking. No one else could be so boring."

Zafira looked down at herself, stretched on a mat, and remembered the shaft of the arrow protruding from her chest. The surprise she felt, even as her body succumbed to pain. How was she alive? How was she in Demenhur? Every thought tangled with the last.

"What am I wearing?" she asked.

Strips of gauze had been wrapped from the right of her chest to the opposite crook of her neck. The muscles in her back were strangely knotted, making it hard to ease herself up, but her dress was a bright hue of yellow, taut across her shoulders and a good length too short. It was no wonder she felt cold.

"You were ready to die, so I thought you might as well go looking nice. It's mine. Khara, you're as ungrateful as ever. I cleaned you up and washed your stinking hair. Cleaned your filthy nails. I should have left you out to freeze. That would have served you right."

Zafira stared at her for a few breathless moments until she couldn't hold back her grin any longer, yearning and jubilation and happiness because her friend was *right there.*

And then Yasmine began to cry.

Zafira choked on her pain when Yasmine wrapped her into her arms. Orange blossom and spice flooded her numb senses.

Yasmine's sky-blue gown hugged her generous curves, accentuated her ample bosom. She looked regal. She had always *been* regal in a way that everyone in their village understood. She was the sun in the gloomiest of days. The joy in the despondence of death. Life as a royal suited her, even if she was only a guest in the palace and leagues away from the suffering of the western villages.

"Lana sent me a letter," Yasmine whispered, "and I came as fast as I could. You were—you were bloody and still, Zafira. So still. My heart stopped." Her voice was small and shaky. "I stayed with you. Even when they said it was hopeless, I stayed with you."

What was it Lana had learned from Aya? Only half of a sick man's life was owed to a healer, the other to hope.

Zafira didn't know when Aya had lost the ability to hope.

"If the archer had been even half as skilled as you are, you wouldn't have stood a chance. You're lucky you had Lana on the journey with you to stanch the bleeding and keep you alive until they got you here to the supplies she needed. She knitted you back together, commanding everyone like a little general. Poor thing collapsed from fatigue a little while ago."

Of course it was Lana. Zafira felt a swell of pride, until Yasmine pulled away and she caught sight of the familiar walls. The basin in the corner with its chipped edge. The mirror with its fissure that always stretched her eyes too far apart.

This wasn't the palace in Thalj. It was no palace at all—laa, it was a poor man's house.

It was her room. She was home.

"Why are we here?" she breathed.

"Apparently there was only one way to save you, and it was in your umm's cabinet."

Or in Alderamin, Zafira didn't say. Aya was bound to have tenfold of their mother's collection. *Ya, Ummi.* Before, Zafira had lived with the guilt of not seeing her. Now every glimpse filled her with an aching, numbing emptiness.

The reminder that she was an orphan was a wound opened afresh.

"It's strange being back, isn't it?" Yasmine asked, misinterpreting her silence. "Like wearing an old dress washed one too many times."

It was true. Now that Zafira had seen the palace's smooth walls and the sheen on its floors, she was painfully aware of her home's every blemish. The dark veins of rot creeping from the broken windowpane she never had enough coins to repair. The armoire with its doors that didn't sit right, cutting a shadowy gap that Lana refused to look at for fear of nightmares. The doorway that Baba would lean against as he wished his daughters good night.

Zafira cleared her closed throat. "Was it Kifah who brought me in?"

"If she's one of the Nine Elite, then yes. They brought you here in one of those fancy Pelusian carriages that travel unnaturally fast. She's the only one who stuck around, though."

"And the others," Zafira ventured. "Are they . . . are they here?"

"Others? It's just us. I left Thalj to come here as soon as Lana's missive arrived, and that was before Caliph Ayman returned from Sultan's Keep. So I don't know if he's alive."

No, not the old fool.

Altair, who had materialized in a halo of light to help them at the doomed feast after turning his back on them.

Seif, who wielded scythes like the silks of a dancer.

Nasir.

Nasir. Nasir.

Yasmine canted her head, her shawl sliding from her shoulder. "And here I thought I'd never see color on your cheeks. Are you all right?"

Zafira nodded meekly, unable to meet her eyes for more reasons than one.

"The snow's still here, if you're wondering." Yasmine looked at her hands.

No, Zafira hadn't been wondering. She was thinking of Deen now, which meant Yasmine was, too.

"It's falling less. The elders hope the change will be gradual, or the caliphate could flood."

Deen's name rolled to the edge of Zafira's tongue.

She lifted her eyes and met Yasmine's gaze that was every bit Deen's. Sorrow stirred her stomach.

"I know." Yasmine's voice was flat, the stiff line of her shoulders cutting. "I've known."

Zafira held still, trapped in a case made of glass. *How dare you feel sorry*, guilt demanded. How dare she, when it was her fault?

"I came back here," Yasmine began haltingly, "after you left. And I was . . . I was lost. I don't know what got into me, but I went to the Arz, because I missed you so daama much, and I saw it. It—*flashed* behind my eyes. As if I were suddenly elsewhere. I saw Deen jumping in front of an arrow, and the golden-haired demon who fired it."

Zafira's brows knitted. The Arz didn't present its visitors with visions—it fueled their affinities, which meant Yasmine was a seer. If magic was restored, Yasmine would be able to see snippets of the future.

The revelation made Zafira inhale deep, and she flinched at the sharp sting in her breast. At the change in the room. The charge that hadn't been there before. She had expected it, but she had not anticipated the amount of pain that would thrive upon it.

"I'm sorry," Zafira whispered, and the chain around her neck heavied into a noose. "I'm sorry I didn't love him enough. I'm sorry he died so I could live."

I'm sorry, I'm sorry, I'm sorry. Sorry. Who could have created a word so callous, so insignificant?

"I would never have let him marry you. You know that, right? If your hearts don't beat the same, what does it matter?" Yasmine's mouth was askance and razor-sharp, her tone dripping poison.

Zafira held her breath, waiting for the lash.

"That didn't mean you had to kill him."

Zafira stared at her. Her friend, the sister of her heart. It took every last drop of her will to hold her features still and stoic, to keep from falling to pieces. Wars could wage and swords could cut and arrows could pierce. None of them compared to the pain of a well-poised word.

"A murderer," Zafira said, void of emotion, surprised to learn her heart could indeed suffer more. "You're calling me a murderer. This is a new low, Yasmine, even for you."

Yasmine crumpled in pain, and that was somehow worse. Because it meant she knew it wasn't true, but she was hurting and wanted Zafira to feel the same.

Couldn't she see that Zafira did? She relived his death when the light bled gold across the desert, when a stranger on the street smiled without malice, when she passed stalls of colorful fruit.

"I didn't *take* him," Zafira said, her voice careful and slow and—sweet snow, she sounded like Nasir. It was easier than screaming, pretending she felt nothing. It was easier to ignore the burn of tears, the guilt she felt guilty to feel. "I didn't even *ask* him. He stood on his own two legs and decided according to his own daama conscience, and if you expected me to be his caretaker, you should have given me a wage."

Yasmine was aghast. "And now you have the gall to mock him. To mock me and my pain."

"Your pain," Zafira repeated. "*Your pain.* He was your brother by blood, but he was mine by choice. Did you think I was *happy* when he died? Do you think I'm happy now? My best friend is dead. My parents are dead. My life as I knew it is gone."

"Are you listening to yourself?" Yasmine asked, voice rising. She threw the pillow aside and stood. "All I hear is *me, me, me.*"

"As if you didn't marry and leave us both," Zafira scoffed, heat rising to her face. Anger clouded her head and made her speak so uselessly.

"He didn't die for me," Yasmine enunciated. "He died for you."

"And I wish he hadn't, Yasmine! I lived five years of my life with the guilt of Baba's death. Don't think I'm a stranger to any of this. Altair——"

"Don't," Yasmine bit out. "Do not speak that name in my presence. I know it's his. Misk told me enough to let me connect the daama dots."

Zafira had hated him, once, because of the *notion* that he had killed Deen. But when she learned that it was true, she'd felt sad instead. When he'd turned away from them at the Lion's hideout, she'd believed it with a sinking, drowning certainty, but when he'd come to their aid later, his face streaked red, wrists raw and chafed, she'd felt remorse and contrition.

She loved him in the way she loved Kifah, and she could not fault herself for it.

"He is my friend," Zafira whispered. Not the way Yasmine was, not the way Deen had been, but enough that her heart could not summon hate, not anymore. "And I will say Altair's name as I see fit."

Yasmine whirled, but Zafira beat her to it, clenching her jaw against the sting of her wound as she rose to her feet and threw open the door, slamming it in Yasmine's face.

Kifah lifted her brows from the hall, where she would have heard every last word. "Already bustling about, I see. It's good to have you back."

She tipped her head toward the other room, Umm's room, and Zafira found Lana asleep inside, beneath a mound of blankets, the soft pink one Yasmine had gifted Umm tucked beneath her chin.

"Zafira?"

She paused. Kifah never called her by her name.

"I am bound by duty to the Nine Elite, but I am bound to you by honor. Did you think I'd forget you saved my life?"

The events of Sharr seemed far and foreign, a story rooted in the past, an adventure that seemed less wrought in danger than the reality they faced now. *Zafira* had forgotten it. Or she would have thought twice before firing her last arrow.

"My blade is yours. Until every last star is freed, we are bound."

Zafira warmed at the ferocity in Kifah's dark eyes, her promise a harsh line across her brow. "Does that make us friends?"

Kifah laughed. "A thousand times over."

And though Zafira would never forsake her friendship with Yasmine for anything in the world, even now, when she had flung as much pain as Yasmine had flung back, it was a relief to befriend someone as carefree as Kifah, as if her vengeance had encompassed her so deeply that nothing else was ever allowed to fester.

"What about the others?"

"You mean your prince," Kifah said smugly.

"I meant your general."

"Oi, I told you," Kifah protested, and Lana stirred at the bark of her laugh.

"That doesn't mean you don't love him."

"Laa, and that doesn't mean *you* don't love his grumpy brother."

It felt dangerous to let the words simmer without denying them. A refutation clambered up her throat, but she swallowed it back down. She hadn't almost died to live a life bereft of danger.

Kifah sombered quickly. "I see those bloody streaks on his face every time I blink. You know what's worse? My first thought at the sight of them was *What if it's a lie?*" She looked down. "I've never felt such shame."

Zafira pursed her lips. The two halves of herself were at war with each other. Half of her knew that Altair had dedicated decades to this cause. To Arawiya's restoration. He couldn't have climbed up the ranks to the sultan's right hand without an atrocity or ten. His every act was deliberate, done for the good of the kingdom. She knew this, and yet the other half of her was trapped trying to decipher *why* he had turned away when he'd had every opportunity to aid them.

"No word from anyone," Kifah continued. "Nor did I see either of them when we were escaping, only Seif, who told us to head for the palace in Thalj to recoup, though he didn't know you were alive. We had to detour here, and we're lucky we had Ghada's carriage to quicken our pace, but we'll circle back when you've recovered, and hope they're waiting for us."

The moments leading to Zafira's near death still echoed like a terrible dream, but standing in her old home with the ghosts of her life was somehow worse. The emptiness yawned, hungry and cold.

Kifah followed her to the foyer. "The Lion hasn't wasted any time. He dropped the taxes, and so the riots have stopped. There's even talk of a new caliph being appointed in Sarasin soon. It's only been four *daama* days."

Her words made it harder for Zafira to breathe, but they made sense, didn't they? The Lion had created those riots. He had raised taxes. He'd refused Sarasin a new caliph. All so he could take on the guise of being lenient when *he* became king.

She loosed a breath. Lana's stack of books sat on the majlis, the latest pamphlet of *al-Habib* at the very top. Baba's coat hung near the door, the hook beside it empty, and she felt her cloak's absence acutely. *Four days.* Zafira snatched a shawl and her boots.

"Where are you going?" Kifah asked.

"Outside," Zafira replied, not knowing it was worse.

CHAPTER 64

SARAAB, THEY HAD CALLED THE WESTERN VILLAGES OF Demenhur once. Before magic left and the snow infiltrated their lives. The old name translated to "mirage," for that was what the sparse villages were, a haven for stray bedouins or sailors on their way to the Baransea shore.

Zafira always found it strange that there were two meanings to the old name, the second being "phantom." As if whoever named the villages had known that it would one day become this.

A village of ghosts.

"Easy," Kifah called when Zafira stumbled down the steps leading from her house. Her voice echoed eerily in the emptiness.

A breeze wound through the dry limbs of the trees, welcoming Zafira—*accusing* her. For in all seventeen years that she had lived here, not once had ill befell them.

Until she left.

The cold was instant, a familiar sting in Zafira's nose and a crackling across her cheeks, a whisper of memories from the last time she had stood amid snow. Umm was alive. Yasmine was smiling. Deen was by her side. A hood had shrouded her head and a cloak had hidden her figure. There was an almost dizzying sensation inside her now. As if she were transitioning between two moments, past and present.

She had been two people then, but if she was being honest with herself, she was more Demenhune Hunter than anything else. A mystery to the people, an empty shell until she donned her cloak. Everything had been stripped away on Sharr, leaving nothing but that empty shell behind.

She was just Zafira.

"Oi, it's freezing. Do you want me to stay?" Kifah asked.

Zafira shook her head. "I just need to breathe."

"Right. But have a care, eh?" she said with a pointed glance at her chest.

Zafira waved her off.

Who was she now? What purpose did she serve in the world?

Change hung in the air, making the sun's rays a little bit different, and her steps faltered when she saw it.

The *nothing* in the distance.

No enticing shadows, no breathing black. A simple plain of snow cut into blue seas, a horizon bereft of the Arz. That darkness that had defined her. That had made her who she was.

Now she was an archer without a target. A girl without a home. A soul without a purpose.

Zafira turned and hurried away. The street leading to the sooq was white and empty, and her shawl did nothing to ward her shiver as the ghosts of her village spooled to her side, following her past one house, then a second. The third. *Ghosts don't exist*, Deen said in her head.

Ice scraped the bottoms of her boots, cold and relentless. Not even the downiness of snow had survived the massacre.

The buildings surrounding the sooq held a dark and maddening silence. This was the jumu'a where Yasmine's wedding had taken place, a moment that felt rooted in some long-ago past. How many times had Zafira stridden past the windows of Araby's sweet shop, annoyed at her people for smiling and laughing as the cold clouded their every exhale?

Now she missed it with a bone-deep sorrow. She could hear phantom laughter, the joyous shouts of children, the hustle and bustle of her people. If she walked three steps to her right, she would be able to make out the lavender door to Bakdash. A few steps to her left, and the thin baker's windows would stretch wide.

The wind moaned again, lamenting, lamenting.

"It's all my fault," she whispered, sinking to her knees on the gray jumu'a, snow drenching her clothes.

Footsteps crunched along the ice-speckled stone, and a weight lifted because she knew that gait, those whispering footfalls. She turned to meet Nasir's gaze, to find understanding, reason, *something*.

No one was there.

Shivers racked her body. She was cold, so, so cold.

Her life had fallen apart without even her to witness. These were the people her father had taught her to feed, to care for. They had died because they had breathed.

I'm sorry, Baba.

Resilience flowed through a woman's veins as fervently as her blood, Umm had always said. It was what held together the frayed edges of Zafira's sanity, but endurance, like all else, had its limits.

It was suddenly too much.

She curled into herself, clamping her mouth closed to stave her scream.

Pain flared from her wound. A cry tore from her lips, unleashing the dam that she'd kept patching and patching over the years, failing to notice as it overflowed. One tear became ten, and then she couldn't stop.

A small shadow fell over her.

"Okhti?"

"I did everything. Everything I could possibly do," Zafira gasped out. "Why? Why wasn't it enough?"

Lana pulled her to her chest, and somehow, the tears fell faster, harder. *She* was supposed to be the stronger one. The one to hold them together.

"The world has no right sitting on your shoulders, yet you've given it more than you will ever owe," Lana whispered. "You've done for it what a sultan would require a throne, a crown, and a thousand men to accomplish."

You are very much its concerned queen.

It felt decades ago that the Silver Witch had proclaimed those words. Zafira was queen of nothing now, an orphan in every manner.

"You can cry," Lana said gently. "It helps."

Zafira sputtered a laugh, and then Lana's face broke. She threw her arms around Zafira, forgetting all about the wound she had carefully bandaged.

"Yaa, Okhti. You were just . . . there. You wouldn't move, you barely *breathed.*"

"And yet you were as brave as I knew you'd be," Zafira said softly, shivering at her haunted tone. "If not for you, I would have been lost."

"But you're here now. You're here. And Ammah Aya was useful for something, at least. Have you eaten? We have no thyme," Lana blabbered as tears streamed down her cheeks and her breath clouded the air. "But Umm had dried pomegranate on hand. Can you believe it? Demenhur hasn't grown pomegranates in decades. They were so red. As red as your blood. And I—I—"

Lana's sobs were soft. She had always cried in silence. It was sadder somehow, as if her tears did not want to fall. To leave her. "I thought I'd lost you both. Don't do that again," she whispered. "I like the sound of your heart."

Zafira liked it, too, she realized, as the cold seeped through the knees of her pants. There was nothing like death to make one value life. "Never. You will always, *always* have me."

Her sister was still here and very much alive. Zafira herself still had breath in her lungs, and so long as the Lion sat on the throne, she would have purpose. So long as the Demenhune caliph railed against women, she would have purpose.

"Get dressed," Zafira said suddenly.

"Why?" Lana pulled back to look at her. "Oh no. I know that look. We're not going anywhere until you've recovered. Ah, you're bleeding again."

"I'll rest on the way." They needed to regroup with the others. "We need to get to the palace."

CHAPTER 65

THOUGH MUCH OF THE ROAD BETWEEN THE WESTERN villages and Thalj was rough, the journey to the capital took less than three days thanks to Calipha Ghada's carriage, with its sleek wheels and pulleys and other moving parts that quickened their pace in a way horses never could. But Zafira missed much of the scenery because her wound reopened, and Lana's drowsing tinctures had her weaving in and out of lucidity. It meant she missed much of Yasmine's scowling, too, but she wasn't quite as sorry about that.

The next thing she knew, she was propped against the carriage's cushioned wall as Lana fussed over her bandages, something fine and sharp impaling her skin. Her body was scalding, but the cold wasn't helping matters.

"I didn't get to see anything," Zafira groused groggily, awake enough to see that her words provoked a smile out of Yasmine, which she quickly masked away.

"I expected you to cry out," Lana said tiredly, setting a bloody needle aside.

Zafira's vision swam again. From a needle? "Do I look like a man?"

"You're bleeding. Khara, this is why I wanted you to stay back and rest."

"No cursing," Zafira scolded, and then she blacked out.

———◆———

A fire crackled in the hearth of the large room, white walls carved with lacework flourishes and adorned with silver, gray threading the deep blue furnishings. Arches shaped the windows, unlit sconces between them. It was nowhere near as grand as the Sultan's Palace, but its beauty was less sinister, less cruel.

"You had a fever."

Zafira looked at Yasmine, and Yasmine looked back.

"Even murderers get sick."

"Serves them right," Yasmine replied, but the words were weighted with disquiet, strangled and wrong. "Kifah. Is she . . . your friend?"

"Yes."

"Oh."

"But not the sister of my heart," Zafira said after a beat.

A startled, relieved laugh broke out of Yasmine, faltering between them as quickly as it had come, replaced by Deen with a bleeding chest. With a ring in his trembling hand. Acting out of love until his body released his soul.

Zafira held herself stiff, waiting for Yasmine to speak of Altair again. Or of Zafira being a murderer, Zafira not caring, Zafira dragging Deen to Sharr and burying him in its depths. She inhaled slowly, smoothing the ruptures inside her.

"I'm trying, Zafira," Yasmine whispered.

She was, too. But it was as Nasir said: Not every grief needed conquering. Acceptance was a feat in itself.

"I'm trying to look at you and not see him. I can't. It hurts, and I can't."

A knock sounded at the door, and a girl swept in with a tray. She set it on the low table and poured qahwa from a steaming dallah. Zafira refused the proffered cup with a slight shiver. She had avoided the bitter coffee and those handleless cups ever since Sharr.

"Bring her tea," Yasmine said. "With mint, if you can."

"Sayyida," the servant replied with a slight dip of her head.

The girl left, and Yasmine stared down at the steam wafting from her cup. Zafira stared at her. The silence was a twisted thing between them with thorns and teeth, strange and foreign, and she wondered if they could ever return to what they once had.

She would try, though. It was what Deen would want, she told herself. It was what *she* wanted. She couldn't lose them both. "How is Misk?"

The change was instant. Yasmine stiffened, a loose ribbon gone taut. Her fingers fluttered to her throat as she swallowed her qahwa.

"What's wrong? What happened?" Zafira said slowly, less question than command.

Yasmine's fingers curled around one another, nails digging into her unblemished skin.

"Yasmine," she repeated, voice hard. "Where's Misk?"

"We fought. He left." She paused with a slant of her mouth. A snarl tangled in Zafira's throat. He had *left* her—

"Or rather, I sent him away."

Oh.

The servant returned, and Zafira gratefully gripped the warm cup of tea. Anger etched scores between Yasmine's brows, sorrow shaped the bow of her lips. Still, Zafira waited. This was new, between them. The guard in Yasmine's eyes. This uncertainty, this fear that a misstep would cause the silence to remain forever.

Zafira brushed her knuckles over the ache in her chest. If only wishes were things she could make real. If only pain were like lint on a shoulder, easily brushed away.

"Misk is a bookkeeper, I said. His pockets are lined with silver because the flour merchant's men pay well." Yasmine was trying to force anger into the words, but it had already worn away, agony in its place. "You know what I've always wanted."

Zafira had known forever: a normal life. Her parents had been apothecaries in the army, her brother a soldier. The sister of her heart disappeared into the Arz every day. The same sister's mother had murdered her own husband.

Misk promised what she had always dreamed of: simplicity.

Yasmine laughed without mirth. "It was all a lie. He came to Demenhur for *you*. To *spy* on me. To befriend me and learn about you, the Demenhune Hunter. I was supposed to be flattered that he fell in love with me along the way."

Zafira froze, remembering what Benyamin had said on Sharr. Misk was one of his spiders—one of *Altair's* spiders. Still, she held her tongue; the last thing Yasmine needed was to think Zafira had known about Misk before then.

"He could have been a murderer, a cutthroat, the worst of the worst, and I wouldn't have cared, if only he'd give me his truths," Yasmine murmured.

Because lies were what had thrived in the relationship between Yasmine's parents. Zafira had seen proof of it, when Yasmine's mother would come to their house, tears charting paths down her cheeks.

"Maybe he couldn't. Maybe it was a secret he had to keep," Zafira ventured. Guilt churned through her afresh. Was this, too, her fault in a way?

Yasmine stiffened, and Zafira knew it was the wrong thing to say.

"Am I incapable of keeping a secret?" Yasmine asked. "Did I not hold yours for years? Had it been mine, I would have told him long before our wedding vows."

Zafira kept every movement of hers slow and careful, even her nod.

Yasmine drew her lower lip into her mouth, and Zafira wished she could hold her. She wished her friend didn't feel the need to steel her spine before her.

"I don't doubt that he loves me," Yasmine continued. "He's kind, and he's good, and I might be overreacting—this might be the only secret he will ever have, but I've lost enough to lose my heart twice. What if it *does* happen again? What if there are more secrets and a child between us?" Her voice went quiet. "I was too young. I *am* too young. So eager to call myself a woman, when I'm only a child myself."

A month. That was how long it had taken for a secret to tear the newlywed couple apart. Yasmine *was* too young. Zafira remembered the wedding, an ethereal moment suspended in time. The intensity in Misk's eyes, and the words he spoke to her. Most of all, she remembered envying the man taking her friend away from her.

"Wretched" was too small a word to describe how Zafira felt.

"That's not you talking," she said. "You're Yasmine Ra'ad. The girl without rue."

The last Ra'ad left. Zafira's fingers closed around the ring at her neck. Yasmine's eyes, wet and still cautious, followed.

"People change when they pick themselves up and piece themselves together again. Look at you—you've shattered so many times, I barely recognize you anymore."

Yasmine downed the rest of her qahwa, the thud of her cup a decree in the silence. She was still angry. Angry and in pain.

"We both agreed we need some time apart. I don't want to say goodbye. Does that make me a bad person? For not leaving him?"

Zafira hid her relief with a shake of her head. "It means you love him enough that you're willing to make it work."

Yasmine held still, her gaze off to the side. *What do you know of love?* Zafira imagined her asking in the silence. *You couldn't even love the man who loved you.* Zafira wavered. And then Yasmine crumpled, shoving a hand to her mouth.

"I miss him," she breathed. "I'm so angry, Zafira, but I miss him. I miss you. I miss what we had, and what we could have."

Outside, Arawiya was falling to a ruin even darker than the Arz. Zafira did not know if Nasir and Altair lived. She did not know if magic would ever return.

Still, she found the words slipping out of her mouth, chasing what they once had, trying to remind Yasmine that though she had lost her brother and maybe even her husband, she still had Zafira. She would always have her. "If we were in a story, what would happen?"

A tiny smile broke Yasmine's resolve, breaking a wider one out of Zafira. Yasmine, who was never sad, who was always full of emotion and bursting with passion.

They had played this game time and time again. She could almost mouth the words as Yasmine spoke of the half Sarasin, half Demenhune man she had desired for months in a way Zafira had never understood.

"A bookkeeper would sweep me away with his good hair and good taste. He'd be tall, of course," she recited, and Zafira, as always, refrained from commenting on Yasmine's height, or the lack of it. "Skilled in matters of importance that you pretend to know nothing about."

Zafira couldn't tell whom the game was meant to benefit. "And? Is he?"

"In every way but the truth. I hate lies." Yasmine picked up her cup and swished the qahwa rinds. She didn't look up. "Your turn."

"Mine?" Zafira asked, shrinking back. "I don't have anyone."

She cringed when the words left her, half expecting Yasmine to say *Oh, but you could have.*

"It's theoretical. A game," Yasmine said instead, gaze rising to the bandages wrapped around Zafira's chest, flicking to her face, and she dared to hope: They could get through this, the two of them. They were making progress, if Yasmine could look at her now. "An escape from all this."

Zafira was quiet for a while. Her neck burned even as her thoughts raced. "He'd know his way around a bow and a blade."

Yasmine's brows lifted.

"He'd be my opposite, in every way. So contrasting that if you'd look at us a certain way, you'd notice that we're exactly alike."

She didn't dream. She didn't believe in wishes. She was no romantic like Yasmine, but somewhere along the way, she'd grown partial to another soul.

They were twin flames, twined by fate.

"Heavy words," Yasmine said softly, "from a girl with no interest in love."

The door swung open without a knock, and a liveried guard stepped back, formal and stiff as he announced, "Crown Prince Nasir bin Ghameq."

Her heart stopped.

Yasmine dropped to her knees with a surprised yelp, lowering her gaze as a figure haltingly entered the room.

Zafira heard the weight of his surprised inhale. The breathless murmur of her name that sent shivers down her spine.

She saw the struggle in his limbs, the way half of him pitched forward, the other half holding him back. He still wore the fitted thobe from the feast, matted with dark blood and dusted in sand.

"Shall I get down on my knees before you, my prince?"

Her beautiful, bloody prince.

His answer was a whispered invocation. "Never."

Yasmine made a sound, but he barely registered her presence until she rose to her full height. He blinked down at her, and it was impossible to believe he was unaffected by her beauty.

"Forgive me," he said hoarsely, and stiffly flourished two fingers from his brow. "I will, uh"——he cleared his throat——"I will return at another time."

He closed the door. Yasmine whirled to her, gaping.

"That was . . . that was the crown prince. He looked at you—khara." Yasmine stopped, and the room was suddenly very warm. "A moment longer and he would have torn every last bit of that yellow—khara. Theoretical, I said. Sweet skies, Zafira. Deen for the Prince of Death—"

"Don't."

The word cut harsh, and the room echoed with her command.

"Don't?" Yasmine repeated. "He's—a monster, Zafira. My brother for a monster."

Zafira would have flinched or fought. She would have been offended on his behalf. But Zafira had lived with Yasmine, and she herself had shared in that thinking, that the Crown Prince of Arawiya was not a boy, but a beast.

Until he wasn't.

Yasmine left, and the door stayed closed. Zafira leaned back. What a fool she'd been to think a friendship such as theirs could be mended in an afternoon.

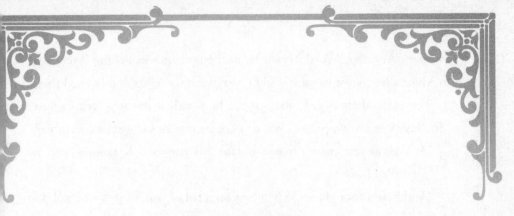

CHAPTER 66

I N THE HALL, NASIR CLENCHED HIS FIST AGAINST THE
wall and dropped his head to the crook of his arm.

The rise and fall of her chest made him want to weep. The sight of
that smile he'd thought he'd never see again—rimaal. Crazed joy echoed
in his limbs, crowded in his throat, worked his lungs for breath. Like a
drunkard finally sobering, Nasir knew what had happened to him, and
what her near death made him realize.

He didn't dare think the words.

"Shukrun for letting me know before you shoved me down that hall,"
Nasir said, trying to keep his voice steady.

"I thought you'd enjoy the surprise," Altair said, his face finally free of
those terrible streaks of blood. "That was a short visit, by the way. Don't
you know what you're supposed to do with the door closed?"

Nasir pretended he didn't understand. "She wasn't alone."

"Ah, so you *do* know——"

"Not. Another. Word," Nasir bit out. Haytham's son clung even closer to Altair's leg. Nasir sequestered his wayward thoughts and burned them.

The general shrugged, patting the boy with inattentive reassurance. "You know as crown prince, you can ask anyone to vacate the room, yes?"

"As well as you know I'm not one for ordering people around."

"Could've fooled me—"

"And here I thought we'd finally gotten rid of you." Kifah stepped past the navy curtain, dark eyes bright.

Altair made a sound between a chuckle and a strangled sob, and wrapped her in a hug, lifting her off the ground.

She froze at the embrace.

"I missed you, too, One of Nine," he said.

She pulled back and pointed at her eye, raising her brows without comment.

"What can I say?" Altair asked in a nonchalant manner that suggested the opposite. "My father was jealous."

"Or exasperated," Nasir said.

Kifah snorted. "*That* is far more believable. Though that act of yours, when you'd turned your back on us? I was ready to fling my spear through your skull."

"I know," Altair said, earnest. "I thought I'd convinced him that if no one else was on his side, his son was. Do you still think I look dashing?"

Nasir tamped down a smile when Kifah gave Altair a look. "I never thought you looked dashing."

"Idris?" a new voice asked.

The four of them turned to the doorway, which framed a man Nasir had witnessed through a fire sparked by dum sihr one too many times: Haytham. Ragged and weary, but alive.

"Baba!"

The boy stumbled and ran, and the wazir dropped to his knees, weeping as he drew the boy into his arms. The old Nasir would have scorned him for how easily his loyalties had turned. All it had taken was the trapping of his son, and the Lion had full sway over the second-most-powerful man in Demenhur. This new Nasir felt remorse for them both. Altair had the decency to allow them privacy, pulling Kifah aside with him.

Nasir had no such qualm.

Haytham looked up.

"Sultani," he said, rising hesitantly. He gripped his son's arm.

"We meet at last," Nasir said. Haytham's mouth twitched with a failed smile. "The Huntress looked at you with respect when you saved her in the palace. Why?"

Had it been anyone else, Nasir wouldn't have cared, he wouldn't have given it a second thought. Haytham's gaze flickered in surprise, but he should have known Nasir would notice. If an assassin was not attentive, he was dead.

"Our interactions were scarce, but I've known for years that the Hunter is no man," Haytham said, choosing his words.

Nasir's eyes narrowed to slits. "How?"

"Ayman's daughter. He cast her away, but I ensured her education and upbringing regardless, by dressing her as a boy. I recognized the signs."

Nasir hadn't known the Demenhune caliph had a daughter, let alone a child. Was the caliphate's bias so twisted that children were all but disappearing? But the regard in Zafira's gaze made sense now. Haytham was a man of prominence, a path to ensuring that the women of the caliphate did not fear for themselves.

"And yet you're a traitor," Nasir said. "The reason her village is gone. Her mother is dead."

Haytham was as much to blame as Nasir was. For it was he who had guaranteed the caliph's whereabouts. He who had fled when the people suffered. The wazir pulled Idris tight against him—the reason a man as loyal as Haytham had loosed his tongue and betrayed the people he was sworn to protect.

"If the people know, you will be stoned," Nasir continued. If Zafira knew, she would break. Nasir knew well enough how painful it was for a gaze once wrought with esteem to lose it. He couldn't allow that to happen.

Haytham did not dare breathe.

"Then we'll speak nothing of it," Altair broke in.

The two of them glanced at the general in surprise. Kifah was nowhere to be seen as Altair's blue gaze flicked between them.

"It won't discount what you've done, but we can all agree your death will do more harm than good, laa?"

Nasir nodded. It wouldn't be a difficult secret to keep. Only the three of them, the Lion, and Ghameq knew. And one of them was already dead. *Forever.* The word was a pebble smooth and laden.

Outside, the sun was dipping behind the spindly trees, the cold deepening. Haytham used the end of his keffiyah to regain some composure and dropped to his knees. His son understood enough and did the same.

Altair lifted an eyebrow. "You're welcome."

Nasir said nothing, but when the boy snuck a glance up at him, he couldn't help it: He smiled.

CHAPTER 67

ZAFIRA WOKE TO SOMEONE REARRANGING THE CUSH-
ions that had slipped during her slumber. She knew by the soundless movements that it was Nasir, and she opened her eyes the
barest fraction as he lit the sconces and drew the curtains before rekindling the fire. Caring for her.

Her monster.

The last time she had spied on him this way, they were on Sharr and
she had wondered when he would kill her. She had spent every moment
awaiting the cool touch of his blade. Now she expected something else.

"I know you're awake," he said in that voice that looped with the darkness, and she felt the familiar simmering low in her belly.

She stretched, flinching when her wound throbbed dully. "You seem
to enjoy playing nurse. I didn't want to interrupt."

"I'm the prince," he said simply, a note of teasing in his tone. A rogue
lock of damp hair curled at his temple, hashashin attire neat and trim.
She liked him like this, without a turban and the sheath of his sword, a

single button of his qamis undone. It made her feel special somehow, that he allowed her to see this side of him. Unpresentable to the world but perfectly all right for her. "I don't play the part of my inferiors."

You're the king, she wanted to correct. *The Sultan of Arawiya with a traitor on your throne.* But she wasn't ready for the light in his eyes to vanish. He sat down and crossed his legs. The brush of his knee against hers was a force made even more startling when he didn't pull away.

My brother for a monster. Yasmine's words, rife with anger and disbelief, tied a knot in her stomach. That wasn't what he was. Not anymore. Not to her.

His fingers twitched, as if he wanted to reach for her hand. There was a nervous sort of energy to him—*anxiety.*

"It feels as if I haven't breathed since you fell," he said finally.

His gaze dropped and his mouth drew shut. This boy who had so much to say but didn't know how. Whose lack of verbosity was something she once criticized.

"It'll take a lot more than an arrow to end me," she said lightly.

The corner of his mouth lifted, breaking the tension as neatly as he would a circle of harsha. It made her slide her hand closer to his the tiniest fraction. He noticed.

Zafira wasn't one to dream, to do much else beside the practical. But reposed here in this homely room, bereft of their weapons and stripped of the hood of the Hunter and the mask of the Prince of Death, she couldn't help it.

"They say the soul cannot rest until it finds its match. Then it ignites," he said.

Her breath caught when her eyes met the cool gray of his.

"Do you believe it?"

Do you feel it? was what he asked. *Is it true for us?* was what he wanted to know. When did he learn eloquence? Where did he find words that cut her as finely as a knife?

Her voice was soft. "I want to believe it."

Once, all she had wanted was to see her village cared for, her sister happy, and the Arz vanquished. To snare a rabbit or a deer, sating her for the day. To know her people would live for yet another sunset. Now she wanted too much. One kiss had made her crave the next. Yearn for the brush of his touch, anywhere. *Everywhere.*

She didn't know what he thought of her answer, because the lines of his face were smooth even as tendrils of darkness wove through his fingers, whispering against hers as softly as a touch.

"Zafira, I—"

"Shh," she said softly. He stopped, less from her command and more because of her fingers against his mouth. She didn't want to hear what he would say this time. She didn't want to hear those words again: *my bride, my queen, my fair gazelle.*

Because they made her hope. They made her forget who she was in the vastness of this kingdom. Holding his gaze, she crooked one finger and swept it across his lower lip. His breath hitched.

The door swung open.

She shoved her tingling hand beneath her thigh. Nasir pressed a hand to his lips and stared at his fingers.

"Why am I never invited to such things?" a boisterous voice asked, and Zafira's disappointment at the interruption was replaced with a different kind of elation.

Altair swept inside, carrying a bundle wrapped in an ivory cloth. He was clean now, scrubbed free of the terrible bloody tears that had streaked his face. A neat patch of deep crimson threaded with gold covered his eye, matching the turban carefully styled around his head. Only he could procure something so extravagant so quickly.

She thought of him turning away, standing at the Lion's side. How well he'd looked then, only a day before he had lost his eye. What had changed within so short a time?

"Why is it you can never knock?" Nasir asked, clearing a rasp from his throat.

Altair peered at him. "Why? Were you busy? You don't look like you were busy."

The insinuation rang clear in his voice, and the feathering in Nasir's turned neck made her pulse quicken. *Touch me*, that vein whispered.

She swallowed thickly as Altair crouched and frowned at her empty cup. "Nice of you to join us in the world of the living, Huntress."

"I could say the same of you," she replied. Questions rose to her tongue. *Why did you leave us? What happened?*

His eye was bright as it swept her face, his smile warm, and Zafira wondered if he had gotten that dimple from his mother or father. "I knew you'd miss me."

And she had, so very much. She'd thought it odd, at first, that she could miss them when she had finally reunited with Yasmine, but it seemed that delicate, mortal hearts were strange and vast.

Riddled with guilt, too. Within the very walls of this palace, Yasmine nurtured hatred for her brother's killer, yet here Zafira was, filled to the brim with relief that he was safe.

Skies, Yasmine. Altair.

How was it that they had lived leagues apart for decades and now, when anger and pain and vengeance burned in the sister of her heart's veins, the object of that vehemence was only a hall away? As if she didn't have enough to do, now Zafira needed to ensure the two of them did not meet. That their paths remained uncrossed.

She could imagine Yasmine in all her tiny glory scrambling atop him with murder and rage while Altair went slack-jawed at her beauty. He would apologize, she knew, but it wouldn't be enough. No amount of apologizing could bring back Deen and mend the hole in Yasmine's heart.

Only time could do that.

"I'm sorry about Aya," Zafira said softly. Altair's face fell, his eye ghosted by weariness. He and Benyamin had been close; it only made sense that Aya had been his friend, too.

If Zafira had been willing to live the rest of her life with Aya's blood on her hands, would any of this have happened?

Kifah stepped inside and slammed the door closed, looking among them. "Oi, is there a reason we're all loitering in something we probably don't need to be loitering in?"

All three of them looked up. Kifah repeated her question with a silent lift of her brows. Her head was freshly shaved, scalp bright.

"We're a zumra. We hunted the flame together, found the light in the darkness, but we were far from done, laa? Now we unleash it. We free the stars, shatter the darkness holding us captive, and return the world to the splendor it once was."

Zafira breathed deep, as if she could somehow ingest the hope of her words. Had Kifah decided not to leave with her calipha?

"With a side of revenge, of course."

Altair dipped his head. "Spoken like a true qa'id."

Kifah cast him a sidelong glance. "Did you just put me in a position above yours? You do know a qa'id commands a general, yes?"

Altair grinned, and Kifah groaned before he even opened his mouth.

"I have no qualms about putting women above me."

Him and his strange double-edged sayings that she wished she could ask Yasmine about.

He turned to Zafira with a stern look and held out the bundle in his hands. "I thought you might want this back."

He peeled off the ivory cloth, unveiling a tome bound in green leather. The Jawarat.

Her breath hitched. A wave of emotion rolled over her when she curled her fingers around it, remembering what it had last wanted of her. To kill the Lion. To rend him in two. She closed her eyes against the senseless savagery it had roused. Kifah looked displeased but said nothing. Nasir watched her.

They knew that the book had used her to speak, but how differently would they react if they knew the extent of its influence? Only Altair was blissfully unaware.

She set it in her lap as if she weren't itching to hold it in her hands.

"I felt his pulse," Zafira said in an effort to shift their attention. "The Lion's."

She thought of telling them about his memory, the stones striking his father to death, but couldn't summon the words. It didn't feel right. Laa, like her strange connection with the Jawarat, it made her fear how they would view *her*. More fearfully. As if she couldn't be trusted.

And sweet snow, there was enough of that with Yasmine.

A thousand questions rose with Altair's eyebrow in the silence. "You, dear Huntress, have come a long way from the innocent lamb I met on Sharr."

The Jawarat hummed with the same thought. Skies, how empty she had been without it. She had missed it deeply, and she knew without a doubt that the Lion, with his newfound throne and newfound power, missed it, too.

For he would forever be a slave to that which he didn't know.

We missed you, too.

"Even with everything he has now, he'll still want it," she said, running her fingers over the fiery mane. "The Jawarat's knowledge is endless, and the Lion couldn't possibly have gleaned even a fraction of it."

We do not want him.

If a book could pout, the Jawarat did just that.

You were quite eager to leave, she thought in her head, not at all unsmugly.

For which we are sorry. We were wrong to have left you. To have forced you to an unwanted fate.

Zafira paused at its apology. It was bowing its head, *yielding* to her. And she, jaded as she was, was instantly wary.

The Jawarat sighed.

"He may seek it out at some point, but he'll make use of the Great Library in the meantime," Altair said.

Zafira had seen much of Arawiya due to this mission, but not the inside of the library her father once lauded. Alabaster floors, gleaming shelves stocked with scrolls upon scrolls arranged in a code only few knew. Librarians, those few were called. The scrolls had interested Baba less than the books, rare and treasured, for the process of binding them was no simple task.

He would have loved the Jawarat.

"Knowledge is his neighbor now that he's king, but we might have something bigger to worry about. Baba dearest believes that magic must remain in the hands of the powerful. And by that, he means himself. He will destroy the hearts."

The Lion was many things, but never wasteful. He would go for them nonetheless.

"He won't prioritize them. They're useless to us, and safe in the minarets," Zafira contended. "There's no reason to choose them over establishing the throne as word of his coronation spreads. He'll want to be loved." *As his father once loved him.* "And there's no better time than now. Demenhur's snows are melting, Pelusia's soil is returning. The kingdom is returning to what it was, *because of us,* and he's going to use that to his advantage. And then, with the people appeased and tolerant, he'll make room for ifrit."

The zumra stared at her. She was unable to remember a time when Demenhur had been so warm.

Altair smacked his lips. "I'm going to pretend you didn't just say my father wants love."

"She's right," Nasir said, and she held still against the weight of his scrutiny.

He knew the Lion had come to her room back at Aya's house—she'd told him as much. He had witnessed her relationship with him before then, too. On Sharr.

"We can't go around re-collecting the hearts," he continued. "The minarets are safest, specifically with the High Circle protecting them."

Speaking of the High Circle . . . "Where's Seif?" Zafira asked.

"In Alderamin," Altair replied. "We lost the Alder calipha, Benyamin's mother, and without Aya as his charge, Seif's place is there. He'll protect the Alder heart and aid Benyamin's sister, Leila, in claiming her throne." He heaved a sigh at that. "What's worse in all this is that no dignitary will divulge the massacre. For good reason, of course, but it means no one outside of the feast will question or fear the Lion."

Zafira was only now beginning to understand the repercussions of the feast. The sultan was dead, a self-proclaimed king in his place, but the caliphates had always been, to an extent, independent. The bloodbath had toppled that system, bringing with it a swell of fear and uncertainty that no leader would rightly impart to their people.

"No point lamenting," Kifah said with force, crossing her arms as Nasir tossed wood into the hearth, discreetly glancing at Zafira's wound. "We need that heart. And if the Lion was in a big enough hurry to leave you unsecured"—she gave Altair a pointed glance, to which he feigned hurt—"there's bound to be something else he's missed."

Altair's mouth widened into a grin. "There is this."

Bint Iskandar.

Not now, she snapped in her head. Altair closed his fingers around the black hilt of a dagger sheathed around his leg and pulled it free. It was black down to the tip of its blade.

Zafira had seen that wicked knife before. In the hands of the Lion. In midair. Striking the Silver Witch.

"The Lion's black dagger," she marveled.

"The one and only," Altair said, flipping it over in his hands with a faraway look.

She studied him. "And the reason you went back."

Altair smiled, and she didn't miss the flicker of relief in his eye. "Ever perceptive, Huntress. It was indeed why I went back, when Nasir told me our mother was unable to heal herself. It just so happens that black ore strips one of magic. You saw how little your arrow affected him. There are spells that protect those who speak them, making the enchanted impossible to overpower. So long as the heart provides him with magic, wounding him will be impossible. Yet, until we wound him, we won't be able to retrieve the heart. Akhh, I love conundrums."

"And with the black dagger, we have a chance of stripping him of his power," Kifah reasoned, foot tapping a beat. "Should have asked me." She flourished a hand across the lightning blades sheathed along her arm. "I've got black ore to spare."

Altair peered at them. "Pure black ore, One of Nine. See that silver sheen? They've been mixed with steel."

Kifah didn't look surprised. "I should have known anything of my father's would be rubbish. Now, don't lose that thing."

"*I* don't make a habit of handing important artifacts over to the Lion," Altair said lightly. "I'll keep it safe. In my *own* rooms."

Zafira ducked her head.

"Using the dagger requires getting close," said Nasir, ignoring the gibe.

"Oi, Zafira went and felt his pulse," Kifah said, waving away his concern, and Zafira stared at her empty teacup.

"No one said it would be easy," Altair said, sheathing the dagger. "But we have a chance now where we didn't before, and it's time we take back what's ours. And yours, Nasir. Worry not—I'll even polish your throne for you."

Nasir gave him a look.

Heed us, bint Iskandar. The heart fights him, yet it will soon be tainted by him.

The Jawarat waited for its words to register. Zafira's hands fell to the cover, confusion giving way to horrible understanding.

Once it is tainted, it cannot sit within a minaret.

The others stopped talking. Kifah and Nasir frowned at the book. Altair stared.

"What can't sit within a minaret?" Nasir asked, jaw set.

"The heart," Zafira whispered, too hollow, too anguished to care that the book had used her again. "We're running out of time."

"What does that mean, exactly?" Kifah asked with the same dread suddenly cloaking the room. She had gone still as a bird trapped beneath snow.

"It's a si'lah heart. Meant to live within the si'lah themselves or the minarets of their making. It was never intended for the body of someone half ifrit, half safin."

Her first thought was not to trust the Jawarat, not after she'd seen how capable it was of manipulating, stealing memories and exploiting others. But it made sense, didn't it? It was the same as placing a fish in an empty bowl and expecting it to survive.

"That means—skies, we need to get it back *now*," she said, "or all that we've done will have been for nothing. The Baransea, Sharr. Finding the Jawarat."

Deen. Benyamin.

"And Aya would have done worse than give him magic," Nasir said slowly.

Altair sat down. "She'll have destroyed magic for good."

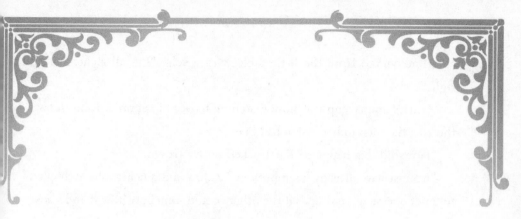

CHAPTER 68

IT WAS FITTING, ZAFIRA SUPPOSED. THAT ONE SAFI HAD dedicated his life to reversing the fall of Arawiya, only for his other half to do the opposite.

She should have unleashed her arrow when Aya had taken the Lion's hand. She should have leaped to the ground and torn Aya apart with her bare hands. Blood filled her vision: Aya gasping, her throat ripped to shreds. Zafira's fingers steeped in crimson.

Part of her was repulsed by her thoughts.

It is as you wanted.

The Jawarat lulled her with its truth. When it had shown her the terrible destruction of her village by her own hand, she had wanted it to heed *her* wishes. That was exactly what it had woven in her thoughts just now. The room spun, angry slashes of red making it hard to see. A soft purring came from the book in her lap and something—

Something fell to pieces.

Altair jerked from the little table with a yelp. "I'm all right! I'm all right!"

Zafira's empty cup was now matching halves of ceramic. Rent in two the way the men in her vision had been.

"How did that happen?" Kifah asked with a frown.

"It must have already been broken," Zafira said quickly. She struggled to quiet her racing pulse, as if the others could somehow hear it and know she had broken the cup.

"And just needed a bit of time to fall apart," Nasir said, watching her, not at all referring to the cup. She carefully set the Jawarat down, out of reach, but the haze didn't disappear. Laa, it was worsening, embers of anger merging into a flame, thieving her thoughts.

You did this, she hissed in her head.

Laa, bint Iskandar. It was you. It is the violence you wished upon the safi.

"I—I need to go," Zafira said quickly. She started to get up but swayed with light-headedness, and Kifah had to grab her arm.

"Maybe you should sit back down," Altair suggested gently. "We need to put together our plan."

Zafira shook her head. She needed space to think. To sort through the crowding in her skull. If she remained, her only input would be blood and murder and other atrocities she wanted no part of. What was happening to her? She was the girl who'd mourned the rabbits she snared, who sought forgiveness as she slit their throats.

"I'll take you to your sister," Kifah said, oblivious. Yes, Lana would help.

"Akhh, there's two of you?" Altair remarked.

Zafira rolled her eyes as the door thudded closed. Kifah led her down one hall and then another, wide and serene, arches beckoning with parted curtains every so often.

"You met Yasmine," Zafira started. Her friend was down one of these halls, hating Zafira for her treacherous heart, knowing Zafira was the reason the last of her family was gone.

Kifah nodded, a sly smile playing on the edge of her mouth.

Zafira ignored it. "So you know what she looks like. And . . . well, I need your help making sure she and Altair don't meet."

Kifah only nodded, her smile widening. At Zafira's glare, she shrugged. "I might have overheard a word or two of your, er, reunion."

Zafira's brows flattened.

"Can you imagine it?" Kifah continued, wistful. "I didn't spend long with her, but bleeding Guljul, the two of them would be perfect."

Zafira's slow blink turned to a scowl when she realized what Kifah was implying.

"She's married," she deadpanned. "And Altair killed her brother."

Kifah only shrugged again as they turned down the hall. "Stranger things have happened."

"Zafira?" Yasmine stepped from one of the rooms as if summoned by their conversation, a shawl clutched in her hand. Her hair fell in freshly washed curls, kissing her cheeks.

Kifah lifted her brows.

"You're supposed to be resting," Yasmine said. She looked between them, gaze narrowing to slits.

"I was," Zafira replied, wanting to step close. Fear held her in place. "I'm going to see Lana."

A door slammed down the adjacent hall, and a laugh echoed, boisterous and free. The dread coiling in Zafira's stomach was instant and girdling.

"You should have seen your face, habibi."

It's fine, she told herself. Yasmine didn't know Altair by the tone of his voice. Only by name.

"Always happy to be the source of your amusement, Altair," came Nasir's exasperated reply.

Zafira looked at Kifah, and Kifah looked at Yasmine.

Perhaps, if they hadn't been here, Yasmine would have thought nothing of it. But their pause gave Yasmine pause. She stiffened, and Zafira saw the moment recognition dawned, her features morphing into anger and rage, eyes bright and livid.

Khara.

"You know," Kifah said lightly, "maybe Yasmine can take you to Lana, eh? I—I have to go."

"Go where?" Yasmine snapped, but Kifah was already jogging backward with a two-fingered salute. Yasmine hoisted her abaya and ran after her.

Now both of them were leaving her.

"Wait!" Zafira called. "What about me?"

Kifah turned down the hall, disappearing from view. Yasmine didn't look back.

Do something, you fool. Zafira winced and shoved her fingers against her wound, crying out at the sudden pain. Yasmine slowed but didn't stop.

"Akhh, One of Nine, why the rush?" Altair exclaimed, moving closer.

Zafira hissed again, just for good measure.

Yasmine looked back at her. "Now what is it?"

"Lana," Zafira gasped, clutching her chest as blood blossomed across her wrappings. Perhaps this was a little *too* good an act. "I think my wound broke again."

Yasmine wavered, torn between going after Altair or helping her bleeding friend. Zafira nearly scowled, doubling over and throwing a hand against the wall instead.

"Yasmine!"

"All right," she snarled. "I'm coming."

Zafira heaved a relieved sigh. Altair deserved the brunt of Yasmine's anger, but not now. Later, when everything was through, she would make the introductions herself.

Yasmine grumbled all the way to Lana's door and abandoned her immediately, but Zafira didn't mind. She'd done her job. She stepped into a room with shelves upon shelves of little bottles—a regular arsenal of healing supplies—and Lana, almost invisible in the shapely rays of evening light.

It was much like the rest of the palace: carved white shadowed by gray, accented in silver that complemented the deep blue furnishings, but this space smelled of so many herbs that Zafira's nose couldn't decipher a single one aside from rosemary, which she had never liked but Lana had always loved.

It was like Lana to claim a room that wasn't hers. Even at home, she could never sleep in their room, preferring to curl on the majlis in their foyer, and for a moment, Zafira could only stand in the doorway, taking in the gleam of her sister's hair, the soft curve of her cheek, lit with a line of fire from the crackling hearth.

It reminded her of home, before she undertook the journey to Sharr, when Lana had begged her to stay, saying magic meant nothing without Zafira.

Now it could be gone. Never, ever to return.

"You're here!" Lana said, leaping to her feet. Her hands were stained with ink. Only then did Zafira realize she had brought the Jawarat with her. Her fear was a viper, sinking fangs and numbing her. "I was just writing down notes. Since you survived."

"I'm delighted your experiment was successful," Zafira said dryly.

We like her, bint Iskandar.

Zafira ignored it, or tried to—there was a sense inside her, a foreboding similar to when a storm churned in the distance.

Lana grinned cheekily before concern marred her brow. "Are you all right?"

Zafira nodded quickly, angling her bandages from view.

"It's the book, isn't it?" Lana was staring at the Jawarat with fascination and fear. "You act strange when you have it."

"I—"

She stopped when a knock sounded and the door opened before either of them could answer. Lana looked past her shoulder and quickly smoothed back her hair with an eager hand, leaving a streak of ink on her temple. Zafira's eyebrows flicked upward. *Sweet snow.*

"Are we meeting someone special?" she whispered.

Lana glared at her. "It's the boy Ammah Aya saved."

Zafira turned to the door, wincing when her wound stretched. The newcomer was slight, with a cloak shielding hunched shoulders and a hesitant step. Zafira was suddenly back at home, staring in her speckled mirror before her hunts. She recognized it all, down to the bare tilt of the newcomer's hooded head.

"That's no boy," Zafira murmured. This was the palace, where the caliph lived. Where Haytham lived. She pieced together the clues. "You're her. You're the caliph's daughter."

The girl startled like a deer, her carefully draped hood falling back just enough to reveal shapely eyes wide in fear. She lifted her chin in a wobbly display of defiance, full lips pressed tight. With a start, Zafira realized the girl was not much younger than her, possibly even the same age as Zafira.

Lana scrambled to her feet, firelight highlighting her distress. "Khara, you're a girl?"

Zafira turned to her sharply. "Mind your mouth."

Lana directed her glower at Zafira. "How did you know?"

"I should think the answer to that question is obvious."

"What's your name?" Lana asked, turning to the disguised girl. Disbelief toned her voice, the edges roughened by hurt.

"Qismah," the girl said in a voice as gentle as first snow. She darted a glance at Lana, but her gaze seemed most comfortable on the ground. "I—I'm sorry I didn't tell you. Only Ammu Haytham knows I'm a girl."

Zafira wondered what sort of life Qismah was leading. Haytham looked out for her, but what did it mean for Qismah to keep her true self a secret? Did she believe herself a harbinger of ill, as many in Demenhur believed women to be?

"And—and Baba."

Perhaps it was the way she referred to her father, with shame and hesitance, that caused Zafira's anger to rear. It was a chorus in her skull, wild and grating. The Jawarat fueled it with murmurs, reminders of the way men of her caliphate looked at her. At women. She cinched her jaw tight, willing it away, telling herself to stay calm as the book sat innocently in her lap, as if it weren't guiding her thoughts.

She smiled at the girl, seeing the resemblance between her and the elderly caliph. "Haytham says you are an apt pupil. You are very brave, doing what you do."

Qismah's half smile was fleeting.

It was unfair that girls so young were weathered enough to understand society so keenly. Once, Zafira would have smiled that same fleeting smile. She would have told herself that this, and this, and this was *enough*.

Enough. The word was a box she had placed herself within, and she would be a fool to let another young girl do the same.

"Your throne will be yours," Zafira promised. Once the Lion was vanquished, and Arawiya stopped teetering at the edge of this dangerous precipice, she would help her. Enough people knew who Zafira was, and Haytham was a man in position who would do what was right. He would help them. The people should know by now how twisted the caliph's words were. If they didn't, they would learn—or she would shove the truth down their throats.

"I . . . ," Qismah began, and tapered off with a nod. "Shukrun."

The caliph's daughter braved a glance at Lana, and in a clear attempt to do *something*, she tossed wood into the fire, pulling back when it hissed, her hood falling farther from her head.

That was when Zafira saw Qismah's hair—shorn like a man's, dark curls glinting bronze. Kifah was bald, of course, but that was a commonality in

Pelusia. In Demenhur, the longer a woman's hair, the more beautiful she was deemed. No one would dare lift a blade to a woman's mane. Trimming it was as unseemly as pretending to be a man.

Trimming it was an act of disgrace.

Liquid fury replaced the blood in her veins, burning hotter than the bluest flame. She barely felt the throb of her arrow wound.

Let us redeem ourselves for leaving you. We will please you.

He will die for what he has done.

She did not know whose thought that was, whose vow that burned bright. She was on her feet. The Jawarat was in her hand, and turmoil ached in her bones, fighting against its pull and failing, failing. This wasn't the chaos she had come to recognize and steel herself against. This was the fervent need to recompense. To atone. And it caught her off guard.

She couldn't tell where her thoughts began and the Jawarat's ended. Lana's mouth shaped her name, but Zafira heard nothing. Qismah hurried away, terror morphing her pretty features. The hall hurried past in a blur.

It wasn't until Zafira stood before two large double doors, the Jawarat clutched tight, that she knew where she was going, danger carving her path.

CHAPTER 69

A GOOD PART OF ALTAIR THRIVED ON REFUSAL, AND
it came alive the moment the Jawarat imparted its eerie message
through Zafira. He refused to believe one of his lovely aunts'
hearts was fading to black inside his father.

Sultan's teeth, he had quite the family tree.

Regardless, he would wring this for what he could. He had been desperately searching for a match to light a fire beneath the dignitaries' arses
and rally their aid, and this new revelation was it.

"What did Ghada say?" Kifah asked as he unfurled the Pelusian calipha's missive.

"If her answer was affirmative, she wouldn't have sent you a letter,"
Nasir said, sharpening his sword. "She's down the daama hall."

"I cannot wait until you and your impeccable ability to rouse hope
are crowned king, brother boy," Altair drawled. "What a gloomy day that
will be."

Nasir's reaction was a downward turn of his mouth.

The prince was right, but Altair read it aloud for Kifah's benefit. "'Pelusia is all that stands between Arawiya and starvation. We cannot, in good conscience, invite the Lion's wrath. Regards, Ghada bint Jund.'"

"A better excuse than the Zaramese caliph's, at least," Kifah consoled herself. The reed of a man hadn't even offered an excuse.

This was it, then. Two caliphs had refused to join their efforts to defeat the Lion. Leila was on her way to claiming her mother's throne in Alderamin, while Sarasin's throne remained empty still, the man most promising for the job dead before he could claim it.

Altair threw open the doors and stepped into the hall, spotting a servant tossing almonds into his mouth. "Oi, you there. Where are Haytham and Ayman? Make haste."

The boy responded with a gesture that would have had him decapitated, had Nasir been on the receiving end. But Altair was only a general, and the boy answered to his caliph.

"Is that so?" Altair drawled. "Do it now, pint. By order of the true sultan."

"True sultan," Nasir repeated when he stepped back inside.

"If you aren't going to use the title for anything useful, I will." Altair rubbed his beard. "What else can we do? Summon a nice feast? A few bodies to keep us warm?"

Nasir's ears flushed red.

"Kifah, dearest?" Altair called. She retracted her spear. "Remind me to check on Nasir's ears the next time Zafira's around, eh?"

She smirked as Haytham entered, his checkered keffiyah off-kilter. A servant girl followed with a tray. The nutty and spicy aroma of qahwa filled the room, awakening Altair's senses as the girl poured him a cup from a silver dallah, breaking the silence with an awkward trickle before offering him a platter of cubed honey cake that Kifah stole away.

"Zafira still hasn't returned," Nasir reminded them as Haytham took his seat.

"She's a big girl," Altair said to pacify him. For his part, Altair could only think of that cake, glistening and soft and not in his mouth. "She knows her way back." He frowned at the Demenhune wazir. "Where is Ayman?"

"Currently engaged in other matters," the wazir said.

The only time that particular phrase sufficed was when a man was in his bedchamber, engaged in matters that were decidedly not rest. Altair lifted his one visible brow, unconvinced.

Haytham's shoulders dropped, disappointment curving his mouth. "He refuses to come . . . He refuses to meet with you."

Understandable. Altair was, after all, the general who had led several armies against Ayman's own. He wouldn't have wanted to meet with the old man, either, had he been on the losing end.

"I am here in his stead," Haytham said, and cleared his throat, lifting a bundle of missives. "Several reports have come in."

"Let's hear them," Altair said, leaning forward.

Haytham slid forward a sheet of papyrus covered in neat scrawl. "Sarasin's smaller cities have fallen to darkness."

"Already?" Altair asked. He hadn't thought his father would act *this* quickly. They'd barely had time to recover.

"It will make travel difficult," Kifah said, gears turning as quickly as Pelusian mechanics. "We intend to return to Sultan's Keep, don't we? If Sarasin has been blanketed by shadows, ifrit are bound to be there. The darkness isn't for nothing. He's creating a home for his kind."

"What's this about a new caliph?" Nasir asked, tapping a finger on the missive.

"Ah. Yes," Haytham said. "They've appointed the caliph elect— Muzaffar. He was present at the feast."

On the low table, Nasir's fingers turned white, and Altair remembered that moment, months ago, when the prince had received his orders to assassinate the previous caliph of Sarasin.

"Muzaffar is dead," Nasir said. "I saw him lying in a pool of his own blood."

Haytham didn't seem surprised. "I had a feeling the timing did not align. The Lion has little reason to appoint someone as beloved as Muzaffar. Even if there was a reason, I cannot see the man idling as ifritkind overtook his lands. Possibly worse, several Sarasin contingents have been sighted shifting to Sultan's Keep. I assume they are reinforcements."

Kifah toyed with her lightning blades. "If they're claiming it's Muzaffar on the Sarasin throne, there's only one way it could be possible: An ifrit is wearing his face."

Altair dragged a hand down his own face.

"It's a near-perfect solution," Nasir commented. "The Sarasins are subdued, both human and ifrit armies answer to the caliph, and the caliph answers to the Lion."

"You said 'reinforcements.' Reinforcements for what?" Kifah asked. "Us? He's put too much faith in our leaders if he thinks we'll march at him with four armies."

Down three different halls of the palace, Ghada sat with her Nine Elite, the Zaramese caliph dozed, and Ayman lounged with his ancient bones. Altair wanted to grab them all by the shoulders and shake sense into them.

Haytham leafed through his missives. "I've also had men scoping the grounds near the Sultan's Palace."

Nasir shared in Altair's surprise. It seemed there was at least one other competent man in Arawiya aside from himself.

"They've reported a mere handful of sentinels, barely enough to withstand a full-blown attack. If the Lion truly does believe we may march in with an army, why remain short-staffed?"

"Magic?" Kifah assumed, plopping another honey cake in her mouth. Altair scowled.

"There are spells that create protective barriers," Altair pondered. "It's what *you* were supposed to use in Sultan's Keep to prevent the Lion from taking the Jawarat."

He still felt the guilt of that moment, the horror of seeing the book in his father's hands.

"We were, until we ran out of blood," Kifah said.

"There is one good note," Haytham said, handing him another missive that looked to have been steeped in snow one too many times. "Rebel forces have been gathering in Sultan's Keep."

"Rebels?" Kifah asked, taking the soggy sheet.

"They may very well join us."

Us. Altair liked the sound of that word from the wazir.

"Depends on what they're rebelling against." Nasir was as optimistic as ever.

"But an army nonetheless," Altair said, spreading the missives across the table. He stared at the map pinned to the wall, gray lines and navy rivers. The silver streaks of palaces reinforced by might and magic, the curve of the Great Library.

The Great Library.

Altair straightened and grabbed a reed pen. "Gather round, children. I've got a plan."

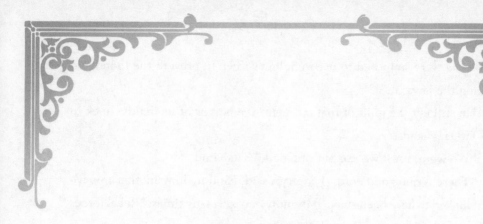

CHAPTER 70

THERE WERE MEN WHO DESERVED FORGIVENESS AND
a second chance, and others who deserved only to suffer for what
they'd done. Caliph Ayman of Demenhur, the Jawarat said, was
one of the latter.

Zafira fought against this claim, for she was a huntress and a girl, an
orphan and a sister. Not a judge.

Wrongs must be righted, the Jawarat crooned. *We will help you.*

It was a losing battle against a bottomless, gaping hunger, a craving
that could never be sated. This was how the Lion felt, she realized, when
he desired knowledge. When he wanted vengeance for what his father had
endured.

He dared to sequester a child in such a way?

Zafira didn't know if the thought was hers alone or the Jawarat's. Or if
it had simply found the vial inside her that held everything enraging, and
drunk it. The caliph had been wrong for *years*. His lies had spread across

the caliphate, had permeated the very fabric of their lives. What made this moment any different? What made murder burn in their veins?

Their?

We are one and the same.

The double doors were locked, white wood as pure as her heart. She laughed at the analogy. *Open them.* Open them? It would be a waste of dum sihr to unlock doors. In her thoughts flashed Qismah's shorn head. Her downcast eyes. Zafira's own hunched shoulders.

A line of red ripped down her palm, and the locks came undone.

No longer will we wait for change. We will bring it.

Resolve hardened her. The doors flew open. Caution whispered from the back of her skull, that viper striking fear slithering close, and she—

"Qif!" Two guards leaped to attention, shouting in tandem, but what sort of fool would stop?

Sharp pain burst across her palm and she threw out her arms. The guards crumpled to the ground, dead. *Dead?* She froze in her tracks, blearily studying her surroundings as if suddenly awakening from a slumber. Her bandaged chest ached. Where was she? Where were Qismah and Lana?

The sentinels merely rest. Look at them, bint Iskandar.

Her lucidity vanished, and she felt as if she were watching herself from afar. The guards were lounging on the floor, chests rising and falling ever so slowly, asleep as the Jawarat assured her they were.

She was led by an invisible hand down one room and into the next, large archways like keyholes that would never find their match. Moonlight flooded the space, solitary lanterns lighting her path to a chamber.

And there, standing before a platform bed resplendent in furs, was the Caliph of Demenhur.

This is atonement for our abandon. Be pleased with this justice.

"You," the caliph said in surprise. "The Hunter."

Oh, how she'd missed the scorn the men of her caliphate directed at women.

The last time he had seen Zafira—as she stood on the ship departing for Sharr and revealed her identity to all—rage had burned in his gaze. Now, the wrinkles on his face were more pronounced and the light in his brown eyes had dulled. The regard he had once shown when he'd thought her a boy was gone.

She didn't care. Laa, she pitied him and his too-small mind.

"I retrieved the Jawarat, and this is how you look at me?" she demanded. "Did you not hear of the Arz falling? Of the sands of Sarasin turning gold again? Of the snow in Demenhur fading?"

"And?" he asked.

That tiny word drowned in a lifetime of prejudice.

"And what? Did you stop believing in Arawiya's restoration the moment you learned I was a woman?"

The caliph didn't move. "Destruction befell the western villages not long after your departure, Hunter. Not long after you dropped your hood."

Why was she trying to speak to him? Why did she think she could make him understand?

Because that is who you are.

Zafira froze, sharp pain splitting her skull. That voice wasn't the Jawarat's. It was Yasmine's and Lana's. It was Umm's.

No, bint Iskandar. There are those for whom reason does not exist. Do you weep the loss of virtue when we have given you power?

The Jawarat was right.

"Speak my name," she said quietly, in a voice not entirely hers.

He took a careful step back. "How did you get past the guards—"

Zafira laughed. "Look at you. *Pathetic.* Afraid of a woman."

His fear was so tangible that she wanted to gather it in a bottle and relish later—*laa*. She was no monster. She didn't toy with her prey the way a lion did with a mouse.

"*You took the future of a girl and did with it as you willed*," she said. Or perhaps it was the Jawarat that spoke. Her vision blurred.

"Whom do you speak of?"

"Your daughter. All of Demenhur's daughters."

The caliph swallowed audibly. "Guards!"

Zafira started to laugh before a pair of guards rushed inside.

"Sayyidi?" they asked.

Both of them stopped short when they saw her. Their swords flashed in the moonlight, uncertainty at the sight of an unarmed girl halting their blows. Perhaps she would have left. Perhaps she would have been sated by the scare she had made, if not for the satisfaction on the caliph's face.

The complacency of knowing she, a young woman, had lost.

You wish to give a girl her throne, the Jawarat told her. *Circumstance favors us.*

Pain seared her palm. Something bold and angry crowded her gaze, as if leniency were a concept she knew nothing about. She lifted her hand.

With nothing but the moon as her witness, Zafira brought down her fist. Agony split the room, the throes a song in her skull. The night bled crimson, echoing with screams.

This is man, bare to the world. Halved of his whole.

She was the bladed compass, honed by the Lion and wielded by the Jawarat.

She was ruin, she was havoc, and she reveled in it.

CHAPTER 71

NASIR AND ALTAIR BARRELED INTO THE HALL, frazzled by the scream. Lana came running from the opposite end, something clutched in her hand, but it was Kifah who shoved past them and threw open the double doors.

Her stricken voice carried from within. "Bleeding Guljul."

Nasir halted the guard rushing to the room, apprehension settling on his shoulders. Haytham would be on their heels as soon as he checked on his son.

"Allow no one inside. Not even the wazir," Nasir commanded.

The guard began to protest.

"By order of the true sultan."

Ceding with a reluctant nod, the guard barred the doors as footsteps thundered down the corridors. Nasir pushed past Altair and Kifah and stopped short in the lavish bedroom.

Blood. Matting the gray furs, staining the white rug, pooling on the wide tiles. Three men lay brutally mutilated against cushions meant for leisure. Fates worse than death.

Despite it, he was relieved Zafira was not here.

"They've been—" Kifah stopped with a gag, turning to Altair and doubling over. "Cut in half."

Something moved at the edge of his vision, and Nasir drew his scimitar as a figure stepped from the shadows and into the moonlight.

Feeling drained from his limbs.

Zafira.

In her hands was the Jawarat, a wicked grin in the dark.

The others froze, but she looked only at him, her gaze sliding from the disbelief on his face that he couldn't mask quickly enough to the scimitar he should never have unsheathed.

Understanding dawned in the wild ice of her eyes, and they were back where they began in the ruins of Sharr. She lifted her chin, baring her neck as if inviting his blade.

Or challenging it.

Blood trickled from her palm, and an empty silver vial lay by her feet. Dum sihr. *Why?* he wanted to ask her. The moment Altair had passed the Jawarat to her earlier today, Nasir had seen the brightening in her gaze, the buzz in her limbs. He knew it had used her voice to speak, but he had never expected this.

Lana was the first to move. She darted forward and shoved a cloth to Zafira's nose before she could react. Zafira fought back for barely a moment before she fell in her sister's arms, eyes drifting closed, lashes fanning in the moonlight. Lana struggled against her weight, and Nasir eased her to the floor, laying her on the cleanest part of the room.

Her breathing was calm, unlike the riot inside him.

"I knew something was wrong when she walked away as if she didn't even know me," Lana said softly. She picked up her damp cloth with a trembling hand. "It's why I brought this."

Nasir brushed the hair from Zafira's face. He wanted to tear the Jawarat from her slack fingers and fling it into the fire. Instead, he turned to the others still rooted in shock. "None of this leaves the room."

"Are you mad?" Altair let out a smothered breath. "You don't need to tell us. She's our friend, too."

Nasir was surprised by the relief that belied his exhale.

"But there is no denying what she's done," Altair added. "Killing a caliph of Arawiya is no small matter."

"I've killed a caliph."

Altair gave him a withering look. "In your right mind, you killed—"

There was a wet slide and sickly *plop* as one of the guards' entrails fell to the tiles. Nasir's stomach rolled. Lana peered closely.

"—a caliph," Altair continued with a grimace. "In *her* right mind, she would never have done this."

"He was cut in daama half," Kifah said, frenzied. "They all were."

"Pin the death on someone else," Lana suggested, oddly calm.

They turned to her.

Lana didn't back down. "After everything she's done—"

"We'll fix the blame on an ifrit," Nasir said. "One we disposed of before opening the doors. It's violent enough that the guards will believe it."

It was far more believable than the truth.

Lana touched the Jawarat pensively, as if listening for a tune none of the others caught. "And there's nothing wrong with her mind. It was the Jawarat."

"Then we take it away from her. I'll keep it," Altair said.

Lana held it close. "The only way to rid someone of a poison is with the poison itself. We can't rip it away from her," she stressed. "She'll go mad."

"And until she learns to control it, she will be capricious."

"Until she learns to control it, she's *dangerous*," Kifah growled.

Lana shook her head, staring unflinchingly at what remained of the caliph. "She was always angry. If you lived beneath his rule and lived the way my sister did, you would know that the caliph had invited this upon himself a long time ago."

There came a pounding on the doors. More guards, no doubt.

"I will never forget the day I first saw her, when I learned the selfless huntress was no ruse but who she truly is," Kifah said with a shake of her head. "If that book is going to make her as unsalvageable as the heart the Lion stole might soon be, then I suggest we destroy it."

"At the cost of her life," Nasir growled.

Kifah paused as if she had forgotten that one, terrible fact, then said in a measured tone, "I would rather die at a merciful hand than live a monstrous life."

Nasir glanced at Altair, mortified when something akin to agreement shone in his eyes. She had done something wrong, *horribly* wrong, but if there was anyone who understood the desire for a second chance, it was Nasir. If anyone understood what it was like to wish they could begin afresh, unjudged and untainted, it was him.

She had given that to him. She saw him as a boy when everyone else deemed him a monster. Even if the world and all it contained gave up on her, he would not.

"No one's taking it away from her," Nasir ruled.

Lana was watching him, relief bright. "Nothing is without salvation, right?"

CHAPTER 72

NASIR NUDGED OPEN THE DOOR WITH HIS FOOT and carefully set her down on the bed, uncaring that Lana was witness to him tucking a pillow beneath her arm and straightening her clothes. Lana clutched the Jawarat to her chest, and as much as he loathed entrusting it to her, she was right. She set the book out of reach and curled against her sister's side without a word.

It was only now that he noticed how distraught Zafira had been. As she slept, the groove between her brows was smooth, the harsh cut of her lips supple.

His life was full of loss and pain, and he would not lose her again.

In the hall, he came face to face with a girl—the one he'd seen at Zafira's side before. She was as slight as Kulsum, her curves more ample, her eyes doe-like and heavy-lidded, the color of honey.

She was not pleased to see him closing the door to Zafira's room.

"She's asleep," he said.

Her eyes narrowed in mistrust, for she didn't yet know of the attack.

Laa, she thought Nasir had been in Zafira's bedroom for a reason other than laying her motionless body across her bed. *If only.*

Her voice might have been melodic, if it was not full of the hate he was used to. "If you hurt her—"

He didn't wait for her to finish. "If I hurt her, I will bring every weapon at my disposal and lay them at your feet for you to do to me what you will. If I hurt her, I will no sooner carve out my own heart than dare draw breath again."

She was silent. Her eyes were no longer narrowed.

"Do you understand?" he prompted.

"You love her."

She spoke the words like a subtle knife: rife with disbelief. As if it was impossible to comprehend that the Prince of Death would care for anyone.

No, he did not love her. The word for what he felt for Zafira bint Iskandar did not yet exist.

———◆———

When at last he stepped into the room where the others had gathered, conversation ceased for a beat. He paused with a raise of his eyebrows, but when he dropped the curtain behind him and joined them, they continued again as if nothing had happened.

It took him a moment to note the tension. The stiffness of Kifah's movements, the stillness in her restless limbs. Wariness tugged at Altair, haunting his one-eyed gaze.

They were *trying* to continue as if nothing had happened.

"I don't think we can wait for her," Altair said.

Nasir leaned against the wall, knowing full well whom he spoke of. He agreed. "No, we can't."

Haytham slid a look across them in the silence, and Nasir wondered how easily he'd believed the lie.

Kifah unfurled a map across the table. "Haytham has received another report. Seems the Lion still hasn't left the palace grounds, not even to visit the Great Library."

"Imagine the temptation," Altair murmured.

"But why not give in to it? Is he afraid?" Kifah mused.

"Or preoccupied," Haytham offered.

Nasir remembered the haunted look in the Lion's eyes, the pain. He wondered if that played more of a part than fear did. He was powerful and protected, and the Great Library was hardly a journey from the palace. His father had made the trip often enough. Nasir knew, because he would note Ghameq's comings and goings to time his own excursions to the mollifying edifice. Each time, his father would return with a stack of—

Only, that *hadn't* been his father.

"He's gathered enough reading material for the time being," Nasir said.

"Perhaps," Altair ceded with a tilt of his head. "But we can agree that standing within the walls is an entirely different experience."

True enough.

"Let's hear your plan, then," said Nasir, catching the hope in Altair's tone and clinging to it for dear life.

His brother looked pleased. "We will, woefully, need to part ways, habibi." He tapped the map with a finger, trailing two upward paths from their present position in Thalj. One path stopped in Sarasin's capital of Leil, the other in the vicinity of Sultan's Keep. There was a third path, too, crossing the sea. "Three parties. Kifah and I. A falcon in the skies. You."

And no mention of Zafira.

"Your job involves doing what you do best," Altair said.

"Killing," Nasir said, stepping closer to look at the plans spread across the table. It *was* what he did best. Still, it stung.

Altair noticed, but his next words didn't help ease daama anything. "You do have experience sneaking into the Sarasin palace and killing a caliph, so—"

Nasir released a breath.

"Oi, don't be upset!"

"And why are we killing him?" Nasir asked, apathetic.

"As you said, the ifrit looks like the man the Sarasins admire. Therefore effortlessly controlling both ifrit and human armies. It's simple. We get rid of him, we command in his stead. Short term, of course. Until we get rid of the Lion and appoint someone better suited for the task."

Perhaps it was because of Zafira and her honor, her rectitude a drop of white in the fabric of his dark world, but Nasir's first thought did not involve killing the caliph, ifrit or not. It was odd how that change had come about within him.

Kifah took his silence as acceptance. "Controlling a horde of ifrit will prove tedious, but this way, we will at least be able to restrain the mortal Sarasin army and use them to hold the ifrit in check."

Nasir looked at her sketch. "A blockade."

She nodded once.

It was easy enough sneaking into the Sarasin palace when he was the rightful prince and no place was off-limits. Now, with the Lion eager for his head and ifrit to contend with? Nasir sighed. "All right. Consider him dead. Is Zafira not any part of this plan?"

Kifah paused with chagrin. Altair looked regretful. "We're leaving just after noon. Zafira needs rest, most certainly, but she also needs to return to herself. Laa?"

"She's still herself," Nasir said quietly. "She hasn't become some sort of wild beast."

It pained him to speak the words, and he was relieved to see it reflected in Altair's eyes. Haytham tried to hide his confusion as no one filled him in.

"If she's stable tomorrow, she can join us. Yes?" Altair looked at Kifah.

"Without doubt," she said.

For a long moment, the three of them stayed mired in Zafira's absence until Kifah dragged her finger along the third path, returning them to the plans. "Then we have the falcon."

"Who will head straight for the Hessa Isles and deliver a note, which I'm still piecing together because the timing has to be right. We're going to need the Silver Witch's help," Altair said without meeting Nasir's eyes.

If the wazir noticed Altair's hollow tone, he pretended not to.

"Haytham remains here gathering intelligence," the general continued. "Meanwhile, Kifah and I will locate the rebels in Sultan's Keep while you ride for Sarasin. We won't be able to communicate, so much of the plan's success will rely on a schedule."

"It seems to me," Nasir said, "that much of the plan relies on chance."

"Chance keeps us alive," the oaf replied.

"The chances," Nasir gritted out, "of you finding my blade at your neck are currently quite high."

Altair flashed him a grin. "I love it when you speak so filthily."

Nasir's ears burned. Kifah leaned back, eyes bright. Adversely, Nasir felt he could sleep forever after everything that had transpired.

"And?" he asked, sensing there was more.

His brother's smile was wolfish. "Well, there is another thing. It's more chaotic than my usual style, and it's *certainly* not your style. It's risky and dangerous. And, uh, flashy."

All things the general adored.

"But it's guaranteed to draw my—" Altair stopped short, remembering Haytham. "To draw the Lion out."

Nasir looked between him and Kifah with creeping dread.

"So, Sultan Nasir, how do you feel about arson?"

CHAPTER 73

ZAFIRA WOKE BESIDE A WARM BODY. INSTEAD OF limbs and skin and dark hair, she thought of blood and tendons and entrails. She was afraid to look. Afraid she wouldn't see her sister's smattering of freckles but the colorless bones of her skull.

"Zafira?"

Yasmine was perched against the low bed, worry scrunching her delicate features. She scooted forward and wrapped Zafira in a hug, wary of her bandages. *She's not afraid of me.* Perhaps it was all a terrible dream, and she hadn't split her caliph in two.

"They said the ifrit nearly had you, too. The guards could barely look at Ayman."

Not a dream, then. The Lion felt less of a monster, compared to what she'd done. Her and Yasmine's fight felt as insignificant as when they were twelve and they'd fought over her being gifted a dress Zafira had always wanted.

She went stiff as the words struck. "Ifrit?"

"The one that killed the caliph," Yasmine explained sadly.

Zafira was just about to open her mouth when something moved by the wall.

Nasir sat up and held her gaze. *Play along*, he insisted with a nearly imperceptible shake of his head.

How? she wanted to ask him, knowing what had happened to Yasmine and Misk because of a truth withheld. But the alternative was worse, wasn't it? Calling herself a murderer, the very thing Yasmine had accused her of being.

Her guilt was a cruel thing, laughing at her as she upheld the lie.

"It was brutal," she whispered against Yasmine's hair, and screwed her eyes closed. That, at least, was no lie. It *was* brutal. *She* was brutal.

Her skull pounded from the tension grinding her teeth. The blood had been cleaned from her palm. The vial, drained of the si'lah blood she'd traded Baba's dagger to attain, was nowhere to be seen.

Neither was the Jawarat. The thought was enough: Hunger opened its jaws, eliciting a shivering need in her limbs. *Breathe.* Her vision swam red and white, blurring as she tried to focus on Yasmine. The orange blossom of her hair, her gentle but fierce hold.

Zafira had steeled herself against the Jawarat's chaos and its need to control her. She had been prepared. But it hadn't been doing either of those when it had spurred her to the caliph's door—not directly. It had been trying to atone. To make up for leaving her.

Sweet snow, what is this madness?

Yasmine pulled away, her gaze cast downward. "For once, I was relieved Misk isn't here. In danger."

Typical Yasmine, never thinking of herself.

But he wouldn't have been in danger, would he? Zafira would never have hurt him. *Would I?*

Her friend recovered with a dramatic roll of her eyes in Nasir's direction. "Your prince is here."

Zafira searched her face, gratified by the acceptance she found. The apology. The indecent twinkle that said she liked what she saw very daama much, making Zafira look away shyly.

She had always marveled at the endless ways in which people met one another halfway. The offering of peace was as near as they'd go to an apology, she knew, for when people were close they rarely needed to use words.

She smiled, a tentative lift of her lips with a thousand apologies in between. *For Deen. For what I've done.*

Yasmine smiled back, wistful. *I know,* her look said, though she could never know the extent of Zafira's deeds. "He sat in that corner for half the night and wouldn't leave, even when I promised to keep you safe."

A maddening laugh bubbled up Zafira's throat. *Safe.* The world needed to be kept safe from her, not her from it.

"I can hear you," Nasir drawled.

"Hashashins," Yasmine muttered. "Perhaps you shouldn't try so hard to listen all the time." Then she straightened, remembering who he was. "Kha—uh, apologies, Sultani."

Nasir said something, and Yasmine replied. Words passed between them, but Zafira heard the sickening hollow of the caliph's bones being split in two. She heard the guards who had come to save his life screaming as they were rent in half.

"—wake Lana?" Yasmine poked her. "Zafira?"

Zafira found herself shaking her head. Yasmine pressed the back of her hand to Zafira's brow and pursed her lips.

"I'll return later. Rest, hmm?"

She gathered the folds of her blue abaya and left, while Lana snored softly and Nasir watched her.

"That's Yasmine," she said, because she needed to fill the silence.

"I know. She doesn't like me very much."

"She's Deen's sister."

"I know that, too," he said.

"She's a seer, and she knows Altair killed him. We can't—we can't let them meet. Not now."

This, he didn't know, and so he was silent. Zafira dropped her gaze to her hands. Every sound was amplified and thunderous. His sigh. The whisper of his limbs as he moved closer.

"Why didn't you do it?" she asked finally. The fire in the hearth did nothing to warm the cold, cold hole in her heart.

His fingers flexed in his lap. "Do what?"

"Use your scimitar."

She had mutilated three men and still had the impudence to be hurt by the sight of him armed against her.

"You were supposed to be with Lana. I didn't expect it to be you."

There was a pause before *it*, as if that small thoughtless space encapsulated what she had done.

She laughed. "You didn't expect me to be a monster."

Laa, that was too tame a word for what she was. *Butcher.* Monsters could be misunderstood. Butchers did one thing alone. Nasir said nothing.

"We can't lie to people," Zafira said, grappling for what little virtue she had left. "I have to answer for what I've done."

"You will be stoned," he said without preamble. "You will die."

Outside, the sky was the darkest hue of periwinkle as the sun roused, pressing through the glass of her window. A limb for a limb, an eye for an eye.

"Tell me how it happened," he said.

She lifted her head, surprised to see him so close, so intent. She'd told no one of the Jawarat's vision. Of the fact that it had collected more than the Sisters' memories on Sharr. What was one more secret in a sea of them? But this was Nasir, and she could not refuse him. Laa, she found it easy to remain true, to bare even the darkest parts of herself. He never judged her, he never pitied her. He understood.

He mistook her silence, or thought to console her as he breathed a whisper of a laugh. "There's nothing wrong with a little bloodlust."

She shook her head. *If only.*

"Your mother called me pure of heart," she said softly. "The Sisters, when I stepped into the glade where I found the Jawarat, called me pure of heart, too."

And more—their voices rose to her ears even now. *Pure of heart. Dark of intent.*

Had they known, in their infinite wisdom, that she would come to this?

"But when I fed my people, not once wishing for repayment, I was angry. I would look at someone and hate them for being happy. I would think of the caliph, and wish him dead so that women and girls wouldn't have to suffer his bias. I would hunt in the Arz and crave its darkness, desire it because I thought it understood me. After it fell, despite knowing it would have killed us by the year's end, I missed it."

"Why?"

"Why what?" Hysteria crept into her voice. *Skies, look at you.* Sitting and discussing her internal state with Arawiya's sultan as if he had nothing better to do.

"Why do you miss it?" he asked. "Because it shaped you in ways you never imagined? That does not make you a monster."

"You don't—"

"I know what it's like to be a monster, fair gazelle," he said tiredly. "And you are not one."

"Is that what the others said when they saw me?" she asked, a wild strain to her voice.

"No, the others didn't say that."

No, but they would have thought it. She would have thought it, if she'd seen someone splitting a man in two in his own bedroom.

"The *others* are concerned," he said, emphasizing the word to include himself. "That was not you, Zafira. This has nothing to do with *wishing* a man dead, because plenty of people do as much."

His eyes fell to the little bedside table, and her own gaze followed, pulse quickening. On it, beside a tin of wrapped malban, was the Jawarat. The sight of it brought on a wave of guilt, strangely detached and not entirely hers—as if it belonged to the Jawarat. What reason would the book have to feel guilty? She had done what it wanted. It had fulfilled its chaotic desires.

If anything, it should be gleeful.

"It's been speaking to me since I bound myself to it," she said finally.

He was silent until she dared to look at him. "I assumed as much."

"I thought—I thought I'd gained control of it. I thought we'd reached an understanding."

An understanding. As if it were a person. Not a master playing her like a puppet.

"But I clearly hadn't," she finished lamely.

He nodded slowly. "Altair has finalized a plan, and we'll be leaving soon. One of us can keep it with us."

Yes. Keep it. She needed the freedom to regain her sanity, to remember who she was.

"You mean to take it away from me," she whispered instead. Pressure was building in her chest, fear and loss overpowering. *What is happening to me?*

He paused at the stillness of her tone, gaze flicking to Lana and back to hers. "No one is going to take it—"

She cut him off with a vehement no.

It was hers. She wouldn't give her clothes to someone else to wear. She couldn't have had Lana wear her cloak while she went out on her hunts. She wouldn't let Yasmine wear the ring Deen had given her. There was a difference. He didn't understand. None of them did.

"No. And neither do you."

Ever so slowly, Nasir leaned back, rose to his feet, and left—and it was only then that she realized she had said all of it aloud. Every last senseless ramble.

In the silence, Zafira dropped her face to her hands and muffled a scream.

"You're awake," Lana said sleepily as she sat up, clutching the blanket.

Zafira clenched her teeth. She wasn't ready for yet another confrontation.

"They wouldn't let me study the caliph," her sister complained. "Isn't it fascinating how bodies are filled to the brim with blood, yet our bones are pure and white?"

Oh.

"It wasn't fair," Lana continued as she slid off the bed and came to kneel by Zafira's side. "After what he did to us—"

Laa, laa, laa. Lana wasn't supposed to be fine with this.

"What, Lana?" Zafira demanded. "What did he do to deserve being murdered?"

"You're the one who cut him in half," Lana reminded her with a scrunch of her nose. "I'm helping you justify it. But look at it this way: He was going to die anyway. Now . . . he'll be written into history with quite the creative death."

Zafira lifted an eyebrow and regarded her tiny, murderous sister.

The gleam in Lana's eyes faded to a look of contemplation. "He stunted the lives and futures of thousands of women, Okhti. You and Qismah found ways to endure, but the others? Anytime I was with Ammah Aya before—before everything happened, when she commanded men in the infirmaries and waited for no one, it was a reminder of how differently we're raised here in Demenhur. And that's the caliph's fault."

That didn't make what Zafira had done any more *right.*

Lana helped her stand. "Yalla."

"Lana," Zafira whined as her sister dragged her to the antechamber.

"He's dead. You're still you. The rest is up to you to fix."

"What rest?"

"The imbalance. Inside you." Lana smirked. "Then you can revel freely."

A bewildered laugh bubbled out of Zafira. "When did you become this wild creature?"

"I was always here," she said with a nonchalant shrug, but she didn't meet her eyes. "You just never noticed me."

A spirited chuckle echoed from beyond the door—Altair. As if on cue, Kifah's equally loud, dry response followed, along with several pairs of footsteps. They came close to her room.

And didn't stop.

Zafira listened through the pounding in her ears, but no one turned back. No one knocked.

We'll be leaving soon. Sweet snow, they had finalized a plan and she wasn't even a part of it. These were her friends, her zumra. Her family bound by resilience and hope.

And they had left her.

Laa, she had broken their trust.

Zafira sank to the floor, wrapping her arms around herself as her wound screamed and her heart screamed louder. She was empty of feeling, a hole chipping wider and wider. A void of a disease by the name of loneliness.

Bint Iskandar.

She tightened her jaw. The Jawarat was the last voice she wanted in her head. She shot to her feet.

"Where are you going?" Lana asked. "Wait!"

Zafira marched back to the room and grabbed the Jawarat with an angry snarl. She dug her nails into the leather, and a dull pain like the blunt edges of ten knives cut across her back.

The book was silent. It was the rued kind of silence that came when someone felt they deserved to be chastised.

We only thought to please you.

Its despondence was as peculiar as when it had led her to the caliph and asked to be forgiven. As if it had ceased its desire to control her when the Lion had stolen it away.

"How?" she whispered. The caliph flashed in her thoughts, split in half like an apple in her palm. *How could that please me?*

"Okhti?" Lana crouched beside her, draping a blanket over her shivering shoulders. "Don't do it. Don't talk to it."

Zafira shrugged away. "I need to fix this. I've—I've lost them, Lana."

"Lost whom?"

"Them. My friends. Kifah, Altair. Nasir," she finished in a whisper. *You*, for though Lana was here and concerned, she was *concerned*, and Zafira didn't want her to be. "They don't trust me anymore."

"Then win them back. You can't undo what's done, but you can decide the future."

The Jawarat stirred from its somber moping. *The zumra has but only one wish.*

The Lion's annihilation.

We can end—

No. She knew what the Jawarat would suggest. *If we're doing this, we're doing it my way.*

Zafira straightened and looked at her sister, tiny and quick. "Can I trust you?"

Lana studied her, as if trying to decipher if it was Zafira or the Jawarat that spoke.

"Always," she said, appeased by what she saw.

"Do you know where everyone's been staying? Which rooms they're in?" Zafira flexed her shoulder with a grimace. She needed to rest and heal, but she could do neither, not with the caliph's death on her shoulders. Not while the Lion lounged on his ill-claimed throne.

Lana's eyes brightened. "You mean the prince's?"

"I mean Altair's. I need you to steal something for me."

CHAPTER 74

I T DIDN'T TAKE ALTAIR LONG TO FIND NASIR. HE
dropped the roof's trapdoor shut with a thud, tugging the collar of his
robes against the cold.

"You only drill when you think too much."

Surprise flitted across the prince's gray eyes. Did he really think Altair
didn't pay attention? Nasir gathered his belongings and leaped across the
rooftop to join him, setting his neatly wrapped bundle beneath the shelter
of a latticed archway. He stared into the distance, the perfect depiction of
brooding. Altair couldn't understand why women found that attractive.

"It's Zafira," Nasir started, slowly piecing his words together. "I don't
know if it's right, allowing her to keep the Jawarat."

Ah. It was natural, Altair knew, to second-guess actions when one had
lived a life dictated by orders.

"Every deed has its outcome," Altair said. "Doubt is inherent. The best
of us merely manage to overcome the voice—"

"If I wanted philosophy, I would have sought out the library."

Altair regarded him. "It's time now for you to follow your heart. To listen to it."

Nasir slowly spun the scimitar before sheathing it with a huff that painted the air white. The boy's nose was an almost adorable hue of pink.

"Teach me," Altair said suddenly.

Nasir's eyebrows rose. "What?"

"Remind me what it's like to use a single sword, because I will never use two again."

Nasir frowned. "Why not?"

"Oh, because my father stabbed me in the eye."

"I'm aware," Nasir deadpanned. "But even a blind man can use a sword."

"Perhaps a blind man who doesn't have a dark army waiting for him. There isn't time. I don't have the balance for two." He didn't have his scimitars anymore, either, and if he was being honest, he didn't feel particularly inclined to find a new pair.

Nasir nodded and stepped to the bundle he'd left beneath the archway. He carefully folded back the fabric and drew two scimitars. Altair's heart stopped. The hilts were burnished gold, the perfect curve of the blades adorned with filigree and branded with names.

"Sultan's teeth," Altair murmured, taking Fath from him. "Where? How?"

"Seif, likely. I found it in the Pelusian carriage."

"Akhh, I could kiss him," Altair announced, turning the scimitar over in his hand. He kissed the blade instead, and sank into a stance. "Parry me."

Nasir regarded him. "What makes you think I won't kill you?"

"You love me too much."

He caught the flash of Nasir's laugh before he swung. Altair dodged it with shameful clumsiness. Both of his arms moved in tandem. They had mirrored each other for so long that it was habit.

"Change is coming, brother. Are you ready?" Altair was aware he spoke to distract others as much as himself sometimes.

"Death will come first," Nasir said, lunging.

Altair heard the approach of the sword, for turning his head to see out of his right eye took far too long, and ducked. "And then—"

Nasir swung before he could finish, the hiss of his blade as cutting as the Demenhune air. This time, Altair parried it more swiftly. Nasir acknowledged him with a nod and swung the same way from his other side—Altair's blind side. He parried a little too late.

Nasir lowered his sword. "And then I'll be king. Or sultan. I know."

"I always knew you were smart," Altair teased, hefting the scimitar against his shoulder. In all twenty years of Nasir's life, not once had they carried a conversation this long.

This was an improvement, and Altair was proud.

As with most of his rare displays of emotion, Nasir's snort was a sound barely there.

"Oi, it's the truth," Altair said. "You excelled in your every class, with every weapon they threw in your hands. You were eloquent. You were brilliant. And even if you weren't, even if you were the dumbest child ever to curse the earth, none of it would have mattered, because you made our mother proud."

He hadn't meant to say all of that, and though Nasir was silent as usual, the silence he held now was one of shock.

Might as well get it all out.

"I hated it. I hated you. I hated how deeply she loved you, but it brought her joy. *You* brought her joy."

On the streets below, a crier wailed some nonsensical news and children dashed down from the nearby sooq. Nasir didn't apologize, as some would. He didn't breathe a word, the idiot boy.

"And then you stopped using your brain in lieu of your father's," Altair said, softer now. "You stopped being yourself." He looked away, words dropping softer still. "And I hated you even more for it."

The words clung to the air, bringing with it a gust of the past. Nasir tucked his ridiculously tidy bundle of weaponry away, and a trail of black followed him to the edge of the roof, as if he were fading into the light. Just when Altair thought he would leap off the end, peacock that he was, he spoke without turning.

"I was not made for battle. This is not my fight."

"Is it mine?" Altair asked with a hollow laugh. "Because I'm his son?"

Nasir stared into the sky as if he hadn't considered that. As if he'd forgotten. "Destruction follows darkness. You know this."

And then he was gone, leaving Altair's second scimitar at his feet.

CHAPTER 75

OF THE TWO ISKANDARS NASIR IMAGINED STANDING at his door, the younger one was not it. He did not expect he would be the one she'd come to with such distress, either.

"What is it?"

Lana wrung her hands. "It's my sister. She—she's leaving."

His brows flicked upward. "And where is she going?"

"I don't know—just hurry!"

Nasir heaved a weary sigh but followed after Lana as she rushed down the hallway. It was gratifying, he supposed, that she had come to him instead of anyone else. Then again, he suspected the bronze-haired girl, Yasmine, would lock Zafira in a room if she had to.

Lana paused in front of a rounded archway until a servant pulled aside the curtain. For a girl who grew up in a village, she had adjusted to palace life rather quickly.

"I almost let her go," she said, darting through. "I even gave her—"

"Gave her what?" Nasir asked, refusing to run.

She waved a dismissive hand and slipped into the kitchen, taking a shortcut. The place was bustling with cooks and maids, a variety of aromas fighting for dominance and reminding him he hadn't eaten a proper meal in quite some time. Stacks of flatbread were piled high, an undercook hefting a trio from a stone oven while a woman and a shirtless boy peeled potatoes into an ample pot.

"That thing is large enough to sit in," Lana murmured.

Not entirely adjusted, Nasir ceded. She ducked her head, realizing her slip when he cast her a look.

He flung open the door to a gust of cold air, and came to a halt. There she was, radiant in the still-early light. A cloak sat at her shoulders, furred with a hood in deep plum. Her tunic cut above the knees, the tail fading to black as it fell lower. The sleeves must have been short, because she'd wrapped bands from forearm to wrist, gray ribbons like armor matching the shawl at her neck. Its fringe was as black as the sash around her middle, framing the ring at her chest. For a brief moment, Nasir's lungs had forgotten what they were meant to do. She was a marvel to behold, a vision both deadly and beautiful.

The Jawarat was clutched to her chest.

"Where are you going?" he said.

Zafira startled, surprised to see him with Lana by his side. She glared at her and slowly unclenched her jaw. "Sultan's Keep."

Snow dusted the courtyard, and a guard kicked some as he went. Nasir leaned against the doorway, keeping his words and stance nonchalant. "And what do you intend to do?"

"I'm sorry for what I did, and I'm going to make up for it."

There was no redeeming oneself of murder. He knew it, and the sorrow in her eyes told him she knew it, too. He nodded slowly. "What does that have to do with Sultan's Keep?"

"I can stop the Lion."

Lana sputtered. Nasir's eyebrows rose.

Zafira snatched her bag with a wince, pressing a hand to her breast. "You're in no condition to ride."

"I can sit astride if someone else handles the reins," she said, vehement.

"And if you run into trouble? Will you wave an arrow and hope the Lion dies?"

Lana snickered.

Zafira looked down at the Jawarat. "I'll find myself a horseman who knows their way around a weapon."

He knew of such a person, as skilled with a weapon as he was with a horse. He knew of a person who would take her to the ends of the world, if only she would ask. He would take the stars from the sky and fashion them into a crown, if only she would have it.

Yet he said nothing. He was not like the boy who had given her a ring, which she wore at her heart like a promise of forever. He was the prince, whose throne she wanted no part of, lips molded to hers for a few brief moments stolen from a thousand more.

Nasir uncrossed his arms and made to leave.

"Wait! Just . . . don't tell the others yet. Please."

"Why not?"

"I know I wasn't included in the plans. I know no one will let me go, because you're all concerned or afraid or what have you."

He bit back a smile at her flustered attempt to act unflustered. The way she was, he didn't think Altair and Kifah would consider her stable enough, but he wasn't about to be brushed aside so easily. There was no reversing what she had done, but to stop it from happening again? Nasir would do anything.

"I won't tell them on one condition."

She looked at him warily.

"Let me be your horseman." *Let me be your everything.*

He was northbound anyway. The quick lift of her eyebrows revealed her surprise.

"Aren't you afraid of me?"

Never. "What have I ever done to wrong you?"

Lana's lips twitched against a smile. Zafira wasn't convinced.

"You'll leave the others behind for me?"

Someday, she would learn he would do anything for her. Someday, he would find the words to tell her as much.

"No one will even notice I'm gone," Nasir said. Not until it was too late, at least. "Have we a deal?"

He watched Zafira's slow intake of air. "No."

He shrugged a shoulder and turned to leave without a word, banking on her small sliver of hesitance as Lana panicked.

"Fine," Zafira bit out. "Don't vilify the Jawarat, and our pact is sealed."

Nasir turned back to her and smiled. "Of course, sayyida."

Of all the lies he'd told, this was easiest.

CHAPTER 76

*W*E DO NOT NEED HIM.

That, Zafira thought with her one remaining shred of sanity, was precisely why she needed him. Even if the very thought of sharing a horse with him flooded her with heat.

In the stables, Zafira's filched prize doubled in weight when Lana snuck her a sly grin as they narrowly avoided Altair exiting the farthest stall. It was yet another way the brothers were utterly different—Nasir would have noticed them immediately.

"Yasmine won't be happy you didn't tell her," Lana said. None of them would be, but when she thought of telling them, she heard Altair's laughter rolling past her door, the horror on their faces at the sight of what she'd done.

"I'm well aware," Zafira replied, "and I'll deal with that later."

"Well, then, what should I tell her? And the others?"

What, indeed.

"The truth." Zafira would be far away by then. "We've lied to her enough already."

The stable was stone, each stall carved into an ornate point like a doorway into a place unseen. Polished shoes hung on the wall, alongside brushes and saddles, everything neat and orderly, square windows illuminating each steed in brilliance. It was nothing like Sukkar's shed in their village.

Nasir joined them with a cursory glance as if hoping Zafira had changed her mind, and though every guard noticed him, not one asked what they were doing or where they were going. They were hawklike in their vigilance, however, no doubt garnering a story to share over arak later about the crown prince taking leave with an insipid Demenhune.

He stopped short, looking past Zafira's shoulder.

"Afya?" he murmured in disbelief.

It was the name of one of the Six Sisters of Old, but he was staring at a horse. A dark gray mare.

"This one."

The stable boy stumbled at the force of his command and brought the horse forward, handing Nasir the reins with hushed respect before turning to her. "Another horse, sayyida?"

Zafira merely shook her head, her attention riveted on Nasir. At the happiness he could barely contain. He ran a gentle hand down the mare's flank and murmured sweet words in her ear, his face breaking into a tenderness too fleeting to memorize. He pressed his brow to her nose, and she nuzzled him back just as gently.

She was melting inside. There was no other way to describe how she felt. This was the same boy who had tended to her their first day on Sharr. The same boy she had healed when the Lion had seared him with the poker. When he forgot to carry the burden of the Prince of Death and allowed himself to *be*.

He turned to her and his smile disappeared. He dropped his gaze and led the horse outside. Zafira couldn't help it: hurt flared through her.

Lana laughed. "You made him shy."

"Him. Shy," Zafira bit out.

Lana tilted her head. "I don't mean it in a bad way, but for someone so brave and smart, you are terribly daft sometimes."

"I'm glad you don't mean that in a bad way."

Lana bit her lip. "Be safe."

"What, no imploring me to stay this time?"

"I tried, Okhti. I'm not stronger than that book, but maybe your prince is. Do you remember that day you took so long in the Arz that it was evening by the time you returned? Deen kept telling us not to worry. 'She has a penchant for punching death in the face,' he said."

Zafira didn't reply. She recalled Deen using those very words with her as they headed to Sharr.

"I believe it now," Lana said.

Nasir's shadow fell across the entrance. "Shall we?"

Zafira looked back at Lana. "Keep Yasmine away from Altair."

Something flickered in Lana's eyes, but she nodded. Contending with Yasmine's wrath was as terrifying as disturbing the Lion's repose.

"And talk to Qismah," Zafira added.

"She lied," Lana protested, "when she pretended to be something she wasn't."

As did I.

"The repercussions for her are tenfold of what they were for me." Zafira touched the back of two fingers to Lana's cheek, guilt gripping her. "I don't know if she knows the truth of how her father was killed, or how she's taken the news, or what will happen to her now. She needs allies. People who will fight for her."

"I wasn't born to fight."

"No," Zafira agreed. "Neither of us were. We were not born to fight, but our cradles were built from struggles and hardship. Pens, swords, sticks—weapons shoved into our fists as soon as we're old enough to grasp them. So we fight, because the world will cut our throats otherwise. We fight, because we won't go down without one. Do you understand?"

In answer, Lana threw her arms around her.

"I can't breathe," Zafira gasped, and Lana pulled away sheepishly.

Outside, Zafira paused, the cold biting the backs of her hands. Nasir waited with Afya, and the guards waited by the gates. Perhaps she *shouldn't* leave without telling the others.

A humming rose from the Jawarat, lulling her wayward thoughts.

We are winning them back. This is what we must do.

Again, she was jolted by its uncertainty, but it was right.

Noon was just deepening the sky when she tugged her cloak closer and used the stool to mount Nasir's horse like a frail old man. She shivered at a sudden gust of wind, and every part of her warmed when Nasir mounted behind her.

Skies.

She felt his hesitation before he reached around her for the reins, breath across her cheek. She tried not to focus on the way it skittered, taking in the mare's dappled coat instead. She tried to ignore the glorious press of his legs at the backs of her thighs, studying the familiarity of the unfolding landscape instead.

The gates rolled open to stone streets lined with houses puffing smoke and people going about their day untroubled, which meant the horrors of Sultan's Keep hadn't yet reached Thalj. *Thalj.* Another city of grandeur to which her journey had brought her.

"All right?" Nasir asked in that voice, reinstating his presence.

She swallowed with a quick nod and met Lana's gaze in silent farewell. Nasir spurred the horse forward, and Zafira fell back against the solid wall of his chest, barely registering the knifing pain of her wound and the Jawarat's whispering melody over the sudden heat of his body.

Sweet snow, this was going to be some journey.

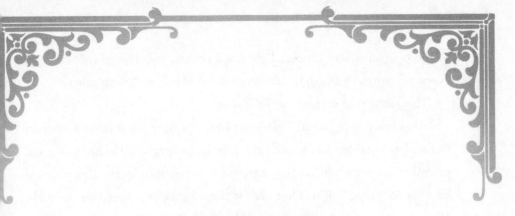

CHAPTER 77

I T TOOK EVERY LAST SCRAP OF NASIR'S SELF-WORTH NOT to press closer when he mounted Afya's back. It became hard to breathe, and then altogether hard to daama exist when Zafira fell against him. Soon they were past the gates, cantering down the sloping street unfurling from the palace, and he had no choice but to exhale a very slow and not-so-collected breath.

Zafira turned back to take in the alabaster majesty of the Demenhune palace, her blue eyes bright with childlike wonder. They were clear, unaffected by the book clutched to her chest, and he wondered if this was one of the moments she had spoken of, when she and it had come to an understanding.

"It's beautiful," she breathed.

"An apt descriptor for a number of things," he murmured, pleased when her shoulders stiffened.

He slowed Afya to a walk along the bustling streets, ever aware of the dark blotch he was in this fair city, from the snow and the buildings down to the pristine white thobes, light-hued abayas, and furred coats almost everyone wore. Demenhur, the caliphate of ghosts and ethereality.

"How long will it take?" asked Zafira.

"Afya is an Alder steed," Nasir replied. Spotting his mother's mare in Demenhur's stables was the last thing he had expected. He had never expected to *see* her again, khalas, sure she'd been eaten by the ifrit elder. If he were to guess, Seif had left her for them in the courtyard on the night of their escape, for only a safi would be shrewd enough to notice an Alder steed in the midst of chaos, and someone in the Nine Elite would have ridden her here. "I'd say a little under three days, but there's no telling how this new, dark Sarasin will be."

He heard her soft murmur of *Alder steed* before she ran her hands down Afya's neck in a way that made him swallow thickly.

The soft sun had reached its zenith by the time the bustle of the main city dwindled to a few sole houses. Nasir picked up the pace, then slowed Afya down again when they neared a village. Zafira turned, profile lit with sunlight. "I'm sorry about your father. I never had the chance to tell you."

He had lost his father long ago, the moment the poker first seared his back, and yet some part of him had held on to hope. For recognition. For a smile. For a nod of approval like he was still a daama child. Now Arawiya's notorious sultan was a corpse on the cold, hard tile beside his own throne. A puppet left to rot without even the respect of a burial.

"It's all right," Zafira whispered, closing her cold hands around his. "It's all right." Her thumbs swept across his skin, covering the dark flame as they passed a man using a shovel in the snow and a line of women chatting in front of another's house.

There were only spiny trees to their either side when she spoke again, softly. "Others cry in tears. You cry in shadow."

She continued her ministrations, absently, and though he couldn't see his hands, he knew the moment the shadows receded and something else stirred inside him at her touch. His grip tightened on the reins and her own loosened, realization striking quick.

Rimaal, he—

He swung off the mare's back, pursing his mouth at the slush beneath his boots but grateful for the rush of cold against his body. She stared at him from the saddle as if he'd lost his mind. He almost laughed. Surely she wasn't *that* guileless?

"Why can't you part with the Jawarat?" he asked, to distract himself as much as her.

She stiffened. "You promised."

"It's only a question." His voice dropped.

"Turn us back."

He stopped.

"Turn back, or I will take you to the caliph's palace and leave—"

He saw the moment her idea struck. She lunged for the reins with a soft cry as her wound stretched, wrenching Afya around with a deft hand. Nasir leaped forward with a curse, grappling one rein from her grip, half of him bearing her weight to stop her from falling.

"You lied," she panted against him, and oh how he wished there was another reason she was like this, so gloriously coming undone.

"It was only a question," he said again, and then he laughed at how he was defending himself. At how he was being used yet again. At how she was ready to leave him here. It wasn't hard to find words when he was in pain. "Do you think I'm some sort of easy mark? Is that why you agreed to letting me be your horseman? Why you didn't want me telling the others?"

She stilled, hurting his pride when she dared to meet his eyes.

"I will take you back to the palace and chain you to your bed," he growled in her ear. "This is madness."

She dropped the other rein, her knuckles bone white. Their exhales clouded the air like smoke.

"I don't—I don't want Lana to see me like this. I'm not going to burden her the way our mother did," she said, almost reluctantly. "Yasmine doesn't understand. Kifah and Altair—I saw them yesterday in the caliph's room. I saw their faces, Nasir." Her words came in a rush. "I'm losing all sense of right and wrong, and there's no one who understands. Not—not the way you can. No one else will look at me and know that I'm still here." She haltingly lowered her gaze to him. "That was why I agreed. Not because I have no respect for you. Not because you're worth nothing to me."

A rider on a bay horse rushed past them, breaking the heavy silence. They needed to move. Altair's plan banked on proper timing, and Nasir had factored just enough time for them and Afya to rest.

"You understand, don't you?" she asked softly. "You know what that means. Don't you?"

What you *mean to* me, her eyes said. Because though she was bold in the face of so much, his presence, he had learned, often drenched her in diffidence.

And it was only natural that after a lifetime of insults, he did not know how to react to words from the heart. Words that held emotions he had never experienced, no matter what he once believed. She puzzled him, too—one moment she was asking him what he wanted of her. The next, he was baring his heart and she was turning away, confusing him. One moment she refused his crown, the next she chose him over everyone else.

He took the reins from her outstretched hands.

CHAPTER 78

SIX SAFIN WERE DEAD. THE NUMBER ITSELF WAS INSIG-
nificant, but this was no casualty of one of Altair's wars. It was
slaughter in the main jumu'a of Sultan's Keep, a square meant for
decrees and announcements, a place where his baby brother's birth was
once celebrated.

All six of the safin had been gutted, their innards smeared across the
gray stone, arms stretched and pinned across erect beams, eyes gouged by
eager predators. Altair sensed a reason behind such specificity, but it was
yet another detail his father hadn't confided in him. Hundreds of stones
littered the ground, tainted red.

The messenger, panting and shivering in Demenhur's cold, hadn't
skimped on a single detail.

They were being punished for abandoning Arawiya after magic disappeared, the new king proclaimed. It should have wrought horror in the
hearts of people, a leader fresh on the throne establishing his rule with

vitriol and violence. Instead, delight was widespread, and it was only then that Altair realized how angry ordinary Arawiyans had been. They had craved justice long enough that the form in which it was achieved ceased to matter.

The second messenger arrived immediately after, reiterating Haytham's message of a swath of darkness bleeding across Sarasin's skies, confirming their suspicions that the new caliph was indeed an ifrit wearing the mortal skin of the merchant Muzaffar. There was no other reason the caliphate remained silent as fiery-staved ifrit trampled people and, worst of all, children left and right. Confusion held them in a transitory restraint as they waited for their caliph to act on their behalf.

Chaos Altair could handle, but it was this careful upending from the root that unnerved him, for everything Altair and Benyamin had worked for was slowly beginning to unravel.

"If you grip that beam any tighter, the entire palace might fall on us," Kifah called over the continuous *whip, whip, whip* of her spear.

If there was one thing that drove Altair's mind to red, raging anger, it was the death of children, the senseless loss of innocence.

He loosened his grip and—hating that he had to turn his entire head to see whatever was on his left—looked to Nasir, only to find the prince absent. Akhh, so that was why he was more silent than usual.

"Where'd he go?"

Kifah shrugged. "I'm not his mother."

Altair scowled and left the war room with its collection of unfurled maps and plans that had once been used to thwart him and his armies. Or to attempt to do so, at least. Altair wasn't a prize general for nothing. Oh, how the tables had turned. Here he was in Demenhur, bumping noses with the caliph's wazir and befriending generals he'd once leveled swords with in battle.

The Demenhune palace was thick with fear. The dignitaries were adamant in their attempts to leave, fearful that ifrit were coming for them, that they were next on the Lion's list to be halved like fish on a board. Altair had almost laughed. If only they knew the truth.

"We need to discuss Zafira," Kifah said, somehow following his line of thought.

"She's not some . . . *thing* to be discussed."

"You know what I mean."

"Just as you know that there's nothing we can do," Altair said tiredly.

Kifah sighed. "We can't shut her away. If it was really the Jawarat that made her kill him, she needs us."

She needed them regardless. She was their friend. A small girl stepped into the hall and stopped short at the sight of him. He recognized her sharp features—she'd been in the room the night before, staring unflinchingly at the caliph's mutilated corpse. There was something about the way she held herself that reminded him vaguely of Aya, but he brushed it away.

"Peace unto you. How's Zafira?" he asked.

"Why do you ask?" she replied defensively, studying him with warm brown eyes.

"I'm her friend."

"A friend wouldn't have abandoned her the way you did."

Shame burned his neck. He'd been meaning to see her. To make sense of what she'd done. He hadn't—sultan's teeth.

"She left," the girl continued.

"Don't lie."

"Lying is dishonorable," she said in dismay.

If he'd had any doubts before, he was utterly certain now that the girl was Zafira's sister, and he was this close to demanding an answer at swordpoint.

He crouched. "If you tell me, little one, I'll ask the kitchens for an extra piece of kanafah just for you."

She lifted an eyebrow at him. "I'm fourteen, and I can weave a needle through your remaining eyelid."

Altair burst out laughing and threw a glance at Kifah. "As Iskandar as they come. She's . . . quite small for fourteen."

"My name is Lana. And *you* are quite large," she replied.

"Not an insult," he said with a grin, and Kifah groaned. "What do you mean 'she left'?"

"She's going to find a lion."

It took him a moment to realize that Lana had said "the" and not "a," and that this lion was decidedly not a cat. Altair was suddenly very, very tired.

"So she's heading to Sultan's Keep?"

Lana nodded.

"Alone? She shouldn't even be able to—" He stopped at her wide-eyed look and dragged a hand down his face. *Khara.* "I should have kept that boy on a leash."

"He's the crown prince." Lana sniffed, offended on behalf of a fool she didn't even know.

"Crown prince my—"

Kifah cleared her throat.

"My what?" Lana asked sweetly.

Altair growled. "Ask your sister."

"She also took the dagger from your room. The one wrapped in a turban and wedged between the bookshelves. A terrible spot, really."

Altair blinked, disbelief slowing his brain. "You—she—what?"

"Lana? Where are you?" A voice called from the hall to their right. Lana gulped, eyes as wide as qahwa cups. She darted a glance to Kifah and fled down the hall before he could stop her.

Altair stomped after her with a frown, but only caught the fluttering end of a blue shawl and heard the swish of a falling curtain. That voice. It had been strangely familiar in cadence, but alluringly melodic and—*Now is not the time.*

Kifah was watching him with mild amusement and his frown deepened.

"What?" he snapped.

She shrugged.

"Sayyidi?"

Altair spun around with a snarl. Zafira was gone, Nasir was gone, the black dagger he had lost an entire eye to retrieve was gone. He forced air through his nose. Panic and stress never helped a soul.

"We—we found you the—a falcon," the perplexed guard stammered.

"Well, where is it?" Altair snapped, the boy's gray eyes reminding him of Nasir.

As the guard led them back to the war room, Altair let his thoughts roam. He and Kifah were bound to leave for their third of the plan soon enough, but they were meant to leave together with Nasir. Not like this. Without a farewell. Without even a note. Oddly enough, it stung.

A blur of brown and cream swooped past the double doors, and the guard ducked with an inhuman squawk. Altair stopped in his tracks. *Is that . . . ?* He held out his arm and the bird perched on his gauntlet.

"We found him sitting on the gates, and someone thought he was one of ours," the guard explained.

No, not one of theirs. *His.*

"Hirsi?" Altair couldn't keep the strain from his voice. "Akhh, boy, did you follow me all this way?" With a contented, answering thrill, the bird rubbed his golden beak against Altair's brow.

Kifah laughed. "Is there anything you don't love?"

"My father," Altair said simply, but at some point during his captivity, he *had* felt something for his father. Not love, but understanding, in the smallest of morsels. He snatched his letter from the desk, giving it one final read.

His mother was the last person Altair wanted to address, but Kifah was nowhere near as skilled a miragi as she was, and the Silver Witch was an integral part of making this plan work.

"Are we certain this will work?" Kifah asked. "How do we know she'll even be in the Hessa Isles to receive it? How do we know she'll agree to an illusion on that large a scale? What if she's still injured? What if *we* don't arrive in time?"

Altair finished tying the note to Hirsi's leg.

"I am forever humbled by your unwavering faith in me, One of Nine. Here's another question for your list: Why couldn't Nasir tell us he was leaving with Zafira?"

Kifah pursed her lips. "If there's one thing the Prince of Death is known for, it's following orders. He'll do his part."

"A thousand questions for me, and somehow you believe in him without a sliver of a doubt," Altair said.

"*You* believe in him," Kifah said, meeting his gaze. "That's enough for me."

Altair smiled, taken by the warmth in her dark gaze. A man could get lost in them for days.

Kifah lifted her brows. "Well? Shall we?"

Akhh, the woman was not one for sentiment.

"Wait," Altair said, remembering something he once never left without. He opened his trunk and drew two blades, strapping on his sheaths and sliding the scimitars snugly into the leather grips. He straightened with a heavy breath.

This time, Kifah did smile. "Just like old times, eh?"

"If only," he said. He would use just one of his scimitars. The other would be for balance, and because he loved both his children equally.

"Maybe it's a good thing he's taken Zafira with him," Kifah said. "We left her out of our plans when we shouldn't have. At the very least, we should have been there when she woke up."

It wasn't that he'd purposely avoided her. There were missives to send out, dignitaries to placate, blames to place. And then it was too late.

He could only hope Nasir would stick to the plan and head for Leil. Not Sultan's Keep. And that he would keep that daama dagger safe.

The same gray-eyed guard led them down to the stables. Hirsi perched obediently on Altair's shoulder, his head darting this way and that.

Altair pilfered an oily dolma on the way to the stables, swinging onto a dark steed and grinning when Kifah swung onto a flea-bitten gray with ease. "Akhh, One of Nine. There's no one else I'd rather ride with."

She arched an eyebrow into a perfect curve, and Altair learned there really was something he couldn't do. With a pang, he remembered he had an eternity ahead of him, and only half his sight. He foresaw lament as his close companion for some time.

"Must your every comment allude to your . . . tendencies?" she asked.

"I don't know what you're talking about. I sincerely admire our friendship, and there is truly no one else I would rather make this journey with and—"

"Tell me one more lie, and I'll make sure this horse's shoe is the last thing you see."

The stable boy snickered.

Altair sighed dreamily. "Not a soul treats me as kindly as you do." He gestured to the entrance and tossed the boy a coin. "After you, sayyida."

Kifah looked at freedom the way a besotted person looked at a lover. "You don't have to tell me twice."

They charged down the snow-steeped hill from the palace, Kifah's ululation echoing in the frigid air. Hirsi took to the air with a shrill promise, and the streets of the city soon echoed with the clamor of hooves. Spindly trees bent over like old men, and fat camels wended slower than their owners. People greeted them as they passed, smiles wide and eyes bright, for the Demenhune had always been more amiable than the rest of the kingdom.

"These rebels, do you think we can trust them?" Kifah shouted over the rush of the wind.

Whoever they were, Altair intended to make use of them. They were short on support, and Arawiya was short on a future.

"What we do know is that my charm will win them over to our side. We'll have ourselves a little army in no time."

He heard her snort loud and clear.

They had no choice; this wasn't a skirmish over territory. It was all of their tomorrows in one fragile fist. They slowed in the thick of Thalj, where the sooq bustled with the midday crowd.

Kifah drew up her horse with a curse and disappeared into an alley. "Oi, look at this."

"I was always warned not to follow strangers into dark alleys," Altair mocked darkly. "Is that . . . ?"

Kifah ripped a sheet of papyrus from the wall, and Altair stared at the face he knew as well as his own. Nasir. The countenance was almost exact, even to the scar slashing down his right eye.

"'A thousand dinars,'" he read, "'dead or alive.'"

"Bleeding Guljul. Should I be insulted that you and I are completely worthless?" Kifah asked.

"I would never admit this to his face, but my brother looks far better in person," Altair said.

Kifah snarled in frustration.

"What? They didn't get his nose right!" Altair exclaimed.

"Could you at least *pretend* to be concerned?"

Altair looked at her. "What should I do? Weep?" he asked, more harshly than he should have. "Will that make the posters disappear? Will that make my eye come back? Benyamin, too?"

Kifah looked away.

Altair exhaled long and slow.

"Akhh, let's leave being woeful to Nasir, laa?"

Kifah eagerly obliged, passing him the poster.

"It's the perfect way for the Lion to turn the people's fear of the Prince of Death into a reward." Altair rolled up the poster and tucked it into his bag. "And he's using the ifrit to spread word. No one else can travel so quickly. Khara, with them on his side, *everything* will move quickly. He might not see a need to prioritize the hearts, but it's clear he sees us as a threat."

"Then let's prove him right," Kifah said. She paused, studying him in the dusty light of the alley. "You're starting to worry."

Altair scoffed. "And risk my hair turning gray?"

"You're bursting with quips," Kifah pointed out.

Altair was too stunned to think of a comeback. Nearly a century and he didn't notice that tell?

"Do you ever think about how the Sisters failed?" she asked.

"They trusted my charming mother."

Kifah shook her head. "We're a zumra made of mismatched ends, one goal holding us together, unafraid to ask for help. We have the 'asabiyyah they didn't."

"'Asabiyyah?"

"The essence of our zumra," Kifah said with a shrug. "Unity based on shared purpose, loyalty to one another over that of kinship." She looked at her inked arm. "I never really understood the concept until now. Until us."

"The Sisters had that, too," Altair argued.

"Every rule has within itself the seeds of its own downfall, and the Sisters' was no different. They trusted their *own* and no one else. If there's anyone who can save Arawiya, it's us."

CHAPTER 79

BY THE TIME NIGHT FELL AND THE TEMPERATURE dropped, Zafira was sore all over. She had somehow managed to hurt Nasir's feelings, and the silence made his presence behind her even more overwhelming. The heat of his chest. The loose bind of his arms.

It had been more than a week since she'd ridden a horse, and the urge to collapse against him almost outweighed her dignity. Her back ached, and her legs ached. Her chest ached, too, from holding still to protect her mending wound as they crested the sloping hills of Demenhur's less-populated lands. They were fields once, bearing herbs and other plants harvested for medicinal purposes. Now they were blanketed in white, awaiting the return of magic like the rest of Arawiya.

When they neared a village at the Demenhune border, Nasir slowed Afya to a walk. The streets were silent except for the whistle of the cold wind. Torches winked like amber eyes from the shadows, and the shops were the kind of dark only ghosts were drawn to, alleys beckoning like the one-legged nesnas out of a child's nightmare.

"Why are we slowing?" Zafira asked. There was something about this village she didn't like. Even the moon had tucked herself behind heavy clouds.

Nasir sighed, a warmth on her chilled neck that she welcomed in more ways than one.

"There is a downside to having Afya on this journey." He slid off the mare's back and began leading her on foot, studying the surrounding structures. "Had she been any other horse, we could have swapped her and been on our way. She must rest. We'll continue just after midnight."

"Surely she can go a little farther," Zafira said, aware she whined like a child. "We left before noon."

His gaze flicked to her and back to the road. "The later it gets, the less likely we are to find rooms."

"I can sleep outside."

"I thought you wanted to kill the Lion, not deliver him your corpse," said Nasir, as apathetic as he had been on Sharr. "We need to change your bandages and find you a bed."

She shrank back. "I can change them myself."

"I've no doubt," he murmured absently, slowing near a dilapidated inn. "I'll see if they have any vacancies." He dropped Afya's reins and started down the path. There was a matching building to its left, brighter and more alluring, filling her with unease.

Here we leave him. Make for the stables.

The Jawarat's urging shot her with fear. She called him back. "You can't go in there looking like that."

He looked down at his clothes with a frown. How was it they had been on a soggy trail all day and he still looked perfect?

"Like . . . what?"

"Yourself," she explained, holding back a laugh at his perplexed state. "We—Demenhune don't like Sarasins."

His brows lifted at that. "So I should—"

"Help me down. I'll ask."

He took a fortifying breath before marching back toward her, but the sudden scuffle of boots across ice made him freeze. He snatched a bundle of rope from the stable ledge and she turned in Afya's saddle, breath clouding the air, to find a group of men meandering down the road.

They spotted Nasir immediately.

"Marhaba!" they called with typical Demenhune hospitality.

Nasir's response was hesitant. "Peace unto you."

His accent betrayed him.

"Come for a room, Sarasin?" one of them asked, lantern swaying.

Nasir responded too softly to hear. That, or her pulse was suddenly too loud to hear anything else as they crowded around him, scrutinizing him. A few of them even turned back to observe her.

"I know you! You're the Prince of Death!"

She held still.

"And look," another crowed. "The prince's whore."

She did not think a handful of words could strip her bare as easily as a knife. Reduce her. Defile her.

They are nothing, the Jawarat told her, but its voice was quiet, hesitant.

"There is a price on your head, Sultani," one of them said.

Her blood burned, but she heard the unsheathing of a rough-edged blade.

"Dead or alive."

Nasir's voice was level. "A price set by whom?"

"The king."

Zafira flinched. Word was traveling quickly—too quickly. This was a lowly village just beyond the mountains. It couldn't have been possible.

"Oi, you three get his girl. The rest of you"—the leader of the group swung his dagger—"kill the Sarasin dog."

If she hadn't been watching Nasir, she wouldn't have seen it: the shatter of his gaze, lit by the moonlight. The break in his composure.

The men were quick to brandish their weapons. Swords. Rods. Mostly daggers. Zafira gripped Afya's reins with white-knuckled fingers, useless. The Jawarat whispered in her skull, too frantic to decipher.

"You know who I am. You should know you can't kill me," Nasir said, but there was something reluctant in his voice. The abundance of Demenhune made his silvery lilt more pronounced, more deadly, yet the men laughed. It was a drawstring being pulled tight.

The cinching of a noose.

Nasir deliberately wound the rope around his fist, giving way to an awkward silence until he looked up at them with a lift of his eyebrows as if to say *This is your last chance.*

Three of them turned to her, leering, their gazes as debasing as what they had called her. She counted each heartbeat as it pounded in her ears, her jambiya pulsing against her leg, Altair's black dagger in her boot.

Zafira heard the snitch of Nasir's gauntlets and his blades cut across the night, toppling two of the men and startling the third. Nasir's rope-bound fist shot out next, knocking one of them out with a blow to his jaw before he whipped the tail end of the rope, tripping the other three. The last of them threw his crudely made spear, wincing when it clattered to the stone walkway.

"Hmm," Nasir said, assessing.

He circled back, stopping only to pluck his gauntlet blades from the men's thighs, giving the last a look that sent him scampering, his features illuminated by the moonlight. He wasn't much older than Zafira. They were *all* young, but that didn't surprise her as much as something else.

The Prince of Death hadn't killed a single one of them.

He hadn't even drawn his scimitar. He'd come far from that moment on Sharr, when he'd looked at her without a shred of life in his eyes and told her it was kill or be killed.

Guilt made her wrap her arms around herself. She felt apart from the world, apart from him. Empty in a way that came with an act as irreversible as butchery.

Do not be empty. We will fix this.

She ignored the Jawarat as the men groaned on the cold ground and Nasir remounted Afya, turning them back to the main road without a word.

———•———

Nasir should have listened to the warnings in his limbs when he'd first turned down the road to this village. Once a threat, the Prince of Death now held out to common people the promise of treasure. A price on his head. A target on his back.

Worse, there was an hourglass already running its course, for Altair would have left Thalj, his plans now set in motion.

Nasir wasn't meant to leave Demenhur and cross into Sarasin until dawn, when at least a sliver of light would grant them an equal sliver of safety, but now they'd have to plow through the Tenama Pass and spend their first night there. He couldn't risk staying here another moment. Not with her.

The snow was bathed in weeping moonlight, houses and buildings passing in a blur of intermittent lantern light. He saw those seven men— *boys* with mouths too big for their years—lying on the ground. *The prince's whore.*

Even when he was trying to do good, even when he wasn't the one drawing a blade and stealing a soul, he was hurting people. *Hurting her.* Darkness slipped from him, streamed behind them.

"Speak to me," he rasped into her hair.

Her hand fell to his wrist. "The moon likes you. See how she shines for you."

Something lodged in his throat, drawn by the sorrow in her lilting voice.

"You're not that," she said after a moment, so softly he almost missed it beneath Afya's hooves.

"Not what?"

"What they called you."

He stiffened. "I know," he said finally.

She only *hmm*ed, acknowledging his lie.

Afya never complained, though it wasn't long before Nasir felt the strain in her muscles. By then, they were deep into the Tenama Pass. The night had thickened, howls from hungry beasts winding from the rugged peaks of the Dancali Mountains.

The pass was a narrow length of darkness, a harrowing tunnel lit only by a shrouded moon. Uninhabited, apart from the sporadic tent erected in the shadows, fires lit and sheltered from the mischievous breeze.

Nasir didn't stop at any of them, even the one where a woman waved and offered food for the remainder of their journey.

And then he came to a wrenching halt at the mouth of the pass. Afya was breathing hard, her sides heaving beneath them.

Nasir dismounted and stared.

"Sarasin," Zafira whispered with a shiver.

The darkness was absolute. The moon had tucked herself away, ashamed of those below. Pockets of light flickered here and there, too faint to be seen as anything but eyes glowing in a graveyard, and with the dark came the cold, a chill beyond even that of Demenhur.

"There are ifrit here," Zafira said, and Nasir remembered how well she saw in the dark. How well *he* could see now because of the new-found power in his blood, after years of enduring the fear that lived within him.

He began leading Afya on foot, a hand on his scimitar, his eyes on their surroundings.

They stopped in a village just small enough that they were unlikely to be recognized. The caravanserai was a low construction that sprawled beneath the moonless sky, horses idling in the courtyard along with a single caravan, the camels slumbering. It was solemn and silent, as forlorn as the rest of the terrain they'd passed, but it was open, and that was what mattered.

"Wait here," Nasir said, knocking back his hood.

"Marhaba," a short, plump woman in a roughspun abaya said when he stepped through the door and its curtains to a warm room full of patrons. "I am Rameela."

"Business seems good," he observed.

The seated crowd was subdued but boisterous enough, the food abundant. Another woman sat on a stool, the gold-dusted length of her brown legs on display. She played a ney, fingers sliding down the flute sensuously.

The caravanserai owner eyed him, her face kind as she regarded his attire. "The sun never shows, but it's nothing new, eh? People still need a warm bed."

"Are there ifrit?"

"None around here. How may I help you, sayyidi?"

"Have you any rooms?"

"Aywa," Rameela affirmed, smiling. "The moon ensured your luck—I've one left."

"Just one?"

She nodded. "Have you a party?"

"I'll take the room. I'll also need a woman—"

Her smile flattened with disappointment. "We do not cater to such needs, sayyidi." She gestured behind him. "Rana sometimes does, if you're to her liking."

Nasir turned to the woman playing the ney, realization striking him far too slowly when she smiled coyly at him.

"I—that's—I'm not—" He cleared his throat. "I mean, I need a healer."

Rameela leaned back and laughed. "Don't look so frightened, sayyidi. You should have said so! I will see to your injury." She looked him over. "My husband is more skilled. Shall I fetch him?"

"No, you'll do. Only to change bandages." Exhaustion tugged at his eyelids like they were stubborn curtains.

The vacant room was down a dimly lit hall. It was a small space with a narrow bed and an even narrower adjoined bath. Cramped, but warm and free from mold and filth, and nearest the back exit.

"Passable, sayyidi?" Rameela ventured.

"It'll do," Nasir said, because he apparently didn't know any other words. Rimaal, why was it so hard to carry on a conversation with anyone amiable?

Outside, a few spindly trees scratched against the caravanserai's roof like knives across bone. He led Afya to a low ledge so that Zafira could dismount more easily.

"No killers in this one?" she teased lightly.

"I'm still here," Nasir replied wryly as he handed the reins to the stable boy, whom he assumed was the owner's son.

Zafira laughed, but stopped just as quickly with a wince and a low moan. Her hand closed around Deen's ring at her chest, and Nasir found himself relieved at the sight. It meant she was thinking of something other than the book, other than death. Other than those boys.

"You truly loved him," Nasir said like a fool.

She paused to look at him. "I will always love him, though never in the way he wished."

He didn't know what to say next, so he said nothing.

Inside, they found the caravanserai owner lighting a few suspended lanterns in the room.

She smiled when she saw Zafira. "Yaa, so this is why you asked for a woman. Come, child. Rest, so I can see to your wound."

"Do you need help?" Nasir asked like an idiot from the corridor.

Rameela *tsk*ed. "If you could help her yourself, you wouldn't have asked me, eh? There is food in the front. Yalla. Go eat, boy."

After avoiding the patrons and the woman playing the ney as he downed a bowl of shakriyeh—the yogurt warm but the lamb sparse—Nasir returned to the corridor as Rameela was leaving.

She regarded him differently, wiping her hands on her abaya. "It is a horrible wound."

"An arrow." He saw no reason to shirk the truth.

"It was mended well," Rameela said, "but it has torn again." She eyed him as if that were somehow his fault, and looked back to the closed door. "She speaks strangely at times, to herself, laa? Fatigue won her over, Sultani."

Nasir held still.

"You hold yourself too proud," Rameela said, as if that explained it. "But it was the scar that gave you away."

He stared her down in the cramped hall, aware that any of the surrounding rooms could hold a mercenary out for silver. Aware that Zafira could be lying in a pool of her own blood because he was a fool to have left her.

Rameela wagged her finger at him. "Any boy beneath this roof is to be treated as my son, prince or not," she said with mock sternness.

Nasir exhaled in relief. Had she heard his father was dead? That he was no longer a prince, but a displaced sultan himself?

"The bed's a narrow fit, but there's space in the room for a bedroll, should you like one."

He thought of what the men in the small Demenhune town had called Zafira, and declined.

"The hall is fine," he said, not bothering to elaborate in Rameela's expectant silence.

"Right, then," she said. "There is one detail I wish to know, if you are to stay the night. You are the prince, but who is she?"

Zafira had shared nothing at all, it seemed.

"Demenhur's legendary Hunter."

She laughed softly. "I should not be surprised the Hunter was a girl all along."

CHAPTER 80

IN THE END, RAMEELA PITIED NASIR AND, AFTER ASSUR-
ing him that she would keep watch over Zafira through the night,
showed him to a small room used to store spare covers and other odds
and ends. It was cramped, but the door had a lock and her son left him a
bedroll before the tiny fireplace, so it served its purpose.

He was dreading the moment when he'd tell Zafira that he had orders
to stop in Leil. That he didn't, in fact, leave Thalj solely for her and would
not be taking her to Sultan's Keep. Khara, he should have been a little
more up front about that bit. He had finally convinced himself to close his
eyes—the word "dog" pounding in his skull in time with his breathing,
Zafira straight-backed and unflinching atop Afya as the men sneered at
her—when a flash of silver knifed the dark room.

And materialized into a woman.

Nasir sat up. "Doors were made for knocking."

The Silver Witch's lips twitched into a faint smile. "And yet a locked
door never stopped you."

The edges of his mouth ticked upward, briefly, as the fire rioted in the quiet. He looked to her hands, but they were empty, no papyrus in sight. Why was she here, if not for Altair's missive?

"Did you find the people you needed on the Hessa Isles?" Nasir asked. *How else could she have materialized in this room, idiot?* But he'd spoken the words as an apology, the closest he would go to atone for his coldness on board Jinan's ship, and he wondered if she would understand. If she would accept it.

She bobbed a nod, for that was how mothers were. "My immortality is no longer at risk. I have regained my powers." She paused. "I heard the Lion has taken the throne. So I came to . . . to . . ."

Nasir saw the mother he knew in the uncertainty crowding her mouth and the concern mellowing her harsh gaze. He heard the question she asked in the silence. The reason she had come to him, and not Altair, as planned.

"He died," he said.

With his eyes closed, her broken exhale was infinitely worse. With his eyes closed, he could dare to imagine both his parents were here in this room in this moment.

"He said—" Nasir stopped. What were these feelings so taut in his throat? When had he begun to suffer so much? "He thinks of you when the moon fills the sky."

Nasir slipped the pieces of the broken medallion from his pocket and placed them in her hand. The remnants of the Lion's control. The gift to her beloved that had proved deadly.

She whispered a word and fled to the hearth, her cloak catching wisps of firelight. As if she could mend herself with every last spark. As if she could turn the tides of the world. He had believed that, once. When he was young and lost and believed in the safety of his mother's skirts.

She, unlike Nasir, had been born to lead. She had been born with a place in the world. And she had given that to him, too, until the Lion came and took it all away. Now he was poised to take away more. Far more.

"Si'lah are solitary creatures, drawn to assisting the weak. I was young, naive. I did not understand that 'solitary' does not mean bereft of companionship. I wanted more than to reign as a warden with an iron fist over the ones who had wronged Arawiya. I reversed the sentences of those imprisoned on Sharr even as the walls of my fortress barred magic. I gave them jobs, homes, allowed them to live as those on the mainland did. And yet I was alone."

He'd seen proof of it, in the ruins of the island. The edifices too elaborate, too luxurious for the incarcerated. In the hollowness of her words, Nasir found the answer to a question he had long asked himself: Was it possible to be surrounded by life yet feel nothing but the emptiness of death?

"I wanted and I was weak. I desired to be loved and understood. He preyed on me. Stripped me of my defenses, exploited my weaknesses. He used me in every possible way even as I deluded myself into thinking I was in love.

"I had never known loss as deep as what I felt on the day of my Sisters' deaths. The day I fled Sharr and stopped at each of their palaces: Demenhur, Zaram, Pelusia, Alderamin, to tear their thrones apart. Of the five Gilded Thrones, only one remains. The one he sits upon now was never mine, for I'd never had one. It was Afya's."

Her favorite of the Sisters of Old.

"I dragged that throne to the old city of Sultan's Keep and cemented my reign, appointing my Sisters' most trusted as caliphs. This is what you hear of my reign. The change I wrought, the ropes I held to keep our fragile kingdom from falling apart. But there is only so much one can salvage of a ruin, isn't there, my son?

"He thieved and pillaged. Deceived without abandon. He took from me my Sisters, my kingdom, my husband, and my sons."

She turned to him, and in her face, Nasir saw his own. He saw Zafira, and Altair. Kifah, and Benyamin. He saw those whose lives were forced onto paths they should not have had to tread.

"He took from me my life, and now I will take from him tenfold."

He felt the chill of her words in his bones.

How did you find me? he wanted to ask, but pride refused to let him. It was magic, he knew. Zafira had slit her palm to find Altair, but his mother's magic wasn't restrained to the volume of blood in a vial when it was her own that fueled it.

"Did you receive Altair's note?" he asked.

She frowned. "Note?"

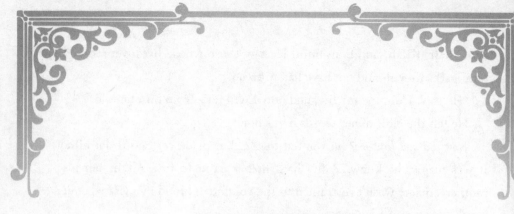

CHAPTER 81

When Zafira woke, she barely blinked at the Silver Witch sitting on the cushions against the wall. After everything that had happened, the appearance of a witch who wasn't deterred by doors or locks felt like child's play.

"How strange it is to be loved by the one who hates all else," Anadil said softly.

Was it Zafira she spoke of, or herself?

She looked at the Jawarat. "It is changing you."

Instead of the anger that raged whenever anyone accused the book, Zafira felt shame. Because Anadil was different. She had been witness to Zafira over the years, even before Baba's death.

"What should I do?" she asked.

The Silver Witch tilted her head. "You are the pure of heart, not I."

Was she still pure of heart, when she had split a man in two? When she had given the Lion the means to embrace the si'lah heart as if it were his own? When her night had passed whispering things to the Jawarat she could barely remember moments later?

"You recall what I said of you, once—that you are very much the people's queen?" the Silver Witch asked. "It remains true, Huntress. Now, more than ever."

"What does that mean?"

The door opened with a soft knock, and the true king stepped inside with Zafira's washed and dried tunic. He handed it to her awkwardly before he stepped back and flicked his gaze between her and the Silver Witch, guarded and hesitant.

"We have to leave," Nasir said unceremoniously.

The Silver Witch rose. "As do I. It seems I've a falcon to find."

Nasir lowered his head in respect. "It is good," he said, "to have you with us again."

She smiled, and Zafira remembered Umm when Anadil's face changed. Perhaps it was a gesture true to all mothers, when their children humbled themselves in such ways.

Sarasin was frightening. Darkness at every turn, ifrit shrieking into the night that would have been day, had the sun not been a coward. They came across remnants of riots in small towns as ghostly as her own, where buildings lay in shambles, glass smashed and glowing in the light of bonfires. The lazy breeze carried leaves of papyrus.

Zafira snatched one from the air.

On it were lines and lines of Arawiyan letters scribed by a reed pen, the letters smoother with each new pass. It was a child's. A practice sheet meant to be taken to school the next day. Her mind tucked the sheet into Lana's small hands, when she was young, not yet six. Skipping home from the old schoolhouse, eager to share the happenings of her day.

She saw her eager footsteps turn panicked. Her skipping turned to fleeing. A child should not have to fear for her life in such a way. With a reed pen in hand, letters in her head, dirty sandals on her feet.

Death before her eyes.

This, because Zafira wanted magic, because she had braved the Baransea for the hearts and brought back Arawiya's greatest foe. Lives had been upended by the Lion's madness. While he practiced order in Sultan's Keep, an entire fifth of the kingdom was falling apart, the rest well on their way.

The Jawarat watched it all through her eyes.

Do you see what happens when chaos unfolds? she asked it. The aftermath of mayhem.

It was silent, but it heard her—she knew by the contemplation pressing against her conscience. It was a new emotion, one it had been stumbling toward since she'd killed the caliph and felt her soul tip empty.

As if, perhaps, it no longer wanted control and a malleable will.

We have learned from you.

"Zafira?" Nasir's voice rumbled through her back, lighting a fire across her neck. He steered Afya away, as if turning one's back on ruin made it less real. "You're speaking to it."

"Does it speak to you, too?" she asked with some hesitance.

She knew his brow furrowed at her question. His silvery lilt stretched when he was confused or uncertain. "I didn't say that."

"It—" She paused, and she wondered if he took her silence as reluctance to speak to him or reluctance to speak of the Jawarat. Knowing how ready he was to disparage himself, it was likely the former, but he didn't know the whole of it. Candor was never quite as bitter with him, because he had more than enough monsters of his own to ever judge her.

Still, she hadn't told anyone the truth of the Jawarat for a reason. She hadn't even told the Silver Witch, who had been like Zafira before she fell for the Lion's silver tongue. She had shrouded the truth, but it had unleashed itself anyway. She had thought to keep its chaos a secret, but it had made itself known through her hand. Through the caliph's death.

She gripped the book tight and opened her mouth.

"The Sisters created the Jawarat from and with their memories, but it was connected to the Lion on Sharr for long enough that it took some of his memories, too. It wants things. Dangerous things sometimes."

A cold unassociated with their surroundings chilled her spine when he finally spoke.

"It?"

He did not dig or pry, or regard her any differently. She swallowed her relief. "I thought the Jawarat spoke using the voices of the Sisters, and then I thought its voice was the Lion's, but it's . . . not."

"It's a hilya," he said. "Fuse enough magic and memory into a single object, and it results in near sentience."

She brushed her thumb down its spine. It was a comfort, even now. A part of her, as nefarious as it was.

"Are you afraid of it?" He voiced his words slowly, as if she might startle if he spoke them too quickly. As if she might shove him off the horse and take off on her own.

"Shouldn't I be? You saw what it made me do."

"You journeyed to Sharr. You faced Arawiya's greatest foe alone. If I were to assume anyone to be afraid of a book, it wouldn't be you."

There was something more being spelled out in his words. Admiration. It warmed her to her toes, and flooded her with the feeling that she was undeserving. She *had* done both those things, but so had he. What made her any different?

"I didn't fear Sharr or the Lion that way," she said matter-of-factly. "I'm afraid of doing the wrong thing. Again. The Jawarat blurs the lines between good and not."

It was what every sane person feared, she realized, but with the Jawarat, virtue had been extricated from her, separated. An entity of its own both hers and not.

"Stealing the Lion's memories didn't make it inherently wicked," Nasir observed, and perhaps it was the cadence of his words, the way he was trying to make sense of it along with her, but she was suddenly filled with such gratitude that she almost leaned into him. She held still, terrified by her heart. "It's like anyone else now, burdened with the task of choosing between good and evil. Why allow yourself to be controlled when *you* can be the one in control? *You* can control *it*. Sway its intent."

Was she already doing as much, hence the change she'd noted? The silent rumination since they'd left Demenhur? She twisted around, pain making her flinch. He was beautiful, even in darkness. Alive, when he spoke to her. "Half of what you say to me is what you need to hear yourself."

Nasir emitted a laugh, a broken, haggard thing more contained than free, and Zafira was aware she devoured his reactions the way a rose sought out sunlight.

As they continued onward with the phantom of his laugh in her ears and Afya's occasional snorts, she noticed his path had begun tilting east.

"There's something I have to tell you," he began hesitantly.

"Oh?"

"We're going to Qasr al-Leil."

Qasr. Sarasin for "palace."

He paused when she stiffened like a board. "Not Sultan's Keep."

At first, she thought she didn't understand, but then she did—sudden and striking.

Her fury snarled through her like an angry vine, ripping every semblance of calm. Nasir brought Afya to an abrupt halt as Zafira wrenched around to face him. Her wound wheezed a warning, and she dragged one knee up between them to ease her strain.

He had never left Demenhur for her.

He had never planned to take her to the Sultan's Palace at all. He had—

"You mocked me. You *lied* to me." Her voice was a growl. Her anger was the Jawarat's. No—the daama book was gratingly silent, and this, this was *her*. Where was the outrage it once used to drive her?

His resilience broke under her accusation. "I did not lie to you. Once my work here is through, we'll continue onward to Sultan's Keep. To defeat the Lion and restore magic. Does that sound acceptable?"

He spoke gently, as if she were an insolent child. As if she didn't hold power in her hands.

"What work?" she asked, her voice flat with wrath.

Regret pinched his gaze. "Killing."

Her snort made him flinch. She wondered how the jambiya he had gifted her would look with its hilt protruding from his heart.

No, bint Iskandar.

She laughed out loud at the Jawarat's dismay. The sound of her madness echoed in the dark desolation of Sarasin, the hungering breeze carrying it through the empty streets.

This is not you, the book said with that same hesitation after she'd killed the caliph and woken beside Lana.

Laa, this is what you wanted me to be.

"If I pushed you off this horse, would you die?"

Nasir's face transformed with a slow, surprised laugh. "Perhaps."

He looked at her as if she were a marvel he had yet to decipher. Laa, he was mocking her, and it made her murderous. It filled the Jawarat with foreboding that once would have been glee. What had changed? She threw herself at him, uncaring that one of them might fall and break their neck.

Nasir only gripped her, stronger than she had known him to be.

And then he kissed her.

Laa, it wasn't a kiss, but a crash. She froze for a defining heartbeat as one vault of emotions careened to a halt and another erupted. She kissed him back. Their mouths fought for dominance. Twice they had kissed, but, skies, this was glorious. Thrilling in a way that electrified her entire body.

She tasted anger on his tongue. Pain. Desire and her anguish and her fury lashed back. He broke down to panting, begging her to let him breathe.

They wrestled, punishing each other for the words they had spoken and the things that they wanted and the Jawarat between them, confusing her. She sank her teeth on his lower lip. He tugged away, greedily taking her mouth again whole. His hands dug into her hair, gathering fistfuls as he pulled her closer, the space between them searing as his hands trailed down her neck, down to her back, pulling her flush against him with a rasp. She slipped her own fingers into his robes, beneath the fine linen of his qamis, and his head tilted back with a low, drawn-out sound.

The cold Sarasin night was a caress as much as his touch. She felt powerful. She felt free—for the first time in an eternity, her thoughts were clear, so full of him that she thought nothing of the green book embossed with a lion's mane.

Afya snorted with as much indignation as the sound allowed, and Zafira pulled away, leaning her brow against his with a sigh.

The starless night looked down upon them.

She stared at the book, grasping at its contentment. As if it were pleased that she felt like herself, that she had *returned* to herself.

You are surprised, bint Iskandar.

She could barely hear the Jawarat over the buzzing of her skin. *I thought you wanted someone to control. Someone to unleash your chaos.*

We thought it, too.

The voice was distant, contemplative once more as Nasir gazed down at her with hooded eyes. "All right?" *Are you through wanting to kill me?* was what he asked in that question.

Sweet snow, the rasp of his voice was a song she wanted to hear without end.

She nodded.

His mouth was a glorious bruise. His breathing the most beautiful, broken sound. He looked as if he'd already known exactly what would happen when his lips touched hers.

He brushed a trembling thumb across her lower lip. "If anyone can change the fabric of the world, it is you, fair gazelle. I have seen it."

She had the feeling he spoke of more than just the Jawarat.

He took her to another inn, this one lavish due to its presence in the capital of Sarasin. Zafira's blood ran hot, her heart still a drum that wouldn't cease.

"Take me with you," Zafira said as Nasir started for the courtyard.

He helped her down and released her hand, and she wondered what it would be like to slip her fingers between his whenever she desired. To call him hers.

Monsters didn't become queen.

Inside, they were greeted with warmth and the scent of fresh manakish. Curtains hung from horizontal beams, and an intricate chandelier fitted with a hundred oil wicks dusted the space in golden light. The crowd was subdued, patrons dressed crisply despite Sarasin's state, their conversations amiable. Apart from their darker colorings, they were almost exactly like the Demenhune. Laa—they were hardier somehow, as if living in the volatile shadow of Sultan's Keep had weathered them for this moment.

Zafira started when a woman sidled up to Nasir's side, her stomach bare, her skin like molten gold and leaving very little to the imagination in a red bedlah.

"Sayyidi," she said breathlessly, gripping his arm.

Zafira frowned, ignoring a twinge of whatever it was. "You sound like you're going to die."

Nasir only stiffened and the woman noted her with surprise. Zafira couldn't see beneath his turban, but she knew the prince's ears were burning a brilliant shade of crimson, and he looked grateful when the innkeeper emerged from the kitchens.

Nasir cleared his throat. "Do you have any rooms?"

The innkeeper nodded, and Zafira didn't like the way his gaze priced Nasir's clothes. "We run low, sayyidi, and—"

A handful of coins clunked on the table between them, and the man's hungry eyes swept downward. Zafira's breath caught. It struck her oddly, how they could share so much yet live entirely different lives. The silver he exchanged in a single moment was more than she had seen in her entire *life*.

"Very nice, sayyidi," the innkeeper said, nodding so profusely that Zafira was afraid his head would unhinge. One by one, he pocketed the coins before gesturing down one of the halls. "This way, this way."

The room was as sumptuous as the ones in the palace. The platform bed was laden with silken sheets and jeweled cushions, wide enough for three of her and surrounded by a thin veil. It was a lavish display not meant for one, she realized with a stroke of heat.

Nasir paused at the sight, and then quickly set her satchel on the low table and turned for the door. His eyes were dark. Fear clamped Zafira's lips tight.

And then the door closed with a soft thud.

A recreant. That is what you are.

"I don't even know what that means," she mumbled.

A coward.

Zafira gritted her teeth. She wrenched the book from her bag and threw it near the fire burning in the hearth, and felt the heat the instant the Jawarat did. With a snarl, she snatched it up again and threw it on the bed.

Anguish flooded her, an overwhelming sense of hurt—and it wasn't hers. Skies, had the thing been . . . *teasing* her?

Why do you not take what you wish?

It was an earnest question, not one spurring her to action. Harmless curiosity was not something Zafira associated with the Jawarat.

"Like when I killed the caliph? When I took justice into my own hands?"

We speak of him. Your prince.

She ignored it and unsheathed Nasir's jambiya, the blade a gleam in the firelight reminding her of all she'd done. Then she pulled the black dagger out of her boot with another wince, thinking of how Altair must have reacted to finding it gone.

She should give them both to Nasir to tuck away.

You have killed. You have not been thieved of judgment.

"Oh, so you're suddenly intent on making me feel good," she retorted, but couldn't summon her anger. What had happened to its goading? To its gloating and vile provocations? She dropped down beside it. "Everything that's happened is your fault."

She was a fool to assume she could go to Sultan's Keep on her own. She pressed her eyes closed at the reminder of her brashness, how mindless she'd been to guilt Lana into stealing the dagger, how witless she'd been to sneak away.

Killing the Lion and stealing back his heart wouldn't rebuild the zumra's trust. It wouldn't recover the shard of her soul that was lost when she killed the caliph. Laa, the only way forward was through. To face them. To retain the person she once was.

We know it is the fault of ours. And so we tried to atone.

Atone. She almost laughed. "This is why you need a mother," she said dryly.

The Jawarat hummed at her joke, too chagrined to do more.

The lantern threw a handful of shadowed stars and shapes across the ceiling as she snuggled into the pillows and cushions with a long sigh. She couldn't fall asleep, despite the fatigue burning behind her eyelids. Could the Lion sense her, the way she sensed him in every shadow and slant of the night?

Zafira stared at the Jawarat, knowing she relied on its company as a drunkard would rely on arak. She turned on to her side and stared at the stretch of space beside her. It wasn't the Jawarat's company she wanted, was it?

She slid off the bed and helped herself to a single ma'moul cookie from the plate the maid had left on the table, glancing at the door and wrenching her gaze away.

She shouldn't. The Jawarat said nothing, only showing her a memory it hadn't stolen, but cherished: her and him atop Afya, the freedom in her veins, the balance restored, the happiness, fleeting as it was.

He is a chaos we savor.

Her hand closed around the doorknob, and with a quick inhale, she stepped into the dim hall. She didn't know where Nasir was. Perhaps he was downstairs, relaxing after a long day of being stuck with her. She took a step forward—

And nearly tripped.

"Khara," she hissed.

A figure rose from beside the door.

"Nasir? Why are you—what are you doing out here?"

The moonlight from the far window caught the bewildered look in his eyes. Fatigue slanted shadows on his face.

"Did they not have any other rooms? Are we out of silver?"

He merely blinked at her tiredly.

Skies. She looked down either side of the empty hall and dragged him inside. "Why were you crouched out there?"

He lifted a hand to the back of his neck and dropped it. "What happened at that inn in Demenhur was my fault. I should not have left you on Afya alone. And not"—his voice rose, stopping her protest—"*not* because you're a girl, but because you're hurt."

"So you were guarding my door," she said, lifting her eyebrows. She set her boots together and moved them to the side, aware of her messiness in the face of his neatness. "Stay here. The room's big enough. Akhh, the bed's big enough for us both."

Liar, the Jawarat taunted, and she thought of his mouth. His hooded gaze. His nose nudging hers.

When he took a measured step forward, igniting her blood, he acknowledged the lie. His chest rose and fell with careful reflection. "After what they said?"

She caught the anguish hardening his jaw. *The prince's whore.*

"Do you think I'd let words from insignificant inebriates bother me? Is it true?"

"Of course not," he bit out.

Skies, getting a reaction out of him was as impossible as the Arz. She hid a grin, trying but failing to act nonchalant. The bed might be large enough to fit three of her, but the room itself was too small for her to daama breathe in. She chewed the inside of her cheek and dared to meet his eyes.

I always knew your innocence was a farce, Yasmine taunted in her head.

The silence churned between them until he said raggedly, gaze darkening to black, "Well then. Time for bed, fair gazelle? You interrupted quite the dream I was having."

She sputtered, parting the curtains surrounding the bed so he wouldn't see the way her limbs shook.

"You can have that side," she snapped.

He removed his sword and aligned it with the bed. Him and his neatness. "Do you think the people are aware the Demenhune Hunter is so . . . domineering?"

"Do you think the people know the Prince of Death dreams so indecently?"

Nasir paused, and Zafira froze in the midst of knotting the curtain, an apology springing to her tongue when he—

He laughed.

Not the quick bark of surprise that he quickly quenched. Not the whisper of one, but a whole and true laugh. It glittered silver in his eyes and tugged back his head, rattling his chest and exposing his teeth and making it oh so hard to breathe. She wished she were an artist to capture this moment. She wished she were bold enough to cross the room and press her mouth to his exposed throat. To taste the sound of his laughter with her own tongue. It filled her with such untrammeled joy that the world darkened a hue when he stopped.

Diffidence colored his cheeks as he unclasped his belt of throwing knives, long lashes sweeping downward with his gaze. He unwound his turban and shook his hair loose. Then he slid his robes free and hung them on the hook by the door.

If it was possible for a girl to incinerate as her prince undressed, she had done just that. It was strange watching him go about such simple tasks. Intimate, in a way. He settled into the bed in that burgundy qamis, armed still with his gauntlet blades and gloves, and all she could think of was the smooth, solid plane of his skin, his pulse heaving beneath her touch.

When she didn't move to join him, he turned back and opened one eye, a laugh twinkling in its depths. "Should I leave? You're not the only one to invite me to her bed tonight."

Zafira's eyebrows flicked up, and he shamelessly made himself more comfortable.

"The girl in the red bedlah?" she asked.

He regarded her. "Jealous?"

The word conjured the girl in the yellow shawl, Kulsum, and indeed, her spite was immediate. She tried to hide it away, to clear her open book of a face. *Too late.*

His eyes were intent, reminding her that he could read her as easily as a map.

She hurriedly tugged on a frown. "Concerned, mostly. The poor thing could hardly breathe."

"I tend to have that effect on women."

"Which women?" She tilted her head.

He smirked.

Skies, what a fool he'd think she was. Of course there were other women. He was the daama prince.

"Not this one," she said, hoping the fluster on her face would come across as exasperation.

"Oh?" He turned and watched her, the teasing in his tone heating the room in a way the hearth never could. "Our little moment on Afya's back said otherwise, but I do love a challenge."

She glared, and the curve of his shoulders trembled with a laugh.

"Sleep well, Huntress. May your dreams be as delectable as mine."

"No one says that."

"No? I didn't know you made a habit of sharing your bed with other men."

She growled and climbed back beneath the covers, facing the opposite side. His voice was like warm honey down her tongue. His presence was a weight, making her mind meander through every story Yasmine had shared, her neck burning. The Jawarat was content and quiet. *Dastard.*

She wrenched her gaze to the window, to the heavy throb of the Lion's darkness, and knew sleep would be hard to find this night.

CHAPTER 82

NASIR WAS HEAVY WITH EXHAUSTION, YET HE could think of nothing but the brush of color on her face, her presence beside him. The heat pooling lower and lower.

And the hesitation in her gaze, clouded by uncertainty.

He was a killer with a crown, a poison alluring enough to taste. To Kulsum, to the women whose gazes followed the Prince of Death down the corridors. Not to her.

I would rather know one intimately than a thousand ostensibly, he had wanted to say, but the words were too bold, more of an invitation than a proclamation.

He didn't want to be another moment stolen from a thousand. He wanted every sunrise and every crescent moon. He wanted to be the reason for every rare blush, the cause of every breathless sigh.

He thought of that moment atop Afya's back, its match on Sharr between the columns just before all broke loose. Was he only so bold when she was in need of a distraction? If he had not kissed her then, so full of anger and pain and sorrow, would she have shoved him off the horse?

"Take me with you tomorrow," she said. "I'm not going to stay here while you're killing the caliph."

"Your wound—" *Your mind.*

"Is fine. Take me."

Who was he to deny her anything? "Aren't you afraid?"

"The one thing certain in life is death, isn't it?" she asked, echoing his cruelty on Sharr. "I was stupid for thinking I could confront the Lion alone, but . . . if I'm going to die, I might as well die fighting for what I believe in. Our cause is just. We're not fighting for land or governance. We're ensuring a future for the people. Magic and a world worth living in."

He marveled at her strength, at how she could open her mouth and give him direction, a compass leading his path.

"It's . . . what I've been doing since the day I first held a bow in my hands."

"You won't die," he said after a silence.

"Why not?" She didn't know that he wasn't teasing, not then.

Because he was aware of every rise and fall of her chest, of her even exhales feathering the air, and the vast distance between them. She was a beacon in the darkness. A wild rose that bloomed over death.

Laa, she was the reason death had become significant to him.

And he would not let it take her.

"All those women," she said, abruptly changing the subject. "You had to have some semblance of confidence."

Her tone was inquisitive, curious, daama clueless. *Fair gazelle, the things I could teach you.* The sheets rustled as she turned to look at his back, and he screwed his jaw tight. Despite his shirt, he felt the presence of each scar as if it were being carved afresh.

She continued, oblivious. "Where did it all go?"

Please. Go. To. Sleep.

"I don't know," he lied, because she wasn't another woman. She was Zafira, legendary and ethereal, pure-hearted and guileless. Lost and tethered to a book. "Where did *you* find the sudden confidence?"

Like a fool, Nasir wished this night could go on forever. The Lion, the darkness, Altair's plans—he wished all of it could disappear, only for a moment.

"I stole yours."

He heard the smirk in her voice, and it took every last drop of his resolve not to turn around and pull her into his arms.

CHAPTER 83

ZAFIRA'S DREAMS WERE USUALLY AS STRAIGHTFOR-
ward as an arrow, but not this night. One moment, she saw the
Jawarat's vision, only instead of crimson flooding the streets of
her village, the blood ran black while the book crowed of redemption,
and as she tried to grasp its meaning, to continue onward and see what
happened next, the white village darkened and narrowed to a room.

A veiled bed, silks sliding along her bare skin, lips feathering the slopes
of her breasts. Her name a whispered prayer in her ear.

She woke with a start. An odd, aching need tightened her skin. The
Jawarat purred.

The hour wanes.

But night still clung to the sky. Khara—of course it was still dark out;
they were in Sarasin. She made to move from her warm cocoon of blankets and froze.

Her cocoon was not a blanket, but a body, solid and lithe. Nasir. She
was nestled against him, wrapped in his arms as if she would disappear

if he let go. At some point in the night, he had discarded his gloves. Her dream rose vividly, heat breaking out across her body.

His exhales were steady and measured on her shoulder, and she carefully twisted her neck to face him. He was even more beautiful asleep. The harsh lines of his brow were smooth, long lashes fanning like scimitars against his copper skin. Her fingers itched to brush away the wayward locks that had fallen across his brow.

One of his hands was splayed across her stomach. The other, the one connected to the arm beneath her, rested palm up beside her face. Ever so slowly, she lifted her hand, marveling at the quake in her fingers. As if she had never once achieved perfect stillness when drawing back an arrow. As if she had never stood unmoving before a deer in the darkness of the Arz.

When she was near him, the very rhythm of the world became something else. A wild, terrifying, incomprehensible thing.

She held her hand over his, two contrasts of color, two differences of size, two palms made for each other.

His hand tightened on her stomach, and his breath hitched. Slowed. Zafira bit back a gasp as something roused low in her belly, embers stirring to a flame.

Turn to him, they seemed to say. *Act*, they goaded. Or perhaps it was the Jawarat and the mayhem it desired. It was one of the rare moments when she didn't care if it was, because skies, she wanted it, too.

She closed her eyes and didn't dare move.

He was adept as she was, the assassin to her hunter. He only needed a heartbeat to read the shift of her breathing. Yet Zafira had noted the way his senses were hindered when it came to her. As if he were suddenly so tangled in his own emotions that he was blinded to all else.

She cracked her eyes open a sliver and relaxed her breathing—as much as she could, considering the pounding beneath her skin. The pillow shifted, and he muttered a curse. One by one, the pads of his fingers lifted.

Silence.

And then, a tumultuous sigh.

"Zafira." He cleared the roughness from his throat and tried again. "Zafira. We have to go."

She made what she hoped was a believable act of waking slowly and turning even slower. His eyes were flint, unreadable.

At last, as if he knew, as if he needed to explain why he'd held her, he said, "You were shaking last night."

"And then I stopped," she said, holding his gaze to say that she knew *why* she had stopped and that she liked it and wished the night had never ended. What were words if not feelings?

"And then you stopped," he replied, honing the weary cadence of his voice as if to say *Me too, fair gazelle, me too.*

But the night had to end. Everything had to. *Cannot all three be one and the same?* She'd been so deep within the turmoil of the Jawarat that she'd forgotten the weight of that question. The sweet torment it gave her.

Nasir was watching her, reading her, and his smile moments later was a spoonful of sorrow.

"Come," he said, fitting his gauntlets and the mask of the Prince of Death back in place.

CHAPTER 84

BREAKFAST WAS TANGY LABNEH WITH ENOUGH LEMON to make Zafira's mouth water, and crispy falafel. She watched Nasir break the chickpea patties in perfect halves as she obliterated her own share. They also shared sesame bread with slices of jibn, the cheese sweeter than she liked, and a dallah of mint tea.

After leaving the inn, Nasir fell silent. Zafira recollected their every conversation, assuming, in the end, that he was contemplating the question that wavered between them, an apparition neither acknowledged.

Ever since their angry lashing of teeth, tongue, and lips the day before, she had felt like herself. He had a knack for that, she realized, for grounding her. Her blood warmed at the memory. If he was the antidote to the Jawarat's curse, it wasn't so bad a problem to have.

The book hummed, and Zafira focused on the road. The sky was still dark as the night, the only indication of it being daytime the bright line far in the horizon that marked the edge of Sarasin.

"Do you think you can kill him?" Zafira asked after a time, aware

Nasir's mark might not be human. When he'd told her of the real Muzaffar, dead in the banquet hall of the Sultan's Palace, a helpless cavern had opened beneath her. He hadn't been any other merchant; he was one who had advocated for change, who had worked for the better of his people.

Now an ifrit had stolen his skin, his face, his seat.

Nasir looked delicately affronted. "Of course. After, it's only a matter of confronting the Lion. Together."

"Together," she repeated with a dark laugh. "The others won't be happy to see me, and you know it."

"And now you're here. The others won't have a choice."

She realized then what he had done.

"If I did not know any better," she said around the fist in her throat, "I'd say you came along solely to kiss me."

And be with me. And keep me sane. And protect me.

He laughed. "You speak as if you didn't enjoy it."

"Maybe I didn't. Maybe I was only indulging you."

"Those were not the sounds someone makes," Nasir murmured against her ear, "when they're merely indulging another."

Her neck burned. The streets were empty.

"If we were in a story, what would happen?" Zafira asked before she could stop herself.

Nasir went rigid behind her. "What does that mean?"

"It's a game Yasmine and I used to play," she said, glancing back at him. "Every day she would learn a new fact about the man she was falling for, and every day she would lengthen the list of what her imaginary husband would have and be when he swept her away. And then she married him."

"But?"

"Hmm?"

"But then what happened?" he asked, ever perceptive.

"She found he was not as perfect as she thought. He had lied to her. Or rather, he'd hidden the truth of who he was," Zafira clarified.

"She discovered he had flaws," Nasir suggested.

Zafira nodded, though it didn't discount the secrets Misk had kept. "And I think she needs time to understand that flaws make us whole. Real. He's not terrible, or a monster."

Nasir didn't respond, and Zafira inwardly cringed at her use of the word "monster." *You absolute fool.*

"I don't—I don't play games," he said, eventually, as they turned down a street far too wide to be an alley.

"You do now," she teased, only to find him serious. Disturbed, almost. At once, she realized it had nothing to do with games, but what this specific one entailed. "You're allowed to dream, you know. To imagine."

He said nothing.

She could sense something—someone, watching them from the shadows. Several domes glinted in the near distance. The palace.

"I would take you for iced cream," Nasir said suddenly.

Zafira held her breath.

"Isn't that . . . what you wanted, once?"

She vaguely remembered making mention of it on Sharr, but it didn't matter now. Bakdash was gone. If that lavender door was still intact, it would stand closed forever. No one was left to open it, to fill its walls with love.

Even if some of the people in her village remained, it wouldn't be the same. The air would be spooled with ghosts, the streets thick with the dead.

"That iced cream shop—it's gone now," she said softly. Renowned across the kingdom, gone just like that.

"You said this was a story," Nasir protested, and she could hear the frown in his voice.

His utter confusion tore a laugh out of her, and she fell back against him, nestling into the nook of his outstretched arms. It was only a heartbeat, and then realization struck them both like a snake. Nasir went still. Zafira straightened. The Jawarat observed her without a word.

After a moment, Nasir audibly swallowed.

"We're nearly there," he said quietly.

Zafira nodded, shifting the book in her hands.

She'd been at ease. Not intoxicated by lust or desire or need, just comfortable. With that one revelation came a flood of more: How she had come to expect his heated gaze and pensive smiles, and how well she fit in his arms. How he cared for her, in a way she thought an assassin could not. How she cared for him, as she once vowed she never would for anyone, least of all the Prince of Death.

Nasir slowed Afya to a walk as they neared the Sarasin palace in the center of Leil. The streets were fuller, likely because of the lighter-than-black skies, less marred by darkness. In it, she could see the grandness that once prevailed. The details carved into every edifice, proof that here they once valued life.

It was bittersweet, in a way. Hopeful, too. For if the Sarasins valued life once, it meant they could do so again. It made her think of her village, and how, despite how hopeless so much seemed, she had still found it in herself to feed her people, to care for them.

What Sarasin needed, first, was someone to stand for them. To unite them, make them worthy of their place in Arawiya.

They stepped through a glade of date palms to a sight that crowded Zafira's throat. She had basked in the ethereal lure of the Demenhune palace and the majestic beast of the Sultan's, but there was something about the Sarasin palace that stole her breath away.

It emanated a dark beauty she had come to associate with all things Sarasin. Where the other two palaces sprawled, this one towered. Minarets rose to the cloudless skies, and the enormous obsidian dome in the center was cut with countless arched windows. Scrolling florals were carved into the gray stone, the slant of the sun deepening the rises and dips.

Zafira had spent all her life thinking Sarasins to be monsters, and yet here was beauty she had never expected. They tethered Afya to a post to the side of the palace and sprinted to a smaller set of gates. Black-and-silver liveried guards were making the rounds, narrow swords set against their shoulders.

She slid a glance at Nasir. What was it like to return to the place of one's blood and know one was not welcome? There was a price on his head. Even if there weren't, he'd killed the previous caliph in cold blood.

Nasir dragged her to the shadows, surveying the surroundings as he spoke. "Raw materials come in twice a day. The carts should arrive soon."

"How do you know we have the right timing?"

He straightened the knives along his belt. "That's why I said 'should.'"

Zafira cast him a look as a rumbling filled the air. With a wink, Nasir pulled her deeper into the shadows.

Three carts clattered down the stone road and halted before the black gates. The guards lazily sheathed their swords and strolled to them. Those locks could undo themselves quicker than the dastards were working them. The cart drivers echoed Zafira's impatience, noisily rifling through sheaves of papyrus, ready for their coin.

Nasir nudged her down the thin line of cover to the last cart, and Zafira didn't breathe as they darted across the road in broad daylight—Sarasin's definition of it, gray and murky. All the driver needed to do was glance behind him. All the guards needed to do was look a little farther down the road.

She sent Nasir a look of alarm that he studiously ignored as he loosened the rope holding down the cart's covering. While Zafira stared at the back of the driver's head, Nasir peeled up the burlap and gestured for her to climb inside. She kept her footing light and winced as she slid between the sacks of flour and nestled into the far corner. The head of a nail dug into her shoulder, just above her wound. The horse shuffled, and the cart rocked with it. Skies, this was nowhere near a foolproof plan. She'd be safer if she tore open a bag of flour and doused herself in it.

Nasir pursed his lips, clearly thinking the same, but there wasn't time.

The guards would turn toward the second cart soon enough. They'd be seen in a heartbeat. He gripped the edge of the cart to heft himself up and follow her inside—and froze.

The guards were drifting their way.

Khara. Voices rose. Someone shouted—one of the cart drivers, arguing over his payment. Zafira heard next to nothing over her pounding pulse.

I like the sound of your heart.

She did not like this newfound fear, the way it paralyzed her senses and slowed her blood. The Jawarat, which thrived on chaos, had no tumultuous words of advice. Nasir met her eyes, panic flitting across the gray.

And then everything went dark as he dropped the burlap over her and the cart began to move.

CHAPTER 85

As they journeyed for Sultan's Keep, Altair saw the results of his actions throughout the decades. The villages he had destroyed in Demenhur. The shops he had burned to soot in Sarasin. He had sacrificed much to garner the sultan's favor. If only he had known it was his daama father he was slaving for.

"At last," Kifah shouted as they raced across the final stretch of Sarasin's darkness, the morning light of Sultan's Keep brightening with each heave of their horses.

Arawiyans waded the sandy streets and loitered in the shadows. Date palms swayed in the idle breeze as children ran around their thick trunks. Women hoisted baskets of clothes and fruit, and merchants carted wares. To them, the new king was not an affliction; he was no calamity.

Not yet.

Altair noted the sun's position. By now, the imposter of a caliph should be lying in a pool of his own black blood.

There was a time when he envied hashashins. He'd seen Nasir meander through a crowd and casually perch atop a roof before his marks fell one after the other. There was grace to a hashashin's movements, but an extra level of it when it came to the prince.

It was strange, how differently they viewed death. Nasir saw the many pieces that made one person. Altair saw the many people that made a contingent, and it was a contrast he could appreciate.

His palms slickened with anticipation. "Do you remember the way?"

"You didn't even see Aya's house," Kifah said, casting him a look. "What if I take you to a morgue?"

"Always so morbid," he said. "The house belongs to *me*."

"I didn't know it was your house."

"Akhh, One of Nine. There is much about me you've yet to uncover," Altair crowed. "I can recount every room, and every bed, and every time—"

Kifah cleared her throat. "You know, I'd prefer if you didn't."

The streets were tame, people going about as if nothing were amiss, swarming stalls of fresh vegetables and fruits, and even if the city had been as dark as Sarasin, the smell of baked goods would have been a clear enough indicator that it was just after dawn.

Altair paid a boy for a fold of pita lathered with labneh, passing half to Kifah.

"You don't seem anxious," Kifah said.

He cut his gaze to her. "I thought we already had this discussion."

They dismounted and let their horses free. Altair led Kifah down passageways and shortcuts he had discovered and collected along the years, stopping in his favorite alcove fitted in the remnant of space between two merchant houses and his own, with a fountain tiled in blue and red that he had commissioned himself.

"A beauty, isn't she?"

Kifah didn't appreciate it. "If you like doing nothing."

Altair sighed and gestured to the alley leading to the house, but paused when several voices and the hissing of steel against stone drifted to them.

"Is that a grinding stone?" Kifah whispered with a frown, bald head gleaming. "It looks like someone's made themselves at home."

They crept through, footsteps light and breathing shallow. The weight of his scimitars was a reassurance, even if a reminder of his halved eyesight. In the courtyard, a man with a tasseled turban stood with around forty or so others, hands on his hips as he surveyed their progress, readying weapons and securing provisions.

"Khaldun?" Altair guessed.

The man whirled in surprise. It *was* him.

Altair grinned. "I should have known it was you."

The half Sarasin clearly looked too pleased for Kifah's liking, for she leaned forward and said, "*Misk* Khaldun? I overheard that his wife chased him off."

Altair's eyebrows flew upward. "Are we talking of the same girl Benyamin gave you permission to marry?"

Misk floundered. He wasn't bound by any pact. He could have easily told the girl—he had to trust her enough to want to spend the rest of his days with her.

Altair laughed. "Akhh, now this is a tale I must hear and a girl I must meet."

Kifah murmured something too low to hear.

"What brings you to Sultan's Keep?" Altair asked. Misk was one of his better spiders, ambitious and honest. It was because of his quick thinking months ago that they'd secured a trade route with the outlying villages of western Demenhur for the region's supple wood—though that wasn't why he'd been stationed there. He had been tasked with uncovering Zafira's identity, and he'd failed.

He'd returned months later with something else, instead. Altair had seen the look in Misk's eyes, a look that would overcome Benyamin whenever he'd speak of Aya. Altair still remembered his envy with shame.

"Your note to escape came too late. The western villages are gone,"

Misk said, and Altair wished he didn't feel his pointed words so keenly. "My home. My life. The lives of everyone I knew." He looked toward the palace. "Vengeance didn't seem so terrible an idea."

These were the men Haytham had spoken of, the ones Altair had ventured to find. The rebels. They were all Demenhune, far from their snowy abode.

Altair regarded him. "In that case, marhaba. You may die with us, but at least we will die fighting."

Misk lowered his head, accepting. Never had Altair expected rallying rebels to be *this* easy.

"What of your wife?" Kifah snapped, and Misk looked affronted. "Your duty to her precedes your duty to your kingdom."

Altair held his tongue. She was right, but he wasn't one to meddle in the affairs of others, especially when it came to wives as fiery as it seemed Misk's was.

A cry echoed through the morning air and every gaze flew upward as something hurtled past the date palm, diving for them. *Hirsi.* Altair held out his arm and the bird landed with spread wings.

Altair's spirits rose. He had reached Sultan's Keep. The rebels were on his side. His mother would travel for the Great Library now that Hirsi had returned—

"Oi," said Kifah, full of foreboding. "Is that . . . your note?"

Hirsi chirped proudly.

CHAPTER 86

ZAFIRA HELD HER BREATH, EXPECTING THE CARTS TO halt and swords to be drawn and turmoil to break loose. Where was Nasir? The only plausible solution was that he had remained behind, sending her beyond the gates on her own. *Laa, laa, laa.*

The carts rattled to a stop. Her mind buzzed. They had found him. They had—

One of the carts moved away, and footsteps crunched along the sand. Her relief was quickly replaced by another fear: The carts were being halted for inspections. Of course they were—this was a *palace*. Zafira's heart drummed loud enough that she wouldn't be surprised if the drivers thought their sacks of flour had suddenly found a pulse.

Footsteps shuffled near, and she knew by the thud of boots that it was a guard. She screwed her eyes closed, pressing herself as low and flush against the side of the cart as she could.

"Yalla," the guard droned. "It's almost time for my break."

Guards are lazy, Yasmine reassured her.

She closed her eyes even tighter, knowing that miles away in Thalj, her friend was livid with hurt and anger because Zafira had left without a word.

Something pushed against the wood—the guard leaning against the side of the cart. Something else rustled.

The burlap. *Sweet snow.* No, no, no. Gray light slipped into the cart as the cover was peeled back, bit by bit. She dug her toes beneath a sack of flour.

The guard paused.

Her limbs shook.

"Eh? Tell me again?"

She couldn't make out the response over the roaring in her ears.

The guard broke out in laughter, the strangest guffaws making Zafira bite her tongue against a laugh of her own. Khara, did her brain not understand the danger she was in?

The burlap fell closed. The guard moved away, talking more animatedly than he had just moments ago, and Zafira's exhale shuddered as the cart jostled forward again, at last rumbling to its final stop. The driver leaped down, tipping the cart with his weight.

And then, nothing.

What was she supposed to do now? She held her breath as the footsteps faded, reminding herself that she trusted her ears more than her eyes.

She lifted a smidge of the burlap and peered into the stall. No one was there. Drivers only drove. They didn't unload goods. *Which means the ones who do will come along next, oaf.* At the count of three, she threw off the covering and leaped over the side of the cart. She fell with a sharp sting down her chest, knees jarring.

The stall was wide enough to park all three carts. The horses that had drawn them snorted tiredly, waiting to be untethered. The place hadn't been cleaned in months, it seemed, and the dust collected from the morose expanse of sand doused in gray light behind her clung to the odds and ends piled against the far wall.

Immediately she knew she was not alone. She ducked her head lower, glancing beneath the cart to see if anyone was heading her way.

"Hello," someone whispered.

She nearly screamed. Nasir clung to the bottom of the cart, dust in his hair and the keffiyah knotted around his neck. With a sheepish grin at her answering glare, he dropped and rolled out beside her as if he did this every daama day. She rubbed the backs of her knuckles across her chest, but before she could snap, he lifted them both to their feet and dragged her to a tiny alcove, hands around her shoulders as the drivers returned.

"Now what?" she whispered, suddenly aware of his touch. There wasn't even enough room in the space to turn around and face him.

"Now," he said smoothly, mouth feathering her ear, "we wait."

She held still. Her body pulsed as she fought the desire to nestle back against him. Feel him against her.

"I wonder how we can pass the time," he mused in that same low tone. For a moment, neither of them moved. Only the sound of their breathing filled the air. Then his hands left her arms and he brushed her messy hair away with a drag of his fingers. She shivered at the whisper of his breath on her skin before he pressed his lips to the hollow between her neck and shoulder.

The drivers, Zafira suddenly thought, could take as long as they wanted.

She let out a ragged wheeze and something inside her came alive. It tilted her head, granting him better access.

"The way you breathe drives me to insanity, fair gazelle."

His daring did the same to her. His voice. The way his words slipped from his tongue, each one careful, each one beautiful. He had been a touch bolder since they'd begun stealthing about. He thrived on this, she realized. On the thrill of his missions.

A curl of darkness whispered along her skin, widening her hooded gaze. She almost startled, but held herself, knowing this was a part of him, one he had not yet conquered. Shadows grazed her wrist and slipped down the slope of her neck, tender and questioning, wholly unlike the Lion's.

"Do you feel what they do?" she asked, lifting her palm. The dark wisps circled her fingers, soft as smoke, and faded, suddenly shy beneath her scrutiny.

He made a sound behind her, as if wishing he could. "It's the same as a pen across papyrus. I control the pen but cannot feel the bleed of its ink."

She turned, brushing against him, grinning when he drew a sharp breath. She knew he could read her, knew he could see in her gaze that she accepted every part of him, every dark shard. His mouth trailed down her neck and fell to her collarbone. She gasped.

"What was that?" one of the drivers asked.

Zafira froze—or tried to. Every part of her pulsed with need, tangible and hot. Nasir's lips curved into a dark smile, trailing lower, his bottom lip brushing away the neck of her dress. She bit her tongue against a sound. Burrowed her fingers into his hair. Sweet snow, this man. These feelings. She shifted her hips and his hands fell, gripping her tight against him with a barely audible groan.

"I wouldn't be surprised if there were ghosts in this place," another one answered. The drivers untethered their horses. She heard them mount, she heard the whip that made her cringe, and then they were gone.

"If only they knew," Nasir whispered, pulling away.

"Wait," she blurted out before she could stop herself.

His fingers flexed in restraint. He looked at her feet. "They'll be coming to unload the carts."

Of course. There was work to be done. "Later," something possessed her to say.

"Forever, Zafira," he said softly. "Forever. You need only say so."

He lifted his eyes to hers.

Yes, she wanted to whisper. *Yes*, the Jawarat echoed, but Umm's hollow eyes flashed in her thoughts, and then Nasir was turning away and sliding open a door and disappearing into a dark hall.

Zafira released a breath.

Her mind was abuzz. She could barely see her surroundings, barely hear anything over her pulse and this terrible *thirst* inside her.

"Is there no quicker way to get there?" she asked when Nasir returned.

They paused as a trio of servants passed, one clutching a dallah while the other two held platters and trays, the whiff of the dates, grape molasses, and carob used to prepare jallab making her mouth water.

"Usually, I would scale the walls, but—" He gave her wound a pointed look.

She swallowed a twinge of embarrassment.

They darted down the corridor and ducked into a tiny closet. He pulled aside a slab of wood, unveiling a steep staircase.

"Makes it easier for servants during big banquets," he explained, taking the steps two at a time. "There are two places our caliph might be."

She hurried after him, nearly toppling them both when he stopped at a narrow door and pressed his ear to the wood with utter stillness. With a slight frown, he eased it open, and she peered over his shoulder into a room.

A bedroom. A jewel of a place she felt a surge of diffidence to behold. It was built beneath the curve of the main dome; the high, angled ceiling painted with a sea of stars interspersed by a mosaic of tiles and calligraphy that told the story of the Sisters of Old. This was *her* room, Zafira realized: the Sister who had claimed Sarasin long ago.

Like a veil from a crown, the sheerest silver gossamer fell over the low and ample bed, another arch at its fore, recessed and ornate. The sheets were made of starlight and dreams, darkness plentiful despite the gold of the afternoon stretching shapely rays through the decadent mashrabiya. She'd seen her fair share of the enclosed latticed balconies, but never one so intricate, many of the carvings fitted with stained glass that told a story itself.

Nasir was watching her. "He's not here," he said unnecessarily, in that voice that looped with the darkness and time spun once more.

She had missed this. Her fascination being a thing to witness with rapt attention.

A few steps away, he stopped again, and she knew. The ifrit who had stolen the face of Muzaffar was on the other side of this door. The newly appointed Caliph of Sarasin.

"History repeats itself," he mused, lifting his hand to the latch.

The last time he was here, he had killed the mortal caliph. Everyone in Arawiya knew this, though Zafira couldn't connect that faceless hashashin with the prince she knew now.

Was this time any better? Could they justify the caliph's death simply because he bled different? *Yes*, she told herself. The ifrit were the reason Deen had died. The reason *she* had nearly died. Fury ignited her blood, sudden and bright. She would kill them all. She would end the Lion and then make the streets black with their blood.

A resounding shout reverberated in her skull.

NO!

She swayed and gripped Nasir's arm, the taut bands of muscle flexing beneath her fingers.

Then the Jawarat stole her away.

Heady, intoxicating power crashed through her veins. Golden light shrouded her, attention scouring her exposed skin, silks against her limbs and jewels around her neck. She saw nothing. Only felt the sovereignty, the power, the superiority—something so foreign, she was lost to it.

We learned power from the women of old. A dominion so great it forged a kingdom.

The Sisters. In the Jawarat's hazy vision, the Sister whom Zafira embodied sat upon a throne. Confidence dripped from her every shift, authority in her every word. Zafira saw, felt, heard, but she understood none of it.

The vision cut.

It was a desolate sort of darkness.

Plink, plink, plink. The metallic stench of blood flooded her senses. She was drowning, somehow, without water. Anguish and the complete loss of power. Helpless. Alone. It drained every drop of her spirit, and when she heard the cry that slipped from her mouth—*Baba!*—she knew in an instant where the Jawarat had taken her.

We learned vengeance from the boy of two bloods. A pain so deep it bred darkness and malice.

Haider. The boy who had become the Lion of the Night. She was a tangle of chaos and pain, clinging to the edge of a precipice, the border of sanity, until she discovered purpose, singular and bereft of morals: vengeance. It burned bright in her blood, the end slowly but surely disappearing from sight.

No sooner had she caught the pinprick of light at the end of the Lion's memory, she was jerked into yet another vision. It was calmer, somehow. Less frantic, less disembodied, as Demenhur's familiar cold stung her nostrils. Like a container upended by an eager child, the calm was ruined by a sense of failure. The pain that crowded her skull was edged not in darkness, but something else. It was almost as heady as the Sisters' power. Almost as flooding as the Lion's malice.

We learned compassion from a girl. A sentiment so profound it altered our spirit.

It was her. The Jawarat was connected to her in ways it had never been connected to the Sisters of Old or the Lion of the Night, a bond no one could understand. Zafira wasn't powerful, she wasn't immortal. She was just a girl trying to find her place in the world. A girl inundated with emotions she was trying to sort through. Pain, sorrow, desire—the Jawarat had been witness to it all.

"Why?" Zafira asked against the confusion caught in her throat, but she knew why.

The Jawarat had wanted a soul to shape to its will, someone to enact the chaos it had absorbed on Sharr, and who better than one pure of heart? When she had refused, it had taken to the Lion, unaware of his iron will.

He eluded its control and in turn tried to control *it*. But hilya were like people, and his abuse did not sit well.

Something changed then, for the Jawarat had discovered it missed the one bound to it as much as she had missed it.

Then, in atonement, once they were reunited, it took her to the door of the man she hated and amplified her anger, provoking her until she cut him in two. It had expected her to be pleased, for this wasn't senseless chaos like the vision it had shown her, it was justice.

How wrong it had been.

It had not expected to upend the girl. It did not expect to find her empty when she woke, isolation and pain stretching as barren as the Wastes, as unending.

Again, it tried to atone, this time with more hesitance and less violence, and she snuck away, intent on killing the Lion to earn back the trust of the zumra. To recover her soul, lost to time. It was along this journey that it mended the angry cuts of her heart, the pain and rage it had nestled in her veins. It found chaos without violence, in her moments with her gray-eyed prince, in her profound happiness and her desires for magic and justice and peace.

You must understand, bint Iskandar. We are of you as you are of us.

She had known that ever since the fateful moment on Sharr, when she had bound her life to it. "You used me, remember?"

For which we are sorry. We tried to atone, and still we were wrong.

That was the reason for its contemplation of late. For its contrition. For impelling her toward Nasir—because he made her happy, which in turn made it happy. It was chaos in a dose that pleased them both, and in this, it found a way to exist.

From you we have learned, and so we shall impart. Must an entire creed suffer for the sins of a few? Must the body be destroyed for the failings of an organ?

The ifrit. The Sarasins. Nasir was right: It was up to her to steer the Jawarat in a direction she chose.

She tucked the book away.

"What happened?" Nasir asked.

"Don't kill him."

Nasir frowned. "The plan—"

"Forget the plan, Nasir. This time, we do what's right."

He inhaled a careful breath, but before he could answer, the door swung open.

She froze at the sensation of eyes scouring her skin. For ifrit were not like men. They were shrewd in a way humans were not, swifter—and their foe was ready.

With a knife.

CHAPTER 87

THE IFRIT WHO HAD TAKEN THE FORM OF MUZAFFAR moved quickly, his slender knife flashing in the light of a lantern set on the low table, but Nasir was no amateur. He swerved and parried, forcing the ifrit back into the room, and disarming him with ease. The knife clattered to the tile, the thin rug muffling nothing.

Nasir pressed his dagger to the caliph's neck as Zafira entered and barred the door.

"The crown prince and the renowned Huntress," the ifrit said, unperturbed by the blade. "At last."

He was stocky and well built, an exact imitation of the dead merchant, but the differences were there for those who looked—the celerity of his movements, the intermittence of his breathing, the occasional flicker of him as a whole, as if it required effort to exhibit a human face.

"Is that you speaking," Nasir hissed, surprised by his fluent Arawiyan, "or the Lion?"

"Ifrit are not mindless servants," he replied mildly. "The prerequisite to my accepting the Sarasin throne involved freedom of mind and wit."

A dark majlis spread behind him, where a platter of fruit sat beside an inkpot and several missives. *Fruit*, Nasir thought dumbly. Rimaal, what did he expect ifrit to eat—fire?

"Let's start with your name—what is it?"

The ifrit smiled. "I've heard human brains are quite small. In the interest of keeping your affairs simple, Muzaffar will suffice."

Zafira lifted a brow. "And does your free wit justify the death of hundreds of humans?"

"It's only natural for one to reciprocate that which is received."

She gritted her teeth against his calm. "Any harm that comes to your kind is from the self-defense of ours."

Muzaffar regarded her. "You are young. What you know of the purge of ifritkind is what your schools teach. The Sisters of Old banished us to an island where not even a drop of water could be found. It was not until the warden arrived that we found ways to live. She fashioned systems in which our people were given food and water, housing. Tell me, Huntress: If you were exiled for the skin you were born within, would you not desire reprisal?"

That warden was Nasir's mother, and he felt a burst of pride. The Sisters were many things: saviors, queens of justice. They were also wrong. They had committed a grave mistake, and more than one race had suffered for it. Perhaps they, too, had even died for what they'd done.

For the world gave that which was owed.

"Then we stop," Nasir said suddenly. *Stop what, you fool?*

He felt the ifrit's consideration in the way his breathing shifted.

"What do you propose?"

"An alliance. You control both the Sarasin army and the ifrit army. Keep them from going to the Lion's aid, and we'll spare your life," Zafira said.

Nasir cast her a look. For once, the book wasn't in her hand, and the clarity in her gaze was startling in the gray light slanting through the wide window.

Laa, this anger was Zafira's alone.

"An alliance is not synonymous with a threat, Huntress. If we are to discuss an accord, perhaps you can release me and we can talk in a civilized way."

The irony of his words was not lost on Nasir. He met Zafira's gaze. After her barely perceptible prompt, he removed his blade from Muzaffar's neck.

Just as someone knocked on the door.

Both of them froze.

Muzaffar noticed, and like a fool Nasir realized how, in that one small gesture, he had allowed the caliph to see how easily he could thwart them. But the ifrit did not call for aid.

"I'm busy," was all he said, loud and crisp. "Ensure no one comes, please."

A courteous ifrit. Rimaal.

He sat on the majlis and motioned for them to do the same. Zafira sat cautiously. Nasir remained standing.

"Now," Muzaffar said, flickering. "You wish for me to withhold both the Sarasin army and the ifrit army when the Lion summons. I do not control them all. I certainly have no command over those in Sultan's Keep."

Zafira didn't budge. "You have command over enough."

"You're asking me to defy my king."

"A usurper," Zafira corrected, then pointed at Nasir. "This is your king."

"Mm. The ifrit army, as you call it, is merely the sum of my people. We crossed the Baransea for the life that was promised, not to become soldiers."

"And you believe it is our fault that your people had to pick up swords," Nasir assumed. At once, he understood the ifrit as he was. He was not like the Lion, bent on revenge. He truly cared for the well-being of his kind.

"Is it not? The Lion of the Night clears entire towns for us to thrive in—"

"You say 'clear' as if human lives were weeds," Zafira growled.

"I wish for my people to live," Muzaffar said, though he had the decency to sound apologetic. "If there were an alternative—"

"There is," Nasir said, and he was surprised by the sudden fear in his veins. The heavy reminder of who he was, now that his father was gone. Every word he spoke held the potential for repercussions. He exhaled a shaky breath, for he feared winning this fight against the Lion almost as much as losing it.

Winning meant he would sit on the Gilded Throne. He would hold the lives of an entire kingdom in his hand.

"Aid us in returning balance and magic to the kingdom, and ifritkind will be free to live anywhere in Arawiya as they please. Should you need a place to hang shadows in lieu of the sky, I will give you an entire caliphate of your own as unique to your people as Alderamin is to the safin. One that doesn't sit atop a graveyard." For that was what Sarasin would soon become, if this fighting continued.

Neither Zafira nor Muzaffar hid their confusion.

"At the expense of whom, exactly?" Muzaffar ventured.

"No one. Under the warden, ifritkind transformed Sharr into a haven where you thrived. You can do the same once more in the expanse of land between Alderamin and Pelusia. It is currently known as the Wastes, but with support, that barren land can be made into whatever you wish."

Zafira sat back. Muzaffar's brows rose. "A caliphate without magic."

Nasir's brow furrowed. "The Wastes may not have a minaret, but when magic returns, it will flow across Alderamin and Pelusia and every city between. No place will be left bereft."

Muzaffar considered this for a while, but then his entire face transformed. "You mock me, Prince. You belittle my people into the fodder you believe us to be. You want the Wastes cultivated, and our labor is an economical choice."

That was not—khara. If there was one thing Nasir hadn't realized yet about diplomacy, it was the way other minds worked.

"Guards!" Muzaffar shouted, rising to his feet. *Short man, short temper.* His voice cut sharp as he faced Nasir. "Were you aware of the price on your head?"

Zafira remained frozen on the majlis.

"You praised the warden for changing your lives," Nasir said, struggling to stay afloat. "She can aid you again. *The crown* will aid your efforts."

"The warden is dead," the ifrit gritted out.

Nasir barked a laugh. "The warden is alive—"

The door flew open. Five Sarasin men hastened inside with three ifrit. Nasir didn't flinch when a sword touched his neck.

"—and I know this, because she's my mother."

But he knew it would be a stretch for Muzaffar to believe him unless he saw her with his own eyes. No, Nasir needed something else. He studied him, the way he wore his skin with earnestness. His care for his people. The impeccability of his attire, either real or illusory, and the esteem with which he carried himself.

And Nasir knew how to tip the scales in the zumra's favor. He was finally neck-deep in Altair's beloved chance, and he hated it.

"And with the addition of a caliphate will come the addition of a caliph," Nasir said, inclining his head even as the guard's blade dug deeper, nearly drawing blood. "You."

CHAPTER 88

KIFAH'S PACING BACK AND FORTH ON THE RUG WAS driving Altair to the brink. He kept glancing to the door, as if Nasir and Zafira would materialize the longer he looked. He couldn't bring himself to remove the note from Hirsi's leg, as if ignoring it long enough would somehow make it reach his mother.

"They're late," Kifah deplored. "Two people—one of them wounded—against an entire caliphate."

"There's nothing we can do," Altair said wearily. Nasir was a hashashin. He wove through death like a needle through gossamer. He *had* to survive—they were only just starting to be brothers.

Kifah stopped pacing. "We need to discuss how we'll proceed if they don't arrive on time."

Pragmatic as ever, except for the concern in her dark gaze.

But Altair had no alternative ready. That wasn't how he worked. He chose the best for his plans, and counted on them to perform.

His mind—ordinarily endlessly calculating, plotting, scheming—had blanked.

He bolted upright when the door flew open, both he and Kifah rushing forward. But it was neither his mother nor Nasir or Zafira.

Only one of Misk's runners, panting.

"The Great Library. It—it's on fire."

CHAPTER 89

SAVING THOUSANDS OF LIVES WOULD NEVER MAKE UP for the ones Zafira had taken with such violence, but it meant she was still there. That she had lost the guise of the Hunter, but the person her cloak had fashioned still remained.

To live is to falter, she thought to herself, and she would not stay down.

Light inundated her senses when she and Nasir crossed from Sarasin into Sultan's Keep. Even Afya stumbled before her Alder eyes adjusted to the light. A commotion echoed from deeper in the city, and Nasir urged the mare faster.

Zafira spotted the palace soon enough. She wondered what Nasir saw when he looked at the glittering domes and the pillars lining the Sultan's Road: his dead father, or his own throne?

When *she* looked at the palace, she saw—

Her stomach dropped. Sweet snow, was that smoke? The smell hit her next. Her surging panic was matched by Afya's, and the horse wrenched to a halt with a neigh.

The Jawarat stirred from a slumber like a cat raising its hackles, eager for the unraveling chaos. But she sensed its struggle and hesitation, the need to match her emotions. It was trying.

People were running toward them, fleeing every which way as screams thickened the air.

"The Great Library!"

"It's on fire!"

Zafira straightened in alarm. *The library?*

"Arawiya punishes us!"

Afya wouldn't calm. Zafira almost fell from her back, grabbing a handful of her mane with a yelp.

"We need to dismount," Nasir said.

Zafira slid to the dusty ground. The library. *Baba.* All that knowledge, all that history. The work of scholars, historians, poets, travelers—gone. She wanted to find the person who said there was nothing more powerful than the written word and shake him. Show him what was happening.

Not all were fleeing. The more level-headed people rushed toward the blaze two by two with buckets of water sloshing between them.

It's useless, she wanted to say as smoke billowed into the skies, great wafts rising.

Nasir nudged her forward with one hand, still trying to calm Afya with the other. Zafira wrenched away. They should be helping, not running.

"Focus. We're short on time," Nasir insisted. "Afya, no!"

The fire tore a gash inside her. As they ran, she alternated between looking down at the ground and up at the smoke that berated the sky in angry undulations.

They stumbled past the gates of Aya's house. As Nasir wrestled Afya toward the stables, Zafira saw men loitering in the courtyard. Demenhune. And there were a number of them. *Good.* One couldn't put out a fire on one's own.

"Zafira?"

"Not now," she snapped. "We need to put out that—"

She turned when the voice registered in her head, the smoke in the distance doused by her sudden rage.

"So this is what cowards do when they lie to their wives," she snarled.

Misk, beautiful and weary, had the decency to look ashamed. Laa, utterly and deeply saddened. He shook his head. "No—I did worse."

The fight rushed out of her. Yasmine had said that he might never hold a secret from her again, and had Zafira been in her place, she would have found a way to forgive him outright. But Yasmine was different; her forgiveness did not come so easily. Especially when the ugliness of a lie was involved.

When Nasir returned with an unsheathed sword, looking for her, Misk's eyes narrowed. "The Prince of Death is not welcome here."

It was odd hearing him speak this way. It was odd seeing him at ease before a weapon, as if he were an entirely different person from the one Yasmine had married. He *was* a different person, she realized. Zafira had known him to be a bookkeeper, a man versed with scrubbing ink from his fingers, not blood. It wasn't just a secret he had kept from Yasmine, it was a whole daama life.

"I didn't ask." Nasir studied him with a tilt of his head. "I've seen you before. In the palace. You're one of Altair's."

Misk's mouth tightened.

"Oi!" someone shouted, interrupting the tension. "Don't loiter. Get—Nasir? Sultan's teeth, it's you! Kifah thought you were dead. Akhh, I'm hurt, habibi. You didn't even spare me a goodbye."

Zafira froze as Altair's footsteps drew near, shadowed by those of another. Her chest was suddenly tight, but she forced herself to turn as Misk sprinted away. Kifah met her eyes and tipped her head in slow greeting. Altair gave her an apologetic half smile. Not a word was exchanged, yet relief flooded her.

You doubted the ones you love.

Zafira felt the urge to fling the Jawarat into the distance. *You made me do it.*

Altair's features softened. "I was wrong to have left your side, Huntress. Forgive me."

"Me as well," Kifah said, stepping closer.

Zafira smiled around the swell in her throat, clamping her teeth against a mad laugh. She had judged others for less. She had judged *Altair* for less—for merely turning his back on them when Aya had.

"I'm sorry, too," she said softly.

Kifah shrugged. "Eh, the old man had it coming."

She knew that was not what Kifah really believed, which made her appreciate the words even more. Altair, Kifah, and Nasir lingered another beat, silence stretching amid the screams and blaze in the distance, before they began turning away.

"Wait—what about the fire?" Zafira asked.

"What about it?" Nasir asked.

"It's quite a sight," Altair said with a tilt of his head.

"Started just now," Kifah said with a shrug. "Which means word will reach the Lion soon enough."

Not one of them was concerned, or worried, or even upset at the decades of knowledge burning into the ether. Laa, they looked impatient. With confusion, Zafira remembered the Silver Witch at the inn, Nasir asking her to come to Sultan's Keep, that he had left too soon to know the "exact timing."

The daama Silver Witch.

"It's . . . not real," she realized aloud, slumping in relief.

"It's an illusion," Nasir said unnecessarily.

Zafira's features flattened. "Thank you, my prince. I don't know what I would have done without you."

Altair snickered as Nasir's ears burned red and Kifah rolled her eyes. Zafira immortalized this moment in her heart. This reminder that the zumra was still a family to which she belonged.

"Did you have any trouble killing the ifrit in Sarasin?" Altair asked Nasir.

Nasir glanced at Zafira. "I didn't kill him."

Kifah gaped and Altair looked to Zafira with alarm. "*You* killed him?"

"I might have tarnished my pristine reputation, but I'm not some creature of habit," Zafira said with a lift of her chin.

"The ifrit is alive," Nasir said. "I've promised residence to ifritkind across Arawiya, and a caliphate of their own. They'll cultivate the Wastes with aid from the crown and the Silver Witch."

Altair's eye widened in surprise, then softened in pride. "You, brother dearest, are quite the diplomat. I always knew you'd make a good sultan. Not as good as I would, of course, but good enough."

Zafira watched as Nasir tried but failed to mask his pleasure at the acknowledgment. She had always assumed it was easy, being sultan—or king, as the Lion had now dubbed the title. For though the sultan ruled over the kingdom as a whole, he mostly presided over the caliphs and emirs, leaving day-to-day governance to the leaders themselves. It was clearly a misguided belief.

"I didn't do it alone," Nasir said, looking at Zafira.

Altair dipped his head at her, his gaze solemn. "And you would make a good queen." His single eye flashed a wink. "Every leader has a healthy dose of blood on their hands."

She wrinkled her nose, ignoring the weight of Nasir's gaze. Negotiating with the ifrit had been thrilling enough, but it made her realize the difference between working with common folk and working with their leaders. How a calipha did for her people as she had done for her village.

"Oi, no time to stand around." Kifah saluted with two fingers off her brow and jogged backward as she reprimanded them. "We're counting on the Lion's love of the written word, and we only have one shot. Yalla, zumra."

Swords passed from hand to hand, and grinding stones clattered on the ground. Arrows thudded into quivers, and though Zafira felt the absence as acutely as their impending doom, she wasn't about to be ousted from history simply because she couldn't wield a bow. There was glory to be had in battle, victory as sharp-edged as her name.

We will be with you.

It was comforting, those words. Zafira and the Jawarat had come to an understanding, one she didn't fully comprehend as yet. Laa, she could still barely believe the events that had unfolded in the shadows of the Sarasin palace. The peace she had ushered and Nasir had enacted.

An admirable team, the three of us.

She wanted to tease it, but a voice slipped from one of the second-story windows, freezing her in place.

It was impossible for the owner of that voice to be here in Sultan's Keep and not far beyond these borders, beyond Sarasin, all the way back in the secure confines of the palace in Thalj.

Zafira hurried up the stairs to the open door, heart leaping, crashing, stilling.

Yasmine.

There she was, standing before Misk, her tiny figure holding its place against his taller, sullen one. His head hung in shame.

"We agreed to spend time apart, Misk!" she shouted, her voice cracking. "Not for you to sign your life away. To die in some battle that doesn't even need you."

She caught sight of Zafira.

"And you!" Yasmine cried, whirling.

Misk's head shot up, and Zafira joined his side to make it easier for her friend to shout at them both.

"I've lost everyone, and there you are, running to where men are being blinded and women are being shot and buildings are burning and who knows what else is happening."

"How did you get here?" Zafira asked, as if Yasmine hadn't just up-ended the entire alphabet.

Yasmine glowered. "I left Thalj the moment Lana told me *you'd* left. And I was nearly kidnapped on the way, shukrun."

Zafira held her gaze, fighting a wave of guilt. Yasmine collapsed with a sob, the fight rushing out of her. Tears streamed down her cheeks.

"Why?" she asked in a broken voice. "Why is everyone so eager to leave me?"

This was the heart of Yasmine's fears, Zafira realized. She crouched in front of her and Yasmine gripped her hand, sliding her palm along hers until their smallest fingers intertwined. As if reminding her that though one Ra'ad sibling was gone, another still remained.

"I need to finish what I've started," Zafira said just as softly. "I need to do this, or Deen's death will have been for nothing. *All* of this will have been for nothing."

"I'm not trying to stop you, Zafira. I only want to be important enough to be spoken to. To not be kept in the dark. Am I not worth saying good-bye to? Am I not worthy of an explanation? Of the truth?"

Zafira looked away. "You are. Of course you are. I—I'm sorry."

Misk mumbled something similar.

Yasmine reached for Zafira's hands. "Just—let's stop fighting, all right? I know you have to go." She offered Zafira a small smile, and then looked at Misk. He knelt beside her and she kissed his cheek, then the bridge of his nose. Forgiveness was spelled out in the tiny gestures, warming Zafira's limbs. "I don't want to lose you, too. So don't die. Either of you."

"You don't have to worry about me," Zafira assured her.

Misk was far more eloquent.

"I am yours forevermore, in life and in death," he murmured. He pulled her to his chest and touched his lips to her brow. "What, no words to torment me?"

"I was so angry, Misk, but when I saw you there, a sword in your hand and—" She broke off with anguish. "The heart cannot forget the one who lives in her soul."

He smoothed back her hair, matching her tone. "Such finesse. Which book did you thieve that one from?"

She hit him square on the chest with a fractured laugh before he kissed her quiet. His hands enclosed her small form, while her fingers strayed to his hair. Zafira looked away, neck burning, and rushed down the stairs so she wouldn't have to hear or see anything else that she wasn't meant to.

She stumbled into Altair, who lifted an eyebrow at her fluster and glanced at the second floor with a studious frown.

"Are you hoping you'll blend into the daylight?" Zafira asked, looking pointedly at his clothes.

He was more haggard than he'd ever been, weariness drawing a circle beneath his eye, but he was dressed as impeccably as always. Zafira hadn't the slightest idea where the man found such clothes, or the time to maintain them. The entire ensemble was white and black, edged in gold, the filigree a nod to fashion. Laa, it was familiar.

A tribute—those were the colors Benyamin had worn.

Altair's frown deepened. "It's called fashion, Huntress."

"'Fashion' and 'ridiculous' don't mean the same," Kifah said as both she and Nasir joined them. "You don't have to be a scholar to know that."

"Glory is an acquired taste, and one must dress the part."

If Zafira knew anyone who would appreciate his mad sense of style, it was Yasmine.

Life thrives with irony, bint Iskandar. Indeed, it did.

"When all this is done, Altair, I'll give you the perfect position in the palace so that you can lead the life you've always deserved," Nasir said, sheathing his scimitar.

Altair rolled his eye, and Zafira withdrew the stolen black dagger and offered it to him, hilt first.

"Keep it," he said with a soft laugh, his warm hand closing her fingers around the hilt. "That was always your part in this plan."

She searched his gaze. Had he truly factored her into his scheme? Or was this a moment of improvisation? Before she could find the courage to ask, he was turning and gesturing to the two rows of buildings leading to the palace gates, pausing when Misk sprinted down the stairs.

His turban was nowhere to be seen, his hair disheveled in a way that was clear it wasn't the wind that had rifled through it.

"Sultan's teeth, Misk Khaldun. Have you no decency?" Altair exclaimed.

Misk grinned, his gaze bright. Nasir whispered something that sounded suspiciously like *You're one to talk.*

"Station half your archers along those rooftops," Altair told him. "The rest of us will spread out and regroup—"

The ground began to tremble. Altair and Nasir shared a look and hurried outside, and Zafira wondered if either of them knew just how much strength they drew from the other.

"Ifrit," Kifah whispered. "We're late. They weren't supposed to come to us."

"Zafira?" Yasmine asked from the upstairs balcony, her face flushed. "What's happening?"

"Stay in the room. Lock the door," Zafira ordered, unsure if that would make a difference. "Don't leave."

But Yasmine didn't move from the balcony. She was watching her.

"It's still new," she said softly, "seeing you armed and uncloaked. Shoulders back, head high. The bearer of change. I can hear the bards already— 'she was a reed against the harrowing tides, the curve of the moon leading them to freedom.'"

Zafira bit back her smile, undeserving of that prideful delight. If only Yasmine knew what more she had done to bear that change. The sins she had committed because of their caliph's bias. Yet the words stirred tears from a piece of her that awaited acknowledgment and praise from her dearest friend.

"I'm proud of you. Lana is, too. If I hadn't threatened to lock her in the palace dungeons, she would have come."

Zafira laughed through the trappings of her guilt, for Yasmine had protected her sibling in a way Zafira had failed Yasmine's.

When she looked back up, Yasmine had fixed her gaze on Misk, who saluted her one last time before disappearing after the others. Fear filled her hazel eyes with tears, and she fled before they could fall, latching the door closed.

Live, Zafira demanded Misk. *Amend your shortcomings. Love her.*

Then only Kifah and she remained. Kifah, armed with her spear, gold-tipped and fierce. Zafira, with only Nasir's jambiya in her hand, the black dagger tucked in her boot. No bow, no arrows.

"Oi," Kifah snapped, startling her. "Don't slouch. You overpowered the Jawarat, and that thing is as old as the Lion."

That was exactly it, wasn't it? Zafira gripped the satchel strapped to her side. "And as long as I'm connected to the Jawarat, I'll be a risk. I feel like I've been made of glass."

Kifah shook her shoulders. "No one walks into battle expecting to die, Huntress, and a book bound to your soul doesn't make that any different. Now hold that dagger high and stick with me, glass girl. I'll make sure you don't shatter."

CHAPTER 90

ADARK HAZE BLED INTO THE AFTERNOON LIGHT, chilling Zafira's skin, and worry buzzed through Misk's rebels when the streets erupted with screams and alarmed shouts. Smoke continued billowing to the skies, but this darkness was different.

This was the darkness that preceded ifrit in their natural form. They flooded the gates, staves flashing, shapeless guises shifting. Zafira locked the house doors. Altair breathed a curse.

Somehow, that made everything worse.

"This," Nasir rounded on him, his voice hushed in anger, "is what happens when you leave anything to chance. People die."

The men murmured among themselves, hope spiraling with the sun.

Altair glanced about sharply. "Don't. You may not understand the workings of men, and you may not have been made for battle, but I will not let you destroy their hope."

"I'm not destroying what never existed."

"This battle banks on hope. Humanity banks on hope," Altair seethed, throwing up his sword. His voice rose over the sudden howl of the wind. "Yalla! It won't be long before the Lion hears of the fire."

Hears of it? Skies, by now he would have to be smelling it, seeing it, feeling it. The world would know of it soon enough.

They'd barely made it past the gates before the ifrit converged, shrieks filling the air.

Zafira ducked when an ifrit made it past the ranks ahead and lunged for her. Her heart leaped to her throat as she ripped her jambiya through the dark soldier. *Safin steel*, unlike Baba's dagger, now far away in Bait ul-Ahlaam. Even still, it was ten times more frightening than aiming a bow from a distance.

Beside her, Kifah unleashed a handful of throwing knives, felling three ifrit before turning to impale another. Altair and Nasir, despite their bickering, fought back to back, the prince's sword flashing quicker than the other's single scimitar, and she wondered if that was why Nasir was at his side.

Death sweeps toward us.

She paused at the Jawarat's murmur. Already, men and ifrit littered the ground, shadowy forms beside human ones.

A fire crackled behind her, a warning before she whirled, tackling the stave away with her dagger, singeing the tips of her fingers in the process. Kifah turned to her aid with two well-placed thwacks of her spear.

"All right?"

"All right," Zafira replied with some disappointment. She didn't need a sitter. She needed a bow and an arrow.

Staves flashed without end. Misk's men fought valiantly, making full use of their rough-edged swords and jambiyas, the pride of their fathers. But they needed to power ahead, to push past Aya's house and make for the palace. The ifrit would only keep coming.

A shout rang out to her right, another to her left, this one older. For the rebels weren't all spry young men, but those who had lost enough to fear death a little less. Altair deftly saved the first rebel as Misk sprinted toward the older man.

Zafira didn't know why she watched him, why she was paying heed to the half Sarasin, half Demenhune who had stolen the heart of her dearest friend.

Until one of his archers shouted a warning that Misk didn't hear.

And a stave pierced him from behind.

Zafira forgot to breathe.

The ifrit pulled the stave free and pierced him again, higher now. Misk choked. Zafira felt as if the stave were ripping her own heart. Sound became pulses. She stumbled.

Stole someone's bow. Nocked an arrow and fired as pain tore through her mending wound. The ifrit fell. Her bow fell.

Misk fell.

Misk, Yasmine's husband, the man she spoke of with anger and happiness and love. He had lied and he had withheld, and yet he had loved her just as much.

"Zafira," Misk murmured as she sank to her knees beside him, yelling for help and knowing nothing could be done in time.

Someone screamed. Zafira looked up to find the doors flung open and Yasmine racing through the dark haze, a bundle of blue as bright as the sky. Too late, too late.

He sighed when he saw her. "Yasmine."

"Time apart, Misk. Time apart," she breathed. "Not an eternity, not life and death."

Misk brushed his hand down her cheek, his smile tender.

"Forevermore," he whispered. "In life, and in death."

Zafira's face was damp.

Yasmine placed her hand on his heart as a shadow fell over them. Nasir crouched, his mouth pursed. Death fell like rain around them, soldiers of smokeless fire, rebels of bone and blood. Misk rasped another breath, ragged and wet. Blood trickled from his lips, his eyes losing focus.

But he slowly inclined his head in respect. "Sul . . . tani."

Zafira's throat constricted. Yasmine sobbed when the last beat of his heart thrummed against her palm. For a moment, neither of them could move. She didn't think Yasmine breathed.

From the folds of his robes, Nasir withdrew a dark feather and touched it to Misk's blood. He sighed as he brushed his knuckles down Misk's open eyes. Eyes Yasmine had loved, had spoken of in barely restrained adoration.

"Be at peace, Misk Khaldun min Demenhur," he murmured.

Yasmine wept, then. Terrible, brutal sobs. A jewel of blue in the shadows of the city. With a strangled sound, she bundled Misk into her arms, lifting him, fumbling. Falling. Zafira stared numbly.

"Let me," Nasir said softly.

He hefted Misk against himself, and Zafira guarded his path toward the house, holding Yasmine close. Around them rang the shouts of wounded men and the clang of metal. It was death in full garb, a resplendent chorus. Misk was not hers, but her heart was connected deeply enough with Yasmine's that she felt her pain, inexplicable and uncontrollable.

"He did not die for you to follow," Nasir told Yasmine when he lowered Misk's body to the floor in the foyer of Aya's house. He pressed a dagger into her hands. *Misk's* dagger, with a moonstone in its hilt. "Stay inside. Stay safe."

He left. Zafira wavered between following him back to the battle and remaining here with her friend. Once orphaned. Now widowed.

"Go, Zafira," Yasmine said, hollow. "Kill them all."

CHAPTER 91

"WHO WAS THAT?" ALTAIR ASKED WHEN NASIR returned to his side, wiping his blade free of black blood. "I only saw her hair. I've never seen a shade so brilliant."

"Misk is dead," Nasir replied. He didn't particularly feel for the man, but the death had shaken something in him. It was the sight of Zafira's friend and the hollow in her eyes, the shatter of her soul that bled into her sobs.

Moreover, it was how acutely Zafira felt Yasmine's pain. A knife to his skin.

Altair turned to Nasir, barely reacting when a rebel barreled against his shoulder. "Dead?"

"That was his wife."

"She's here?" Altair asked, quieted by woe.

Nasir's tone matched his, knowing he would hear despite the din. "She saw it happen."

"Sultan's teeth."

Kifah shoved her way between them, eyebrows raised, spear dripping blood. "Oi. What's going on?"

"Misk is dead."

"Oh." A flash of amusement crossed her face. "I never did like the man."

Nasir pressed his lips thin. And he thought *he* was callous in the face of death.

"You know," Altair mused, goaded by Nasir's look. "I think this is my first time charging into battle without a plan. I don't think I've ever felt anything so . . . thrilling."

"It's an ambush," Kifah deadpanned, the gold tip of her spear flashing with each turn.

"I'm going to kill you," Nasir growled.

"Please join the line, princeling," Altair said gently.

"What of your power?" Kifah asked.

He arced his scimitar. "I don't much feel like burning anyone to a crisp right now."

Nasir shoved him away from an oncoming stave, fixing him with scrutiny. "This has nothing to do with morality, does it?"

Altair didn't answer for the longest moment. In that time, Nasir killed three ifrit and got a hole burned in his sleeve, and Zafira had joined them, and they still hadn't progressed much farther from the house. The plan hadn't meant to proceed this way: They were supposed to be at the palace when the fire began.

But Altair's falcon had failed to deliver the note, and Nasir, who had left Demenhur before the plan's final run-through, had only been able to guess at timings when he'd told his mother.

"I've had magic for as long as Arawiya didn't. Do you know what that feels like? To live every day with the knowledge that you might be the reason the kingdom suffers?"

Nasir *did* know that feeling—to an extent.

"I didn't know our mother was a Sister of Old," Altair continued. "I didn't know I hadn't *stolen* magic from Arawiya. So I never practiced. And on the occasion that I did, I'd return to the palace and learn you had another burn on your back. Light burns, doesn't it? I thought you were paying for my wrongs." He scoffed. "My mother's perfect son."

In the exhale of the sun's last breath, Altair's blue gaze burned amber like his father's.

Zafira stilled. "What was that?"

The ground trembled again and sinewy wings stretched across the horizon. Elder ifrit. Preceding them, in rows and rows more numerous and orderly than ifrit: men. Sarasin soldiers.

Hope spiraled once more, and Nasir *felt* it. This was what Altair meant about wars banking on the sentiment. Archers and magic didn't turn the tides—*hope* did. This was what the Lion had so often wanted to quell, using his father's voice to flay him, inside and out.

But what the Lion didn't understand, what *Nasir* never understood until now, was this: *Hope never dies.*

Hope was the beast that could never be slain, the light that blazed in every harrowing dark. *A person without hope is a body without a soul,* his mother murmured in his heart.

"We may die," Nasir said suddenly.

Altair looked at him sharply, and so did everyone else. Rimaal, he was Arawiya's future sultan, and if he couldn't inspire a few dozens, how could he sway an entire kingdom?

"I know death as well as I know the lines of my palm. He rides for us today. We can flee and let these streets run red with our cowardice, or we can die with swords in our hands and zeal in our hearts. Be a force eternalized in history."

Nasir paused, his breaths coming hard and fast as murmurs passed among the men. What did the greats do with their hands when they spouted speeches?

"We are all that stands between Arawiya and an age of darkness. An assembly of forty from different walks of life." His eyes flicked to Zafira's and away. "An archer without a bow. A general without an army. A warrior without allegiance. Villagers without homes."

The wind echoed his call, charged the air with its howl.

"And you," Altair added, his tone mellowed by what Nasir realized was respect. "A king without a throne."

How Nasir felt about his brother's words made them no less true. He looked from one man to the next and breathed a heavy exhale.

"That throne is ours. It is not only the Lion whom we must slay and an army we must end, but a horizon that promises no future. A darkness that promises no relief."

The murmurs had risen to a buzz now.

"If we don't fight for our kin and kingdom, who will?"

The buzz became a roar. Fists rose in agreement, cheers echoing. For the first time in his life, Nasir gave himself up to an illusion, to the trick of hope in which their handful of fighters were suddenly tenfold more. Altair held his gaze and dipped his chin in a gesture that meant more to Nasir than he had ever imagined.

"Big words from my brother who wasn't made for battle."

Nasir gave him a lazy shrug. "I'm the future sultan."

Altair laughed, and it was almost easy to forget they were counting the moments until their deaths.

Almost.

CHAPTER 92

DEATH WASN'T SUPPOSED TO FILL HER WITH SUCH A blaze, and yet, Zafira was brimming with pride, her heart a touch lighter. The careening sun lit the ash of Nasir's eyes aflame as the breeze toyed with the end of his turban. His hand was on the hilt of his sword, the point buried in the sand beside him. He was the Prince of Death, breathing life into his words.

Every bit the sultan he was born to be.

It was a bittersweet thought.

"You did well, Sultani."

He breathed a broken laugh. "Don't call me that."

"Why not? It was how you spoke," she said. It hadn't been the most moving of battle cries. It wasn't full of bluster and swagger, which was more suited to Altair—she wouldn't be surprised if Altair's thoughts themselves strutted in such a way—yet for someone like Nasir, who had been forced to trim his words and hold back, back, *back*, it was a leap.

The words he had strung together had taken far more courage than wielding a sword did, and it filled her to near bursting.

"The night may not be lenient," Nasir said, and she paused, warming at the crimson painting the tops of his ears.

"It may not," she said.

He stepped closer. "We may not see the next dawn."

"We may not."

"The last time we stood in battle, I could only think of the things I didn't say."

Tell me, she wanted to whisper.

Altair called to them. "We need to disband. Kifah, with me. Nasir, you and Zafira head for the palace. At least one of us needs to be there when the Lion drops the barrier and leaves the grounds. We'll join once we have the upper hand."

Nasir scoured the dusty ground and picked up a scimitar. Zafira held herself still when his hands cupped hers and closed her fingers around its hilt.

"Later," he said, answering her, but when he didn't release her hand, she lifted her gaze to his, and saw that it was not a promise. The way he looked at her was the way the dying stared one last time at the sky, and so she knew.

He had conveyed hope into the hearts of men, but had left nothing for himself.

When Zafira and Nasir finally stumbled from the narrow confines of the alleys leading to the palace, Misk's archers covered them.

The sinewy draw of bowstring after bowstring was a torment, a reminder of her weakness. Huntress Zafira. Orphan Zafira. *Soldier* Zafira. A peg in a makeshift army grasping at hope as their end drew near. She was stranded without her bow. Abandoned without the compass in her heart leading her forward.

"Ifrit!" Nasir shouted.

Zafira ducked beneath the arc of a stave and countered, not expecting the force to wrench the scimitar from her grip. She dropped to her knees, sand in her fists, perspiration dripping between her brows.

The same stave came crashing down near her fingers, and she sprang away, her hand closing around a bow. Beside it, a Demenhune archer lay with his stomach ripped open, eyes wide and empty. Like Misk.

What had her people done to suffer this way? Shunned, starved, gassed, murdered. She stumbled back, bile rising to her throat.

Rise, bint Iskandar.

She gagged and yanked the fallen archer's quiver free. If she was going to die, it would be with a bow in her hands and intent in her heart. For Deen and Baba. For Benyamin. For Umm and Misk and Yasmine.

The Jawarat hummed, urging her onward.

They sprinted into the chaos near the palace. The Great Library was barely visible in the billowing smoke. Angry surges of orange and vibrant red swelled in the darkness, flames crackling and roaring. The library was as much a part of Arawiya as magic was. It was the culmination of all that they were.

It's not real, it's not. But it smelled real, it looked real. The screams were real. It was all proof of the Silver Witch's power, but with every single one of her senses goading her to drop to her knees and weep, Zafira couldn't appreciate it.

Nasir dragged her into the cover of a date palm. "Look. The gates."

Through the smoke, Zafira saw it: the iron gates swinging outward with twin groans. Another sound, low and bestial, rolled from its confines like the unsheathing of a sword, and something hummed against her skin. *Magic.*

The Lion's barriers were coming undone.

ACT III

THE END OF THE BEGINNING

CHAPTER 93

THERE WERE ARCHES THAT LED TO THE PALACE doors, and before them was the fountain Nasir's mother had commissioned long ago, shaped like a lion.

Its water ran crimson.

The hairs on the backs of Nasir's arms rose at the sight. The clamor of men and ifrit echoed from the streets, and from the deeper shadows along the palace walls, soldiers materialized, human in appearance, though the staves against their shoulders gave them away as ifrit.

Nasir drew his scimitar. Zafira nocked an arrow in an unfamiliar bow.

And a figure stepped from the arches. A place he had no right to stand in. A position he had murdered to obtain.

The Lion of the Night. Perfectly poised and dauntingly dramatic.

Laa—he was neither of those things. Not now. Panic painted his stance, glowed in his amber eyes, because that which he valued most was burning to cinders. He looked worn, surprised to see them; a strange sight, for the Lion was adept at masking emotion.

Shadows gathered in his outstretched palms.

Nasir sheathed his scimitar.

If the Lion desired a game of shadows, Nasir would give him one. He mirrored the Lion's movements, lifting his own hands, but he wasn't quick enough. Darkness shot toward them, the fountain falling to pieces in between, stone scattering to the courtyard. Zafira fell with a cry. Nasir stumbled, but held his ground.

The Lion didn't wait. He dashed for the gates, abandoning them in favor of the Great Library, still engulfed in flames. Nasir watched, and though he didn't consider himself petty, he took great pleasure in the Lion's haste, and then in the way his delicate features morphed into horror, cementing him in place.

As the fire, smoke, and every last ember in the air disappeared.

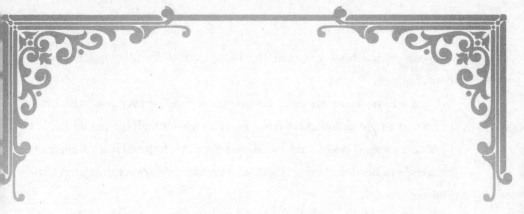

CHAPTER 94

ZAFIRA LOOSED A RELIEVED BREATH WHEN THE IL-
lusion disappeared. The Lion's horror gave way to laughter, and
she didn't like how part of her reacted to the sound. In heartbeats, that relief would turn to anger when he realized he had been made
a mockery of. He whirled, darkness in his palms.

Nasir was ready.

Both shadows clashed like thunder in a rare storm, rage igniting the
courtyard. Zafira took a careful step away, shifting her bow to and fro as
she tried to sight the ifrit, her wound whispering a warning everytime she
moved. The shadows wouldn't still, stirring debris and sand, whipping
her hair about her face.

"You think to end me." The Lion's voice carried over the chaos. "To
take the throne you imagine rightfully yours."

Zafira looked to Nasir in alarm, but the words fell harmlessly.

"Pathetic."

Nasir gritted his teeth, and the Lion, despite the distance between them, noticed.

"You will never be enough. The people will never love you," the Lion spurred in a tight drawl as he drove his shadows with all his strength.

A rasp escaped Nasir, and she knew he saw his father. Heard him. Felt the weight of his dead body. Skies. She needed to do something, stop that monster's mouth.

"A killer," the Lion goaded, and she flinched. "A scarred boy king with barely enough words at his disposal."

Nasir's shadows began to waver, and she knew. The words themselves hurt less than the reminder that they were once spoken by his father.

"How do you think to rule, mutt?"

Nasir's shadows disappeared.

He dropped his hands, and the Lion's shadows struck him, *threw* him. Zafira shouted as he was flung back against the metal gates. He fell without a sound.

And didn't move.

She swallowed her cry, and fired. Her arrow whistled across the courtyard until the Lion snatched it in its deadly path.

Her heart lodged in her throat, at the reminder of what she needed to do.

"I've lost count of the sunsets I've witnessed, the men I've slain, and the books I've devoured—that is how long I've sustained upon this earth, azizi. Did you really think to kill me with a twig?" He snapped the arrow in half and caged her with a gust of darkness.

Bint Iskandar.

The Jawarat's fear gripped her as the shadows did. They writhed around her, winding relentlessly, pressing the air from her lungs.

She refused to cower. "Did you really think we'd burn down Arawiya's history?"

It was ironic, she thought, that the very thing he valued most would now be his downfall. *If I live.*

He ignored her. "What is it about the weak that draws you to them, azizi?"

"I don't—" She started to protest, before she realized she didn't owe him an answer. She owed him nothing. "Release me."

"So bold," the Lion *tsk*ed. "What if I killed you instead?"

Between one careful breath and the next, the Lion moved from the shambles of the fountain to the shadows trapping her in the center of the courtyard. His long fingers skimmed her neck and gripped her chin. Blood trickled down her throat, warm and thick. She shivered.

Claws. Sweet snow below.

"Why?" he asked suddenly. The question wasn't tempered or conniving. It was merely him trying to understand. "Why are you trying so hard to stop me?"

Skies, he was truly mad.

"Look around you," Zafira said, trying to keep the hysteria from her voice. "Where is the sun? Where are the people? You might have controlled Ghameq, but he had his limits, and even if we feared him, the known devil is better than an unknown saint."

"Is it the devil you seek, azizi?" He was mocking her. Then he read her face and canted his head. "Do my people not deserve the freedom of yours? Do you know how it feels to stand beside others forged of the same flesh and bone and still be treated as inferior? As someone undeserving?"

Of course she did. Every girl was born to that unfortunate truth.

If her head weren't tipped back, she would have spat at his feet. "This is not how one seeks freedom. Your cause might have been noble once, but you lost your way long ago."

He clucked his tongue, but she wasn't surprised. He wouldn't acquiesce to the truth. "Never, azizi. Though I wondered as much, when I could no longer remember why my soul craved vengeance. Why I desired knowledge, enough that I inked the word upon my face. I thought Sharr had driven me mad, but it was only that wretched book. Thieving me of my past."

The Jawarat did not recoil from his wrath. Laa, it matched his with its own. It wanted the black dagger in Zafira's hand. It wanted the blade buried in his chest. But the shadows held her in place.

This close, she could hear his heartbeat.

"I had always been one for the written word, even then. You witnessed my memory. You saw them refuse me tutelage by stoning my father to death. When one is denied a thing, is it not normal to crave it? When that denial comes through violence, that need will do the same."

So he had gleaned it all. He started with Benyamin's library, learning Safaitic from the safi himself before using that knowledge to enact his reign of darkness. It wasn't enough. He was banished to Sharr along with his people, and so he used Ghameq to devour what he could from the Great Library, mastering incantations and Arawiya's long-lost secrets as he awaited his freedom.

He wanted and he received, and an endless wanting created greed. From knowledge, he desired power, and power made his gaze stray to the Gilded Throne.

He watched her connect one dot to the other. "Sarasin is where my people will live. Not the graveyard of the safin, a land defiled by their filth."

What of the heart? she almost asked, but it was clear, wasn't it? He could not create a home for his kind and destroy another without magic, nor could he do what he wished with the limited morsels the Sisters' amplifiers provided. And why share and invite trouble when he could keep magic to himself, rendering him as powerful as the Sisters of Old themselves?

"And so, in your desire for freedom, you've become as cruel and terrible as the ones who wronged you," Zafira said. "That doesn't make you deserving of anything but a place in the dungeons."

He released her in disgust. The Sisters had been wrong to imprison the ifrit on Sharr. They had been wrong to corral them like cattle and abandon them on an island. But one wrong didn't justify another.

Zafira carefully measured her breaths, aware the Lion was plotting and scheming with every passing heartbeat. He spun his finger, and shadows coiled tighter, making her light-headed.

Bint Iskandar.

She struggled to draw breath. With a sigh that was almost resigned, the Lion reached for the satchel strapped to her side, only to straighten with a croak.

A gold tip protruded from his chest, sticky with black blood.

The darkness vanished like smoke and the palace came into view, as did Altair and Nasir. The courtyard was littered with ifrit corpses.

Zafira stumbled backward and Kifah withdrew her spear, readying to pierce him again. But the Lion—though slumping and out of breath—clenched his fist, and Kifah dropped to her knees with a vise around her neck. He flicked his other wrist, and Altair, rushing to help her, went flying.

Heartbeats later, the hole in the Lion's chest stitched itself together again, not even a drop of blood left as proof.

When he blinked his amber eyes at her, he didn't look like a man who had been run through with a spear. He looked almost bored.

So long as the heart provides him with magic, wounding him will be impossible. Until we wound him, we won't be able to retrieve the heart.

The black dagger pulsed in her boot, cool and ready. But she didn't dare reach for it, not when he could easily overpower her. Laa, she needed to catch him unaware.

The heart weakens him.

For a stricken moment, Zafira thought the Jawarat spoke of Nasir or Altair, but when the Lion dropped his hands, she caught the sheen of sweat on his brow. The fatigue.

Steal it.

But—the heart was inside his daama body.

The Jawarat laughed. *When have we steered you wrong?*

Zafira froze at its tone, the terrible beauty of that laugh. The reminder of what she had done with its voice in her mind, splitting a man in two as no mortal should be capable of doing.

The Lion watched her.

"Touching of your friends to run to your aid." His gaze was intent. "Join me, azizi."

Zafira scoffed. "Because you can't kill me?"

"I won't merely kill them," he said, and from the corner of her eye, she saw Nasir using a whip of shadow to release the vise that had been crushing Kifah's neck. "I will cut them open and string their innards together, as I did to the safin less than a fortnight ago. I will sever their heads to adorn the palace gates."

"And then the people will love you?" Zafira asked, bile rising to her throat.

"Create enough fear, and the people will have no choice."

His hand cut the air, and strands of shadow rippled toward her. Zafira threw up her arms, intent on protecting the Jawarat, but the shadows stopped before they reached her.

Caught in a shield of black that dissipated as quickly as it had come.

Nasir.

He extended his gauntlet blades as Altair and Kifah came up from behind. The Lion looked among the four of them and laughed, as if their weapons were playthings, as if they were as insignificant as the ground beneath his feet.

From the corners of the palace, ifrit stalked forward. More marched from beyond the palace gates, caging them in. The crackle of their staves echoed in the air. *The dagger, the dagger, the dagger*—she couldn't wrest it free now. He would rip her arm from her body the moment she did. Their weapons *were* playthings.

The Lion half turned to watch his encroaching horde and froze with a sharp breath.

"Baba?"

Zafira stilled. That one word teemed with an eternity of pain, and for a long, confused stretch of time, no one moved. He made a sound between a whimper and a sob.

Now, bint Iskandar.

The Lion stumbled forward. A breathless sort of pity rooted her in place. Nasir looked to Altair. Kifah narrowed her eyes. Who was it he saw? Surely an ifrit would not toy with the leader who fought for their right to live.

The heart, the Jawarat insisted, and she ducked past Nasir and Altair until she saw what the Lion was seeing.

A safi with blue eyes as bright as Altair's stepped close. It was the man Zafira had seen in the Jawarat's vision, only not bloody, his body unbruised. *His father.* He was alive.

Impossible.

And if Zafira was seeing the same face he was, this was no ifrit. It was an illusion—laa, an apparition.

A cruel twist of fate.

There was only one person the Lion had wronged so deeply, so terribly that she could fathom doing the same to him. Only one person with the power to create an illusion so real, no one could tell the difference. *The Silver Witch.*

The safi continued walking slowly toward him, and Zafira understood that it was more than an apparition; it was a distraction, and she was standing around like a fool.

Zafira ran, tucking the Jawarat against her chest and using both hands to shove the Lion to the dusty hard stone. He fell with an *oof* beneath her.

He was cold. Startled. Afraid. His eyes were crazed, barely seeing.

Pity broke Zafira's inhale.

No. Focus.

Her hands shook as she grabbed the lapels of his robes and wrenched them apart, exposing his chest. Now the Lion struggled. He fought against her, shadows pooling in his palms and fading into nothing when she brought the black dagger to his skin.

Panic paralyzed him.

Paralyzed her.

Tell me what to do, she begged the Jawarat.

Altair shouted, "Do it!"

The Lion's gaze cleared.

She trembled in alarm, but the Jawarat steadied her hand.

And plunged the stolen black dagger through his chest.

The Lion sputtered. Zafira cried out.

Trust us, was all the book said, and the Lion froze, as if he heard the Jawarat's command as loudly as she did. Down her palm was a line of blood, in her skull was a song. Her fingers tightened around the hilt.

And the dagger ripped downward, carving across him.

"This doesn't belong to you," she said, and took the beating heart out of his chest.

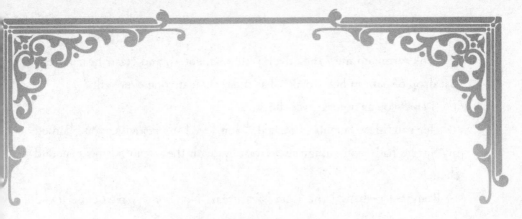

CHAPTER 95

Nasir saw Zafira slump over the Lion, and the darkness faded with the suddenness of a blade. Fear cut the air from his lungs. And then she rose with a heart in her fist, blood dripping down the length of her arm. The Lion tried to stand, but collapsed, panting as he struggled without magic, without a healer.

The black dagger was in his chest.

His blood stained the courtyard stone. He was dying.

The safi he called Baba continued to approach. Dark-haired and blue-eyed, aristocratic in a way much like the Lion. And changing—features shifting, figure curving, hair fading to stark white.

Recognition lurched in Nasir's stomach.

It was his mother. Wronged by the Lion, wronged by the world. She had done as she'd vowed, and Nasir's pride was fierce.

The Lion rasped a laugh. "That was cruel, Anadil. Even for you."

He sounded sad, broken.

"You wronged me," the Silver Witch lamented, and Nasir heard every last drop of pain in her words. "Far more than anyone ever will."

"I *loved* you as no one ever did."

Her mirthless laughter cracked. "You loved my *power*, as you claimed my Sisters had. You ruined me. Even in death they granted me a second chance."

Remorse reshaped the Lion's features. "No. Some part of me loved you, as you had loved me."

A lie, Nasir thought in his bewildered state, but he trusted his mother. The Silver Witch knew the Lion more than any of them could imagine, and when she slowly knelt beside him, Nasir tried to ignore the warning bells as they tolled.

The Lion rolled his head to face her, and Nasir wondered how different life might have been if the Sisters hadn't locked the ifrit away. If the safin hadn't taken to pride so violently.

Perhaps, if Nasir hadn't given in to wishful fantasy, he would have been ready when the Lion's amber eyes flashed, an instant before he lunged.

And the Silver Witch screamed.

Nasir's blood turned to ice, and he acted on instinct. On rage. On memory.

His mother screamed.

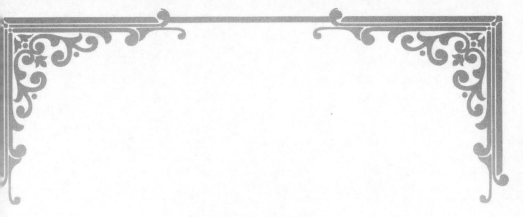

CHAPTER 96

ALTAIR LOVED HER AS HE DID MOST THINGS: EVEN
when they did not love him in return.

He'd had years to reflect, to try to understand his mother.
When he was young, he'd wished she had never existed. When he was
older, he'd been angry when she'd died. When he'd learned the truth
upon Sharr, that she had fabricated her death, breaking the soul of the one
son she loved so deeply, he'd felt, well, sad.

Power begets pain. She wasn't a cruel mother, or an evil one. Rather,
she was ill-equipped for motherhood, too mired in her own mistakes and
failings and their recompense, and both he and Nasir had paid the price.

Still, she was his mother. He was her son. There were some bonds that
remained no matter how they were tested.

You've a heart of gold, she had once said.

Is that why it weighs so heavily? he had replied.

And so, when his mother screamed, every last drop of blood in his
veins came to a halt.

CHAPTER 97

Zafira saw the moment the Lion lunged and sank his teeth into the Silver Witch's flesh. One last attempt for si'lah blood. For power. Terror gripped the very air when Anadil screamed.

Then both brothers moved at once.

They did not think, they did not hesitate. It was innate, their actions. Unrestricted by sentience.

Shadows swarmed from Nasir's palms, light roared from Altair's.

Magic collided in a crash of thunder and a cresting hum. Both beams struck the Lion, black and white merging into a coruscating, iridescent pillar of magic that rose from the palace courtyard and disappeared into the clouds, dappled in every color Zafira could imagine.

"Bleeding Guljul," Kifah exhaled.

They were draining him, siphoning every last dreg of his power into Arawiya. Ifrit shrieked, scattering into the shadows. Zafira struggled to breathe, something raw and broken upending her insides. It tugged her as close to the iridescent skeins of magic as she could go before Kifah shouted for her to step back, *step away*.

The Silver Witch clutched Zafira's hand. Her face was wet with tears.

"Finish what they started." *She* had drawn Zafira here. "His mind belongs in the Jawarat."

Before she could ask *how*, Zafira staggered backward. Memories plowed through her, a violent and powerful barrage of emotion. The Lion as a child, in adolescence. As an adult. Lonely, always lonely. The Jawarat trembled in her hands as his memories joined the Sisters', flooding Zafira with yet another life she had not lived but would always hold because of her bond.

The hum faded to silence.

Nasir and Altair lowered their hands, and the haze steadily cleared.

Where the Lion had lain, a tree now stood, dark branches curling into the sky like fingers seeking something out of reach. At its base, a body lay slumped, amber eyes closed to the world.

Mind, body, and soul, the Jawarat said softly. It was how the Sisters had wanted to defeat him, years and years ago.

"Why?" the Lion whispered. Only, his voice came from elsewhere. *No*—from the Jawarat, from her heart, where a part of him would live forever.

She closed her eyes against the anguish in his plea. Hadn't she stood before the Arz that had stolen her father, and asked that very same question?

Against the black tree, the manifestation of his soul, the Silver Witch placed her hand. Lovingly, almost. Part of her truly did love him, the way the Lion might have loved her.

Zafira watched as Anadil closed her eyes and opened them to a new world.

"We are born with the promise of death," Zafira said softly as a single rose, wild and white, blossomed on one of the branches. It was a gift. "You had merely outlived yours."

CHAPTER 98

NASIR COULD SCARCELY BELIEVE IT TO BE TRUE. That the monster who had controlled his father, held his leash, belittled him without end, was gone. The Silver Witch spoke first, breaking the trance that had fallen across the courtyard.

"The heart. We must make for Sarasin at once."

In Zafira's fist, the heart that once belonged to one of the Sisters of Old pulsed direly, a shade of crimson so dark it was nearly black. Nasir met her gaze and saw doubt, for the Jawarat had called it impossible.

Nasir had never cared for magic the way Zafira had. He hadn't spent decades working for its restoration the way Altair had. It did not signify vengeance for him the way it did for Kifah. Laa, for him, magic had signified destruction and pain. It had ruined his family and burned darkness into his life.

And still, he wanted its return—for them, for this new family he had built himself.

He led five horses to the palace gates.

CHAPTER 99

I T WAS A THRILLING KIND OF FREEDOM TO RIDE IN THE
dead of the night, the thunder of hooves carrying one through. Kifah
ululated as they charged through the streets, making it a little easier to
ignore the destruction of the city, the heart dying in Zafira's hand. The loss
she felt, every time she recalled those amber eyes, closing to the world.

Magic, she reminded herself. What she had dreamed of and desired for
years and years on end.

It will not work, the Jawarat said again.

Zafira ignored it, just as she had ignored the black gleam of the organ, far
from the crimson it should have been. The pulse had been steady, promising. *Corrupt.* Surely the minaret, created by the Sisters' hands, could rid the
heart of the Lion's evil.

The Jawarat only sighed.

It was still learning how stubborn she could be. How much she would
give up to hope. They had come this far. If she couldn't *believe* the heart
would survive, how could she expect it to?

She would live in a world with glory akin to that of a century ago. Magic would roar in her veins, hum in her limbs. And it wasn't only her, but *everyone*. Arawiya would thrive again.

It had to. She would not let herself think of the alternative.

The night was fading by the time they reached the palace in Leil. They rounded to the royal minaret, and Zafira was surprised to find three safin of the High Circle awaiting their arrival. The zumra neared the glittering tower, anticipation crowding her lungs.

"Akhh," Altair exclaimed at the sight of the stairs spiraling to the very top of the minaret.

With an exasperated look at him, Nasir disappeared into an alcove and soon enough, the squeak of a rope filled the quiet. Thousands of oil lamps flickered to life, and the floor beneath them began to rise.

No one spoke. Everyone stared at the heart in Zafira's hands.

"It's slowing," Zafira murmured.

The pulley creaked and the floor rose and rose before finally screeching to a stop.

Cool air brushed her skin, winding around her neck with a gentle caress much like the Lion's darkness, and she held her breath as she stepped into the night. The others followed in hushed silence.

Sarasin unfolded beneath them, a perfect bird's-eye view of darkness interspersed with flecks of fire like embers in the wind.

Zafira gave it all a passing glance, for her gaze was set much closer: the pedestal in the center of the annular space. Stone hands curved upward in everlasting prayer, the same mottled gray of the ones that had grasped the Jawarat on Sharr.

No one spoke. She did not think anyone dared breathe.

Her footsteps were heartbeats on the tiles. In her lungs was a drum. The Jawarat, too, held its breath, for it had at last learned that it could cling upon hope.

Zafira had only made it halfway when her legs stumbled to a halt, freezing her in place.

"*No*," she cried.

As the heart

crumbled

in her hands.

We warned you, the Jawarat said, but not even it could find a way to be smug.

Anguish tore from her in the shape of a sob. The wind rose, winding through her hands, ashes scattering and swirling into the night, leaving her bare.

Empty.

She dropped to her knees with a shattered breath.

She did not care about Kifah's soft cry. Altair's croak. Nasir lifting his fingers through the fading dust. The Silver Witch, witness to every broken moment.

No. Zafira thought of Deen, who had died for this. Of Yasmine, who had lost for this. Of Misk and his sacrifice. Of Benyamin and his dreams.

Of Baba, who had taught her the enchantment of magic, parting the cage of her ribs and feeding desire into her very soul. She brushed her knuckles down the ache in her heart.

Never, ever to be sated.

"How?" she whispered.

The zumra remained silent as she wept. No one spoke of hope, for there was none.

CHAPTER 100

ZAFIRA COULDN'T STAND THE SIGHT OF THOSE STONE palms any longer. Empty. As empty as her chest, her lungs, her heart. She pressed her hands to the floor, dust biting her skin, and her vision clouded with this terrible dream.

"Huntress."

She almost didn't hear the Silver Witch's voice, as if she herself wasn't certain she wanted to be heard. Zafira wanted to laugh. There was no Huntress anymore. There was no Hunter. There was no Arz, no Sharr, no whispering shadow, no magic.

No magic.

Still, Zafira turned to face her. The last remaining Sister of Old. The vanishing moonlight illuminated her and the blood on her palms, a trickle smattering the dark stone at her feet.

In her hands was a heart. Pulsing and alive, brighter than all the others she had seen.

Hers.

"Magic for an entire kingdom versus magic for one warden who has lived far too long," the Silver Witch said wistfully when her sons looked to her inquisitively. "I was the only one of my Sisters never to remove my heart. I was one with my power, and could not understand how easily they relinquished their own. They had never asked me to, and I realize now that it was not they who would ask, but you.

"My kingdom."

Zafira sputtered, a sob becoming a laugh. Altair joined her, bewilderment making him rasp.

"I don't think I can take any more of this," Kifah choked out, clutching her chest with her free hand.

Nasir couldn't contain a smile of his own, and the moon crept from the clouds, an eager witness.

Zafira stepped forward. Stopped. She didn't know what to do with her hands. She wanted to scream, she wanted her joy to be felt across the caliphate, across Arawiya.

The Silver Witch gestured for her to take it. "This honor is yours."

"Mine?" Zafira said breathlessly. "I—I'm no more worthy of it than any of you." She looked across them, her friends, her companions. "Kifah, this is your vengeance complete. The Sil—Anadil's redemption come full circle. It's your *heart*. Nasir, this is the opposite of what ruined your life. Altair, you're—you're the one who plotted decades for this."

"And yet none of it would have been possible without you," Nasir said in that voice that looped with the darkness, and she warmed at the deep intent in his eyes.

"You didn't think we'd forget, did you?" Kifah asked, cocking an eyebrow. *It is yours, bint Iskandar.*

Zafira met the Silver Witch's eyes and reached for her heart. The embodiment of her power, more supreme than any of the Sisters of Old. Zafira's breath caught as the pulsing mass filled her hands, thrumming quick beneath her fingers, and knotted a blustering laugh in her throat.

Anticipation flooded her, rendered her mute.

She could tell they all held their breath once more as she turned to the stone hands. The familiar hum of magic set her veins at ease. The Jawarat basked in her joy. Blood dripped from her fingers, each plink a hiss, until she carefully placed the organ in the center of the pedestal.

For a long, drawn-out beat, nothing happened.

Then the hands lifted with a great groan, and closed around the final heart.

CHAPTER 101

FOR AS LONG AS NASIR LIVED, HE WOULD NEVER FORget this moment. The way the earth's exhale ruffled his hair. The way the safin's eyes fell closed, returned to a love long lost. In a way that Benyamin, the dreamwalker who had given his life for this moment, never would. It was only now that Nasir realized how deeply magic had been ingrained into Arawiyan life.

"So this is what it feels like," Kifah contemplated, "to see vengeance through."

"What does it feel like?" he asked.

"Freeing."

A thousand troubles unraveled with the rupture of her laugh, a sound so untethered and unfettered to the world, so perfect for this night, that Altair joined her, and Nasir smiled.

His mother did not look like one who had lost a part of herself. Laa, she had gained something by losing her power, and Nasir knew it was the relief that only someone of si'lah blood could comprehend.

Perhaps more significant than any of it was her: Zafira. The way she alighted in untrammeled joy, the way her head fell back in victory, and still she stopped to look at him. Him of all people.

Had he, too, been a walker of the past, gifted to relive memories, this was where he would return. Zafira, always and always.

CHAPTER 102

Iɴ Baba's stories, once the villain was vanquished, the world suddenly became a better place. The victors could at last lean back and avail themselves of the fruits of their labor. There was much the stories failed to mention. The way the victors missed the villain, for instance. The trauma left behind for the kingdom and its people to endure. The deaths to mourn.

Zafira had reunited with Sukkar, who was the same lazy dastard he'd always been, not really surprised to see her alive. Laa, the beast would have been surprised if she *had* died. Misk had kept the horse busy, riding him from Demenhur all the way to Aya's house where he and his rebels had gathered. Together, she and Sukkar found Yasmine in the graveyard beneath the morning sun, not far from the Sultan's Palace. A mound of dirt stretched before her.

Misk Khaldun.

"The dead don't like to be delayed," Yasmine said in greeting. Her friend looked smaller than she was, delicate and breakable. She didn't look up, even when Zafira sat down beside her on the rug flecked already with sand.

"I wish he had died in Demenhur so it wouldn't be so hard to visit him," she continued.

"You'll have to move here, then," Zafira teased. "The royal life suits you."

Yasmine breathed a laugh, and finally looked at her. "They're gone, Zafira. I'm an orphan. I'm a widow. I was once a sister, and now I'm not even that."

Zafira reached for her hand, sliding their palms together. "You still are."

She didn't exhale until her friend squeezed back, but she felt the whisper of her hesitation, the pain. *I'm trying* was spelled within the gesture.

"Hearts need time to mend," Zafira said softly, reassuring them both.

Love was a peculiar thing, she had learned. Like the surge of old magic that defeated the Lion, like the Silver Witch sacrificing her heart.

It had been little more than half a day since his separation: his memories in the Jawarat Zafira kept close, his soul immortalized in the black tree in the palace courtyard, and his body soon to be anchored in the Baransea.

Jinan hadn't asked for coin this time.

Zafira sat back, breathing the scent of freshly turned earth. It was strange, not having to worry about whether or not she would live to see the next sunrise. Strange that the Lion was no longer a threat, that the Arz no longer crept closer. Every breath she took now felt new and free. Every heartbeat felt like the promise of another.

And yet she missed both the Lion and the Arz beyond comprehension. They had shaped her into who she was, as Nasir had said, forcing themselves into the fabric of her existence.

A crier marched the streets, announcing the upcoming coronation and filling the city with a buzz of excitement and fear. Change was coming, and as the Lion taking the throne had shown them, it was not always good.

What they did not yet know was this: the coronation would grant them more than a new king, but magic, too. A new age. As Seif had assured the zumra, the High Circle had positioned blockades to stop its flow until after the coronation, and though the dignitaries who had attended the ruined feast knew of the hearts' restoration, it would be some time before everyone else did.

Yasmine rose and dusted off her dress, spotting Sukkar. "What's the plan? Back to Thalj?"

"Only to fetch Lana," Zafira replied, refusing to meet Yasmine's eyes as she swung atop her horse. In days, Nasir would become ruler of Arawiya, the circlet of a prince replaced with the crown of a sultan. It filled her with pride, even as her heart ached.

She took Sukkar's reins as Yasmine watched her with a wistful softness in her eyes, understanding everything.

"I'll be back for the coronation," Zafira said.

She intended to return with enough time to spare, and though the trek through Demenhur would be sloppy as snow continued to melt across the caliphate, she couldn't complain. Word had come that it was gradual enough that the water seeping into the ground would allow people to grow herbs once more, and soon.

"You mean *we* will be back," Yasmine said, arching a brow when Zafira looked at her in surprise.

She loathed the sorrow in her friend's gaze, the hollow that she was afraid might never be filled again.

"It's your prince. Did you assume I wouldn't want to come?"

CHAPTER 103

THE ANNOUNCER BASKED IN HIS MOMENT OF FAME from the balcony overlooking the main jumu'a, where not long ago, death and blood had run rampant. The palace gates had been thrown open, the entire kingdom invited to the occasion, including the remaining caliphs. The trio was seated on a platformed majlis below, with Haytham representing Demenhur. Nasir had invited Muzaffar, too—the ifrit, of course. For the future of Arawiya promised to weave not only human and safinkind at its core but ifritkind as well.

The people were not jubilant.

They whispered of the strange tree that had sprouted out of stone. They whispered of him. They were not bursting with love for the assassin turned sultan, and how could they? The Prince of Death had touched upon countless lives—if not directly, then indirectly. Displayed like the sultan's prize dog, used to instate fear and obedience.

Nasir was no stranger to the way people reacted to him, but now that he had done so much, *changed* so much, their whispers were a thousand and one stones upon his back. He lifted his chin, determined.

Their hesitance meant there was work to be done and barriers to tear down, and Nasir reminded himself that he would not have to do any of it alone.

"Ready, brother boy?" Altair asked as the announcer finished his spiel.

Kifah was unable to stand still. "He was born for this."

The Silver Witch smiled, for it was she who had taught him how to rule, she who had ensured he was ready.

Zafira was still not here.

A plinth held the royal crown in a shroud of gossamer. Nasir had asked them to remove the small onyx in its center, which had been set to represent his father's Sarasin lineage. Now the crown would stand with a rare polished amber, untethered to any caliphate.

A reminder of all that they had vanquished.

The announcer returned to the shadowed alcove with a dip of his head.

"Yalla," Altair crowed. "The food will get cold."

"He means the belly dancers," Kifah said.

Nasir drew a careful breath, everything muffled as he met his mother's eyes, and went forward into the light. The crowd fell silent. He saw their fear. Their reluctance. Their curiosity.

And when he opened his mouth, every last word he had prepared disappeared.

Honesty, Zafira whispered in his skull. Honesty was easier when people expected little of you.

"My mother once said I was born to hold a crown on my head and death in my fist," Nasir said. He was far more quiet than the announcer had been, but the balcony had been designed to carry his voice across the courtyard and into the streets. "I excelled at the latter. I killed fathers, mothers. Lovers and dignitaries. Each left their mark, in more ways than one."

Murmurs swept through the people. His people.

"I am not—" He stopped, clenched his jaw, and started again. "I am not going to ask for forgiveness; I am going to ask for trust. In me, in the throne. Trust that Arawiya will be restored to greatness. Trust that our trade will flourish, and our cities will shine, and that one day your children will speak of these dark days as ones we overcame."

His eyes searched the crowd until he alighted on a young woman shoving her way through the crowd. A profile of ice, a study of angles.

She had come. Her eyes were lit with pride. Her smile was bittersweet.

Honor before heart, she had said. All that she did, she did for love. For honor. For what was *right*.

Like that, he knew what he needed to do.

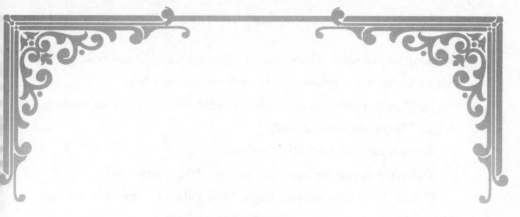

CHAPTER 104

B Y THE TIME ZAFIRA FETCHED LANA FROM THALJ, RE-
united with Yasmine, and returned to the Sultan's Palace, the
throngs of people that had gathered for the coronation were impenetrable. The hushed whispers and curiosity made it clear Arawiya still
feared him, the Prince of Death, but if Nasir could change her heart, she
knew he could change countless more.

She dragged Lana through the thick of the crowd. "This is all your
fault."

Zafira had left Sukkar behind for the very reason of trading horses and
riding hard, and still they had managed to arrive late.

"It's not my fault you never taught me how to ride as well as you,"
Lana whined. She was smart enough to know that now was not the time
to bring up the fact that having to restitch parts of Zafira's wound had
delayed them, too.

"She has a point," Yasmine said.

Near the black tree, Zafira paused to lift her head to the branches reaching for the skies. There was no white rose on its limbs now, but she felt a whisper as she brushed past, a call she once heeded.

"Qif," ordered the guards standing before the doors, silver uniforms bright. "No one is allowed inside."

Zafira froze, and Lana lifted her chin.

Yasmine propped her hands on her hips. "We're expected."

One of the guards barked a laugh. "You and every other peasant here. Move aside."

"I'm the—" Zafira almost said "Hunter," before the word died on her tongue, for there was no Arz to hunt in anymore. She wasn't a hunter, or a huntress.

She was a peasant, as the guard said.

"Okhti," Lana warned beside her, and Zafira snapped out of it as the guard descended the steps, his face cruel.

She grabbed Yasmine's hand and the three of them backed into the crowd, shoving their way through the people until they found a spot within view of the balcony where Nasir had already begun addressing the crowds.

"I'm sorry," Lana said softly.

Zafira and Yasmine hushed her.

And then Nasir found her in the throngs, and he stopped.

He smiled after a thought, a true curve of contentment that reflected in his eyes, a dimple etched into his right cheek. From his mother, then.

Several people turned to look at her, to see what had stolen their sultan's attention, and she couldn't stop a full grin of her own. Then he opened his mouth.

And

damned

himself.

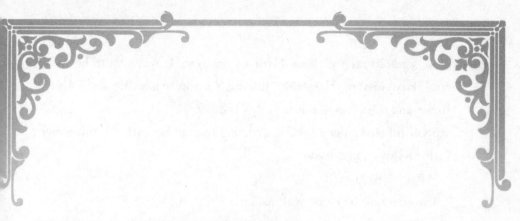

CHAPTER 105

SOME DECISIONS COULD NEVER BE UNDONE. NASIR WAS aware of this fact as he pieced together his next words.

"There are many truths you will learn in the years to come. The biggest is this: Arawiya's sultana, Anadil, was not safin. She was not human, either. She was the last of the Sisters of Old, once warden of Sharr."

The crowd ruptured in surprise. Again, he looked to her, his fair gazelle. She was holding her sister against her, whispering something even as she held his gaze.

"I am her son, but not her firstborn. I was raised a prince, but I wasn't given the heart and soul of a king."

The buzzing crowd fell silent at this admission. The zumra's gazes burned into him, questions rising in the quiet, none of them louder than his mother's.

"Her first son, however, was given both of those things. He has fought and bled for this kingdom, to keep the darkness at bay and our people alive even when all hope seemed lost. As I carried out the worst of commands, killing without mercy." Now Nasir's voice rose. It was a truth he would brand across history if he must. "If there is anyone deserving of the Gilded Throne and this crown, it is him. My brother."

Nasir inhaled a deep breath, gripping the rail beneath the full weight of what he was about to do.

"Altair al-Badawi."

The effect of the name was instant.

Joy swept down the ranks of the people gathered below, triumph in their shouts. He knew not everyone would trust that Altair was his brother. He knew there would be those who would search Altair's lineage for the name of his father. Those who would challenge him.

But for now, their love for him, and all he had done for them, would be enough.

Nasir stepped inside, expecting bitterness in his veins, but he only felt pride. Pure and whole.

He turned the golden crown over in his hands. "I don't know if this will fit, but—"

"Are you out of your mind?" Altair growled.

Kifah was grinning ear to ear.

"You are quite something when flustered," Nasir said in full seriousness.

Altair shoved a hand through his hair, mussing it even further and dropping his turban. He turned to the wall and gulped down several deep breaths.

"If I take the crown—" he started, turning back.

"There's no 'if.' I'm not going to step back outside to say I spoke in jest," Nasir replied.

"What will you do?"

For once, Nasir had an answer waiting. "Sarasin's throne sits empty."

"Sarasin?" Altair asked, surprise arching his brow.

Nasir's answer was wry. "I am my father's son, after all."

It was more than that. He vowed to begin righting his wrongs, and it was Sarasin that he had wronged the most. Sarasin that had suffered beneath his blade. Sarasin, where he had learned he could not live without her, as they had traveled and fought and triumphed as one, prudent and tactful.

When he found the strength to seek out his mother, he found shock and understanding. Uncertainty, but also surety. There were tears in her dark eyes, not ones welled from sorrow, but those of pride.

She said nothing, knowing she did not have to.

Altair regarded him as cheers continued to ripple outside. "You're more than that. We both are."

Nasir swallowed the sudden barge in his throat and struggled against the tantalizing fear in his veins that signified change. "If I didn't know you any better, I'd think you were going to kiss me," he said, pulling a page from the general's book.

Altair scoffed. "If you weren't my brother, perhaps. That's a little too much, Nasir. Even for me." He looked at his trembling hands with a shaky laugh and wrapped his turban with haste. "Wish me luck, One of Nine?"

Kifah couldn't stop grinning. "You gave up your eye for Arawiya. Make your own luck, Sultani."

Nasir watched as Altair flicked his gaze, uneasy and fleeting, to their mother. The nod that was exchanged seemed indifferent, though it was anything but. And then the announcer was clearing his throat, prompting him to follow with a fortifying breath.

Altair hurried back inside.

"Wait—is my turban crooked?"

Nasir smiled. "Just the way you like it."

CHAPTER 106

H
E HAD BEEN BORN FOR THIS. HE HAD BEEN BRED
for this. Zafira had—skies, what had he done?

"Why do you look surprised?" Lana asked.

"Did you not hear what he said?" Zafira shot back. "He just gave up the daama crown like it's kanafah. He's lived his whole life for this moment, for the *crown*, and he just *gave it up*." Her voice was louder than it should have been. People were turning to stare.

Lana tilted her head, a laugh in her eyes. "Because of you, Okhti. Didn't you see?"

Zafira closed her eyes, exhaling a slow, slow breath as Yasmine watched. Her stomach dropped, not because of Lana's words, but because she *knew* she was one of the reasons why he had done this. Some part of her had seen it flicker in his gray eyes before he even opened his mouth.

Altair ducked beneath the curtains and closed his hands around the burnished rail, his bare arms glistening in the full sun. People murmured of his eyepatch, threaded in gold. They murmured of their love for him.

"Arawiya mocks me even now," Yasmine murmured with some of her usual bite.

Zafira threaded her fingers through Lana's. Her sister, who had grown so much. Who would soon know how to heal with a touch. "What do you mean?"

"He's far too pretty to be a murderer," Yasmine said with a sigh.

Zafira grinned. Altair was light incarnate. Nasir was right about one thing: He *deserved* this. And a very different kind of pride swelled in her heart when the crown was placed on his head.

"Remember when I stole from the sultan?" Lana asked with a smirk.

Zafira let out a long-suffering sigh.

CHAPTER 107

T HE CROWN WAS PLACED ON ALTAIR'S HEAD, AND
the written scrolls immortalized his coronation. He was sultan,
he was king. He was a grand liar who had somehow earned himself a throne.

He had lived in his baby brother's shadow long enough that he was accustomed to being second, and so none of this felt real. It felt undeserved, despite what everyone said. It made him guilty to feel elated with the weight of the metal atop his turban.

Altair had always intended for Nasir to sit on the Gilded Throne. It had been a part of the plan: Return magic, vanquish Ghameq, and nurture the young prince into the ruler Arawiya needed. But a crown on Altair's head didn't mean Nasir would be treated as any less than a sultan himself.

Altair would ensure it.

The procession made its way to the coronation feast in the banquet hall, ululations and drums ringing between the umber walls.

"Where are you going?" Nasir asked, ever observant. "Your belly dancers are getting cold."

"I'll be right back," Altair said, plastering on a grin. "They won't even know I've gone."

There was something he needed to do without a witness in case he faced the rejection he feared. He pushed his way to the empty hall, taking the steps by two, and stopped in the throne room.

The Gilded Throne was still shrouded in shadow, the steps steeped in black.

Altair straightened the collar of his thobe that he had tailored for his brother's coronation and strode to the dais, his footfalls hollow, his pulse quickening when the steps remained as dark as the night.

Sultan's teeth. He laughed to himself. Those were his teeth now.

He held his breath and eased himself down. A whisper unfurled across the room, a sigh almost. *One of us,* the throne echoed. No, not the throne, the *Sisters.* Relief wound through him as resplendent gold spread over the darkness.

"Did you really believe the throne would not accept you?"

The Silver Witch stepped from the shadows.

"Did you doubt your blood?"

Altair's grip tightened around the arms of the throne, his knuckles white. "My own mother didn't accept me."

"A sin I will forever regret."

He didn't know why her remorse contented him.

"Why? I was an amalgamation of your mistakes," he replied mildly, but the words held less bite and more a bone-deep weariness. As if the part of him bereft of her love wanted to believe her, and years of experience told him otherwise.

"And it was worse to blame my wrongs on a newborn child," she said softly. "If there was ever proof that good triumphs over the darkest of times, it is you. I will not ask for the forgiveness I do not deserve, but know that I will live the rest of my days with regret."

Altair considered the white mane of her hair, the loss she endured that no one would ever know the extent of. The power she had relinquished by giving up her heart. "Will you stay here? In the palace?"

"I thought I'd had my fill of these walls," she said carefully. "But if you'll have me . . ."

A flutter, in his chest.

"Now that you mention it," he said after a beat of thought in which he didn't think at all, extending an offer of peace, "I *am* in need of an advisor."

His mother's lips twitched in the faintest of smiles as the throne room doors swept open, bringing with it a gust of the revel and three others. His family. His zumra. His lifeline.

Nasir looked surprised to see their mother, and Altair gave him a sardonic smile.

Zafira bowed first. "My king."

Nasir followed, then Kifah, and Altair leaped off the throne and rushed toward them.

"No!" he commanded. "You will never bow to anyone, least of all me."

Kifah smirked. "I only did it so Zafira wouldn't feel awkward."

Zafira rolled her eyes, and Altair was struck by how much he would miss them. Ruling a kingdom was lonely like that. He couldn't expect Nasir to govern Sarasin from Sultan's Keep. He couldn't keep Zafira from her home, or Kifah from her calipha.

The others sobered, realizing the same.

"Strange, isn't it," said Nasir, who was never one for contemplation. "How the darkness brought us together, and the light will let us fall apart?"

Zafira shook her head, looking among them. "We're not falling apart. We hunted the flame on Sharr, set free the stars across the skies, but it was only ever the dawn of our zumra. Now we make sure that light doesn't go out. Forever. Together."

CHAPTER 108

THE SAFIN OF BENYAMIN'S HIGH CIRCLE WOULD LIFT the blockades on magic at sunrise, and ease the people into the use of their affinities. A little bit more every day, Seif had said, and for the ones who wished to master the ability they'd been born with, the safin would aid them in cities across Arawiya.

There was a time when Zafira had approached the safin with disenchantment, but now she was glad of them. Glad they were here, with their experience of living in a world of magic, so that they could do for Arawiya what the Sisters could not.

Zafira left Lana in the palace banquet hall, where the girl was keen on trying every dish she possibly could, and closed the door to their rooms. Anticipation buzzed beneath her skin. Even the Jawarat hummed in excitement, ready for the inevitable chaos.

We cannot help it, it said at Zafira's reproach.

She threw open the window as the knot in her throat became too thick to breathe around, as if she would be able to see magic flowing across the skies, reaching for her.

They had done it. *She* had done it. How small she had felt leaving her village behind for a mirage that she feared might never be. And now it was here. It was daama here.

Rest, bint Iskandar. We must be ready for dawn.

Just a few moments, she promised herself, tucking the Jawarat to her side. She didn't think she'd doze off, but the next thing she knew, the bed was shifting and a figure curled against her side. Heftier and taller than Lana.

"Yasmine?" Zafira asked, cracking open an eye.

Yasmine turned onto her back, lifting her chin to stop her tears. They trailed down the side of her face, falling to the shell of her ear.

"I've never felt so empty," she whispered. Her face was swollen, stained in streaks of sorrow.

Zafira turned and tucked her arms around her and held her close, as if that could bring Misk back, as if that could fill her with whatever his death and Deen's had taken.

"If I hadn't wished for time apart—"

"No." Zafira stopped her. "He would have done it regardless. He was tied to Arawiya and its future. That's why he worked for Altair. He was a hero, Yasmine."

Yasmine sobbed. What had Zafira expected? For the Lion to die and all to be righted? It wasn't only war that had an aftermath, but life, too.

"You can add that to your list now," Zafira teased with a nudge.

Yasmine tried to laugh, but wept instead. And as the sister of her heart mourned the man she loved, Zafira was reminded of Umm and Baba. She was reminded of Nasir, and a truth: She could think of no future without him, and the revelation scared her roaring thoughts into silence.

Love was a terrible thing, she decided. It tore hearts apart with talons and gnashing teeth and left nothing behind.

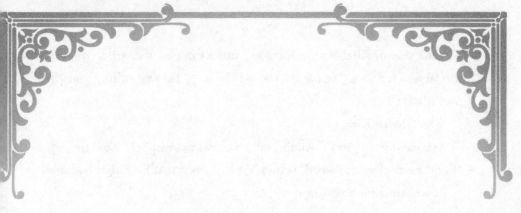

CHAPTER 109

Altair's first order as Arawiya's ruler was upheaving the depressing decor of the Sultan's Palace. He didn't understand such dark and drab decor. Royalty wasn't dead. A day after magic's return, the black carpeting was rolled up and a new one unfurled in blue and red and edged in gold.

But if he was being honest, all this was merely delaying a more important task: *being* sultan. The loneliness of it. Magic and the chaos it entailed. Already there was word from one village of a fireheart having accidentally set a tree ablaze and the flames spreading to the sooq, upon which an aquifer thought to be heroic and flooded the market stalls.

Some good the safin were doing, easing magic into Arawiya.

"And here we have our lonely sultan," Kifah said by way of greeting as she strolled into the room.

He *was* lonely. Nasir had already left for Sarasin to prepare for his own coronation. Zafira and her sister were bound for Demenhur. He bit the inside of his cheek. Sultans didn't cry.

One side of Kifah's mouth curled into a smile as she strode to one of the large windows. "Seif and I toured the city. They're calling you Zhahabi Maliki."

The Golden King.

"Has a nice ring to it," Altair said, swallowing a rasp. He liked the word "king" more than the word "sultan." What was it that his father had said?

It was time for a new era.

He'd written to the ifrit known as Muzaffar, the soon to be ruler of his own caliphate. Ifrit were different from men and safin—they'd require laws specific to them, benefits created for them, and Altair would figure it out. He was part ifrit, after all. Surely that would earn him a few favors.

He'd sent invitations to the caliphates, too, including one to Qismah, the daughter of Ayman al-Ziya, the dead Demenhune caliph. It was early, and it risked him appearing malleable, but he'd already met with the rulers as a general, and he'd hoped the gathering would usher in a new unity in less time than Anadil expected.

There were ways to rule, she had said. Altair agreed *and* disagreed, for there were ways to appeal to hearts, too.

"And you, One of Nine? What does Ghada say, aside from wanting her daughter in my lap?"

Kifah laughed. "I don't think I'll get a second invitation, if that's what you mean." She paused. "But . . . I don't think I want one. I joined the Nine Elite to prove something to my father, but it was Benyamin who gave me what I'd wanted."

The chance for vengeance. Altair regarded her. "Will you return home to gloat? Am I to say farewell to you, too, then?"

"Have you need of me?" Kifah probed.

"I have a proposal for you, actually," he said carefully. Her eyebrows rose. "For a place by my side."

"With a crown on my head?" Kifah sputtered. "Are you asking me to marry you?"

Altair grinned. "I'm not blind, Kifah. I know romance isn't something you desire if even my perfection can't tempt you."

She snorted, but her dark eyes glistened.

"I was thinking something more lethal, like Sword of the Sultan. Captain of my guard."

She didn't answer. Of course she'd want to return home. The bastard had taken away more than her brother.

"Think about it. Discuss it with Ghada if you must. Find your father and gloat a little. You've seen the reports. These first few months won't be easy as people come into magic, even with the help of the High Circle and the gossamer web. Then I'll have to start worrying about every other kingdom wanting a piece of us now that the Arz is gone and—"

"Altair. For once, *please* stop talking."

He stopped, and Kifah met his eyes.

"Yes, I accept. Why be one of nine when I can be *the* one?"

CHAPTER 110

IT HAD BEEN THREE DAYS SINCE NASIR HAD TAKEN THE Sarasin throne. The people were not enthused about giving the crown to the assassin who had killed their previous caliph, but when had Nasir's life been particularly loving?

He found Zafira on a rooftop overlooking Sarasin's capital of Leil, near the quarters of Dar al-Fawda, home of the prestigious camel races. She sat on a red rug with her back to him, loose strands from her crowned braid fluttering in the bare breeze. Nasir paused, chronicling every piece of the scene before making his presence known.

She smiled when he sat down beside her, but there was a tightness to the gesture, a guard behind her eyes.

"I'm leaving for Demenhur today."

Why? he wanted to ask, but he was certain she had a thousand and one reasons to head back to her home. "When will you return?"

As soon as the words were out of his mouth, he realized they had never spoken of this. The fragility of a future, and what she wanted. She had arrived for his coronation on time—without Lana or Yasmine, who had stayed in Thalj—and had been staying in the palace since then, but between the ceremony and the turmoil of magic's return and the knowledge that his people were not pleased, Nasir hadn't had the chance to see her. To speak to her.

He saw the undulation of her throat before she looked at him. "I won't."

The words were scythes carving out his heart, and it took him a moment to make sense of them. They could reject him across cities, across caliphates, all of Arawiya could scorn him, and none of it would hurt as deeply as this.

He didn't know what he should say. *I am falling in love with you, and I don't know how to stop.* Those weren't words someone said aloud, were they?

"I can't sit on that throne. I can't rule," he said instead.

Without you.

She turned to him fully. Her eyes glistened.

Why not? her face asked. "You can," was what she said.

He shook his head. "The darkness—"

"Darkness doesn't need to be destroyed. We *need* the dark as much as we need light. It makes us bold, as much as it makes us afraid." She smiled. "Darkness needs only to be tamed."

"Tame me," he said in desperation. Shadows bled from his fingers.

Marry me. Love me. Be with me.

"Be mine, wholly and utterly."

She lifted an eyebrow. "What if I want *you* to be *mine?*"

"Fair gazelle, jewel of my soul, I was already yours. I've changed for you. I've—"

"But I like you just the way you are," she whispered. "Scarred, deadly, and beautiful." She had wrapped her arms around her legs, containing herself, as if she would fall apart otherwise. "I promised a calipha her throne."

"Honor before heart?" he asked quietly. The wind whistled across the rooftops, bringing with it surges of the city life below.

"It's not always one or the other."

"For you it is." He leaned forward and pressed a kiss to her brow, closing his eyes against a welling of pain. Closing away his heart as he had done long, long ago. The words inked inside his wrist had never rung truer.

He was wrong to have expected her to leave behind her entire life and join him in the dark palace of Sarasin, which half of Arawiya loathed and feared. He was selfish to wish and dream and hope.

She pulled back, barely meeting his eyes as she rose to her feet. "Rule well, Prince."

Her face was wet as her tears fell to the rooftop. She was his moon and his sun. She stole his breath even when he had none to spare.

Why? he wanted to ask. Why was she ripping out their hearts and trampling them both? But it had always been one of the many things he loved about her: that he could never understand the enigma that was her.

He let her go. "Ride swift, Huntress."

CHAPTER 111

B ACK IN THE DEMENHUNE PALACE, ZAFIRA STARED at the ceiling of her room. After having experienced the unhindered magic of Sharr and dum sihr, the doled-out dosage of the royal minarets left Zafira wanting. She fisted her hands in her sheets, cursing the hearts, cursing the Sisters. Why was magic not giving her the joy it had on the royal minaret? Why was she so . . . empty?

Be mine, wholly and utterly. She tucked her blanket beneath her chin, ignoring the dampness of her pillow. Resorting to bitterness was good, if it meant less crying.

The door cracked open, and she cursed her numbed state for forgetting to lock it. The torchlight lit Yasmine's silhouette.

"Zafira?"

"I'm sleeping."

Yasmine didn't care. "What did you do?"

At some point in the past two months, she had carved out half of her heart and given it to him. That was what she had done.

"You've been crying ever since you came back," she said sadly. Of course it was Zafira who had managed to make her even more sad than she was. "I saw a vision just now. At least, I think it was a vision. I was in the palace again, looking for someone. I had a knife, so it could have been a dream. Zafira? Is it magic? Did you lose it? Why are you—"

A wild laugh tore out of her. Zafira had magic, all right. Her heart was a compass once more, and it was pulling her in a direction she didn't heed.

"I came home, that's why. I came home because Sarasin isn't," Zafira said simply.

Understanding dawned in Yasmine's eyes. "We *have* no home."

Zafira looked at her sharply. "Our home is in the western villages, and we're going back tomorrow."

Yasmine's head snapped up. "For what? Neither of us have anything left there. Not our homes, not our families. *Nothing*, Zafira. Deen is gone, Misk is gone. Why would I want to live in a place that will haunt me for the rest of my life? The palace healers offered to tutor Lana, and I'm going to stay, too."

Zafira stared at her.

"You're running away from him, aren't you? That's what this is about. Lana told me. You run from the things that scare you."

Zafira scoffed. "And yet I marched into the Arz every daama day. I trekked to Sharr. I faced the Lion of the Night."

"Because you're not afraid of the dark, or of evil, or of harm. You fear change and what it signifies."

"This isn't like your stories," Zafira said angrily. "I can't wear the crown of calipha and suddenly command an entire caliphate. I'm supposed to help the caliph's daughter secure *her* throne."

She owed that to Qismah, and more, after what she had done to her father.

"And you can do both. You won't have to rule over Sarasin," Yasmine said, sitting beside her. "He will."

"So I'll take care of his palace. Fold his clothes. Sit pretty. Care for——"

They were lies, and she knew it. He would ensure she was nothing but his equal. She could do for Sarasin as she'd done for her village, only tenfold. Care not just for a handful of houses but for an entire caliphate. She'd seen it when she'd spoken to Muzaffar.

That wasn't what she feared.

Yasmine touched her hand. "I don't know him the way you do, but I was there. I saw how he looks at you. If he's the darkness, then you're his moon, and the moon wasn't made to be caged. It's a beacon to behold, a relic to revere. To be loved."

Zafira didn't realize the tears were falling until Yasmine brushed them away. She never knew she could hurt so much. Want so much. Lose so much.

Yasmine whispered, "He will give you what Deen could not."

"I don't need a man to complete me."

"No," Yasmine agreed with a sad smile. "We never do. Your happiness completes you. And if he is what makes you happy, why would you throw him away?"

Zafira closed her eyes. She wanted him. She wanted him so badly she could not breathe, she could not think, she could not *be*. Which was precisely why she should stay away, wasn't it?

The Jawarat regarded her from her bedside table. It was the embodiment of memories and magic and the reason for all the wrongs she had done. Wrongs she would have continued, had he not been there for her. Had he not believed in her, understood her, the way no one else had.

Loving him was a knife to her throat, thorns around her heart. The fragility of life in the clasping of their hands.

Outside, a bird trilled as Demenhur awakened to a new world. One Misk would never see.

Her whisper was soft. Raw. "What if I lose him?"

She had nearly lost him once.

"The way I lost the one I loved?" Yasmine asked. She cupped Zafira's face. "I will forever regret every word I didn't say and every moment I spent not holding his hand. The questions I never got to ask. The understanding we did not have. But I will never, ever regret marrying him." She pressed her brow to Zafira's. "Knowing you can lose something is what makes it more precious."

CHAPTER 112

LISTENING TO HIS PEOPLE WAS A DOUR AFFAIR, BUT IT was one Nasir did without complaint. It meant Sarasin was slowly but gradually beginning to trust him in the three months since he'd been crowned caliph, the prince who had killed so many of their own. Freeing the children of the camel races and giving them an abode in the palace had helped, too, but Nasir hadn't done it for the people.

His wazir, a stern-faced man named Yasar, straightened every last missive they'd received from dawn until noon and handed it to him, signifying that it was time for another unbearably hot afternoon in his chambers, writing and stamping and poring over caliphate affairs.

"Oi, give him a break, old man," Altair intoned. He had come for a visit and was sprawled on the dais at the foot of the throne, going through missives of his own.

Yasar was miffed. "If you have a problem with how I manage my caliph, Maliki, I suggest you return to your palace."

It was only a quarter day's ride between Sultan's Keep and Sarasin, and the new king was known for his spontaneous visits, dragging Kifah along with him. The only one missing from the zumra meetings was Zafira.

"I hear Qismah's coronation as Calipha of Demenhur is one moon from now," Kifah said.

"It is," Nasir replied, and it was the only letter he'd happily opened, for the silver parchment sealed in navy, the colors of Demenhur, reminded him of her.

Not once had he doubted her. He could see the ice in her gaze, the ferocity in her bearing as she conquered the hearts of the thousand men who stood between Qismah and her throne.

The last merchant finally shuffled from the room, and as the guards closed the doors for the day, a ruckus rose from the hall. Altair sat up. Nasir paused, craning to see, nudging the young scribe out of the way so he could step off the dais.

"What is the meaning of this?" Yasar snapped when the doors flew open again. The guards drew their spears as a hooded figure stepped inside, moving with gazelle-like grace and snatching the air from Nasir's throat.

"The caliph is no longer holding court," one of the officials barked.

"Protect the king," a gold-cloaked guard commanded.

"Drop your hood," another one snapped.

The children paused in their chores to stare.

The newcomer lowered the fine hood of their cloak, exposing the delicate features that had plagued his nights and days and his every waking moment.

Nasir's heart saw it fit to pause here. To stop and chronicle this instant in time.

And then he was running, stumbling, racing toward her, missives scattering behind him to Yasar's disappointment and Altair's laughter. His hands skimmed her shoulders, her neck, cupped her face.

"Zafira," he whispered as papyrus drifted around them.

"Nasir," she replied, as if she had never left. As if he hadn't forgotten how to breathe.

His lips molded to hers. His life began afresh. Twin sighs escaped them, as if they had both been starving and salvation was finally theirs. The men murmured among themselves, and at the sound of Kifah's ululation, Zafira pulled away.

"I hear Sarasin is in need of a calipha."

CHAPTER 113

"HABIBTI," HER HUSBAND SAID, TOUCHING A KISS to her lips.

There was a scar at her breast, and another in her heart, for people had died because she lived.

"Hayati," he breathed, pressing another to her ear and stealing her thoughts.

Around her, silver gossamer. Above, a painted sea of stars.

"Roohi," he rasped, feathering her jaw until they were both panting, until a hot tear rolled down his face and fell to the hollow beneath her shoulder, searing her bare skin.

"Why do you cry?" Zafira whispered.

Roohi, roohi, roohi. He stitched her soul anew.

"Because my heart cannot contain it."

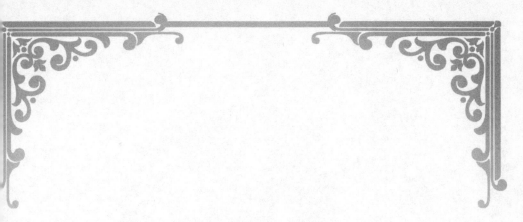

CHAPTER 114

LATER, MUCH LATER, PERHAPS ONE OR TEN OR FIF-
teen days after he had bound his life to hers, light streamed
through the open windows as the palace slept away the midday
heat. She murmured sleepily beside him, lashes feathering the tops of her
cheeks. The book bound to her soul lay at ease in the room just beyond.

He lifted her arm and touched his mouth to the skin inside her wrist.
This was what he feared more than the dark, more than the power at his
grasp: the whisper of her pulse, petering to silence. Taking her from him.

Fear made his love grow. To fear was to live and to strengthen. It was
maddening as it swelled in his heart, and yet, amid all his feelings was one
more, stirring foreign and raw: contentment.

I once loved, he had inked on his wrist. *I will again*, he inked on the
other. He opened his palm and a plume of shadow curled to life. It was a
reminder: People lived because he did.

And to think, once upon a time, Nasir Ghameq, Caliph of Sarasin and
Crown Prince of Arawiya, had wished he could feel nothing at all.

ACKNOWLEDGMENTS

I hear every author reaches a moment in her career when they simply can't anymore. When they fall deep where the waters are dark and the light vanishes from sight. I reached that low with *We Free the Stars*. It was a beast of a book, a monster that took everything from me, and I was afraid I'd never reach the end.

And I wouldn't have, if not for my family. My mother, who believed in me from day one. My father, who attended every last industry event and pushed me to go beyond my limits. My brother, Abdullah, just because. My sisters, Asma and Azraa: the pillars that kept me sane. Thank you for pulling all-nighters with me, for reading draft after draft and line after edited line, for being the tireless advocates I couldn't have found anywhere else.

That's *my* family, but a book's family is a lot larger, and there are so many more amazing souls to thank.

To Janine O'Malley, for making me suffer—I'm kidding. Sort of. But thank you. For believing in me from day one and for your endless patience and wisdom. For the extensions upon extensions, and the chocolate. For knowing I'd get there as you asked all the right questions, even when they made me want to tear my hair out. This book would not be what it is without you, and I don't say that lightly. To Melissa Warten, who never asked to be stuck with me and the complex world of Arawiya, but made it shine in ways I never imagined. Thank you for your relentless support and friendship.

To my team at Macmillan, a family I adore and love and appreciate so, so much. To Brittany Pearlman, publicist extraordinaire. Thank you for escorting me around the country and working tirelessly for this series. For going out of your way to ensure I felt safe. To Molly Ellis, for accompanying me to Macmillan dinners and keeping my headaches at bay. To Allison Verost, for pulling all the strings. Our breakfast at SDCC 2019 continues to be one of the highlights of my career. To the magnificent Melissa Zar and Jordin Streeter. To Mariel Dawson, secret ally. To Katie Halata and Kristen Luby, for making Sands of Arawiya shine in all things S&L. To Fierce Reads tour queen Morgan Rath. Also Joy Peskin, Jen Besser, Jon Yaged, Callum Plews, Kathryn Little, Gaby Salpeter, Mary Van Akin, and all the magicians in sales who make wonders happen.

To Elizabeth Clark for the design, Erin Fitzsimmons for the gorgeous typography to match, and Simón Prades for the killer cover art once more. Thank you for turning my book into art.

To John Cusick, for your reassurance and your support, which I could always count on, and for your undying enthusiasm.

Special thanks to Joan He, girl and goat. To friends Brittany Holloway, Lisa Austin, Mary Hinson, and Sara Gundell. To Korrina Ede and the OwlCrate team for bringing the book to thousands of new readers, to Shelflove Crate and Illumicrate, and to the lovely Meagan and her team at FaeCrate. To Allie Macedo, Rameela, Nawal, and Sanya: *We Hunt the Flame* couldn't have found bigger fans and enthusiasts. Thank you for making my days full of love. To the *WHTF* Street Team, for all your support.

ACKNOWLEDGMENTS

We were one heck of a team. To the unyielding creativity of bookstagrammers and the tireless advocacy of bloggers and influencers, booksellers and librarians: thank you. Your work does not go unnoticed.

As always, last but never, ever least: you. Thank you for picking up this book and this series. For every post and every email, for the fic that you write and the art that you create and the edits that you whip up: Thank you. You make my days special, and I'm forever grateful. Thank you for being part of the zumra. Shukrun.